Also by Elizabeth Waite

Cockney Waif

Elizabeth Waite

WARNER BOOKS

A *Warner* Book

First published in Great Britain by
Warner Books in 1993
Reprinted 1994 (three times), 1995, 1996, 1998 (twice)

A CIP catalogue record for this book
is available from the British Library.

ISBN 0 7515 0713 X

Phototypeset by Intype, London

Printed in England by Clays Ltd, St Ives plc

Warner Books
A Division of
Little, Brown and Company (UK)
Brettenham House
Lancaster Place
London WC2E 7EN

For my husband and son
with my love

My grateful thanks have to go to Darley Anderson. Without his help my writing would never have been published, and his kindness has given me a new lease of life.

Chapter One

London, 1918

WHEN ELLEN KENT came out of the doctor's surgery, every woman in the waiting-room felt sympathy for her. She looked ghastly. Really ill. The receptionist took her card and at Ellen's request made her another appointment. This patient puzzled her; she was certainly not the usual type who frequented the surgery, great idle lumps wearing faded clothing and looking as if their skin hadn't seen soap and water for many a day. Mrs Kent was young and slim with a clear skin and brilliant grey eyes. Her delicate features and the quiet way she conducted herself left no one in doubt that, poorly dressed though she was now, she had originated from an aristocratic background.

Outside, Ellen pulled the collar of her coat up around her neck. This raw November wind seemed to get right inside her bones. She felt so tired she could hardly put one foot in front of the other. Her worst fears had been confirmed. The outcome was inevitable: she was going to die.

What about Patsy? What would happen to her?

That question hammered away in her mind until

she felt as if her head were spinning. The doctor's diagnosis hadn't come as a shock. She had prayed hard that it wasn't consumption, but in her mind she had known all along that was what was wrong with her. Seething with anger at the unfairness of it all, she stood still for a moment to catch her breath. Calm down, she told herself, anger would get her nowhere. She must think about it sensibly, logically. Patsy had to be her first priority.

Patsy, her lovely wonderful illegitimate daughter, who had never known the joy of having a father. For thirteen years there had been just Ellen herself and Patsy – no relatives, no family. If she could turn the clock back, would she have it any other way? She answered her own question without hesitation. No. Definitely no.

Her Patsy. A smile flickered around her lips and she crossed her arms across her chest as she walked and hugged herself. The love she felt for her daughter was total. From the moment she had known that she was pregnant she had been determined to keep her baby. Against overwhelming odds she had battled on and made a life for both of them, albeit in a poor district. Patsy had grown up none the worse for that. She was a tough little nut really, sinewy but strong. Her skin always had a healthy glow, her long thick hair was the colour of a polished chestnut and her eyes so green you'd think they could glow in the dark.

Ellen sighed heavily. There was no child in this

world so dear as her Patsy. She couldn't go home, not yet.

Looking about her in the dim evening light, she realised her footsteps had brought her to the Broadway. On the opposite side of the road were the Public Baths. 'At least that will give me time to think,' she murmured to herself, though what good more thinking would do she couldn't imagine. There were only a few people about and the yellow glow from the gas lamps made the street look sinister and ominous. Around the corner came half a dozen young men, totters, making for home with their barrows. Alongside them, hoping for a handout of specky fruit, ran a group of small boys, all looking the same in their tattered jumpers, cutdown trousers and laced-up boots. She had to wait, then, as a tram rattled by and rumbled towards Balham before she could cross the road.

Once across she held tightly to the brass hand-rail and dragged herself up the stone steps that led to the entrance marked 'Ladies'. A pretty, fresh-faced young woman sat behind the glass partition.

'It's tuppence for the bath, tuppence for the use of a towel and a penny for a tablet of soap.' The assistant took Ellen's sixpence, gave her a penny change, and three tickets.

Along a corridor and through a turnstile, then Ellen was in a long hall which was partitioned into small cubicles. The walls were tiled, the atmosphere steamy. A very tall woman, wearing a sacking apron around her waist and a man's flat cap on her head, yelled for Ellen to go into cubicle number six. A long, glistening porcelain bath took up most of the space, leaving room for only a wooden stool and a slatted wooden platform on the concrete floor. There were no taps. The attendant used a metal spanner to turn two bolts set into the wall at the head of the bath. Water came gushing out and when the bath was half-full she reversed her actions with the spanner, tested the water with her rough red hand, and then shut the door behind her with the parting words, 'Yell out if yer want any more 'ot water.'

Standing on the wooden platform, Ellen stripped off her clothes and laid them neatly on the wooden stool. Then she stepped gingerly over the high side of the bath and, easing herself down into the hot water, let it lap over her. The warmth helped her to relax and she smiled to herself: this was better than bathing in the old tin bath in front of the fire.

As her tiredness eased away, she began going over the events of the last few weeks in her mind. Florrie was right. She would have to do something about Patsy, make sure that someone would take care of her, for one thing was certain – pretty soon she wouldn't be around, and she couldn't bear even the thought that the authorities might decide that Patsy should be placed in a home. Florrie wouldn't let that happen! She'd move heaven and earth to prevent it. Would she be able to, legally?

There must be something that she could do. There had to be.

Turning her thoughts to Florrie, Ellen realised what a wonderful friend she had found. Indeed, fate had certainly been on her side when she had arrived in Tooting all those years ago. She had been on her own, heavily pregnant, terribly afraid. What would she have done if Ollie hadn't come to her rescue and taken her to Florrie's house? Because of Florrie, the whole Day family had taken her under their wing and over the years that had meant her survival. She had much to be angry, even bitter, about – life hadn't treated her fairly – but she had also had many blessings.

Wealth she hadn't amassed, but these years had been filled with friendship, teeming with it, loving, generous, unselfish attachments that no money could have bought. But now, she would have to face facts. There could be no more dithering; if she wanted to leave Patsy safely provided for, she would have to swallow her pride and go and visit her father.

South London boroughs all had their posh areas and their working-class districts. Wandsworth was no different from any of the others. Strathmore Street where poverty was known to all, was decidedly working-class. It was less than six miles from London's West End, with its theatres and shops enjoying royal patronage, but there was no comparison. In Strathmore Street lived disillusioned men, women old before their time, too many under-nourished children. There was overcrowding in back-to-back houses, without proper sanitation. In spite of all that, the people who lived here were the salt of the earth.

In the back kitchen of number twenty-two Strathmore Street, Florrie Holmes sat in her armchair drawn up to the fire, her badly-veined legs stretched out resting on a stool. A homely, fat woman with a florid complexion and hands knotted by arthritis, aged just forty, but looking nearer fifty, not in the least attractive, Florrie Holmes was regarded as a friend by the inhabitants of the neighbourhood It was said she listened to everybody's troubles, solved at least half, and was gutsy enough to give advice even if it wasn't always what people wanted to hear.

It was nearly midnight, on a cold November night, but she couldn't bring herself to go to bed. She wished to God someone would tell her what to do! She had been on to Ellen for weeks to go to the doctor's and get something for that awful cough of hers, now she almost wished she hadn't persuaded her. Was it better to know that Ellen hadn't got long to live? In some ways it *was* probably best that the doctor had told her outright; at least she would have to set to and do something about Patsy.

'It's not fair,' she yelled out loud. 'It's not bloody fair. It's never those that deserve it.' As she spoke, she punched the air with her fist. When a sudden gust of wind blew down the chimney, sending smoke billowing into the room, she gave a cynical laugh. 'Damn chimney. Still needs sweeping.'

For a moment she forgot her grief and anger and managed to smile. Her thoughts had flown back to the day that Ellen had arrived on her doorstep. Still voicing her thoughts aloud she lowered her feet to the floor, then used a rolling motion to get her body out of the chair. 'You couldn't blame anybody for being a bit wary of Ellen, not when she first came 'ere you couldn't. Wearing clothes the likes of which you didn't get to see round 'ere. Boots made of real leather, and by Christ she spoke as if she'd got a plum in her mouth. That wasn't the worse of it though, not by a long chalk! No, to top the lot, she'd been ready to drop a baby and not a sight nor sound of any husband and 'er wanting to rent my upstairs rooms. Gawd love us, that was a day that was! Not that I've ever bin sorry I took 'er in, far from it. Having Ellen and that wonderful kid of hers about the place has just about made my life. What I'll do without them, Gawd above knows.'

Suddenly Florrie felt cold and chilled. Oh, it was too cruel, too horrible to brood over! There was no cure for consumption, not for poor folk; there were probably sanatoriums and such like, but it was too late for Ellen. She began to shake. It shouldn't happen, she wouldn't let it. Ellen was too young – she wasn't going to die, she still had to look after Patsy. Florrie tried hard not to accept what the doctor had said, but deep down she knew he was right and that there was nothing she could do to alter things. But how long? How long before that cough got worse? Before Ellen choked to death?

Florrie was still muttering to herself as she took the kettle to the sink. 'I'll make a cup of tea and take her one up.' A cup of tea was her cure for all ills. While she waited for the kettle to boil she angrily brushed away the tears that threatened to spill over and run down her cheeks. She mustn't let Ellen think that she was fussing too much. It would be Patsy that they would have to consider now. She'd never forget the day that child was born – only ten days after Ellen had arrived.

It had been raining cats and dogs when she had sent young Tommy Day to fetch the midwife, and it had seemed that hours had ticked away as she sat holding on to Ellen's hand. In the end it had been Gran Day and herself who had brought Patsy into this world. Annie Reid, calls herself a midwife – Florrie sniffed in disgust – oh, she'd arrived all right, moaning that she was soaked through and only really worried about whether she was in time to collect her ten bob. Patsy had been a scrawny little mite, but even so the delivery hadn't been easy for Ellen, and when it was all over it had been Gran who had made the tea. Yeah, and I can remember the exact words old Gran said that night as she propped Ellen up on the pillows and handed her a cup: 'I've put a drop of something in your tea and it's no good you protesting, neither. Now drink it up like a good girl and then get yourself a good night's sleep.'

Ah, well, that was all water under the bridge now. So much had happened since then. Ellen had surely paid dearly for her one youthful fling. Florrie would have bet her last penny that things would not have worked out between herself and Ellen. She hadn't known how to handle the situation. Ellen was so ladylike, so beautiful, with deep expressive eyes that held such sadness – almost a hopelessness. Yet it hadn't taken long for Florrie to realise that she not only felt a strong sense of loyalty towards Ellen, but also that she loved her dearly. And as for Patsy! Well, you only had to look at her – she'd grown up into a smashing girl. Full of life. Too cocksure for her own good at times. Despite her heartache, Florrie just had to grin. Patsy only had to flash those great green eyes of hers at you and you knew she could get away with murder.

The tin lid of the kettle began to rattle and the water hissed and steamed from the spout. Florrie put four teaspoonfuls of tea into the pot, added the boiling water and put the cosy on the brown earthenware teapot. Leaning against the wooden draining-board she muttered, 'I'll leave it to draw a few minutes, can't stand weak tea. Ellen likes it good and strong now. There was a time when she drank it weak as dish-water, but I soon cured her of that! Got her round to my way of thinking.'

As she climbed the stairs it dawned on Florrie just how helpless she really was. She still prayed for a miracle, but without much hope. Tears were again stinging at the back of her eyes. Angrily she rubbed at them. 'Bloody crying won't help,' she irritably told herself.

When she entered the room Ellen was sitting in a chair by the fire and her face was grey. An open book lay in her lap.

'You shouldn't be reading, you should be in your bed,' Florrie scolded her mildly.

'I'm not really reading, and I am resting,' Ellen said and she gave Florrie such a soft sweet smile that she had to turn her back, swallow deeply and count to ten, otherwise she would have burst into tears. It took a full minute before she felt calm enough to turn and say, 'Well, put the book down. I've brought you a nice hot cup of tea and a piece of my fruit cake. Patsy helped me make it this morning.'

A grin spread over Ellen's face on hearing that. She knew well enough the antics they got up to in that downstairs kitchen, with as much flour ending up on themselves as ever went into what they were supposed to be baking. No wonder Patsy adored Florrie! She spoiled her rotten.

Having set the tray down, Florrie removed the book from Ellen's lap. 'Mind, it's hot,' she said as Ellen reached for the tea. 'Try and eat the cake.' She nodded her head towards the tray. She was finding it impossible to say straight out what was in her heart, for the truth was that she couldn't find the words to say anything. They seemed to have said it all in the past few days since Ellen had visited the doctor.

'When you've drunk your tea you'd better get undressed and get into bed. I've warned you till I've been blue in the face about overdoing things, ain't I, but would you listen? Oh no! You always think you know best! Well, now you've got to ease up, ain't you?' Fear was what was spurring Florrie on. She watched as Ellen set the cup back down on to the table, lay back in the chair and closed her eyes. She looked so ill, so very tired. She reached across and touched her hand. 'Ellen, have you thought about getting in touch with your family?'

Ellen opened her eyes. 'I've thought about it a lot, but somehow . . .' Her voice trailed off.

'Too proud, are you?'

Ellen smiled weakly. 'I haven't seen them for fourteen years. They didn't want their grandchild. They could have found me if they had wanted to. They never tried.'

'Oh, come on, love, time's a great healer and when all is said and done family is family.' Florrie was doing her best to sound calm and confident but her insides were all of a wobble. She was so afraid. Afraid for Ellen, for herself, and most of all for young Patsy. And she blamed herself. If only she'd insisted on Ellen going to the doctor's sooner! No use harping on all that now, it was too late. Still, someone had to get things organised. Somebody would have to take on the responsibility of Patsy. The times she had wished that Ellen and Patsy were her own flesh and blood, but they weren't and there was no getting away from that fact. If the worse came to the worst, and that seemed more likely every day now, she couldn't see the authorities letting Patsy stay with her. Some bloody do-gooder from the Town Hall would turn up and say that she was not a suitable person to be in charge of a child.

'You know, your mother and father might feel very different now, especially if they were to see Patsy.' Florrie's voice held a note of pleading as she sat staring at her.

Ellen sighed as she reached over and took hold of Florrie's rough, workworn hands. 'I don't deserve you, Florrie.' The tears glistened in her eyes. 'Give me time, give me time,' she murmured.

Time is what she hasn't got, Florrie silently thought.

After all these years she knew exactly what had happened to Ellen to make her up sticks and leave her well-off family and land up on the doorstep of number twenty-two Strathmore Street.

Did her parents know where she had been all these years? Living and working among poor folk? Her father hadn't kicked her out – she had left of her own free will – but he hadn't given her much of an alternative. Disgusting. That was how Florrie thought of him. Him with his sheltered and privileged life, ashamed because his daughter was having a baby on the wrong side of the blanket. Pompous old git! Ellen wasn't the first to be caught, and she wouldn't be the last. Pity her parents hadn't shown a little more kindness and understanding. All that old man had seemed to be concerned about was what his posh friends would say, never mind that his daughter had needed his help. Well, facts had to be faced now. Surely once he knew that Ellen was dying he would want to make some provision for his granddaughter?

Florrie put the cup and saucer back on to the tray and picked up the plate, noticing that Ellen had eaten only a morsel of the cake. She straightened up and took a deep breath before saying, 'Ellen, you can't go on shilly-shallying. Try and swallow your pride, love. Go see your folk, for Patsy's sake, will you? Will you promise me?'

Ellen nodded.

Silently Florrie said, 'Oh, thank God!' and she meant it. She felt calmer now and, in a strange way, relief filled her.

Ellen caught Florrie's hand and held it against her cheek. 'I've been so lucky to have had you,' she whispered.

The tears brimmed up again and the lump in Florrie's throat choked off any words she might have wanted to say. She bent low and wrapped her podgy arms around Ellen's thin body, hugging her close to her large breast. They stayed holding on to each other for a long time until Florrie broke away, brushing her eyes with the back of her hand.

'Well, I'm away downstairs now. And you want to get yourself off to bed,' she said briskly. She sighed heavily before adding, in a very much quieter voice, 'Don't suppose it's any good me asking you not to go to work in the morning, is it?'

Ellen got to her feet. The fear that had bordered on panic when the doctor had told her his verdict had passed now. It was hard, though, very hard to appear to be brave, especially in front of Florrie. Somehow she had to find the courage and inner strength needed to carry on as normal. She couldn't give in. She'd got to persevere until she had set things right for Patsy. 'Florrie, please, try not to worry about me. I am going to go to work in the morning and when I've finished I promise I will set about seeing my parents.' As she spoke the words she truly meant them. She couldn't put off things until another day, as she'd always done in the past. Florrie said nothing, just leaned over and kissed Ellen's pale cheek.

Neither of them was to know that fate would play its own hand. Ellen had left it too late to mend the bad feeling which had existed between herself and her father.

When at last Florrie got into bed she couldn't sleep. She kept shifting about restlessly, uneasily. Had she given Ellen good advice? Would the old man relent after all these years? Surely he wouldn't

be able to resist Patsy? Anybody with half an ounce
of decency would be thrilled to acknowledge that
girl as a granddaughter. She let out a long-drawn
deep breath before muttering to herself, 'Oh, for
Gawd's sake go to sleep. There's no fool like an old
fool and for all you know he might even refuse to
see Ellen.' The very thought made her curse out
loud. 'If he still thinks of our Patsy as a bastard, and
he still won't help Ellen I'll kill him! I'll find the
bugger meself and I'll murder him!' She was still
swearing about Ellen's father when she finally fell
asleep.

The house seemed so silent now. Ellen knew she
wouldn't be able to lie in bed. Sleep would be
impossible. Tiptoeing quietly so as not to wake
Patsy, she went into the bedroom and removed the
blanket and quilt from her own bed. She wrapped
the blanket around her body then, settling herself
down in the armchair, she tucked the patchwork
quilt around her knees and over her lap. Muffled up
she felt warmer. She leaned back in the chair and
gazed absently around the room. Just thinking
about going to see her father brought all the hurtful
memories flooding back.

It was a long time since she had allowed herself to
dwell on the events that had led her to Strathmore
Street. She didn't want to have to remember it all,
yet tonight she couldn't help herself. In her mind the

years slid away and exposed it all: the loneliness, the bitterness and the anger.

Just three days after her nineteenth birthday, her mother had led her into the drawing-room and her father had broken the news to her that Peter had been killed in a hunting accident. Ellen, clinging grimly to the edge of a table, her face as white as a sheet, had pleaded, '*No*. Please, no. Tell me it's not true. Peter and I are going to be married, he promised. He can't be dead.'

Even now, as she recalled that day, the memory hurt so much that her lips trembled and her body shook. For as long as she could remember, Peter had been part of her life. From childhood their relationship had been like that of brother and sister, and she had always idolised him.

It had been the Easter holiday time, and they were out on the moors together, when it seemed as though – for the first time – they really discovered each other. Suddenly he had bent his head and kissed her.

When he drew away she stared up at him. No one had ever kissed her like that before, but she didn't feel angry or outraged or hurt. She felt happy, deliriously happy. Before she had time to think, she was swept up into his arms and he was kissing her again and she was kissing him back. This time, when he let her go, a feeling of warmth, happiness and belonging flooded over her.

Peter realised she was no longer a child. She was

almost nineteen and he was twenty-three. He looked at her differently now, studied her face, the soft skin, the huge eyes fringed with long lashes, the warm generous mouth and he knew that he loved her. This new-found attraction and their love for each other could not be denied. Nothing and no one else mattered. There had been nothing leisurely about their love-making, their kisses long and hard, the coming together frantic. With hindsight, it was as if Peter had known that his life was to be cut short.

Ellen wasn't sure that she was pregnant. Her mother, coming upon her vomiting her heart out in the huge upstairs bathroom with its enormous white porcelain handbasin, had simply leapt to that conclusion. The scenes that followed were dreadful. Ellen had wanted to lay her head on her mother's shoulder and confess how it had really happened. To explain that her love for Peter and his for her had been so sudden, so wonderful that they had let themselves be swept along. Instead, the following days had turned out to be an awful nightmare.

She had thought that at least her mother would be sympathetic. But she wasn't. She indulged in hysterics. Her father became her enemy, shrieking foul insinuations at her. She had been appalled that his love for her could so quickly turn to hate.

So much yelling and shouting. So many horrible accusations.

She couldn't bring herself to tell them who the father was, though many a time she was tempted. It just didn't seem the right thing to do. Peter's mother and father were still so upset at the sudden loss of their son, she couldn't add shame to their sorrow.

Her father's voice hissed at her through his clenched teeth. 'The man had to be scum. No gentleman would have dared touch a daughter of mine.'

His decision was that the bastard, and that was the way he referred to it, could be put up for adoption or go to an institution. He didn't care which, just so long as he never had to set eyes on it.

Ellen pleaded and cried until there were no tears left. She toyed with the idea of having the baby adopted but, strangely enough, she now wanted the baby that was inside her. She had lost Peter and she knew that this pregnancy wasn't going to be easy. The truth was staring her in the face. If she wanted to keep the baby then she could not stay under her father's roof. He had left her in no doubt about that; he was not willing to discuss the matter any further, and his terms were not open to negotiation. His eyes had been black as coal, his face purple with rage, as he had pushed past her in the corridor. 'Just keep yourself out of my way. The very sight of you sickens me!' he had bellowed loud enough for even the staff below stairs to hear.

The tedious weeks of virtual imprisonment had

almost broken her spirit. Only allowed out under the cover of darkness, and then heavily cloaked and commanded by her father to stay within the grounds of the family home, she had had plenty of time to think.

Constantly she turned the alternatives over in her mind. She could stay with her family and be well looked after, which meant giving up her baby, probably without even seeing it, or she must leave there and fend for herself. Finally she made her decision, and as she did so she thought of Peter. So tall, so handsome, so full of life. If only he hadn't died, if only they could have been married, if only . . . Everything would be so safe and secure, she'd be so happy, if only Peter were still here.

Ellen stirred suddenly, her eyes snapping open. She stared into the glowing embers of the fire, wondering what had roused her. Outside a dog howled, then another barked. That must have been what had wakened her, she thought, heaving a great sigh. Snuggling down she drifted off again, her mind still very much in the past.

Making her arrangements hadn't been as easy as she'd thought it would be, but her determination never wavered. Finally the day dawned. There would be no turning back now. Today she was abandoning her whole family. But they had abandoned her weeks previously.

Her clothes lay on the chair by the window, her

valise neatly packed alongside. Daylight was beginning to show through the curtains – it was time for her to get up. Going to the washstand, she poured water from the tall china jug into the bowl and washed her face and hands, then cleaned her teeth.

Trying to do everything quietly so as not to wake Rosie, her personal maid who slept next door, she brushed out her hair and plaited it with a certain amount of difficulty. Usually Rosie would have done this for her.

Then she began to dress.

She would wear a formal high-necked blouse with leg-o-mutton sleeves and long tight cuffs and the full dark navy blue skirt which reached to her ankles. Hastily she pulled on her grey woollen stockings and her boots, raising each foot in turn on to a stool to enable her to button and lace them, for stooping low was now almost impossible. Being in her eighth month of pregnancy, she decided not to add a belt to what had once been her tiny waist. On top of her small attaché case lay her navy straw hat with a silver ribbon. She picked it up and placed it on her head, setting it at a perfectly straight angle.

Next she opened the top drawer of the chest which stood against the far wall. First she took out her gold fob watch and pinned it to the lapel of the jacket she was to wear. Next she extracted a jeweller's box. No need to open it for she knew its contents by heart. Pushing it deep down into her valise beneath the articles of clothing, she felt no remorse.

The jewellery was hers. Finally she put in a leather pouch which held a good many gold sovereigns she had carefully hoarded over the past few months. At least she had sufficient money to tide her over for a while.

She was ready to leave. The minute she walked out of this house she was going to adopt a new identity. She would become Mrs Ellen Kent. She had decided to stick with her own Christian name. Kent was entirely fictitious, a name she had drawn out of the blue, and the 'Mrs' a courtesy title she would bestow upon herself.

Pulling her hat more firmly down on her head, taking up her case in one hand and her valise in the other, she made her way downstairs. Letting herself out into the back courtyard Ellen shivered, thankful she was wearing her heavy top coat. Within minutes she was in the lane which would take her on to the main road. Only once did she pause to look back at the house. Although within easy distance of the city, it stood in beautiful grounds. For a moment she wavered, filled with a longing, a yearning that was almost unbearable, to turn back to become part of her family again. With an effort she pushed down the sadness and walked on. She knew her father wouldn't relent. The bitterness she had felt towards him had lessened during the past months, but as to feelings of love for him, she had none. Resolutely she set off in the direction of Buckingham Palace Road.

She managed to reach the depot and board a tram before the tears came.

'Tooting Broadway,' the voice of the conductor rang out. 'This is the end of the line, madam,' he told Ellen as he gently tapped her on the shoulder. There was nothing else for it; she had to stand up, and with some difficulty she made her way between the wooden seats of the tram car. She alighted into the middle of the road and the chirpy conductor kindly leaned down and handed her her attaché case. Standing still, she watched in bewilderment as the tram rattled to the end of the tracks.

With the crowds milling about, and the commotion that was going on, she wondered for a moment how she would ever make it safely to the pavement. Clutching both her bag and her case, she was scared to death. It was not so very far from her own home, yet she felt as if she were on a different planet. The pavement was crowded with grubby children, the women all wore shawls and shuffled along with large straw shopping bags dangling from their arms. The men and the bigger boys made her nervous. Their language was so strange, every other word seemed to be a curse.

She had to walk very carefully to avoid being jostled off the kerb into the roadway. Wearily she kept going – her head was aching, her back and shoulders were aching. She'd never felt so exhausted in the whole of her life, and her valise was becoming heavier with every step she took. A few yards further on she saw a notice-board nailed to the wall outside a shop which bore the name of 'Smoker's Delight'. Jars of snuff, boxes of cigars, cigarettes and matches were on display in the window. It was however, a carefully printed card pinned to the board which took her eye, for it declared in large letters: Rooms To Let.

With a determined effort she opened the door.

A bell jangled, startling her, so that she stood in the entrance a while before closing the door. The shop was brightly illuminated by gas jets and was infinitely more cheerful and warm inside than the grey foggy November day outside.

There was a man in a white apron behind the counter and another man lounging in front of the counter talking to him. They broke off their conversation as Ellen approached. On reaching the counter she put down the suitcase, but gripped her bag tightly with both hands. Then she cleared her throat and gave a nervous cough before saying, 'Good morning, I'm enquiring about the rooms which your display card states are to let.'

The man in the white apron couldn't have been kinder or more helpful. Taking pen and paper he wrote an address. 'I don't need to look it up for you, love, that's Mrs Holmes.' He stretched out his hand and announced, 'I'm Fred Davis,' then, turning, he added, 'and this is Alexander Berry.' He gave a deep-throated chuckle and added, 'He's better known to everyone around here as Ollie.'

Ellen used her free hand to shake that of Mr Davis and turned to Mr Berry, who was looking at her questioningly. She said, including both men in the statement, 'I'm Mrs Ellen Kent and I need to find suitable lodgings.'

'Well, love, I think you'll find you've landed on your feet if you go along to twenty-two Strathmore Street.' Again he gave a deep jolly chuckle before adding, 'Mrs Holmes is a bit of a rough diamond but she's clean. Yeah, say what you like, that woman keeps 'er place spotless and she 'as a heart of gold. Strathmore Street's not far from 'ere. Just cross the road, go past the pie shop and it's the second on your left.'

While Fred Davis was talking, Alexander Berry, obviously a mate of Fred's, had kept glancing at Ellen. When their gazes met he smiled and she smiled back. He was totally different from this jolly shopkeeper: a much quieter man, and not at all like the working-class men she had already come into contact with. He was a very tall man whose clothes were different, for a start. He wore a dark grey suit that fitted him well and his black shoes were well polished. As their gaze met again, there was something, both in his expression and his general demeanour, that Ellen felt was gentle and kind. His was an open face, and his bright eyes seemed to be full of understanding.

'If you'd like me to, I'll walk with you. It's not taking me out of my way, I live in Strathmore Street myself.'

He had spoken quietly and his speech held none of the cockney twang. Relief gave Ellen courage. She felt herself warming to him, not in the least afraid or suspicious of his offer.

Without further ado, Mr Berry picked up Ellen's case, walked to the door which he held open, making a gesture with his head to indicate that she should go ahead of him. Before doing so, she thanked Mr Davis for his help, to which he replied, 'You're more than welcome, my love. Pop in for a chat any time, it's always nice to see a lady.'

Ellen smiled at this invitation, taking no offence, for it had been offered kindly, and she nodded good-bye as she left the shop.

Fred Davis's eyes followed her. He had already guessed that she had run away from something or someone and she didn't look the type to live in this neighbourhood. Her clothes alone told him that much, quite apart from the educated way she spoke. She was a very attractive young lady, but there was no getting away from the fact that she was preg-nant. Scared, too, very scared, and with good reason – she certainly wouldn't settle easily in this working-class district.

Mr Berry placed his hand beneath Ellen's elbow and steered her across the main road. The hustle and

bustle of people, carriages, tramcars and the huge
great horses pulling the carts had made her hesitate,
but with determination he soon had her safely on
the opposite pavement. They walked in silence, but
she cast surreptitious glances at him from time to
time. He wasn't very much older than she was, but
he certainly was a lot taller – about six foot three,
she surmised, and he was quite handsome with that
mass of dark unruly hair. He walked with the air of
a man who feared no one and was totally at ease in
this locality.

Strathmore Street was narrow, with dingy-
looking back-to-back houses almost pressing
against each other. Ellen thought them wretched
dwellings even for the working classes.

'Here we are, follow me and mind your step!' Mr
Berry called over his shoulder as he opened the front
gate of number twenty-two. Too late. Ellen failed
to see the cracked, raised flagstone. Tipping it with
the toe of her boot, she wasn't able to ward off the
fall. She stumbled badly, fell awkwardly, and ended
up lying on the pavement in an ugly heap.

Her skirt caught up under her large belly, she felt
indecent. With no time to straighten her clothes, let
alone pick herself up, she felt a searing pain shoot
through her stomach, and then she was vomiting
into the gutter. Opening her eyes, which were
brimming with tears, as much from embarrassment
as from pain, she saw Mr Berry kneeling on the
pavement beside her, with little regard for his own

clothes. From his pocket he produced a spotless white handkerchief, and leaning across her, he wiped her mouth.

Disengaging the valise, which still hung from her arm, he bent low, and gently helped her to her feet. Still feeling too sick to protest, she relaxed, letting her whole body rest against this total stranger. She had no idea how much time elapsed before, still feeling shaky, she allowed him to steady her with one of his arms, whilst he held her case and bag in his other hand. Walking slowly, he steered her towards number twenty-two. As he helped her up the short garden path, he whispered, 'You'll like Mrs Holmes. Don't let her appearance put you off.'

Ellen stared at him in dismay, not knowing what to expect.

'Florrie, Florrie! Move yourself, we need your help,' he called through the open doorway.

An ample woman, with swollen ankles, shuffled along the hallway. 'What the 'ell's going on?' she roared, staring suspiciously at Ellen.

'This lady is looking for rooms to rent, but at the moment she isn't feeling too well.'

Just like Fred Davis, Florrie Holmes didn't need anyone to draw a picture for her. She had already summed up the situation with canny instinct. 'Well, don't just stand there, Ollie Berry, make yourself useful. Get her through to me kitchen. No, no, never mind about 'er cases, leave 'em where they are. Just see to 'er.'

Ellen looked around. She had never been in so small a room before. She felt a sense of despair, compounded with weariness and disillusionment. The tears welled up and trickled down her cheeks.

'I'll make us a cup of tea.' Florrie got up and took the kettle to the sink which stood in the corner. 'Sorry the place is in a bit of a mess, but the bloody sweep hasn't turned up.' She let out a cackle of a laugh as she pointed towards the fireplace. From the high mantelshelf hung a ragged green cloth. The hearth was covered with wads of old newspapers.

'Three weeks ago it was I ordered that sweep. Lazy sod! Probably had a win at the dogs and don't need the money. Still he'll be round, and when he does come he'll be sorry he messed me about. If I wasn't so fat I'd crawl up there meself. Later on today I'll set light to some paraffin rags, shove 'em up the chimney. That'll do the trick, and I'll 'ave saved me bloody money.'

Ollie Berry shook his head, even though he was having a hard job to stop himself from laughing. He knew well enough why Florrie was gabbling on so. She was trying her best to put her unfamiliar visitor at ease.

'Here. Blow your nose.' For the second time that morning Ellie was being offered a clean handkerchief, this time by Florrie. 'God above! There's no need for yer to cry. Nothing's so desperate that we can't do something about it.'

Moving at a speed which belied her bulk, Florrie

soon had them seated around a well-scrubbed kitchen table. Steaming cups of tea now stood in front of them, and Ellen found herself smiling as she watched Florrie Holmes slicing bread from a long crusty loaf which she pressed into her soft belly, whilst cutting it into thick pieces with a saw-like knife.

'Have some, Mrs Kent.' Ollie grinned broadly at her as he pushed the plate in her direction. Ellen found herself enjoying it, liberally spread with butter and jam, and admitting to herself that she had eaten better fare, and off far better china, but it was a long time since food had tasted this good or the company had been so friendly.

Although Ellen couldn't have known it then, that meeting was to form the basis of a lasting friendship and great affection between these three ill-assorted people.

Ellen stirred in her sleep again. The fire in the grate, banked down with vegetable peelings and tea leaves, gave off a hissing sound. Suddenly she was wide awake. On her cheeks were tears, which she wiped away with her sleeve. There was also a lump in her throat the size of a golf ball. She took a deep breath, then another. 'Well,' she declared out loud, 'reliving the past isn't going to help.'

So many years since Ollie had literally dragged her over Florrie's doorstep. She'd be the first to admit that she could have travelled further and fared

a lot worse. A smile came to her lips as one of
Florrie's many sayings came to her mind. 'You can
travel this earth and you might find a cockney's
equal, but you'll never find their betters.'

Ellen turned her head, glanced at the clock on the
high mantelshelf and saw it was still early – only five
o'clock. She had time to have a strip wash before
getting dressed.

When all the process of getting herself ready for
work was finished, she set the table with a porridge
bowl and cup and saucer in readiness for Patsy's
breakfast. She still had a good half-hour to spare.

'I'll make some tea,' she said under her breath as
she took the brown china teapot down from the
dresser. Many a morning she didn't bother to make
tea for herself, waiting instead until she got to the
market, knowing that at least one member of the
Day family would be brewing up. A large enamel
mug of good strong tea would be placed in her
hand, often before she even had time to take off her
outdoor coat and don the large wrap-round apron
all the Day women wore.

Sipping her tea, Ellen knew only too well that, but
for Gran and Grandad Day and their family, she
might never have survived in this working-class
area of South London. Her introduction to the Day
family had really started from that first day. Gran,
not wanting to miss out on anything, had made one
of her frequent visits to Florrie, supposedly for a
cuppa, but in reality to see Flo's new lodger. Gran's

house was directly opposite number twenty-two, and it was Gran who had assisted Florrie in delivering Patsy.

The baby had been born almost before she had had time to settle into Florrie's upstairs room and get her bearings, never mind make any arrangements to go into hospital. Maybe it had all happened for the best. From the moment Gran had told her she had a little girl, it was as if Gran's heart had opened to include Ellen. Over the years Gran had loved her and watched out for her as if she were one of her own daughters. As for Patsy, she could do no wrong! The whole tribe of Days loved her. Very quickly Ellen had learnt that with the Days for your friends, you were lucky indeed. As enemies, they were a different kettle of fish entirely. Hurt one and you upset them all.

There were so many of them. Ellen, nor indeed many other folk, had never really worked out the final total. Gran and her husband Jack had five sons and one daughter. To them had to be added the daughters-in-law, one son-in-law and fourteen grandchildren, all living in Strathmore Street. In adjoining streets lived nephews, nieces, uncles, aunts and cousins. Probably not even the Days themselves could give the sum total of their tribe.

Compared with others in the district, this family was quite affluent. It was a safe bet that they owned ninety per cent of all the market stalls. Gran presided over the entire brood with as much command as any queen, and God help the daughter-in-law whose views were contrary to her own. Yet for all that she wielded a rod of iron, she was loved by sons, daughter, grandchildren and in-laws alike. Ellen felt she had been fortunate that Patsy, and she herself, had been included in this love that knew no bounds. She was also well aware of the fact that it was because of Gran's insistence that she had been offered employment on the market.

Ellen bit her lip as she recalled those early days after Patsy was born. Florrie had eagerly offered to look after the baby, but while Ellen would not have hesitated to take her up on her offer, she had found no one willing to employ her. She had applied for several advertised positions and had been turned away. One man, in an office of a local builder's yard, had even gone so far as to tell her that her accent was 'too genteel'.

It had been as she was on her way home from this interview, feeling very miserable, almost at the end of her tether, not knowing how she was going to be able to earn her living, that she had bumped into young Tommy Day. 'My Gran's bin looking for you,' he said as he gave her a cheeky grin. Ellen smiled as she thanked him. It was obvious he hadn't had a wash. His hair was uncombed, his short trousers too big for him, and his wide grin showed that his two front teeth were missing. Yet for all that, he was as happy as a lark and as fit as a flea.

Ellen worked her way down the narrow passage,

squeezing past the children whose names she didn't yet know.

Gran had her chair placed right up in front of the fireplace, a long-handled toasting-fork in her hand and a pile of thick slices of bread lying on the edge of the fender. 'Ellen, come in. Come on, love, pour yourself a cuppa. Pot's under the cosy on the hob. Could you eat a bit of toast?'

Ellen had to smother a smile. When wasn't the teapot on the go in this house? In the short time she had known the Day family, she had come to the conclusion that they drank tea day and night. Gallons of it.

Ellen took a cup to the draining-board and poured milk into it from a quart bottle which stood in a bowl of cold water on the window-sill; that was the way to keep the milk fresh, Gran had told her. Having filled her cup with the strong brew from the pot, she sat down on a chair facing Gran.

'Any luck?' Gran demanded eagerly, knowing Ellen had been up to the builder's yard after an office job.

'No. My way of speaking wouldn't suit the customers, the manager told me,' Ellen said ruefully and shrugged.

For a moment there was silence between them. Fancy putting the girl down just because she spoke a bit posh-like, Gran thought. Probably the old bugger was jealous!

'You're going to work for my boys,' Gran stated

emphatically, staring at Ellen, who couldn't believe she had heard right. Gran wasn't one for beating about the bush. She'd come straight out with it.

Ellen's head dropped. She couldn't find words to answer Gran. The very thought of working in a marketplace terrified her. It wasn't that she was too proud, but that she feared she would not be able to do the work. God knew she would try.

Things worried her now which previously she had never even had to think about. She needed to buy coal; the rent had to be paid; food had to be bought; and her store of money was running low.

'Ellen, did you 'ear me?' Gran leaned forward and gave her cheek a gentle tap. 'Look, love, it'll be all right, you'll see.'

Ellen's eyes were brimming with tears. Emotion clogged her throat. She hadn't expected to feel grateful for charity.

As if reading her thoughts, Gran lowered her voice, and said softly, 'It's not charity my boys will be giving you. Bleedin' hard, dirty work, that's what it will be. All hours that Gawd almighty sends and grubby, grimy jobs. I know what I'm talking about. I worked on that market long before it was covered in. Yeah, and I 'elped my Jack push a barrow around these streets of an evening.'

Watching Ellen trying to suppress her amusement, Gran said, 'You can laugh my girl. Go on, laugh, it'll do you good.' Grinning broadly now, she went on ' 'Course, that was before me bloody legs swelled up like balloons.'

'You're having me on, Gran.'

'Gawd's truth, love. There was something else an' all that put a stop to me working.' She threw back her head and let out a great belly laugh. 'Yeah, it were my Jack! Put me in the club regular as clock-work! He only had to hang his trousers on the end of our bed and I'd end up with another bun in the oven.'

The expression on Ellen's face set Gran off again. They were both clutching their sides and tears were trickling down their faces when finally they stopped laughing.

Gran sighed. 'I wish you weren't so bleedin' thin, Ellen. Like a rake you are. It's a wonder you don't slip down the drain 'oles out in the street.'

'I'll be fine, Gran. I'm perfectly fit. If the boys will just show me exactly what I have to do, I'll soon learn.'

'Oh, my Queenie will see you all right. She's a good 'un is my Queenie, you'll see.'

Well, see she had. She'd worked for the Day brothers in Tooting Market from that day to this, and had cause to be eternally grateful to the fat, coarse, common woman, known to all as Gran, whom she had come to love so dearly.

Most evenings she came home with dirt-grimed fingernails and her eyelids dropping with exhaustion. Nevertheless, it had been a good life, good company, rough cockney humour, not many dull days!

She had missed having a man, a husband, but Patsy had more than compensated her.

Time to go. With grim determination, Ellen donned her coat. Wrapping herself up warm, even down to the woollen mittens she had persevered so hard to knit. Quietly she went into the back bedroom and bent low over her sleeping daughter. 'I wouldn't change a thing about you,' she whispered as she placed her hand gently on Patsy's head.

A moment later she let out a long sigh. Patsy was so beautiful. The distinctive colouring of her chestnut hair and that healthy bloom to her skin set her apart. 'Patsy, Patsy, Patsy,' she murmured as she lightly pressed her lips to the top of her daughter's hair.

At the door she paused, staring backwards, as if to imprint the picture of her daughter firmly in her mind.

Chapter Two

As ELLEN LEFT the house, the raw cold of that November morning struck her immediately. When the pain hit her, she panicked. She was gasping, drawing in great gulps of air. She stood still, clutching herself around the chest with both arms crossed. When the spasm eased, she cleared her throat, the rasping sound of her coughing echoing down the street.

'That you, Ellen love?'

She heard the voice before she saw the man. Harry Watkins – so familiar was she with his routine and daily greeting, she knew his voice well. 'Morning, Harry. Nippy, isn't it?'

'It sure is,' he agreed.

It was not yet daylight, and the lampposts positioned at regular intervals still shed their ghostly yellow light. More out of politeness than anything else, Ellen watched as Harry, the lamplighter, raised his long pole shaped like a shepherd's crook. He carefully wielded the hook to catch in a brass ring that hung at the end of a long chain. Harry then applied pressure and pulled. The mechanism gave a loud click and at once the area where they stood below was plunged into darkness.

'Think they'd leave the lights on, dark days like this, wouldn't you?' he grumbled as he mounted his bicycle and precariously wedged his pole across the handlebars.

'Bye, Harry,' Ellen called, moving off quickly for already her feet were freezing cold.

'Ta-ta, Ellen. Take care, gal, and git yerself something for that cough.' His words came back to her through the foggy darkness, and she smiled to herself. What a nice old man Harry was!

When she turned the corner into the Broadway, the accustomed sight stimulated Ellen. Whereas at first, all those years ago, the activity and commotion each day as the preparation for trading got underway had horrified, even appalled her, she now felt excitement stirring within her. It was here that she had been given the opportunity to earn her own living. If the Day family hadn't taken her under their wing, and Florrie hadn't taken them into her home, what then? Where would she and Patsy have lived? How would they have lived? She pushed these questions to the back of her mind.

What about Ollie, the very first person to have befriended her when she had first arrived in Tooting? Over the years his love and companionship had meant so much. He had been the nearest thing Patsy had ever known to a father.

Oh, if only Peter hadn't been killed, if they could have been married, things would have been so different. She just couldn't imagine life without Patsy, but had she done the right thing? Had she been selfish wanting to keep Patsy, giving her a life that hadn't held many privileges?

This was no time to be having nagging doubts, she reprimanded herself. It would be far better to be thinking how she could safeguard Patsy's future, but she was still struggling with her conscience as she stood at the edge of the kerb.

The fog obscured the entrance to the market on the other side of the road. Once safely inside, she saw the large, naked gas jets were going full blast, giving out not only light but some degree of warmth. Hissing blue flames, with no protective covers, were positioned over every stall and at intervals the length of the market. On a day such as this they would be burning continuously until the market closed in the evening.

Although it was only a little after six a.m., the hustle and bustle which preceded every day's trading had begun in earnest. There were vans, barrows, handcarts and drays. Horses stood stamping and pawing the ground with their iron-shod hoofs, their breath coming from wide nostrils, hanging stagnant for a moment before mingling with the swirling fog. Then this warm vapour rose, as if from a boiling kettle, momentarily forcing the murkiness away, clearing a space around the huge horses' heads.

Men jogged and jostled each other, shoving and thrusting their way through. Everyone was anxious to get unloaded. The prospect of the market café and a good hot breakfast added weight to their vigour and strength. The task of unloading fell to the younger men, ferrying the goods from vehicle to stall. Hurrying to and fro, burdened down with bulky boxes and crates, some preferred the freight to be humped on to their backs, while others heaved their loads on to one shoulder. Hand on hip and breathing heavily, they slanted their strides because they carried their burdens on one side only. God help anyone who got in their way.

'You silly born bugger! Wait for the ice blocks before you unload that fish. How many more times do you need telling?' Blower Day's voice rang out sharp with authority. Ellen removed only her top coat, putting first her wrap-around pinafore over the top of her woollen jumper and cardigan. Then in front of that a bibbed apron, which she tied securely around her waist.

Queenie Day was a beauty and to her parents and her brothers none was her equal. Extraordinary-looking, she was of medium height, buxom, with thick, wavy blond hair. She had marvellous skin and a colour to her cheeks which came from her outdoor life.

Queenie had been eighteen when Ellen first came to Strathmore Street. What had most impressed Queenie about Ellen was her gentle face and form, her soft-toned voice and her obvious good breeding. Queenie had never before come into contact with a young woman such as Ellen. A kindly mateyness had developed between the two right from the start. As the years passed, their friendship had grown to become great affection.

'Morning, Queenie,' Ellen said to Queenie's bent back.

'Morning, Ellen.' Straightening herself, Queenie looked directly at Ellen and for a moment she was startled. Her friend's usually fine features looked gaunt. Indeed, her whole appearance had changed. Haggard was the only word Queenie could think of to describe Ellen's looks this morning.

'You all right, Ellen?' she asked, concern apparent in her voice.

'Yes, thank you, Queenie.'

'You sure? You don't look all that great to me.'

Ellen smiled, pleased that Queenie cared. 'I'll be fine. I just didn't sleep very well last night.'

'Well, if you're sure. Would you get some beets going in the copper?'

'Right away.' Stooping, Ellen picked up a wooden box full of dark, dirty, raw beetroots and walked towards the rear of the market. Reaching the end door, which led into the outside yard, she was about to put the box down in order to have a free hand to push the iron bar upwards and so unfasten the door, when suddenly it opened. The man about to enter stepped back quickly, allowing her to pass, and at the same time murmured 'Okay, Ellen?'

'Yes, thank you, Leo. Is the copper on?'

'I built the fire under it and put a match to it a good half-hour ago. The water should be nearly boiling by now.'

'Thanks, Leo,' Ellen said, giving him a grateful smile.

It was raw cold outside in the open. It came to Ellen's mind that the men like Leo, who hung about on the off-chance of earning a tanner here and there in return for doing odd jobs, certainly earned their money.

Lifting the wooden lid down from the top of the copper, Ellen dragged an empty crate nearer. Placing it upside down, she stood on it. Then, raising the box of beetroots waist-high, she proceeded to lower them by their cut stalks into the boiling water. Having added two handfuls of rough cooking salt, which she took from the stone jar standing against the wall, she replaced the lid. Wiping her hands on a coarse towel hanging from a nail in the brickwork, she thankfully went back into the comparative warmth of the market.

There had been a time when the fresh rabbit stall had nauseated Ellen. Now there was no squeamishness in her actions. On to the blood-smeared wooden block she threw half a dozen carcasses. A quick cut with the knife, pull, rip and the fur was removed as far as the head. One blow from the cleaver and this was severed. The smallest rabbits

Ellen chopped into joints, to be sold separately. The best specimens she skilfully prepared to go on display. Pulling back the skin each side of the belly, she nimbly inserted a wooden skewer, thereby creating an opening which allowed the kidneys and the fat that encircled them to show to the best advantage. Then, having laid them out in rows and placed sprigs of parsley to embellish the presentation, she stood back. Queenie cast a critical eye over the stall, gave Ellen a thumbs-up sign and, laughing together, they moved across to the fruit stall.

With his usual flourish, Danny had by this time set out a decorative arrangement of fruit. All that remained for the two women to do was to polish a few apples and select the best of the oranges. Then they folded and crushed the coloured tissue paper which the fruit had been wrapped in, to use it as a nest to set the fruit in on top of each display. Finished, Queenie banged her cold hands to her sides.

'It's enough to freeze a brass monkey,' she complained.

Ellen laughed, well used to Queenie's raw humour.

'You go and collect the mugs up and I'll put the kettle on,' Queenie offered. Ellen didn't hesitate. She was more than ready for a hot drink. The cold and damp from outside had penetrated right through the entire market. The walls were wet and unpleasant to the touch. The fog seemed to be creeping through, shrouding the stalls with swirling smog.

They drank their hot tea and chatted about life in general. Ellen listened to Queenie's bawdy, cockney witticisms and chuckled when she let out great belly laughs. As Queenie loaded a tin tray with mugs of the strong brew for her brothers, Ellen made for the yard.

'She's a good-humoured girl is Queenie,' thought Ellen, feeling much better for having had those few minutes' rest.

As Ellen removed the lid, the steam that rose from the copper made her gasp momentarily. She used her forearm to brush her hair away from her forehead. It felt clammy and dank. Using a long-handled dipper bowl, she extracted a few beetroots from the murky water. From her apron pocket she took a matchstick and used it to prod the largest beets. They didn't bleed. To make sure, she used her thumb and forefinger, easing the skin back. Satisfied they were sufficiently cooked, she marvelled to herself what a difference boiling made to the humble beetroot. Before cooking they were hard to the touch, and rough and dirty in appearance, whereas boiled and skinned they were soft and deep red in colour, with a gloss all of their own.

Having got out as many as she could, Ellen changed the dipper for a long-handled fishing net. Even so, to remove the remaining beetroots from the bottom of the copper she had to bend over almost double. Finished at last, and grasping the two handles of the tin bath which now contained the steaming beetroots, she used one knee to raise the bath almost chest-high.

About half-way across the yard Ellen staggered. The pain in her side was excruciating, but she continued on. Customers were already swarming into the market as she threaded her way between the stalls.

Blower Day, his arms full of empty crates and boxes, paused in his stride. 'Put that down, Ellen. I'll get one of the lads to carry it,' he shouted.

Ellen attempted to open her mouth to answer him, but a burst of coughing came instead. Involuntarily, she let go her hold on the bath. As it hit the ground the tin clattered and clanged, sending its steaming contents in all directions. She continued to cough. Her hands flew to her mouth and blood oozed out between her splayed fingers.

A loud crash echoed down the building as Blower threw his load of boxes to the ground. In two strides he was beside Ellen. As he reached her she slumped forward on to her knees. Her face was ashen and her lips blue.

'Jesus Christ Almighty. Get Danny,' he yelled.

There was no need to call him. Blower's frantic shout and the hullabaloo caused by Ellen dropping the tin bath, followed by the throwing of the boxes, had brought all his family running. Danny and

Blower, one on either side of Ellen, caught hold of her, lifting her as gently as they knew how.

Blower cursed loudly. The front of Ellen's white apron was splattered with blood and, looking down at her face, he could see that her nostrils were blocked with blood. Tough as he was, Blower Day was so distressed at the state Ellen was in that alarm, fright and dread all swelled up in his throat, making him want to retch.

He turned his head to the crowd that had gathered. 'Don't just stand there. For Christ sake, one of you call a bleedin' ambulance!' he screeched at them.

The market traders knew that what had happened that morning would remain in their memory for a very, very long time.

Chapter Three

PATSY WAS READY to go. She tucked her clean handkerchief into the pocket of her thick winter coat, wound her scarf twice round her neck and tugged her woollen hat on to the top of her thick, shining hair.

She gave a last look round the kitchen to see that she had left everything tidy. These upstairs rooms in a back-to-back terrace house were the only home she had ever known. To her it was a nice home. Her mother scrubbed the floors, polished the odd pieces of furniture with wax and constantly washed the two hand-made rugs. Their living-room was cosy, always bright, clean and tidy. Even the bedroom held two real beds. Many of her school friends were not so lucky. One girl she knew even had to sleep on a straw palliasse laid out on the floor.

There had always been just her mum and herself. When she was little she had often wished she could have a father, but wishing didn't make it so; and since she had grown up she had tried her best to close her mind to the fact that she hadn't one, and not think about it. Anyway, she told herself, she was very lucky.

She had Florrie downstairs – she was a real old

sweetie, even if she did go on a bit sometimes. Then there was Ollie, just up the road. He was their best friend, her mother was always telling her that.

Her mum was different an' all! She had a job. A real job, not going out cleaning which most women round there did; no, her mum worked full time on the market, which meant that she brought home lots of vegetables and fruit. It also meant that she had to get her own breakfast, because Mum had to start work real early. Sometimes she did wish her mother didn't have to work such long hours; not that her mum ever grumbled, but she was often dog-tired when she got home at night.

How much longer, though, could her mum continue? For months Patsy had known her mother was ill. A group of women chatting in the roadway below, oblivious to the fact that their voices carried, had seemed to assume Ellen Kent had consumption.

Consumption!

On that day, Patsy had flown downstairs to where old Florrie lived, trying her best to fight off her nagging fears.

'Flo, Flo. Where are you?' she demanded, bursting into the back living-room. 'Do you know what consumption is?'

Good-hearted Florrie had been taken by surprise, but down-to-earth as ever, she understood immediately what must have happened.

'Aw, Patsy, you don't want to take no notice of them gossiping women.'

Patsy repeated her question, 'Do you know what consumption is? And has my mum got it?'

Florrie knew only too well and yes, if she faced the truth, she knew Ellen Kent was riddled with that terrible disease.

She loved Ellen as she would her own daughter and this bright young child, now standing terrified before her, even more so. Florrie made up her mind to tell her some half-truths.

'Your mum's got a really nasty cough, you know that. She's not strong. She's not built to rough it like most of us round 'ere. It's this blinking awful winter. You'll see. Come the warmer weather, she'll buck up.'

Florrie closed her eyes and prayed that she had spoken the truth. When she opened them again and looked into Patsy's face she said, 'Oh, Patsy!' Her double chins were quivering; her whole fat body had been quivering. This was what she had feared for some time now – Patsy finding out the truth.

'You're a good girl, love. You 'elp yer mum a lot and when you leave school and git a job, yer mum will be able ter take things a lot easier.'

Since that day, Patsy had done everything she could to make her mother rest. After school she would haul a bucket of coal up from the yard, put a match to the fire her mother regularly laid before leaving in the morning and light the gas under the black enamel pot containing shin of beef or neck of mutton stew. Every evening she would help her mother prepare the vegetables for their next day's dinner. There was never a shortage of vegetables, thanks to the kindness of the Day brothers.

When her mother came home, the two of them would huddle around the fire and drink hot, strong tea until their meal was ready.

Just now and again, Patsy would think her mother's health was worse. The cough persisted and her face looked so thin. Always her mother insisted it was only a bad cold.

Well, now there were only three more weeks after this one and she would be able to leave school. She didn't for a moment think her mother would be able to give up work altogether. Patsy knew she herself would only be able to earn a few shillings each week. Still, it would be a great help. Perhaps her mother could cut down on the hours she did and rest a little more.

It was ten minutes past eight. If she didn't go now, Patsy knew she would miss the tram and be late for school. She opened the kitchen door. At the same time, Flo's voice boomed out from below.

'Come on, Patsy love. You're going to be late.'

Having known Patsy from the day she was born, her warmth and natural love came through in the sound of her voice. Patsy ran down the narrow, steep flight of stairs. In the passageway, Florrie took Patsy in her arms.

'Now, don't you 'ang about when you git orf the tram at Wandsworth. You 'urry along to the school.

This bleeding fog is 'orrible, gets down on your chest. Are you wrapped up well?'

Patsy kissed Flo's lined cheek and squeezed past her bulk. She was smiling when she went out into the cold.

Florrie remained leaning against the wall. If anything happens to Ellen, it'll break that girl's heart, she told herself. Lumbering back to the warmth of her kitchen, she flopped down into her well-worn armchair. Her feet were badly swollen today.

'I love that kid. Me, Ollie and Gran Day, we're all she's got.' Florrie's face, never a pretty sight, was now distraught with anxiety.

Outside, Patsy was hurrying along the street, head bent against the cold.

'That you, Peggy?'

'That you, Patsy?'

Through the swirling fog each made out the shape of the other. Peggy Woolston linked her arm through Patsy's.

'Blinking cold, ain't it?'

'It sure is,' Patsy answered. 'Come on, let's run.'

They shot off down the street together.

'Come along now, girls. It's too cold to dawdle.' Miss Bennett, class mistress and deputy head of the church school in Shine Water Lane, paused for only a moment.

'Yes, Miss Bennett.'

'Morning, Miss.'

The voices of the girls dimly echoed behind her. Soon she was out of sight as the swirling fog hid even her silhouette. The fog that morning seemed to be eliminating all the usual noise, and because of the raw cold the girls felt indisposed to talk amongst themselves. Instead, they buried their chins deeper into the mufflers they all wore wrapped around their necks. To hurry was not in their nature. Many of these schoolchildren were far too undernourished for their movements to be hasty.

' 'Allo, 'allo, my luverleys.'

The policeman's voice boomed out bright and cheerful even before the girls could see him.

'Close in tight. Come on, tuck up and we'll all cross the road together.'

Now they could see the familiar sight of their friendly bobby. He was a firm favourite with all the girls. They regarded him as a friend and he was always good for a laugh.

The policeman's mackintosh cape was damp. His face beneath his helmet was red and raw, as were his hands. He fumbled to switch on the flat, black torch he had strapped across his chest. Those nearest to him could see a beam of light, but beyond ten yards it made little or no difference. The dirty yellow fog swallowed up all in its vicinity. His face, however, was a joy to behold. Beaming from ear to ear, his eyes sparkling and twinkling, he spread his arms wide, gathering the children into a tight group.

'Stay here for half a mo while I stop the traffic,' he ordered. Stepping briskly out into the road, he waved a large square of white rag he had taken from his pocket. Then, one hand in mid-air, he made a motion with his head and the girls trooped out together to reach the other side of the road safely.

'Thanks, bobby.'

''Bye, bobby,' they called back.

Shaking his head, he returned to the pavement. Poor, pathetic kids, he thought. Bet not many of them have had a decent breakfast, even on a morning like this. Ah well, we do what we can. No one man can set the world to rights.

Buttoning up his cape again, he proceeded on his beat in a thoughtful frame of mind.

While the children were crossing the bridge which straddled the dirty River Wandle, the Tannery Works opened up its steam vents. It was an awful, disgusting smell but the children were well used to it. The brewery, on the other hand, was a source of entertainment: barrels being rolled across the forecourt; teasing from the big, brawny draymen. This was their part of London. The horses which drew the drays were lovely – huge animals covered in heavy harnesses and gleaming brasses, always standing quiet and calm, so patient. This, however, was not a day to linger.

'There's the bell going. Come on, the lot of you. We don't want t'be late!' It was Peggy Woolston, the self-appointed leader of the class, who hurried them on.

The school gates were in sight now and, beyond the railings, the playground. It was a church school, neither in a good environment nor in a good state of repair. However, compared with the hovels most of these girls lived in, it was a warm, friendly place.

The school had six female teachers and one male. They all had a reputation for being kind and dedicated. Featured first every day was the morning service. At a nod from Miss Burgess, the headmistress, Mr Herbert took his seat at the upright piano. Mr Herbert had no teaching qualifications, but made himself indispensable in numerous ways.

The whole assembly was quiet now.

'We will sing the hymn "All things bright and beautiful".' As she mouthed the words, Miss Burgess felt herself to be an absolute hypocrite. How could she be so insincere as daily to ask these children to sing about the goodness and love of God? More than half of them were physically ill through undernourishment.

The sweet voices of the girls of all ages rose clear and pure. Miss Burgess cast her eyes over and around the assembled pupils, tormented by her melancholy thoughts. Was it only a fortnight since the Armistice had been signed? Bells had rung throughout the land, promising a land fit for heroes. That was, for those left alive to return. Even the soldiers spared were not now all whole men. For the past eighteen months she had worked as a volunteer orderly at the Infirmary. Within yards of London Bridge, that hospital had seen some sights.

Oh, yes, on the eleventh of November, people had hugged and kissed each other. Whistles had blown. Tugs on the Thames had hooted.

'Peace, peace at last. The war is over.'

But was it? Not for everyone. Families were mourning a son, brother, husband or friend. What of those who were returning? Would they find work? Who would care for the disabled? Men deprived of their limbs, some with their lungs torn to shreds due to the diabolical, fiendish use of gas in the trenches.

The sudden hush brought Miss Burgess back to the present. All verses of the hymn had now been sung. Bowing her head she said, 'Let us pray,' and began to recite the words of the Lord's Prayer. The children's voices followed her. The words were uttered in a sing-song tone, reeled off by heart without heed being given to their meaning.

'*Amen.*' Prayers for the day were over.

Outside the door of form five, Miss Bennett paused. From within came the sound of talking and occasional outbursts of laughter, with Peggy Woolston's voice raised above everyone else's. Throwing open the door, she walked briskly to the front of the class to her desk which was placed centrally in front of her pupils' desks. The girls stopped talking and started to fidget, nervously.

Miss Bennett was not over-qualified but what she lacked in academic honours she made up for in enthusiasm. Her passionate soul burned to ease the plight of these girls. She had become resigned but never immune to the fact that there was little she could do to alter their miserable lives.

Their future would vary little from that of their mothers: early marriage, almost yearly pregnancies and the long, endless struggle against dirt, disease and poverty.

'This morning, girls, you are going to help me with some administration work.'

Nodding to a girl seated in the front row she said, 'Come forward, Jenny. Take this box and hand out one pencil and a sheet of paper to each girl in the class. Now, this exercise is mainly for the girls who will be leaving the school in three weeks' time, when we break for the Christmas holidays. For those of you not yet fourteen years old, it will still be good practice and give you a lot to think about.'

Going to the blackboard she wrote in large capital letters:

INTERVIEWS   JOB PROSPECTS   NIGHT SCHOOL

Turning again to face the girls, she asked, 'Have you finished heading your papers?'

'Yes, Miss Bennett,' they chorused.

'Then please copy the three subjects I have chalked on the blackboard. I would like you to list beneath the first two anything that has happened or is likely to take place in the near future. Regarding Night School, if you have enrolled or even tried to register at any institute, please write full details. You may begin.'

Seating herself at her own desk, Miss Bennett stared hard at all her pupils in turn. The whole thing was hopeless, really. There was hardly a girl present who had the remotest chance of securing employment.

She allowed her gaze to fall upon three girls in particular. These three were, or could have been, bright pupils. Sadly, their minds needed nourishment just as much as their bodies in order for them to function to their full ability.

Take Peggy Woolston. She was loud-mouthed and common but with a mind capable of soaking up information. Given the chance and the encouragement, she could go on to win a scholarship. Miss Bennett deplored the fact that her mother was a money-lender, charging enormous rates of interest to those unlucky enough to have been driven to borrow from her in the first place. Having said that, one did have grudgingly to admire the woman. Peggy was, without a doubt, the best-nourished and probably even the best-dressed girl in the class. It would be futile to approach Mrs Woolston again, however. Further education, to her, was a waste of time. She was an ignorant woman. Two visits had already been made by the school governors. Both had proved ineffectual.

Then there was May Higgs – such a frail, tiny girl. May had the ability to pass examinations and to succeed. Her parents were good, hard-working people. Mr Higgs was fortunate in being in full-time employment. However, the fact remained that, as well as May, her parents had eight other children. Mr Higgs had listened with great attention to the school board officials, proud to hear of his daughter's achievements. As to her being allowed to continue her education, he couldn't see any advantage in that. He felt the officers could serve him better by finding jobs for his three sons.

Patsy Kent was the oddity in the class. Miss Bennett found herself thinking perhaps rarity might be a better description. Though she was cleaner in habits and dress than most of her classmates, the clothes she wore were as shabby and as dowdy as those worn by the other girls. Unlike the rest, however, Patsy's were always patched and mended neatly and fitted her body. When it came to footwear for the children, much was left to be desired. In this Patsy was no exception, often attending school in boots at least two sizes too large and regularly showing signs of being in need of repair.

Mrs Kent was so different, she was unique. A slight woman, she had bright, grey eyes and a

pleasant face with fine bone structure. It was, however, the smiling, gentle quality – almost an aura –
that seemed to draw people to her. Men and women
alike trusted her. Most felt affection for her. It was
as if Patsy's mother were a breed apart. Miss
Bennett wondered how she came to be living in a
district such as this. Though Mrs Kent was never a
healthy woman, and certainly not robust, it was
obvious to all members of the staff that she had had
the advantage of a good education. Yet she worked
on the market stalls!

As for Patsy, she was a typical cockney sparrow,
darting here and there and bubbling over with good
humour. Witty, alive and incapable of giving
offence, this girl was hungry for knowledge. Poring
over what few books were available on loan from
the school, she came top of her class in almost every
subject. Patsy Kent seemed to absorb knowledge as
a sponge soaks up water.

Teaching these children was the joy of Miss
Bennett's life. Even their shabby clothing was forgotten and life was endurable so long as she was
able to teach and encourage them to use their lively
minds.

The disadvantages with which these girls were
starting out certainly weighed heavily on her consciousness. Having by now exhausted her own
thoughts, she decided that any sympathy she might
or might not have felt for these pupils and their
families must not be allowed to influence her judge-

ment. Despite the fact that their mothers' lives had been an endless nightmare, it was deemed quite natural for their daughters to face the same prospects. Tradition had a lot to answer for.

Taking up a stick of white chalk, Miss Bennett rose from her seat and walked towards the blackboard. She paused as she heard a knock on the classroom door. Before she even had time to call out 'Come in', the door opened and Miss Burgess entered, accompanied by a gentleman. This was an unusual event and for a moment Miss Bennett stood stock still, her hand in mid-air still holding the piece of chalk.

With a nod of his head, the gentleman indicated he wished Miss Bennett to withdraw to the furthermost corner of the classroom, close to the door. The three adults huddled together, their backs turned to the pupils, their conversation whispered. Each minute took a long time to pass. Restless movement from the girls ceased abruptly when the man turned and faced the class. He knew his task was an unpleasant one, particularly as he became aware of the frightened looks on the faces of the girls.

Arthur Walker was a paid social worker attached to the Grove Infirmary. He would have gladly relinquished many tasks which came under his jurisdiction, but none more eagerly than what he was required to do today.

In his middle thirties, married with two children of his own, he usually planned things down to the last detail. Today, however, he was finding it very difficult to cope with this particular situation. Resolutely, he cleared his throat, coughed huskily, raised an arm chest-high and said, 'Would Patsy Kent please come to the front of the class.'

All other thirty-seven pupils breathed a sigh of relief. Their canny instinct told them that only disaster would be allowed to disrupt their lesson.

Patsy's heart began to pound rapidly, partly from surprise but also from dread. Taking a few steps towards her, Mr Walker said, 'Hello, Patsy.' She appeared not to hear. Arthur Walker knew a little of this girl's background. No father. The headmistress's opinion of the mother was that she was very well-bred and accepted by the neighbours as clean and hardworking. Her origin was a mystery.

There certainly was an indefinable quality about this girl who stood before him. A London child's face. Shrewd, sharp, green eyes, now dimmed a little with fright. He was aware that, in spite of her shabbiness, she was clean and tidy. The patch on her skirt was neatly sewn, her long black stockings darned in several places. With her thin shoulders protruding through her navy blue cardigan, this girl was as spare as a street sparrow.

Miss Burgess cut into his thoughts. 'Do you wish Patsy to go with you now?'

Patsy had been about to ask, 'Go where?' when Miss Burgess took hold of both of her hands. Holding them tightly, she bent her head saying in a soft voice, 'Your mother has been taken ill. She's now in the local infirmary.'

'No!' Just the one word escaped from Patsy's lips. Her face fell. Her heart was beating so fast she thought her chest would burst. It took a great effort to raise her eyes to Miss Burgess. An unspoken question showed clearly: was it true? Staring down at Patsy, Miss Burgess's heart ached with feelings of pity.

Arthur Walker kept his thoughts to himself. Why were these children so underprivileged? They were doomed from the beginning by the circumstances of their birth. Bitterly he accepted the fact that there was no justice for the poor.

When he spoke it was with quiet resignation, his voice low and sad. 'Come, let's get your hat and coat, Patsy, and we'll go together to see your mother.'

Some seconds passed before Patsy, turning to her teacher, muttered, 'I'd better go to the cloakroom, then, Miss?'

'Yes, yes, of course, Patsy. Go along with Mr Walker.'

In the cloakroom Patsy sat down on the wooden form, her head resting against the green painted brick wall. She wished she could go home or, rather, see her mum by herself. Her feet felt frozen. She shook her head, determined she wouldn't cry in front of this man. He was a stranger.

Doing his best to ease the tension, Mr Walker

remarked, 'That's a nice long scarf. I bet it's lovely and warm.' Expertly, Patsy wound the scarf around her neck and tied the long ends securely across her waist.

'My mother knitted it and the hat – these as well.' She proudly showed him the thick woollen gloves she had drawn from her coat pocket.

Ready now, quiet, submissive, Patsy stumbled as she went through the cloakroom door into the corridor. Mr Walker put out a hand to steady her. As if sensing now that she had to trust this man, Patsy allowed him to take her hand.

'I've a motor car outside. Have you ever ridden in one before?'

'Of course not,' Patsy retorted, without stopping to think.

'Well, there's a first time for everything. Say goodbye to Miss Burgess and we'll be on our way.'

Outside the fog had not lifted. It was a real pea-souper, strangely muffling all sounds. The air was damp and moisture-laden.

She settled herself in the back of the car, which on any other occasion would have been an experience she would have revelled in. Patsy turned to have a last glimpse at Miss Burgess and to give her a wave, but the dense fog had obliterated not only her headmistress but the entire school building. Crawling, Mr Walker steered the car away from the kerbside. Visibility being down to a few yards, he had no option but to drive slowly.

Turning her head to the front, Patsy began to ask herself questions. 'Where have they taken my mum? I wonder what will happen to her.' Then, with wisdom beyond her years, she added a prayer: 'Please, dear God, let my mum be all right.'

Although she was unaware of the fact then, schooldays for Patsy Kent were over.

Chapter Four

UNDER NORMAL WEATHER conditions, the journey would have taken little more than twenty minutes. Today it had seemed endless. With a sigh of relief, Mr Walker steered his car through the main gates, bringing it to a halt outside the porter's lodge. Twisting his shoulders round, he spoke to Patsy. 'We're here, love. Let's find out to which ward your mother has been taken.'

Even with the swirling fog making day almost as dark as evening, the brass plaque mounted on the brick wall was visible, illuminated by the lamps which glowed brightly from within the gatehouse: The Grove Infirmary.

A gasp, which sounded like a long, drawn-out sigh, escaped from Patsy's lips. 'But this is the fever hospital.' Her tone was one of utter despair.

Everyone knew this was a place to be dreaded. People didn't get better in here. It was known as the 'No Hope Hospital'. Florrie always said that it was an undertaker's goldmine.

'What's the name of the patient and when was the admission?' the loud, rough voice of the gatekeeper boomed out.

Barred from entering by a half-door, like that of a stable, Mr Walker leaned against the wide top ledge.

'Mrs Ellen Kent. I understand she was brought in this morning. Here's my credentials.'

'No need for identification, Mr Walker. I knows you well enough by now.'

The porter thumbed through a large ledger. Licking his forefinger and thumb as he turned the pages, he said, 'Kent, Kent, Kent. Ah, here we are. On open order. Ward Four B.'

Peering out into the gloom, he nodded his head to where Patsy stood. 'Tough luck on the kid. Her muvver, is it?'

With a nod of his head and a murmured 'thank you', Arthur Walker took hold of Patsy's hand and led her back to the car, not bothering to give an answer to the porter's question.

A slow, hazardous crawl and minutes later the car was safely parked. 'Come along, Patsy. We'll soon see how your mother is now.'

Up the ramp they walked, into one of the covered walkways which connected the sprawling wards. A brighter atmosphere now, with all the lights on. The ward ahead was closed off with a double screen made out of pretty, bright yellow material.

'We have to climb a lot of stairs now. Are you feeling fit?' Mr Walker knew it was a silly question.

Patsy merely nodded her head.

Wards seemed to stretch endlessly, to the left and right, on each landing. The rows of beds were clearly visible. Three flights up and they stood at the doorway of Sister's small office. The Sister looked up from her desk. Mr Walker let go of Patsy's hand.

'Go and sit on that bench, Patsy. I'll just have a word with Sister. I won't be more than a few minutes.'

It wasn't fair. It was *her* mum they were talking about. Why did she have to wait outside? Patsy rested her elbows on her knees and cupped her chin in her hands. The stink of disinfectant was horrible. If only Florrie were here. She wouldn't put up with all this hanging about. She'd put a flea in somebody's ear. Yes, Flo would have got them past that Sister. Oh, come on! When am I going to see my mum?

At last! The Sister in her starched uniform stretched out her hand and ran a finger lightly down Patsy's cheek.

'Come along, my dear.'

Everyone keeps telling me to come along!

Mr Walker stood aside, allowing Patsy to approach the bed first. Standing at the far end of the side ward, he thought for a moment he had brought the child too late to see her mother. That was until the woman in the bed moved – he was shocked by the sight of her grey face.

'Mum, Mum, it's me. Open your eyes . . . Please.'

The head on the pillow moved slowly. 'Patsy.' It was only a croak.

Hardened as he was by everyday events in his job, Mr Walker wanted to gather Patsy into his arms to comfort her, but he could only talk to her to try to give her some hope. 'It's all right, Patsy. You'll see. It will be all right.'

He didn't believe his own words. How could he convince Patsy?

Time seemed to stand still. Patsy stood motionless, her two hands still gently holding one of her mother's. 'She's very ill, isn't she? My mum's really ill?'

Patsy's eyes were enormous – blank and staring. As she saw the colour drain from Patsy's face, the Sister moved forward quickly. Taking Patsy firmly by an elbow, she pushed her from the room. Outside in the corridor she sat beside her on the wooden form.

'You should leave now. Your mother needs a lot of rest. I promise you will be able to come back later.'

Patsy's large green eyes were swimming with tears. They gazed at the Sister, full of pleading. The child expected her to perform a miracle. Sister put a hand to her forehead in an involuntary gesture. Her head was throbbing. Tired out after a long shift, what could she do? Watching the suffering of this little girl was heart-rending. She couldn't lie to her, but how could she tell her the truth? There wasn't much hope for Mrs Kent.

Mr Walker took his leave of the Sister. Was she,

he wondered, as hard-hearted as she seemed? He
doubted it.

'Ollie! Oh, there's Ollie.' Patsy pulled herself
away from Mr Walker's grasp and was away down
the corridor.

The tall, broad-shouldered man stood erect, his
arms held wide. Without hesitation, Patsy started to
run, not stopping until those two arms enfolded
her.

A long drawn-out sigh came from Patsy as she
uttered, 'Ollie. They've got my mum in here. I
think she's ever so bad.'

'All right, Patsy. All right, my love. Take it easy,
there's a good girl.'

Patsy eased her body to the side of the man, then
she lifted her face upwards and he bent down and
put his lips to her cheek.

Mr Walker, standing silently by, felt the compassion in Ollie's action. Then, as if she realised
the need for an explanation, Patsy said, 'This is Mr
Walker. He came and got me out of school. We've
been to see my mum, but the Sister said I have to go
home now.'

Ollie thrust out his hand. 'Alexander Berry. I
know you, or at least I know of you, Mr Walker. I
work at the Town Hall and my job often covers the
same ground as yours – housing and such-like. I
came straight here, as soon as I was told about Mrs
Kent.'

'Oh, I'm pleased to meet you.'

Mr Walker shook Ollie's hand, but it was seconds before he could bring himself to ask how Mr Berry came to be involved with the Kents. 'No offence meant, but are you a relation?'

Ollie, his face solemn now, said, 'No, more's the pity. I live in the same road as Mrs Kent and Patsy. Our friendship goes back over many years.'

Mr Walker felt reassured. This was someone who might accept responsibility for this child. He noticed from his voice that Ollie was an educated man, with no cockney intonation here. The two men continued speaking, taking a few steps backwards so that Patsy could not hear.

She felt rejected and very scared. Tears burned at the back of her eyes, but she wouldn't cry. Patsy marched forward now, full of indignation, asking herself why grown-ups had to behave like that – as if she weren't there. Anyone would think that what they were talking about had nothing to do with her.

'So what you are saying is that there has never been any evidence of a father. In the time you have known Mrs Kent, she has always been alone.'

'Nosy parker! What's it got to do with you?' Patsy rounded on Mr Walker, her temper well and truly roused. 'I've got my mum and my mum's got me. I don't need no father.' She accompanied this statement with a punch which glanced off Mr Walker's arm, causing him to stagger a little.

Amazement showed on his face. Patsy's eyes

were flaming. The docile child had changed into a tigress!

When he had heard that Ellen Kent had collapsed, Ollie's stomach had turned over and it was hard for him not to show emotion. He had known her days were numbered but, surely, not yet, not suddenly like this. He knew the full story of Ellen's life except for one thing – the name of Patsy's father.

Since his first meeting with Ellen he had loved her. Over the years, all the love he had to give he had bestowed on Ellen and her illegitimate daughter. Now, although his heart was aching, he had to suppress a grin. Patsy worked up and on the defensive, as she was now, was the Patsy he knew. She was tough – a kid of the streets. Even Ellen's refined influence had not been able to suppress this trait in Patsy.

'Hey, hold on, Patsy. Mr Walker didn't deserve that.'

'I'm . . . I'm sorry,' she forced the words out. Then, to Ollie's astonishment, Patsy burst into tears. Choking, rasping sobs shook her body. She tried to speak, to tell them she wanted to be with her mother, that she was frightened, but her crying smothered her words.

Mr Walker stood bewildered. Ollie drew Patsy to him, stroking her hair, looking around the depressing corridor as if searching for words of comfort.

Mr Walker came to a decision. Raising his voice a

little, kindness in his tone, he bent and spoke to Patsy. 'Mr Berry has said he will be responsible for you. Would you like him to take you home?'

Barely audible came the answer, 'Yes, please.'

Mr Walker felt very relieved. A big worry had been lifted from his shoulders. 'Thank you, Mr Berry. I'll be in touch.'

Mr Walker was only too aware that he could do little to help Patsy. He was grateful that not every case he had to deal with ended in tragedy, but experience told him that only tears and heartache were in store for Patsy.

Keeping close to the inside of the pavement, Ollie and Patsy walked home. With the fog as thick as ever, it was useless to wait around for transport. Neither of them felt like talking. With Patsy's arm tucked through his, Ollie gave it an occasional squeeze, doing what he could to reassure her. At last they reached familiar surroundings. Their steps quickened on turning into Strathmore Street.

At the doorway of number twenty-two, Ollie bent and kissed Patsy's cheek. 'I'll be up as soon as I can, love. Florrie's waiting for you.'

As she watched him walk away, Patsy felt she would never be happy again. Suddenly, all the fun and joy had been wiped out of her life. She was filled with a longing to run after Ollie. Throughout the whole of her life she had turned to him with her troubles. Ollie was to her a father, uncle and elder brother all rolled into one.

'Ollie. Go and fetch my mum home. Make her better. Don't leave her in that horrible hospital,' was what she wanted to yell after him.

Patsy pushed open the front door. In this street no doors were ever locked. Florrie came out from her kitchen, wiping her soapy, red hands on her apron of coarse sacking.

'Aw, Patsy, my love.' Cautiously, her hands went out touching Patsy's shoulder. Then, quickly, she gathered Patsy into her arms, pressing her to her own enormous chest. Slowly she began to pat her back, caressing her, soothing her, as she had when Patsy had been a babe-in-arms. It was too much. Patsy's body shook with her sobbing.

'That's it, love. Let it all out.' The more Florrie tried to console her, the more Patsy wept. Florrie became anxious and her tone changed. 'Aw, Patsy, give over. Come on, love, no more. You'll make yourself ill.'

Patsy's sobs petered out. 'I'm sorry, Flo. I'm sorry, but you should have seen my mum. She looked ever so bad, but they wouldn't let me stay with her.' The tone of her voice was pathetic, it tore at Florrie's heart.

'Never mind, love. We'll both go and see your mum later on.'

'Will we? Will you come back with me?' A ghost

of a smile came to Patsy's lips. 'They won't tell you to go away, will they?'

'*No*. They bloody well won't. We'll get in to see your mum. Don't you 'ave any fears about that.'

Pushing Patsy before her into the kitchen, Florrie busied herself making what she called 'a good, strong pot of tea'. Patsy's attitude was too quiet for Flo's liking. Too subdued. It wasn't natural. Patsy was a cockney kid, born upstairs in this very house, brought up amongst tough children. Patsy could stand her own ground, chirpy and bright she was, with more than enough to say for herself at times.

Gawd, what a day! Yes, and only the God Almighty knew what the next few days would bring. What a bloody life this is! What the hell would happen to Patsy now?

It was three o'clock in the afternoon of the same day and Ollie and Florrie had brought Patsy back to the hospital. There was silence between them as they sat grouped around the single bed in the small side ward. Patsy wasn't too frightened now. Her mother looked a lot better. Bravely, her mother raised her head, smiling at each of them. 'All I need is a rest.' The words were softly spoken.

'The doctor would like a word with you, Mr Berry. You, too, Mrs Holmes.' A different, uniformed nurse held the door wide.

There was deep quietness in the room now as

Patsy gazed lovingly at her mother. 'Do you really feel better now, Mum?'

There was a pause before Ellen said, 'Yes I do, dear. I'm just very tired.'

'Can I get you anything, Mum? Florrie bought you this bottle of lemon barley. Would you like a drink now?'

'No, thank you, dear. Florrie is kind, isn't she? You be a good girl and do what she tells you.'

When Ellen closed her eyes, Patsy took her mother's hand between her own and sat staring at her mother's face. She lifted the hand and held it to her face, rubbing it gently against her cheek. Why couldn't her mum sit up and put her arms about her?

Ellen's eyes opened, looked towards her daughter and she smiled. Patsy smiled back but she had to bite hard on her bottom lip to stop herself from crying.

Florrie's chin jerked upwards. 'Are you telling us there's no hope?'

The doctor was struck by the misery of these two people seated before him. No relation to the patient, he had been given to understand.

'That is not what I said, Mrs Holmes. Should Mrs Kent recover sufficiently, we may be able to send her to a sanatorium.'

Florrie was moving her head slowly from side to side. Why didn't the bugger tell the truth? She couldn't bear this. Ellen was going to die. Not in six months' time, but now.

With Ollie it was different. Although he dreaded the worst, he still hoped and prayed, sending up an earnest entreaty that Ellen would be spared for a while. There were things Ellen had yet to do. Should she die now, with matters left unsolved, what was to become of Patsy?

Ollie and Florrie tiptoed back into the single ward.

'She's sleeping now,' Patsy told them. Patsy's hands were clasped together on the pink checked counterpane. Her head moved in small, pathetic jerks as if she were willing her mother to get well.

Ollie had the desire to lay down his head on the bed and cry. To thump the mattress with his large fists. His pent-up anger at being absolutely unable to change this unfair world welled up inside him. Ellen's daughter would be cruelly affected if her mother were to die now.

How well he remembered when Ellen first came to Strathmore Street. She had stuck out like a sore thumb. At first, neighbours had felt uneasy in her presence, sensing she came from a very different environment, but she quickly won over everybody who came into contact with her. The few who did not feel real affection for her admired her for her endurance.

Patsy, who now looked so downcast as she sat

opposite to Ollie, was probably in many ways a disappointment to Ellen. As things were turning out, maybe it was as well. Patsy was not refined in speech or manner as was Ellen, yet she did have the benefit of her mother's breeding. In looks, Patsy was a miniature replica of Ellen, the only difference being in the eyes. Ellen's were soft and grey as a dove, but not Patsy's. Cat's eyes she had been born with and so they had remained, green and as bright as any Ollie had ever seen. He knew only too well the fiery glances Patsy could throw if the mood took her. Ellen's daughter was the product of two worlds. Maybe now the privileges she had been denied, and the fact that she had had a harsh start to life in many ways, would stand her in good stead for what undeniably lay ahead.

The fog had cleared and the clouds were massing dark in the sky as Patsy left the house next morning. As she turned into the High Street the rain began to fall.

'Patsy, Patsy, come over 'ere!' Irish as they come was Mary Brett. Whatever the weather or the season, Mary was there. Standing at the entrance to the market behind three huge wicker baskets she sold cut flowers – an assortment of blooms, the combination of their colours a joy for all to see.

Thrusting a nicely wrapped bunch of flowers towards Patsy she told her, 'Now, you're to stop worrying yourself. It's praying to our Blessed Lady

I've been, and I've asked her to watch over your mother.' With her right hand Mary made the sign of the cross. 'Before you know it, your mum will be home again. Yes, t'be sure she will. You just tell her we all send our love. Don't you forget, now.'

'I won't, Mary. And thank you for the flowers.'

'My pleasure, love. On your way now, and God bless you.'

Ellen was awake and as Patsy came towards the bed her whole face lit up. Bending low, Patsy kissed her mother's cheek before seating herself on the chair which stood beside the locker. On the counterpane, Ellen's fingers fluttered like a trapped bird beating against the wire of its cage. Patsy took hold of her mother's hand and held it tenderly between both of her own. Ellen lay back against the pillows. She had made one attempt to talk but was quickly cut off by a rasping cough. She seemed to take comfort from Patsy holding and stroking her hand. Her breathing became quieter and soon she appeared to be sleeping.

From the windows of the ward, Patsy could see the corresponding wards on the opposite side of the hospital, connected by glassed-in walkways. Some patients' beds had been wheeled out onto balconies and verandas and they lay propped up by many pillows. In the courtyard below, large wooden tubs had been planted with various shrubs. She sat watching the falling rain washing away the dust, the shrubs now glistening and shiny green. Vases of flowers in the ward soon wilted. Those Mary had given her to bring to her mum were still lying in their wrapping paper on the bed. She longed to go and fetch a vase, fill it with water and the flowers and place it on the table at the side of the bed. She didn't dare. Everyone in the corridor and adjoining rooms seemed too busy for her to stop them and make her request; they bristled with efficiency as if all members of the staff had secret and comprehensive knowledge of what was taking place.

Patsy felt a hand on her shoulder, gently shaking her. 'Oh, I'm sorry. I must have dozed off.' She blinked several times before her eyes focused on the nurse at her side and her surroundings became more defined. Her mouth was dry and her heart pounding as she made to rise quickly. 'Is everything all right with Mum?'

Gently pressing her back down on to the chair, the nurse smiled at her. 'Yes, everything is fine, but you've been here for hours. No one with you today?'

'No. Mr Berry had to go to work.'

'Well, you had better go home because it's getting dark. Come along, I'll help you on with your outdoor things and you can have a hot drink in the kitchen before you leave.'

'Thank you. I'll just say goodbye to my mum.' Bending over she whispered, 'See you tomorrow, Mum. I love you.'

Ellen gently stirred as Patsy laid her cheek against hers for a brief moment.

★

On the fourth day Elien died.

Patsy knew it the moment her mother's hands were still, though she had never seen death before. Raising tragic eyes to where Ollie was seated on the opposite side of the bed she spoke, calmly and quietly. 'Mum's just died, hasn't she?'

He looked across the space that divided them into those big, green eyes, now so full of sadness and tragedy that he had to lower his own eyes. It was heart-breaking to look at her, yet he could find no words to say that would half-way heal her hurt.

Time didn't matter. It was as if the world had stopped turning. The room was soundless as the two of them tried to suppress their grief. Only Patsy herself knew she couldn't live long enough to erase the picture of her mother's death from her mind. At the moment she wasn't even capable of dealing with the pain inside her and all the other strong emotions she was feeling, including hate towards the doctor. He had failed her and this aroused in her deep resentment. Why, oh why hadn't he helped her mum?

Outside in the corridor the doctor, long used to death, drew Ollie aside and told him the death certificate would read 'Consumption', although he felt that many other factors had contributed. Eventually, there was nothing left for them to do but leave.

In the cold, fresh air of the grounds, Ollie led Patsy to a wooden bench. For a while they seemed to find solace in each other. Their need for each other, established long since, now became necessary for all time. Worried about her, afraid for her, Ollie's voice was quite sharp as he asked, 'Are you listening to me?'

She lifted her eyes to his face for a moment before lowering them again. He thought she had retreated so far into herself that nothing and no one would be able to penetrate.

'Patsy, please talk to me.'

With her head so low that her chin almost rested on her knees, she let out a groan which soon turned into a wail. It sounded like a puppy yelping after being kicked. As Ollie made to draw her trembling body to his she blubbered, 'Why couldn't she get better, Ollie?'

'Oh, my love, how can I answer that? Sometimes things just don't happen the way we want.'

Her mouth quivering, she murmured, 'Poor Mum. Poor Mum.'

This tough, strong, big man who had been involved in Ellen's life for the past fourteen years, who had known and loved this child since the day she had been born, didn't know what to do or what to say. He wanted so badly to cry but knew he mustn't let go, not yet. His heart lurched with pain as he watched her. Her whole body was tense until suddenly he felt her slump against him, and his arms tightened around her small body as great dry sobs wracked her. When she had calmed down a little she was so deep in her own misery that she made no objection as he drew her to her feet. His arm still across her shoulders, they left the hospital grounds and began to make their way home.

Coming home to Florrie's opened the floodgates. One look at Patsy's face told them it was all over. Florrie couldn't move or speak. Tears welled up in Gran's eyes but she made no move to wipe them away. She stood there, her whole body shaking as she held out her arms. Patsy, sobbing softly, went forward and let Gran hold her. For what seemed an eternity, the young girl and the old woman held tightly to each other, neither wanting to break away.

'All of you sit down, and I'll make the tea.'

Patsy felt the tension within her ease. This big man with his kind, gentle ways would take charge. She loved Ollie, really loved him. So had her mum; she knew that now.

Suddenly, the door burst open, bringing all heads around to focus on Blower Day. His raised eyebrows asked the question.

'Yes, son, Ellen's gone,' his mother told him.

His strong body quivered.

'Pull yourself together, lad. Here, drink this.' Ollie handed over a tumbler which held a good measure of whisky. 'I'll join you.'

Watching the two men, Gran shivered. It said a lot for Ellen, didn't it? A great bloke like her son cut up about her dying. He wouldn't be the only one neither, not by a long chalk. Folks around here had taken Ellen to their hearts – men and women alike. Gran said aloud, 'Christ, somebody just walked over me grave.' No one smiled. No one answered.

Six months before the war had ended, her son Charlie had been killed. Well, she hadn't believed in justice then and she didn't now. God's love! Love for whom? Jesus Christ had said, 'Suffer the little children to come unto me.' Well, now Patsy was left to suffer. Yeah, and the worse was yet to come. There would be the funeral to be got through.

Gran heaved herself up and stood gripping the edge of the table. 'I'd better get meself off over home, Flo. I'll see you later.' She placed her hand on Patsy's head of glossy brown hair, aware for the first time that there were glints of red amongst the brown. 'Try and have a sleep, pet.'

'I'll come with you, Gran.' Ollie rose as he spoke. Patsy never even raised her eyes and there was only a silent nod from Florrie.

Patsy's face drained of all colour.

'Is it to be a pauper's grave?'

The ticking of the brass clock high on the wall sounded sinister in the silence that followed. Then, seconds later, Ollie raised his voice, provoked by the undertaker's assumption. Silence again, except for the scratching of the pen nib as it moved across coloured forms and occasionally the scrape of the nib against the edge of the glass inkwell. As the undertaker closed his office door behind them, he pondered on his thoughts. Dealing with death every day and seeing the different ways people handled their feelings, he was still surprised by both Mr Berry's and the young daughter's sensitive and emotional reaction to this woman's death. Mr Alexander Berry, no relative of the deceased, was going to pay the entire cost of the interment.

During the weekend, Ellen Kent's body lay in an open coffin upon a trestle table in Florrie's downstairs front room. It was an over-furnished room at the best of times and now neighbours and friends were obliged to squeeze themselves between the table and the fireplace in order to pay their last respects. Ellen, they said, had been laid out nice. Florrie had placed candles at the head and foot of the coffin.

They came in a stream – old and young alike. Young women left their children outside in the street.

'Don't you dare make a noise,' they whispered to them. Older women, most with elastic bandages around their legs, clutched their shopping bags and sniffed their tears away.

Monday morning at last. Patsy sat quietly, dressed soberly, wearing a black armband on the sleeve of her coat. The main pall-bearer bent low.

'Miss, would you like to say your final goodbye? It is time to close the coffin.' The big-boned man's eyes were very gentle.

Patsy pressed her lips to her mother's forehead. Her mum felt so cold but peaceful, just as if she were asleep. She went out and stood in the passage. She couldn't stay in the room and watch those black-suited men put a lid on her mum and nail it down.

Patsy gazed affectionately at Ollie. He had done her mother proud. Beside her Florrie muttered, 'She's going out like a Queen.'

The hearse was drawn by two black horses, a black cloth draped across each of their backs. People were grouped around the gateway. Florrie, dressed in black, her hat stripped of its usual adornment and replaced by a wide, black ribbon looked exactly what she was – a good, kindly, working-class woman. Ollie today looked exceptionally out of place in the area. He walked tall and upright, smart in his dark suit, white shirt and black tie.

A motor car stood behind the hearse, a rare sight in Strathmore Street. As Patsy was helped inside, her heart began to beat fast and furiously, in spite of her efforts to stay calm.

Women huddled together. 'This raw cold eats right into your bones,' one told another. Men removed their cloth caps, folding them in half and clutching them in their work-stained hands, and bowed their heads.

It wasn't until Patsy stood staring into the gaping hole in the ground, watching the coffin being lowered, that the full realisation hit her. Someone thrust a single, white lily into Patsy's hand. The smell was overwhelming. She thought its huge trumpet and yellow throat ugly. Ollie led her forward and motioned for her to throw a handful of the soft, loose earth down on to the lid of the coffin. Hesitantly, Patsy did so, letting go of the lily at the same time.

At long last the day was over. Alone upstairs, Patsy made straight for the bedroom, closing the door softly behind her. On the bed lay the bag given to her by Mary Brett earlier that day. Patsy withdrew the paper. Slowly she read through the list of names of people who had contributed to Ellen's memory. Pencil-scribbled names. A few coppers from some, as much as a pound from a market trader. Seventeen pounds and ninepence the total came to.

Patsy screwed her eyelids tight. Even so, the tears welled up and rolled down her cheeks. She threw her arms out in front of her, let her head down upon the pillow and at last gave vent to her feelings. Sobs were almost choking her, turning to hiccups. Gradually her crying eased and, finally, she fell asleep.

Chapter Five

ONE DAY BECAME very much like another. Getting herself out of bed, washing and dressing, spending time downstairs with Florrie, going over the road to see Gran.

It was as Patsy was finishing her breakfast that a yell from Florrie made her jump. Florrie's voice, loud and coarse at the best of times, now was ringing through the house so loudly they must have heard her up at the Broadway!

Patsy took the stairs in leaps and bounds.

Florrie's face was bright red and she was visibly shaking. She was muttering to herself, 'Bloody cheek, bloody cheek.'

'What's the matter, Flo? What the 'ell's going on?'

'It's this interfering bugger.' Florrie thrust a pointed finger at a slight, well-dressed man who stood on the doorstep.

'Calm down,' Patsy implored, 'and let's find out what he wants.'

'Never mind what he wants! I know what he'll bloody get if he's not off my doorstep in two seconds.'

Patsy stood there, feeling utterly bewildered. It

Elizabeth Waite

was a minute or two before Florrie got enough
breath back to go on.

'Says he's come about you, Patsy. You know
what he is, don't you? He's the cruelty man. Cheeky
sod!'

'I am not the cruelty man.' The man spoke with
as much dignity as he could muster, pulled himself
up to his full height, which was only about five foot
five, looked at Patsy and said, 'I am a representative
of the Society for the Prevention of Cruelty to
Children.'

'There you are! What did I tell you!' Florrie
roared as, fist flaying the air, she advanced menac-
ingly towards the man.

He, in turn, backed a little way down the garden
path then stopped and stood his ground, looking
very apprehensive as he faced Florrie's bulk.

'Clear off, go on, sling your bloody hook. I'd
give a lot to know who put you up to this. I'll find
out though, you can bet on that and when I do
Gawd help 'em.'

'Mrs Holmes, Mrs Holmes, please will you listen
to me for a moment?'

There was no mistaking the note of pleading in
his voice.

Patsy had covered her mouth with her hand, not
wanting Flo to see her grinning. She felt a little
afraid of this official's visit, but the way Florrie was
having a go at him was enough to frighten anyone.

'What bloody child 'as suffered cruelty around

here, that's what I'd like to know,' Florrie was demanding.

Raising his voice the gentleman said, 'Please, be reasonable. It's Patricia Kent I have to see. I understand she is living alone at this address.'

Patsy thought Florrie was going to burst a blood vessel. Her face had turned a deeper shade of red, and the words exploded from her mouth.

'Well, you understand wrong, she lives with me! Now get going before I really do do you an injury.'

Florrie was prevented from putting her words into actions by Gran. Nothing went on in the street that Gran didn't know about. She wasn't going to be left out of any happenings, and most certainly not when they affected Patsy. She pushed her way past the man.

'Who is he, Flo? Did I hear right? Is he the cruelty man?'

'No, I am not. My name is Mr Ferguson.' He cleared his throat with a nervous cough before continuing. 'Here is my card.' He held it out to Florrie and she took it with a furious swipe. 'I have to warn you that I shall be back this afternoon and with me will be two other gentlemen. If you will allow us to come in, I am sure we will be able to discuss the child's future in a reasonable manner.'

Florrie had the last word. As he stepped on to the pavement she flung at him, 'As far as we're concerned, there's nothing to discuss.'

★

Florrie's kitchen-cum-living-room was cluttered, as always. None the worse for that, it was comfortable, warm and cheerful on this cold winter's afternoon. On one side of her fireplace sat Mr Ferguson and facing him sat Ollie. Two men, one introduced as the District Relieving Officer and the other from the Shaftesbury Welfare Society, were sitting at the kitchen table. Gran was wedged half in and half out of the scullery doorway. She had eased her backside into Florrie's most comfortable armchair and her sticks were perched precariously within her reach. Florrie and Patsy sat on two straight chairs placed against the wall.

The Relieving Officer addressed himself to Ollie. 'I am Mr Litchfield. These other two gentlemen are from voluntary organisations. While their motives are humanitarian, I am here in an official capacity.' He glanced nervously at the sheaf of papers which lay in front of him before speaking again.

'The crux of the matter is that this child is now without parents. Either she goes to an orphanage, although I fear she may be too old for that or, more probably, to an institution.'

The last words spoken by Mr Litchfield were almost drowned. The whole room seemed to explode with noise.

'Take 'er to the workhouse! Over my dead body!' Gran reached out in desperation for one of her walking sticks.

'Not while I've got me 'ealth and strength does

that kid leave this house. She's been like my own since the day she was born.' Florrie's face was a furious red.

Ollie's usual calm was forgotten and he made his fury known. 'I shall be the child's guardian. No harm will come to her and she will be adequately provided for. No workhouse commitment order will ever be served here, I promise you that.' Ollie had put emphasis on his last four words.

Patsy, who had known utter despair on hearing Mr Litchfield's words, now felt relief surge through her. Ollie wouldn't let them take her away. Gran and Florrie would do their best to keep her, but Ollie was different. He worked at the Town Hall. Men looked up to him, he was respected. Besides, Ollie loved her. So did Florrie and Gran, too, in their way but with Ollie it was a sort of 'belonging'. Ollie had always sorted out her problems and he would again now.

'Can any one of you claim to be a blood relative of this child?' This question was asked falteringly by Mr Woodbury, the man from the Shaftesbury Society.

'Or have you legal guardianship, as required by law?' asked Mr Litchfield.

These questions only heightened the atmosphere which could now be felt in the room. Animosity was directed at all three men, whether officials or not.

'No.' Ollie answered for them all. 'That doesn't

mean we are about to stand by and allow you, or any other governing body, to take Patsy off to the workhouse.'

The Relieving Officer looked both annoyed and embarrassed.

'Now, really, Mr Berry, I gave you credit for more sense than that. You should not refer to an institution as a workhouse. Conditions today are not that bad, I assure you. Patsy would be given every care until she reached the age of sixteen.'

'Oh, yeah, and she'd end up being nuffin' but a bloody drudge.' Gran couldn't keep her tongue still and added for good measure, 'Anyway, she ain't going nowhere. My boys will see to that.'

'Madam, you cannot block the system. The child is a waif without kith or kin and no visible means of support or shelter.'

'That's a damned lie. She's got shelter upstairs where she was born and where she's lived all her life.'

At Florrie's outburst Mr Litchfield became irritable. The cases he came into contact with served to make him hard, yet he strove always to show compassion. 'None of you have a say in the matter, I'm afraid. Patsy's future will be decided according to the law.'

Sheer frustration made Ollie tremble. He knew no argument was ever won by losing one's temper. That didn't stop him from wanting to throttle this stranger who, with his forms and the stroke of a pen, could and seemingly would commit Patsy to live in an institution.

'I shall fight every inch of the way to keep Patsy here among people who care for her. It is unfortunate that Mrs Kent did not leave instructions as to her daughter's custodian.' Impatiently, Ollie leant forward, swiping at the papers so violently the top ones slid on to the floor. 'For heaven's sake, this is officialdom gone mad!'

Mr Litchfield was amazed. Would that every child that came into his care be so badly wanted, so obviously loved! Looking around the room he thought, be it ever so humble, there is an abundance of affection here. In his experience, quite the reverse was normal. Relatives fought to get children off their hands, only too glad to have them taken into care.

Patsy, who had kept quiet until now, pressed through the array of chairs, ignoring the fact that she had scraped Mr Litchfield's shins with the toe of her boot. Her small fists thumped the table with such force it rocked on its legs. 'I won't go in no home. You can't make me. I'll run away. I will. I will. I can look after myself.'

Whimpering now, Patsy stumbled towards Ollie. His arms reached out, bringing her to stand between his knees. 'It will be all right, Patsy, you'll see. We will work something out.'

But would they? These men wouldn't listen. They didn't want to understand. They would take her to a place where she didn't know anyone. Gran and Florrie wouldn't be around and, worst of all, she wouldn't be allowed to see Ollie.

When Patsy heard the voice behind her she jumped as if she'd been prodded in the back, turning her tear-stained face to Mr Woodbury, who had risen to his feet.

This man might help her. He knew she shouldn't be put in a home. There was kindness in him, and as he took hold of Patsy's hands she could sense it. As he looked at her his face was gentle, his eyes were smiling. 'Go back and sit next to Mrs Holmes,' he whispered.

Patsy's bottom lip trembled. 'I'm not going in no home. I'm not going anywhere. I'm going to stop here and live with Florrie.'

'All right. Just do as I say for the moment.' His obvious patience weakened her. Tears spurted from Patsy's eyes, running down her cheeks to drip from the end of her chin.

'Come here, my love,' Florrie called to her. Patsy looked towards Flo for a second and when she held out her arms Patsy sprang into them.

'There, there, my pet. Course you ain't going nowhere, we'll get it sorted out. Now stop your crying. There ain't a bugger born that's going to take you away.'

Patsy rubbed at her eyes with the back of her hand. Florrie could always make her smile. She could make anyone smile if she put her mind to it.

'Is there anywhere we can talk in private, Mr Berry?' All four men were now standing.

'You can use my front room if you want to,' Florrie murmured.

Ollie grinned at Patsy and they left the room.

Mr Litchfield had come to a decision. To what extent Alexander Berry had been involved with Mrs Ellen Kent he hadn't yet worked out. That he was definitely determined to have custody of the daughter was obvious. I don't think he has any ulterior motive, he thought. No, I'm sure he hasn't. Mr Berry is stubborn, even obstinate, but he has the interest of that child at heart. If I make the wrong decision it could cost me my job. Momentarily, he felt ashamed. Give the man the benefit of the doubt – at least for the time being. The girl has no mother or father. Be grateful someone is willing to take charge of her. Besides, you've seen his good points – the way he loves that girl. Yes, I'm sure Mr Berry is a normal, straightforward, good man.

Turning around, Mr Litchfield faced Ollie squarely. 'All my instincts tell me to trust you – to leave matters as they are for the time being. However, I shall arrange for my superiors to interview you in order to set up a more permanent arrangement.' With an assertive nod to his colleagues, he asked, 'Do you agree?'

'Yes, yes.' There was no hesitation in their answer.

'If I might add something.' Mr Woodbury knew

he had to tread carefully, very carefully indeed. 'I think I know of a way which might help. I feel the Shaftesbury Society would be willing to contribute towards the rent for the upstairs rooms the child occupies. They might even be willing to pay the full amount.'

Mr Litchfield allowed himself to smile. Assistance from this quarter would give his decision backing. 'So, we are all of the same opinion. It will be kinder to leave Patsy in her familiar surroundings for the time being.' Both men nodded. Mr Woodbury even raised a hand in agreement.

The wind was blowing outside, rattling the windows. The front room was bitterly cold, but Ollie neither heard the wind nor felt the cold. 'That's all I ask. Thank you.' He had won the first round.

Those waiting in the kitchen heard the front door open, then close.

'Thank God for that, they've gone. Jesus, dear Jesus, don't let them take Patsy away.' Both Florrie and Gran were mouthing the same silent prayer.

'You are staying here.' Ollie covered his eyes with his hands. Patsy watched his whole body shudder with a great, dry sob. Gran and Florrie started to cry. Patsy laughed and cried at the same time. Lifting the corner of her apron, Florrie wiped her eyes, then rubbed the whole of her face with the rough material.

'Don't just stand there, Patsy girl. Make yourself

useful and put the kettle on. Christ Almighty, I've never wanted a cup of tea more!'

With Christmas only days away, Blower Day approached Patsy. 'You don't want to stay cooped up here, moping about the place. We could do with you up at the market.'

'Really? Do you mean it, Blower? When can I start?'

It was such a busy period, she was run off her feet. Still, she enjoyed being there. The company, yes, and the kindness, meant a lot. Here she didn't have time to think too deeply.

Suddenly, it was Christmas Eve. The market was packed with last-minute shoppers. The stalls looked great. Turkeys and geese plucked and powdered hung upside down. Pyramids of oranges and tangerines, the top ones wrapped in silver and gold paper. Baskets of nuts and holly and mistletoe between the vegetables – everywhere an air of festivity.

'Keep filling those spaces and get the stuff sold. This poultry won't keep. Knock it out at rock-bottom prices.' Blower was everywhere, dropping crates and boxes off at every stall.

'Come on, move yourselves,' he urged his workers and family alike.

Out on the pavement the Salvation Army Band played steadfastly on. 'O Come, All Ye Faithful' . . . 'The Holly and the Ivy' . . . 'O Little Town of Bethlehem'. Hardly a person passed by without pushing a penny or two into the slots of their collecting boxes.

Christmas morning dawned.

'Do you think I've bought enough food to see us over the holiday?'

Suddenly, Patsy wanted to cry. She felt so alone – but she wasn't alone, was she? She and Florrie were spending the day at Ollie's house.

'Gawd help us, Ollie. We'll live like fighting cocks till the New Year on what we've got here.' Florrie pushed him aside. She was in her element cooking the dinner.

They had all eaten too much. Tradition had it that plum pudding must follow. Ollie came through the doorway, the deep dish held high, blue flames licking around the dark fruit pudding.

'You've never wasted good brandy, have you? Fancy setting it alight! I could have drunk that.' Although Florrie was scolding him, Ollie was pleased to see her face was wreathed in smiles.

In the front room, their chairs drawn up to the blazing fire, they were warm and snug. Outside, the sleety rain drove down the street and the wind blew with the force of a gale. Florrie's eyes were closed in a deep sleep. Ollie's face wore a contented look as he puffed on his cigar. Patsy sniffed – she liked the aroma. She accepted the fact that today could have been much worse. Never once in her whole life had Ollie been unkind to her. If it hadn't been for him, she wouldn't have been there now. It didn't bear thinking about where she might have been spending Christmas. Ollie was so good to her. If he had been her father he couldn't have done more. How many times had she wished that he were. This room was lovely. The floor was covered with proper carpet, not lino. There was a three-piece suite and a what-not in the corner holding real china figurines. Everything was clean and shining.

This wasn't the first Christmas Patsy had spent in this house but in previous years her mum had been with them. She swallowed hard and told herself what a lovely day they were having. Only she wasn't, not really. Her mum was missing. That was not true, either. Mum was not 'missing'. She was gone, she was dead.

In truth, Patsy wasn't alone with her sad memories. The effort to remain cheerful was beginning to tell on Ollie, too. Christmas for him wasn't the same this year either.

Dread showed in Patsy's eyes as Ollie read from the official-looking letter.

' "Mr Alexander Berry is requested to attend the Magistrate's Court, Lavender Hill, South West London, at two p.m. on Wednesday, the tenth of January. The child in question, namely one Patricia Kent, should also attend." '

The tone and wording of the letter sounded far

too authoritative for Florrie's liking. Wisely, she kept her thoughts to herself.

They lived in dread until the actual day of the hearing arrived, though Patsy wasn't sure whether it was a relief or not.

'Turn round. We can't send you off looking any old how. She's all right. You look nice, Patsy. Those boots don't show – your skirt hides them.'

Gran and Florrie had combined their efforts to make her presentable. Flo had washed and ironed Patsy's underwear and her striped blouse. Gran had spent more than an hour steaming her serge skirt. Queenie Day had made her a present of new black stockings. There wasn't much she could do about her boots. Each woman kissed and hugged her. Florrie whispered, 'Your hair is shining so bright it will dazzle those men at the court. Remember now, take your hat off before you go in.'

Walking up Lavender Hill, Ollie raised his eyes to the sky. 'It's going to snow.' Patsy did not look at him or answer. Ollie glanced at his watch. 'We've got plenty of time.' Then, bending down, he said quietly, 'Trust me, Patsy. Just act normal – just be yourself and you'll see, everything will be fine.' If only he could be certain of that. Patsy's small hand was gripping his. 'Florrie wanted to come, but she's better off waiting for us at home.'

Patsy still made no reply. She was in a quiet mood. Who could blame her, he asked himself. She'd been through a lot lately. 'I just hope this afternoon will end the uncertainty,' he thought. He had stopped talking, but his mind was racing. 'What if it doesn't? What if it goes the other way? I'll go out of my mind if they reverse their decision. Best not to get worked up – wait and see what happens. Oh, God. Please let Patsy be allowed to stay with me . . .' He was still fearful of the outcome as they entered the building.

The corridor in which they waited was cold. The wooden bench was hard. They sat in nervous silence. A heavy oak door to the right of them opened.

'Mr Berry?'

'Yes, sir.' Ollie stood up as he spoke.

'Please come in, Mr Berry.'

Ollie made to take Patsy's hand. 'No, just you, Mr Berry. The child will be quite safe waiting here.'

With what he hoped was a reassuring smile, Ollie gently pushed Patsy back down on to the bench and walked towards the open door.

The room was much less formal than he had anticipated. A bright fire burned in the hearth of an enormous fireplace. A deep-piled beige carpet covered the floor. At the windows hung floor-length curtains of the same colour. 'Thank God, it's not a bit like a courtroom,' thought Ollie.

'Come and sit down, Mr Berry.'

Ollie took the vacant chair facing a long, large desk, behind which sat two gentlemen and one lady. Each formally nodded to him.

'Mr Berry, we appreciate your coming here this afternoon. I am Mr Blaire, the gentleman on my left is Mr Shepherd and our lady magistrate is Mrs Wilkinson.'

To Ollie's keen eye, the two men might well be successful businessmen. They were in their fifties, dressed in well-cut suits with white shirts and sombre ties. Each had a pale complexion – a sure sign their work was conducted indoors. Mrs Wilkinson's attire was appropriate – a grey, tailored costume with a high-necked navy blue blouse. Her fair hair was waved. She smiled easily, for which Ollie was grateful. She was not old, neither was she formidable-looking. She wouldn't frighten Patsy. He felt a little more easy in his mind.

'We are here to determine that whatever decisions are made will be in the best interests of the child. We have before us the birth certificate of Patricia Eleanor Kent. It gives full details of the mother but *none* of the father which, unfortunately, makes it an indisputable fact that the child is illegitimate. No relatives have been traced. However, Mr Litchfield has submitted a report to the court in which he states that you are willing, and in his opinion eager, to accept responsibility for this child.' Mr Shepherd paused, leaned across and spoke a few whispered words to his colleagues.

'Yes, yes.' They all seemed to agree.

Turning to the front again he nodded his head. 'Mr Berry. Why do you want to take on this obli-

gation?' Without giving Ollie time to think, let
alone answer, he continued. 'Tell us of your associ-
ation with Mrs Kent, and her daughter. Needless
to say, all of today's conversation will be treated
confidentially.'

Ollie had to take a deep breath. He wasn't prepared for this frank, straightforward approach. He
sighed deeply. He hadn't liked hearing it voiced
aloud that Patsy was illegitimate. This was going to
be far worse than he had thought.

'Please, Mr Berry, begin with your full name,
your age, then your address.'

He still couldn't speak straight away, but had to
swallow first. 'Alexander Berry, 36 Strathmore
Street, Tooting, SW17. I was born in 1882. I have
lived in the same house all my life. I own it outright.
My father left it to me when he died.'

He told how he had first become acquainted with
Ellen and of their subsequent friendship over the
past fourteen years. Then came the moment when
he felt he couldn't go on. Why should he tell these
strangers of his feelings, of happenings that he had
never yet spoken of to anyone? Rightly or wrongly,
he subconsciously felt that these three magistrates
were reading more into his relationship with Ellen
than there had ever been. If only their suspicions had
been true! Why hadn't he ever proposed to Ellen? A
number of times he had been on the point of doing
so. Ellen had never encouraged him to be more than
a friend. If only he had pressed her, taken care of

her, legally adopted Patsy! 'What's the use – it's far too late now,' he thought to himself.

He was brought back from his recollections by the voice of Mrs Wilkinson. 'Would you rather we adjourned the case until a later date?'

Desperate to get it over, finished with, to get out of the place, Ollie's heart sank. 'No, it's all right, ma'am. There isn't much more to tell, only that should you decide to place Patsy in my care, or even appoint me as her guardian, I will ensure that she is well looked after.'

Patsy's future might depend on what he had said. Well, he'd done his best; he could do no more. He relaxed, almost slumped, in his chair. It wasn't in his nature to plead but he had pleaded today.

To the three persons seated behind the oblong desk it had been an impassioned appeal. For a moment they stared silently at each other. Usually, people who came before them were quick with sympathetic words but as for actions, taking on responsibilities, that was an entirely different matter. For each of them, it had been a refreshing change to listen to Mr Berry. Each felt their findings were in accordance with those of Mr Litchfield. His written report stated that in his opinion Mr Berry was a sincere man, with no ulterior motive in his offer to care for the child.

'We'll have the girl in now. You may stay in the room, Mr Berry, if you wouldn't mind sitting over there.' Mr Blaire indicated a chair in the farthest corner of the room.

Holding Patsy's hand, Mrs Wilkinson led her in, seating her in the chair just vacated by Ollie. Patsy looked deathly white, her usually bright eyes now cloudy.

'Patsy. Tell us how you feel about Mr Berry.' Mrs Wilkinson's voice was soft, the words spoken kindly.

Patsy knew that Ollie was seated behind her. She longed to turn round. What should she tell them? Ollie would know what she should say.

'Would you rather we had a little talk on our own, just you and me? We could go into the room next door.'

'If you like,' Patsy murmured.

A quarter of an hour passed, during which time Ollie died a thousand deaths. It wasn't right. No child should be put through this ordeal.

'Right, Mr Berry. If you will take Patsy and wait outside.'

It was agony. Why didn't Patsy fidget instead of sitting so still? What if they came out and said 'No'? The thought filled Ollie with terror. He could find no words to comfort Patsy. He needed someone to commiserate with him.

'Please, both of you, come back in.'

All three magistrates were smiling, and it seemed to Patsy they were inviting her to smile back.

'We have decided the local authority shall become

your legal custodians until you reach the age of sixteen.'

Patsy's heart sank down into her boots. The colour drained from Ollie's face. Mr Shepherd, sensing their despair, quickly remonstrated. 'Let me finish.'

Oh, why did he have to be so long-winded? Why didn't he just come right out with it? Patsy felt that if he droned on much longer, she would have to ask outright: yes or no?

' . . . great deliberation and contemplation of written reports . . .' Florrie would say he'd swallowed a bloody dictionary, and she'd be right an' all.

'We paid great attention to your own wishes, Patsy.' Well, if they'd done that in the first place there wouldn't have been any need for all this.

'The Shaftesbury Society are generously offering contributions.'

Why does he keep on shuffling through those papers?

'We have decided to delegate the day-to-day care of you to Mr Alexander Berry. We shall review the position at least once every six months. You will also be in the partial care of Mrs Florence Holmes.'

Patsy looked long into Ollie's face and he into hers. She wanted to throw her arms around his neck but now he had dropped his head. His face was buried in his hands. In spite of this, Patsy knew it was happiness he was experiencing. For as long as she could remember, Patsy had loved this man. Now that love was intensified a hundred times.

Chapter Six

PATSY WORKED FULL time at the market now. Her life, since the death of her mother more than two years ago, had settled into a humdrum routine. At times, the work seemed hard but she loved it. Here she felt alive, among the crowds, the workers, the bustle and the frenzy of everyone moving at break-neck speed. Turning the corner most winter mornings, even before it was fully daylight, there was her reality. The whole market throbbed from end to end with the pace of life.

Patsy never complained. She sorted eggs, stacked cabbages, cut stalks from cauliflowers carefully so as not to damage the white heads, even scrubbed wooden blocks. She did every task asked of her willingly and with her natural good humour.

There was a slump in trading at the moment but, being January, it was not unexpected.

'You can go and ask Blower for another net of sprouts when you feel like it.'

'If I wait till I feel like it, you'll never get them.'

'Eh, Patsy. You get cheekier by the day.' There was a fondness in Queenie's voice and as she watched Patsy thread her way amongst the stalls she thought, 'That one's a tough little nut, but she's turning out all right.'

'Patsy, would you like to go out on the rounds with Danny today? There's not much doing here.'

Not sure whether Blower was joking or not, Patsy looked hard at this thickset man. To some he appeared hard: shrewd in business, with not much time for people with a hard-luck story. Patsy knew differently.

'Do you mean it, Blower? Can I go with Danny?'

'Yeah, go on, but mind you wrap yourself up well. It would freeze the brass balls off a pawnshop out there today.'

Patsy gave him a mischievous grin, causing Blower to laugh. He sensed Patsy was sad at times, and often very lonely. She was a good kid, though, bursting with life, even though there were days when she exasperated everyone. 'I'll have to keep me eye on her, she could easily become a street urchin,' he thought: the idea caused him to frown.

Chuckling to herself, Patsy ran to find Danny. That was something she still missed, being told to wrap up warm. Tuck your vest into your knickers. Have you got your hat and gloves? No one cared now. No, that's not true, she chided herself. Florrie does, all the Days do and Ollie really does. I still miss Mum, though, she thought.

Two magnificent horses stood waiting, harnessed to the flat-top cart. They were Danny's pride and joy.

'So I've got to put up with you today, have I?' Danny grinned as he lifted Patsy up. Mounting the box himself, he wrapped a large blanket around her knees, tucking the ends under her arms.

Soon they were threading their way through the traffic, heading for Wimbledon Common.

'Blimey. Ain't it posh!' They had arrived at their first port of call.

'Patsy, you're not to talk like that. God will blind you if you do, and you know Ollie hates it when the cockney comes out.'

'Oh, all right Danny! But all the same it is posh, isn't it?' Patsy was happier today than she'd been for a long time. 'Can I come in with you?'

'No, not here you can't. Even the staff are a bit stuck up. I have to work on them.'

Danny winked and gave her a broad smile as he made his boxes ready.

'Who wants to come in, anyway?' she yelled after him.

They were off again ten minutes later, stopping only a few yards down the tree-lined road. In her excitement, Patsy nearly dropped the basket of eggs she was carrying.

The cook welcomed them both with open arms. She was neither old nor fat, as Patsy imagined all cooks to be. The kitchen was warm and bright, bigger than any kitchen she had ever seen. There was a huge, black-leaded range with a roaring fire and shining copper saucepans hanging above.

'Coo, isn't it lovely?' Patsy said the words without thinking.

Cook smiled proudly. 'Come over to the fire, my lovely.'

Patsy sipped the mug of thick soup and thought how smashing it was. Danny talked to the cook and two kitchen maids, their voices low, intermingled with giggles. However, Patsy heard enough to know that Danny was flirting with them.

That wasn't the only time that day that Patsy had to hide her smiles behind her hand. All the houses they called at were nice, the kitchens warm and sweet-smelling. Invited into most, Danny wasn't averse to kissing the housemaids and making up to the cooks. Like all the Days, Danny was brawny with dark, curly hair and full of wit and charm. Gran always said he could sell ice to Eskimos.

Their last call of the day was at a convent. Even here, it was obvious that Danny was a firm favourite with the nuns. The corridors smelled of incense, flowers and floor wax. Although the nuns' voices were soft, Patsy could hear their happiness bubbling through as they spoke and she was embarrassed by her boots making a clipping sound as she walked, disturbing the tranquillity.

The cook here *was* fat – her face flushed as if she had been bending over the long, wide kitchen range. She moved towards Patsy, bringing her forward and sitting her down. A hot scone smothered with butter and a cup of tea were placed in front of her. Patsy wondered how to say thank you to this holy woman, who had a crucifix on a chain hanging around her neck even though she wore a white overall.

The weather had been awful and it was cold riding back on the cart, but not for one moment did Patsy regret going. 'Thanks for taking me, Danny,' she told him as he lifted her down. She stood for a moment, stamping her frozen feet on the cobbles of the yard. 'Can I come out again with you another day?'

Danny regarded her solemnly. Much though she tried not to show it, Patsy was a sad little soul. Her life seemed to be all work and no play. She had been forced to grow up too quickly. Robbed of her childhood, she put on a brave face, sometimes going to the extreme, making out she didn't care about anyone or anything. Those around her knew it wasn't so.

'Of course you can, me darling.' Then, changing his mood, he added, 'But don't you go telling Florrie or Mum what I get up to on my rounds, or I'll never hear the last of it.'

'I won't, Danny.' Nevertheless, she was laughing at the thought. 'Goodnight, Danny, and thanks again.'

'Nothing to thank me for. I was glad of your company. Goodnight, now. See you in the morning.'

As they ate their evening meal together, in spite

of her promise to Danny, Patsy gave Florrie a blow-by-blow account of the day's happenings. By the time she got to the part where Danny had kissed the maids, Flo was continually pushing up her wobbly breasts and chuckling so much her cheeks had turned crimson.

'Goodnight, Florrie.'

'Goodnight, my love. God bless you.'

It was half-past seven when Patsy climbed the stairs to her own rooms. A banked-down fire burned in the grate, thanks to Florrie. Her breakfast mug and plate had been washed and set out again in readiness for the morning. Florrie's kindness never failed. It was cold in the scullery because the window frame had never fitted properly and she gave it a shove upwards. It was no good, it was jammed fast. 'Oh, well, it's my own fault,' she thought. 'I must remember to tell Ollie. He'll soon fix it.' As she moved back she saw it was snowing outside, falling fast and thickly. A few flakes blew in the top of the window, landing on her hair and dissolving slowly, running down her cheeks almost like tears. She wasn't crying and she didn't have the urge to – not tonight.

It was strange; she seemed to miss her mother more as time passed, not less as Gran and Florrie repeatedly told her she would. But she could think happily of her tonight. Life was not really so bad and she'd had a smashing day today. In fact, if she counted her blessings it would take a long time.

Only one thing she wished: if only her mother hadn't died. *If only*. As Ollie said, 'If wishes were chariots, none of us would ever walk!'

How quickly snow changes. For the past week it had quilted the streets, bringing with it a strange silence and even beautifying the squalid houses and back yards. Leaving early for work, Patsy thought Strathmore Street looked clean with the snow not yet marked by footsteps or horses' hooves. Passing the small park in Garrett Lane, what few trees there were had crystals hanging from their branches and the faded, dirty grass was now a bright, sparkling white blanket. Today it had begun to melt. By the time evening came, it would have turned into grey slush, messy, lingering against the walls and gathering in heaps in the gutters.

Saturdays were always busy and that day seemed never-ending.

'Go on, Patsy. Get yourself home. We shan't be long behind you – there won't be many late shoppers out tonight.'

'Thanks, Blower.' It didn't worry Patsy that it was only seven o'clock. Usually it was after eight before she got away on a Saturday. Queenie had gone home more than an hour ago, her excuse being that she had to see to the kids.

Patsy unlaced her boots in the narrow passageway.

'I'm home, Flo.' There was no answer. Patsy's

heart missed a beat, for Florrie was never out when she got home. The empty kitchen looked strange, though nothing was missing except Florrie herself. The gaslight was turned down low, the fire flattened and banked and the safety guard placed in position. A gorgeous smell met her from the oven. At least, Flo had their tea on the go. The brown earthenware teapot had a piece of cardboard propped up against it. A grin came to Patsy's lips as she picked it up. 'Over Gran's. Come over.' The large, irregular letters could have been written by a child.

Patsy had a job to push open Gran's front door. The hallway was thronged with children, but she looked past them, down the passage, to where Gran was emerging from the kitchen.

'Get out of the way you lot, and let Patsy get in.' Gran's shout worked. The children squashed back against the walls, making a pathway for her. Even so, she had to step over two small girls and a crawling baby.

'In there,' Gran told her with a nod of her head. The front room? What was going on? It was only ever used on high days and holidays. A fire burned half-way up the chimney in the hearth of the old-fashioned tiled fireplace. The room was packed with people and more children and so warm that Patsy closed her eyes for a moment in delight.

'Come on, love. Find yourself somewhere to sit and Queenie'll get you a cup of tea. Move over, you kids.' The children stopped squabbling and pressed back against the furniture. They knew better than to disobey Gran.

Ollie was sitting quietly in a corner of the room, observing all but saying nothing. He didn't work on Saturdays and, compared with his normal weekday attire of a dark suit, his blue jersey and grey trousers looked casual and relaxed. Patsy pushed her way through and sat down on the carpet, letting her body lean back against Ollie's legs, her head resting on his stomach. Queenie gave her a cheeky grin and handed her a cup of tea.

'What's all this in aid of?' Patsy swivelled her head round and raised her eyes to Ollie.

'Ah, just you wait and see,' he answered, smiling widely. Ollie placed his hand on Patsy's head. It depressed him to see Patsy looking tired, her lovely hair tied back with a piece of tape and looking lifeless. He remembered how shining and healthy-looking it used to be when Ellen was alive. It was still long, hanging way past her shoulders, yet she no longer looked a little girl.

The heat was making Patsy drowsy as she sipped her tea; her eyelids were so heavy she could have easily dozed off.

'Bet you can't guess where we're all going!' Julie, Queenie's ten-year-old daughter, shot at her.

'No, and you aren't going to tell her. Now shut up, and don't spoil the surprise. Grandad will explain it all when your uncles get home.' Queenie was enjoying the secret.

Florrie bent towards Patsy, her breasts almost bursting out of a pretty cotton blouse she had squeezed into.

'You'll love it, you will, pet. It'll give us all something to look forward to.'

'Oh, come on, tell me. Don't be rotten, Flo.'

Flo let out a great bellow of a laugh. 'All in good time.'

Patsy's eyes again darted to Ollie's face. His head above his broad shoulders was nodding approval, and there was merriment in his eyes such as she hadn't seen for a long time.

A woman Patsy didn't recognise handed her a plate on which were two wedges of crusty bread, sandwiched together with ham and mustard pickle. This woman seemed to be the only thin person in the room. She was not very tall and her dark hair, flecked with grey, framed her deeply-lined face.

'How are you, Patsy love? My, you've got taller but you haven't filled out much, have you?'

Gran, seeing the hesitation in Patsy's eyes, said, 'You remember Lily. She's my Charlie's widow. It's not long since she moved away and now she's moving back with her children, there's two of them.' Gran pointed to the two boys sitting on the floor by the window.

'Oh, of course. I'm fine, Lily, how are you? I'm glad you've moving back.'

'So am I, ducks, so am I. The kids get on me mother's nerves. It's not exactly a piece of cake living with her. Right old bitch she can be at times, I can tell you.' Patsy was smiling. She remembered Lily now. She had always been a card.

'Quiet, quiet, let's have your attention. You kids, if you can't sit still, get yourselves out into the kitchen.' Upturned faces gazed in rapt attention at their grandfather.

'The Fox is getting up an outing. Blower and Danny are on the committee and Ollie is to be treasurer.'

'Yeah, and we're coming and all.' Two children, heads poked round the doorway, made this positive statement.

'You won't live long enough to go anywhere if you don't keep quiet and let Grandad finish.' Queenie's bawling sent the children scurrying away.

'Where's the outing to and when are we going?'

Patsy couldn't contain her excitement. She was thrilled, for it wasn't often that a chance like this came along.

Grandad Day was in a jovial mood. He genuinely loved Patsy as if she was one of his own. She had had some hard knocks in her short life, but she had coped bloody well. He bent now and gave Patsy's arm an affectionate pat. 'My gal's coming with us, aren't you love?'

'Of course, Grandad – but hurry up and tell us where to.'

'Hampton Court and Bushey Park.'

'When are we going?' several voices yelled in unison.

'Easter Monday.'

Patsy clapped her hand over her mouth. She wanted to giggle. How was Grandad going to get this lot, and half the street besides, all the way to Hampton Court?

For the next hour everyone did their share of talking.

'Listen, Patsy. I'll tell you what.' Queenie had sunk into the chair from which Ollie had just risen. 'When the Fox puts on a "do" it's always a good one. So it should be, and all, for that pub does most of its trade from our market men, inside and outside of hours, if you get what I mean.' She flung her head to one side and laughed. 'Not to mention the saloon where Ollie and his friends drink. There's never a day their trade could be called quiet. I'd like a share in some of the bloody profits they make. They'd better make it a good outing, or we'll know the reason why. Eh, Mum?'

Gran didn't even know she was being spoken to. With a wet dishcloth she was wiping pickle from a small girl's mouth then, bending down, she yanked a boy from under the sofa and shook him none too gently. 'Them's new trousers you've got on. Crawling about all over the floor, what do you think you are – a bloody cat?' Gran pushed the child towards the door, giving his backside a smack as he disappeared.

The house was cluttered, untidy and, to be truthful, not too clean. The people were coarse and common in their speech, but they were a family – always together.

'I wish I belonged to somebody's family.' Patsy looked across to where Ollie stood as she made her silent wish.

'Well, love, I'm ready to go home, how about you? Good job I made a hotpot for our dinner, anything else would have been ruined by now.' Florrie lumbered to her feet, almost falling as she tangled with a crawling baby.

Ollie was immediately at her side, placing a protective hand beneath her elbow. 'Steady there, Flo. Thought it was only tea you had been supping.'

'Cheeky sod.' There was laughter in her voice as she added brazenly, 'For that remark, Mr Berry, you can treat me to a drop tonight.'

'I most certainly will, but let's get you home first.'

'Bye, love. Bye-bye, Patsy,' young and old voices called out. Patsy smiled at everyone and kissed Gran and Grandad.

'You're a lucky man, Ollie Berry, taking two girls home!' Queenie called after them. Then, just as she was about to close the front door, she changed her mind, popped her head out and shouted, 'Ollie, if them two ain't enough for you, you can always come back over here. My Chalkie will be up the pub till closing time.'

Florrie tut-tutted. 'That Queenie,' she muttered as she gently pushed Patsy in first over the step. Ollie behind them wasn't doing much to smother his mirth.

As the time drew near, the whole street was excited. Anticipation was high in young and old alike and the only dampener on the proceedings was Gran's refusal to go on the outing.

'Aw, come on, Gran. You'll have a smashing time,' the eldest of the grandchildren repeatedly told her.

'Of course you are coming. Me and the boys will look after you. Besides, Dad won't come if you don't,' Queenie pleaded.

'We all want you to come. You will, won't you, Gran?' Patsy had begged.

All the coaxing and pleading hadn't changed Gran's mind. 'What would I put on me feet? Can't get any bloody shoes on, can I? Perhaps I should wear the boxes they came in. Look good, wouldn't it, me shuffling along with me feet in a pair of cardboard boxes?'

It wasn't funny, quite the opposite. Everyone felt sorry for Gran but didn't know what they could do to help.

Easter Sunday morning, and Florrie was peeling the

potatoes for dinner. 'Hope it's going to be fine tomorrow. Gawd knows what we'll do if it rains.'

Patsy carried the saucepan full of cold water to the table. 'Don't keep looking on the black side. Try praying for the sun to shine.' Patsy grinned as she said this.

'Yes, and who is going to listen to me? I might just as well go out into the yard and do a sun dance.'

'Florrie, Patsy, come out here! You're missing all the fun.' Ollie's voice came to them from the top of the passage.

'What's he on about? I haven't got time to stand out in the street. I want to get our dinner over and done with today because later on we've got all the sandwiches to cut for tomorrow.'

'Oh, don't be so grumpy, Flo. I said I'd help you and I will.' With that, Patsy was away. Florrie wiped her hands on her apron and followed outside. I'd better see what all the upheaval is about, she told herself.

Patsy couldn't believe her eyes. The whole street was out. Women and children gathered in their doorways and the men were in the middle of the road, shouting and jeering. Danny was the centre of attraction. Not minding the remarks, he walked tall down the centre of the road, pushing before him what looked like an oversized cradle on wheels. Drawing level with his mother, he gave her a sweeping bow, inclined his head and said, 'Your chariot awaits you, milady.'

'Now where the hell did you get that thing from? If you think you're getting me into that contraption, my son, you've got another bloody think coming!'

Queenie was warming to the idea. 'Oh, goodo, Danny. It's a great idea, wonderful, bloody marvellous.'

'Oh, you think so, do you?' Gran's annoyance was really to mask her fear. How would she ever get into it? She knew what it was – a bathchair. Up at Balham Hippodrome, where she and Jack used to sit in the gallery on a Saturday night – Christ, that was a long time ago – they always had a sketch where some toff with gout in his foot was wheeled to the centre of the stage in one of them. It was nice and thoughful of my Danny, she admitted to herself, but I'm still not getting in it!

Queenie lined the bottom of the wicker bassinet with a blanket and placed two pillows at the head, beneath the T-bar handle.

'I'll have first go. You watch, Mum. I bet it's nice and comfortable.' Willing hands heaved Queenie into the cradle.

'Right.' Spitting on his hands, then rubbing them together, Danny winked at his brothers and set off. He walked at a snail's pace, both hands tightly grasping the centre push-bar which served as a handle. The crowd laughed. They were having a good time. Danny's high jinks were hilarious and everyone began to cheer and clap. Danny, enjoying all the attention, acted the goat, swerving from side to side.

Ollie, smiling broadly, whispered to Patsy, 'Danny's got a few pints inside him.'

Running now, full pelt, he precariously turned the thing round when he reached the corner of the road. Queenie gripped the sides.

'Cor blimey! Take it easy going back, will you?'

Danny ignored her. With even more speed he returned to where his mother stood. Queenie alighted, to an enthusiastic burst of applause.

Distrust, even fear, was showing in Gran's eyes.

'How did you come by it, son?' This was the first time his father had spoken.

'The nuns at the Convent of the Sacred Heart loaned it to me.' What he really meant was that he had wheedled it from the sister in charge of the convalescent wing.

'And just how did you get it home?'

'On me cart, of course. Not full length like that. It folds up. The cradle comes off the base and the wheels fold underneath. We could easily take it with us tomorrow and Mum would have a great day.'

'Would I, now? That's what you think, is it?' Gran was not going to be so easily convinced.

'Come on, Gran.'

'Come on, Mum, just try it.'

Sons and grandchildren were using their persuasive powers.

Jack Day walked across the front garden to where

his wife was propped against the window-sill. With one arm on her shoulders, he bent his head. 'Wouldn't you like a day out with me? Remember when the kids were all small and we took them to Hampton Court?'

Gran nodded her head twice and her eyes misted at the memory. She had been young and slim then, able to get about under her own steam. What was she now? A fat, old woman of no use to anyone.

As if reading her thoughts, Jack told her, 'We've all got old, my love. It's a good job we've aged together. Nobody could say I'm the same man you fell in love with, but you're stuck with me.'

'Aw, go on with you. You're just trying to suck up to me.'

'Course I am. You're still my girl and I'm taking you on that trip. So, let's have no more nonsense.'

She'd die before she'd admit it, but Gran was moved. Her Jack, after all these years and all their kids, still didn't want a day out without her.

'Danny, you hold that thing still. If it moves I'll flatten you.'

Jack Day turned to his eldest son. 'Now then, Blower, you get the other side of your mother.'

Age and hard work had taken their toll. Stocky and sturdy in youth, like his sons, Jack Day's shoulders were now rounded. Nevertheless, as he directed Blower to place one arm under his mother's knees and the other across her back under her armpit, he did likewise. They both showed compassion as they lowered her into the chair. Jack straightened her legs and lifted her higher in the chair. They plumped up both pillows and placed them behind her back so that Gran was now in an upright, sitting position.

'Out of me way, son, I'll push her meself.'

The whole family was awestruck as he slowly but steadily walked the length of the street. Reaching the corner, he remained still for several minutes. The return journey was different. Urged on by their parents, the grandchildren ran to meet the chariot. Gran, despite her shabby clothes and bedraggled hair, was acting dignified, waving to the onlookers in a haughty manner as if she were the old Queen herself, and no longer showing any signs of terror.

'All right was it, Mum? Was it comfortable? Told you it was safe, didn't I?'

She didn't answer Danny. She merely crossed her arms over her bosom and, with laughter in her voice, said, 'It wasn't bad. Not bad at all, and I'm coming with you to 'Ampton Court tomorrow!'

'Those slices are no good for sandwiches. Here, let me have a go.' Patsy took the brown loaf with 'Hovis' printed deep on its side away from Florrie.

'All right, clever clogs.' Florrie smiled as she watched Patsy slice the bread thinly.

'Where are the eggs I put on to boil, Flo?'

'They're in the saucepan out in the scullery with

the cold water running on them. You'd have let them boil dry.'

'What's the cold water running on them for?'

'Cos, as I told you. That makes them peel easier.'

Coming into the room, Ollie stopped short. Piles of wrapped food, greaseproof paper and bags of fruit covered the table.

'Are you two aiming to feed the whole street? We have got a high tea laid on, remember. Four o'clock in the afternoon and we shall all be sitting down to a hot meal.'

'Yeah, well, since we're leaving at half-past nine, what do you think we're going to live on all day, fresh air?' Florrie was quite put out now.

'There are shops and cafés.'

Before he could say more, Florrie pitched in. 'At bloody fancy prices an' all, I bet.'

Ollie winked at Patsy. 'Well, I'll leave you to it. Do you want me to come and give you a knock in the morning?'

'That will be the day, Ollie Berry, when I rely on you or anyone else to get me out of bed. No. Get yourself off. We'll be ready. You needn't have any fears about that.'

Patsy woke at five-thirty. She had set the alarm for seven, but she switched off the button. She wouldn't go back to sleep now. She felt happy and alive inside. Today she was going on an outing and would be one of a crowd. She stretched her legs over the side of the bed and thought, if only Mum was coming with us. It was just that her mum never had many treats, not that she could recall, and it would have been so nice if the two of them had been going together. Still, Ollie would be there and Florrie and even Gran now. It was going to be a lovely day. The exciting thought made her catch her breath.

The scene at Tooting Broadway was incredible. This was the first Bank Holiday of the year and they were all out to enjoy themselves. Even the weather was being kind, so far. The morning was bright and the sun was shining, even if there wasn't much warmth coming from it. Not too many clouds in the sky and the few there were were like fluffy, white cotton wool. Two tramcars were drawn up, one behind the other, on the track in the middle of the road. Both looked shiny and bright.

The women had their best clothes on, some looking very attractive. Most wore hats, secured tightly to their heads by awful-looking hatpins. The men, too, had made an effort and were well turned out. Small boys ran in and out of shop doorways, unable to contain their excitement. Some got a box around the ears, which they didn't deserve, and were told to stand still. As if they could!

As was expected, the first team was reserved for the Day family, their relations, friends and neighbours. Jack and Blower struggled to get Gran up the high step. There was near tragedy as she almost toppled backwards.

'I'll be all right. Just leave me alone,' snarled Gran. 'I've just got to get me breath back. Take that bloody thing down to the front so's I can get by.'

Willing hands took the folded bathchair, which lay in the gangway, and placed it up with the driver.

Folk were still crowded on the edge of the pavement, clustered around Danny and Ollie. 'Mrs Warner. Is Mrs Warner here? Oh, yes, there you are. Yourself and three children, second car, please.' Patsy watched Ollie walk from one car to the next, checking his lists, assisting the ladies, teasing the children and exchanging bawdy comments with the men. She had not imagined so many people would be going on this outing. Seeing Mrs Woolston and her daughter Peggy hanging back, as if they were friendless, Patsy leaned down from the tram platform and called loudly, 'Peggy, Peggy, get on this one. There's plenty of room for you and your mum.'

Florrie, from her seat just inside the door, bristled. 'We don't want to be lumbered with them.'

'Why not? Why do you always have to be so spiteful? Peggy's my friend.'

'Hum, some friend,' Florrie huffed.

'What did you say?' Patsy turned on her.

'Well, maybe Peggy's not so bad. It's her bloody mother.'

Patsy sighed. She had heard it so often, she was sick and tired of hearing it.

'Mrs Woolston is a shark. You start off borrowing ten bob off her and end up owing her ten pounds. Ought to be locked up, that woman should.' Florrie was like a stuck gramophone record where Mrs Woolston was concerned. Well, Patsy didn't care. Especially not today. She liked Peggy, she was good for a laugh and her mother wasn't so bad. She's always been nice to me when I've called for Peggy, Patsy wrangled with herself. Their home is nice, a bit showy maybe, but that's nothing to do with me.

Waving furiously now, Patsy beckoned to Peggy and as she and her mother drew near Patsy got in the last shot.

'Now shut up, Flo. Try and be nice.'

Red-faced and angry, Florrie wisely kept her mouth closed.

The commotion died down. Men, women and children alike were keyed up. The conductor at the rear of the tram signalled to the driver everyone was aboard, the journey could commence.

At Wimbledon Station the tram came to a stop. The conductor climbed down, taking his blue billy-can into the café to be filled with tea. The children were becoming restless. One or two attempted to run up and down the aisle between the seats, only to be pulled back beside their mothers.

'Wish I'd gone upstairs with me dad,' one boy insolently muttered.

'Well, go on then,' his mother told him. Needing no second bidding he made off. Just then the tram rolled and the boy fell hard against a seat, banging his head. He got no sympathy. His mother lunged at him and, to everyone's amusement, told him, 'If you don't sit still and behave yourself, I'll throw you in the river when we get there.'

The sun was still shining and it felt warm through the glass windows.

'Oh, Flo, isn't it nice to see some different places.' As she spoke, Patsy realised that, apart from going to work and up the common now and again, she hadn't been further afield for a long time.

'Get your coats on and make sure you've got all your bits and pieces, we'll be running into Bushey Park any minute now,' the conductor told Florrie, walking between the seats.

'No need to hurry, me ducks, let the young ones get off first.' Flo smiled her thanks at the young man for his consideration.

Reaching Gran, who had occupied a double seat, the conductor smiled down at her. 'As for you, my beauty, you'll be carried off in the arms of young men. You'll have a fantastic time, but don't forget I'll be waiting to take you home at the end of the day.'

'Mind your manners, young man. Those "young men", as you call them, are all my sons.'

'Well, give us a kiss quick before they come downstairs!'

'Get on wiv yer, you cheeky whelp.' But Gran giggled as she reprimanded him.

'Gran's on her best behaviour today, else she'd have called him more than a cheeky whelp,' Florrie whispered to Patsy, who had been thinking exactly the same thing. They laughed together.

'Have a good time, kids,' the tram driver called to the children. They needed no telling. Off across the grass they streaked, shoes and socks dispensed with. Trouser legs were rolled up, hems of dresses tucked into elasticated knicker legs, and into the river they swooped.

Patsy couldn't express all her thoughts – not out loud. The air was sharp and clean as she took great gulps of it right down into her lungs. There was grass everywhere, no matter which way she turned. It wasn't grass such as in the recreation park or on Tooting Bec Common. This was like velvet – clean, well cared for and springy to walk on. In fact, she felt guilty as they trampled across it. Great tall trees stood majestically, their spring foliage beginning to unfurl. So many different shades of green with heavy great branches stretched up towards the sky as if saying: 'Winter's gone – spring is here.'

Many areas of the ground were dotted with early daffodils. At the base of the great oaks, crocuses still bloomed in colours of brilliant purple, yellow and white. Standing side by side, Florrie's arm came slowly around Patsy's shoulders. 'Different world 'ere ain't it, love.'

Patsy turned to look at her. She was surprised to see that Florrie's eyes were filled with wonderment. She flung her arms around Flo's waist and laid her head on her shoulder for a moment.

'I'm glad we came, aren't you, Flo?'

'Yes, love, I am. I wouldn't have missed it for the world.'

Patsy felt happy, not so much with the actual words Florrie had said but with the depth of feeling with which she had uttered them. She broke away and gazed at that face, so deeply etched, with a character all of its own. The way Florrie was look-ing at her frightened her. Patsy felt that unselfish love, such as this woman had shown her, must be rare.

'Florrie, what would I do without you?'

'You know, Patsy, I'd like a pound note for every time you've said that to me. Well, it works both ways. My life isn't exactly dull with you around.'

They ate their lunch spread out on the grass. All except Gran; she lorded it over everyone from the height of her bathchair. Amongst the women, there wasn't one who wasn't comparing today's sur-roundings with those of their everyday lives.

'Right, everyone finished eating? Well, don't let's leave the place in a mess like this. You kids, pick up those paper bags and those apple cores. There's plenty of rubbish bins about. Chop, chop, look lively.' Blower picked up his coat from the grass. 'That's it, then, all ready to go.'

Ollie took charge of the wheelchair, placing Florrie's now half-empty shopping bag at Gran's feet.

'Flo, walk this side of me and keep a tight hold on to that bar. Come on, don't straggle you lot. When Blower gives the word, we all cross together. Got it?' It amazed Ollie that the whole crowd of them did make it safely across the busy road.

A hoot heralded the coming of a steam boat. One and all leaned over the parapet of the bridge that spanned the wide River Thames. What a sight! The upper and lower decks of the pleasure steamer were packed with bank holiday revellers. An upright piano stood near the rails, its keys being thumped by a man in a straw boater. The songs were bawdy and the voices loud, if not musical. Grown men roared their approval as the steamer passed under the bridge, the children cheered while their mothers hung on to their coat tails, wondering why water held such fascination for them.

Patsy's first impression of Hampton Court Palace was its size. She had gazed in admiration at the enormous gates and the old clock, but now they had reached the palace itself. It was magnificent.

Nothing she had ever before been so close to had
been quite so splendid. 'Private Residence Only.'
The notice barred the way. Her imagination ran
riot. Who was allowed to live here and what kind of
people were they? They must be rich.

'Patsy, shall we go into the Maze?'

'All right, but what about your mum?'

'She doesn't want to walk any further. She's over
there, sitting with your Florrie and Gran.'

Patsy tilted her head to one side and her green
eyes glinted with amusement. Mrs Woolston sitting
talking to Flo and Gran! Wonders would never
cease!

'I'd better go and tell them where we're going.
Shan't be a tick, Peggy.'

Off she darted and found several other women
seated on the high-backed bench with Gran positioned in her wheelchair alongside.

'Flo, I'm going into the Maze with Peggy. Will
you be all right here?'

'Course I will, love. Queenie, Lil and several
others have already gone. They've got all the kids
with them, so watch out.'

'Will you tell Ollie where I've gone, if you see
him?'

'Don't be silly, gal, you won't see Ollie for the
next hour. He's gone for a drink and, come to that,
so have most of the men.'

'That's all right, then, see you later. Bye-bye
Gran.'

Both women smiled and tutted as she ran off.

With every corner they turned in the Maze their mood changed. It was good fun, it was frightening – and it was horrible! Some of the paths were tortuous, bordered by hedges of closely growing trees clipped tightly down the sides but left to grow quite high so no one could see over the top.

'Turn left, now left again.'

'No, Patsy, we're only going round in circles. I'm sure we've just come out of that path.'

They were lost. Would they ever get out? What about when it got dark? They had bumped into a few people as they walked up and down the lanes, but no one they knew and of those they had asked no one could point the way out. Shrills, screams and yells and even once the sound of Queenie's unmistakable voice had come to them from a distance, but their calls hadn't brought forth any answer. Turning yet another corner, they saw a seat.

'Thank God for that,' Peggy said as they both sank down on it panting, short-winded from all their frantic running about. They suddenly started to chuckle; this turned to laughter and soon they were chortling until both had tears running down their faces.

'Oh, Peg, fancy us getting lost! What a carry-on, eh?'

''Tis a bit of a lark, isn't it? We'll have another go when we get our breath back.' Peggy pulled a white paper bag from each of her coat pockets. ''Ere. Have a sweet: buttermilk toffee or humbug. Take one of each.'

'Oh, thanks. I'm ever so thirsty, are you? I hope we get out of here in time to get our tea.'

'Of course we will. It's high tea, isn't it? I wonder what we'll get.'

'Are you two young ladies lost?'

Where had the voice come from? No one was in sight! The little square in which they were sitting was entirely enclosed with the same tight-knit hedges in which no gaps or holes were visible. They bent forward together, peering at the narrow entrance that led to the path they had entered by, but still no person was to be seen.

'Up here. Look up.'

They were flabbergasted. High up in the air, way above the top of the hedges, was a man. At least, his head and shoulders were to be seen and he appeared to be perched on top of what must have been a gigantic ladder. He was certainly conspicuous. The jacket he wore was royal blue and on the shoulders were ornamental epaulettes outlined in gold braid. Their upturned faces stared at him in amazement.

'Don't be frightened. I'm an official here. Listen to me and I'll guide you.'

With his directions of right, now turn left and left again, they were back at the entrance within minutes and they both fell about laughing, rolling on the grass unrestrained in their high spirits.

They were doing their best to tidy themselves up

when Peggy lifted the fob-watch that was pinned to the lapel of her jacket.

'Do you know it's gone one? In fact, it's nearer half-past.'

'Is it? We'd better go and find the others. Wait a minute, though, you've got grass sticking to the back of your skirt. I'll brush it off for you.'

As Patsy picked off the clinging pieces of damp grass she said, 'It's left a stain and it's a new skirt, isn't it?'

'Yes, but never mind. Rub it with this.'

Dabbing at the offending patch with a handkerchief which Peggy had spat on before handing it to her, Patsy couldn't help remarking, 'It's lovely material, Peg. You always have such nice clothes.'

Indeed, it was a good skirt. It was grey serge and near the bottom were three strands of narrow, maroon-coloured velvet. Beneath the hem, Patsy glanced at the boots Peggy was wearing. They were black leather, real leather, the laces criss-crossed over shiny buttons. 'Hey! I like your boots, too.'

Peggy turned round to face her. 'Patsy, you look nice an' all, especially your hair. No one's got hair like you. Look at mine. My mum will make me strand it up in rags of a night and all I ever look is frizzy on top.'

Patsy felt her cheeks reddening with pleasure. Flo was always telling her that her hair was her crowning glory. Dead straight, it lay down her back well past her shoulders. She'd washed it the night before and, looking in the mirror this morning, she had seen the reddish glints shining. Now as she timidly raised her hand and stroked it down, it felt silky and nice. When she'd been at school, Mum had always cut it, making her keep it short because of lice. Lots of kids in her class had had lousy heads. Oh, Mum. How would you think it looks today? She was talking to her mum as if she were still here. She mustn't do that – not today.

'Did you make your dress, Patsy?'

Oh, dear. Was it so obvious?

'I'm not being nasty, honest. It's smashing, you always were good at needlework.'

'My mother taught me,' Patsy said without thinking.

Peggy stretched out a hand to her, trying to show that she cared.

'Does the skirt hang right?'

'Yes, I told you. It looks great.'

'It took nearly four yards of material. I got it at Smith's down Mitcham Lane. It was one and nine a yard, but I told Florrie it was one and six. You know how she goes on, thinks everything is too dear.' They both grinned. 'It's not a full dress, only a pinafore one. Ollie bought me the blouse for Easter. Do you want to see it?'

For just a brief moment, Patsy forgot it was a home-made dress she was offering Peggy Woolston the chance to admire. She liked Peggy. She might have everything that money could buy but, like her-

self, she didn't have many friends. That was mainly
Mrs Woolston's fault. Her loud mouth was feared
by those who owed her money.

Patsy unbuttoned her navy blue winter coat and
took it off. The dress was little more than a skirt
with a bib front. Wide straps went over the
shoulders and crossed at the back, fastened to the
waistband of the skirt by two buttons. She twirled
round.

'Those buttons are pretty.'

'Florrie found them in her button tin for me.
Wouldn't let me buy any.'

'And that blouse is lovely.'

Patsy knew that was the truth and the thought
gave her comfort. The dress material was a multi-
coloured check, the predominant colour blue. The
pale blue silk blouse, which was gathered high in the
neck and had full sleeves that came in tight below
the elbow, leaving long cuffs fastened by a row of
pearly buttons, complemented the outfit. Ollie had
chosen well.

'Oh, Patsy, it's a shame you had to wear a coat.
Still, when we go in for our tea, we can both take
our coats off and show off a bit!'

Patsy nodded. Yes, we'll do that she thought.

'Where have you two been? We were getting
worried about you.'

'We got lost, Flo.'

Florrie and Gran looked at each other and burst out laughing.

'I'm not joking, Flo, it wasn't funny.' Although Patsy tried to be serious, she and Peggy were by now both laughing.

'Where's me mum?' Peggy flopped down on the seat beside Gran's chair. 'Don't tell me she's gone off to the pub with the men?'

Florrie gave her a look of disgust. 'No. She's gone over to the fair with Mrs Warner. She said she'd keep an eye out for you.'

'Aren't you going to go over to the fair, Flo?' Patsy knew full well the answer she would get.

'No, we're not. Too bloody crowded for me and Gran. Danny's going to take us to the café for a cup of tea. You two had better get yourselves off if you are going. All the others have gone over. Do you want something to eat first? There's loads of sandwiches left, or an apple or banana.'

'No, nothing to eat, but I must have a drink. I'm gasping. I couldn't spit sixpence!'

'There's a stall over there, by that clump of bushes. Queenie got all the kids a lemonade. Here, I'll treat you.' Opening her purse, she held out a penny towards Patsy, then as an afterthought she added another coin. 'You'd better get Peggy one as well.'

'Oh, ta, Flo.'

'Yes, thanks very much, Mrs Holmes.'

Florrie's eyes crinkled with pleasure. That Peggy

could be quite polite when she wanted to. 'Well, go on then. No good standing there. You won't have much time as it is, because you've got to be back here by four.'

'We will be. You all right, Gran?' Patsy leaned over the chair and smiled into Gran's face.

'Course I am, love, never better. We're lucky ain't we, what with the weather being nice an' all. Blower and Ollie said they'd look out for you over on the green.'

'See you later, then. Bye, Florrie.'

As the two girls ran off to buy their lemonade, Gran's voice followed: 'Oi! Don't forget to bring us back a coconut!'

Music was blaring and the fair was in full swing. The tents and side shows were in all shapes and colours. The world and his wife, it seemed, had turned out to have a good time. Hundreds of feet had already churned up the grass and in no time at all the girls' boots were covered with grey dust.

'Isn't he pretty?' Peggy clutched a long-eared rabbit to her chest. 'He's all soft and furry,' she murmured as she laid her cheek against its head.

'Whoever saw a pink and white rabbit?'

'Aw. Trust you, Patsy.'

'Come on, I haven't spent any money yet. Let's get some rock.'

'Ha'penny a piece, or seven for threepence.'

Wrinkled hands cut the soft, sugary rock into small pieces with the aid of large scissors. This was not pink peppermint rock like Charlie had once brought back from Southend. Behind the stall a great hulk of a man with jet-black, curly hair pulled beige-coloured rock with stripes of brown running through it into long lengths. Every now and again he flung a length over a metal hook then, with both ends between his hands, he walked backwards, stretching and twisting the flexible substance.

Patsy couldn't resist. She handed over a silver threepenny piece.

'Open your mouth.' Now they were both sucking away at the home-made humbug rock and were sent into raptures of delight over the most delicious sweet they had ever tasted.

'Look over there. Ollie's won a coconut. That'll please Gran.'

As Ollie was so tall he was easy to spot in a crowd. Patsy waved her hand in the air to attract his attention. Immediately, he waved back to her. Both girls gave him a quick, warm smile as he came towards them.

Ollie saw then what he had failed to notice before. Patsy had grown into a young woman. The almost ethereal beauty of her face struck him. She looked so much like Ellen, and he remembered in that moment the years of friendship he had shared with her dear mother. The knowledge that he had loved Ellen deeply brought a lump to his throat.

'Are you going to ride on this?' Ollie had to shout to make himself heard above the throb of the great engine which drove the roundabout, the screams of the riders as they clutched the brass poles of the whirling horses and, loudest of all, the music. Bending down, Ollie put half a crown into Patsy's hand.

'Thanks, Ollie,' she smiled at him.

'Well, are you going on it or not?' He made to lift her as the painted horses slowed down.

'No, I don't think so.' She spoke so low that the clattering of the merry-go-round almost drowned the sound of her voice. She was having a good time. She loved the crowds and the happy atmosphere, but the roundabouts and the high helter-skelters frightened her.

'Well, you don't have to,' Ollie told her, sensing her fear.

'Aw, come on Patsy. It don't go that fast! Look, there's an empty one over there. Be quick, it'll start again in a minute.' Peggy was bawling from her lofty position astride a gaudy horse with a mane of false, white hair.

'Oh, all right then,' Patsy answered with carefully assumed indifference.

Ollie's eyes widened at this sudden change of heart.

The clang of the bell sounded horribly loud. They were moving. She had both hands clenched so tightly around the pole that her knuckles showed white. Patsy relaxed. It wasn't so bad; she wasn't scared now. The coloured horses rose, one up, one down alternately, while the dais beneath rotated quite slowly. She tugged her skirt over her spread knees and looked for Ollie's face among the watching crowd.

'Have yer fares ready, please. A tanner each. Cheap at half the price.'

Sixpence! For one ride! Patsy didn't think it cheap. A brown arm encircled by many coloured bracelets stretched across for Patsy's payment. The gypsy girl smiled her thanks, flashing her gleaming white teeth. Patsy thought she was beautiful. Her long, blue-black hair was held back from her face by decorative combs and the rows of fancy beads around her neck jangled as she moved seductively between the horses. Patsy was so busy wondering how she managed to keep her balance that it was a few seconds before she realised they were steadily gathering speed. The faster they revolved, the louder the music played. Patsy screwed her eyes up tight; the sight of caravans, stalls and a blur of faces whizzing by was too much. She felt sick. She hung her head, her hair falling forward over her face.

'You all right?' Two feet, encased in black boots with pointed toes, were all Patsy's lowered eyes could see. A hand came down on her shoulder. Slowly she raised her head, her hands still gripping the pole as if her very life depended upon it. She heaved a great sigh of relief. Oh, thank God, they were slowing down. All she wanted was to get off. Two brawny, heavily tattooed arms came around her.

'For God's sake, what do you think you're doing?'

'Lifting you down, me darling. Wouldn't want you falling, would we?' the man told her, ignoring her protests. He wasn't a man, not really, just a lad. Patsy took a deep breath. He looked like a foreigner. His skin was so dark, his hair black like that of the girl who had collected the sixpences, though his was a shock of tight curls. She would have fallen as she attempted to avoid him, but was saved by those gleaming, brawny arms.

As he released her he didn't step back, but allowed one of his hands to rest on her arm, too long for Patsy's liking. He was grinning broadly. Was he mocking her? She couldn't be sure but in spite of herself she felt drawn to him.

He made a low, sweeping bow.

'Thank you.' Her voice was barely audible as she turned away and stepped down cautiously to the ground.

She looked back. She hadn't meant to, sensing he was watching her. He was certainly handsome, dressed in the flamboyant way of gypsies. His body was firm and taut, without an ounce of spare flesh.

'Aren't you the sly one?' Peggy's voice, ripe with sarcasm, jerked Patsy back to the moment.

'What? I don't get you.'

'Don't you, now? Well, it seems you got Johnny all right.'

'Johnny? Who the hell is Johnny?'

'Oh, come off it, Patsy. He was with you for most of the ride *and* he lifted you down when it finished. I've got eyes in me head. I saw what was going on.'

'I still don't know what you're going on about. I felt a bit sick and that fella helped me. So what!'

'Felt sick, I bet you did! You had Johnny Jackson goggle-eyed.'

'Johnny Jackson? How do you know his name?'

'Know his name? Every girl for miles around knows Johnny, except you, of course. You never come out, do you? You're too busy working in the market.'

'Well, you never work, that's for sure.' Patsy found herself being spiteful. Peggy's implication that she was a dull, stick-in-the-mud workhorse had made her angry. She wouldn't work six days a week if she didn't have to.

'He lives at Mitcham.' Peggy wasn't prepared to let the matter rest.

'Who does?'

'Johnny does.'

'You seem to know a lot about him.'

'I told you, all the girls do.'

'Whereabouts in Mitcham?'

'Behind all those wooden hoardings on that spare ground back of the Three Kings Pond. You know, it's near the fair green.'

'Yes, I know where you mean. I've seen caravans going in and out of there. I suppose I knew some fair people lived there, but I've never met any of them.'

'Some fair people! Gawd, Patsy, where you been all your life? There's dozens of them. My mum says they breed like rabbits. Two of the girls came to our school, don't you remember? Sarah and Polly Jackson. Always hopping the wag, they were. The boys are all right, though. Often muck about with them up the common. Right laugh they are.'

Now Patsy understood a little of Florrie's disapproval of Peggy. 'Gets the boys around her like bees round a honey pot,' Flo was fond of saying. 'Why? Cos she's coarse in her talk and vulgar in her ways. Like mother, like daughter.'

Patsy suddenly thought, if we keep this up, we'll end up having a right old row and that will spoil the day.

'Anyway, if you hadn't made out you were sick, Johnny would never have looked at you.'

Patsy wanted to be charitable. Peggy was an attractive girl and always so well turned out, but she wasn't going to let her get away with too much.

'Oh yeah! That's what you think, is it? Well, tell me this! How did he know I was feeling sick?'

'Cos you put on a bleeding good act. Anyway, I'm going to see a bit more of the fair. You coming or not?'

Patsy was used to hearing women swear. Flo and Gran could do their share but, as her mum used to say, it came natural from them and it didn't seem to give offence. When Peggy swore, it didn't sound nice at all.

She knew now Peggy was piqued, and all because of that lad. Oh well, one up for me, I suppose, she said to herself as she followed Peggy.

'Come on, boys and girls. Roll 'em down. Hit the middle square and you've won yerself a pound note.'

A tawdrily-dressed woman circled the centre of the stall, tossing a pile of pennies from hand to hand. Every once in a while she raked up the coins which had landed outside a square or were touching a line.

Patsy watched as Peggy let roll penny after penny down the small wooden shute.

'I've won, I've won,' Peggy cried. The stallholder picked up the one coin which had landed dead centre in a square. Beneath it, the number six was painted.

'There you are, love, six for one. Roll 'em, roll 'em down.' The woman continued her bawling as she jauntily flicked six pennies towards Peggy.

'Your friend's doing well.'

Patsy's face immediately reddened. She could feel the blush burning her cheeks. He was beside her again, laughing at her, his amusement at her embarrassment lighting up his face. She couldn't be cross. His manner was infectious, appealing to her to be happy and to laugh with him.

'I don't think Peggy was lucky. She's spent a lot more than she's won.'

'Oh, quite the cynic, aren't you? What's it matter as long as she's enjoying herself. You're not still feeling sick are you?'

This last question was asked with a certain amount of concern, but again Patsy was not sure if it was genuine. This fellow was a complete mixture. His swarthy complexion and his gaudy attire made her wary of him yet his gaiety and liveliness invited her to smile at him, and she did. His laughter became loud as he watched her and gradually her own smile broadened until she began to chuckle, without really knowing why.

'My name's Johnny, what's yours?'

'I know, Peggy told me.' She cast a quick glance in Peggy's direction, glad to see she was still busily rolling her pennies down.

'She would. Is Peggy a friend of yours?'

'Yes. We went to school together.'

'Oh, well. You still haven't told me your name.'

'Patsy.'

'Do you live in Tooting near Peggy?'

'Yes. In the same street.'

'Well, we won't upset her then. I'll take you both round the fair.'

He got no argument from Peggy as he turned the charm on. It was Peggy who rode the swing-boats, roundabouts, dodgem cars and catwalks with Johnny, while Patsy stood and watched. She did try her aim at the coconut shy and was pleasantly surprised when Johnny took her last ball and easily knocked one from its cup-shaped stand with a swift, overarm swing.

'Will you come for a walk with me?' he stage-whispered as he presented her with the shaggy coconut.

'What, now? Course I can't. The time must be getting on and we've got to go and find the others. We're going to have a high tea.'

Again, he was grinning from ear to ear. 'How about next Sunday? The fair will be finished by then.' He gave her no time to answer, the rest of his words coming out in a rush. 'Do you know Dunne's, the men's shop at Tooting Broadway? I'll see you outside there six o'clock next Sunday.'

He stroked her cheek with two of his fingers. 'Be good till then. See yer.'

He didn't even look back. Patsy couldn't define her feelings as she watched him weave his way between the stalls, jumping cleanly over all barriers and obstacles.

'Who was that?' Coming up behind her with her forthright question, Queenie caught Patsy unawares.

'Nobody.' The word came out far too quickly.

'Don't tell me nobody. I saw him.'

Peggy came to the rescue. 'That was Johnny Jackson. His family own a lot of the stalls here. He gave us a great time, didn't he, Patsy? We didn't have to pay on anything.'

Queenie gave Patsy a questioning look. 'Yeah, well, you want to be careful. I know the Jacksons and a scrounging, rough lot they are. Ain't even proper gypsies anyway, just vagabonds they are.'

Following Queenie came Lily, doing her best to keep all the children together. 'Hello, you two. Had a good time? About time we went for our tea. Someone said we're going to have it in a tent. Don't suppose you've seen anything of the men, have you? Always disappear, don't they, Queenie?'

'Yes, and never take any of the kids with 'em.'

Inside the marquee, tables had been set up with wooden forms each side to provide the seating. The noise was deafening. Everyone was chattering and laughing, trying to relate the account of their day. Gran's bathchair had been left outside. She had insisted on taking her usual place at the head of the table and a special armchair had been provided for her. All Gran's kith and kin, plus Ollie, Florrie and Patsy, were at this table. Seated among the men, Ollie leaned forward.

'Here, Patsy. I got you a souvenir.'

A slim book was passed from hand to hand and Patsy was delighted to find it contained information on the history of Hampton Court Palace.

'Go on, read us what it says,' Queenie urged.

Patsy was proud that her captive audience showed interest. 'Hampton Court was erected by Cardinal Wolsey and enlarged by Henry the Eighth.' Her voice gained strength as she read. 'It is one of the finest buildings of its kind in the world. Further additions were designed by Sir Christopher Wren. George the Third was the last king to reside in the palace and Henry the Eighth had one of the very first tennis courts installed here.'

'I saw it! A guide pointed it out to me. It were 'igh up, at the top of a big building. All glassed in it were.' Lily's oldest boy volunteered this information. A serious, white-faced lad, he seemed pleased that everyone's attention was now focused on him.

Patsy stared at the photographs in the book.

'I wish we could have gone inside the palace and seen some of these rooms. Don't they look beautiful?'

'Never mind, love. Can't do everything in a day. Perhaps we can come back another time,' Florrie placidly answered. Patsy laughed out loud. What an optimist Florrie was! She couldn't see this outing being repeated very often.

'Mind yer backs. Excuse me, please. Mind, the plates are hot.'

'Cor, 'addock and chips.'

'Don't it smell good.'

'Pass the bread and butter, I'm starving.'

'Will you all shut up and just eat your tea.' Lily tried not to look as exasperated as she felt.

'I don't want the vinegar, I want some of that tartar sauce.'

'You what! Christ, listen to her!' cried Queenie.

Everyone was eating and, for a while, there was no talking. The silence was soon shattered by a squeal from the younger children.

'Look, we're going to get cakes.'

'I want that pink one.'

'Mum. We ain't got no jam tarts.'

'Mum, Charlie's wiped chocolate all over my dress.'

'Aw, Gawd, why don't the kids ever yell for their dad? Why does it always have to be for their mum?'

Home time and, as was to be expected, two children were missing though not from the Day clan. That, at least, made a change.

'No harm done, we've found them.'

Finally, the conductor rang the bell and the two trams trundled homewards. It was nearly eight o'clock when they all dismounted from the tram at the Broadway.

There was a party that night in the Fox. It was supposed to be a party for the families, but the women were tired and they had to put the children to bed. That didn't deter the men. They had done their duty; now it was their turn to have fun and they made the most of it.

Pints lined the bar. The piano played non-stop. Probably for the first time in his well-ordered life Ollie kept up with the Day brothers, matching drink for drink until he was well and truly drunk.

Patsy would have had trouble recognising him and Florrie would have given him a right ticking-off.

At closing time, he was literally dragged home by Danny and Blower and shoved, fully dressed, into his bed. Grinning from ear to ear, Blower closed the front door.

'Let him sleep it off. He'll have a damned thick head in the morning.'

With an undignified lurching, each holding on to the other, they made for their mother's house. It would be safer to sleep there tonight, rather than face the wrath of their wives.

At number twenty-two, Patsy, lying alone in her single bed, pondered on her day. Johnny Jackson was like no man she had ever known in her humdrum life. He was exciting and made her feel important. He'd touched her face, hadn't he? Maybe he thought she was pretty. Just thinking about him was nice, because he was so . . . so full of life, with his tanned skin and dark eyes and his strong, broad body. And his hair – coal black, thick and curly. When she finally fell asleep there was a smile of contentment on her lips.

By Sunday, Patsy was still undecided. There was no promise to break, for she hadn't said she would meet him. No, she wasn't going to go, of course she wasn't. She'd argued with herself all week.

Thursday, Friday and Saturday had been wet and

windy, but when she had woken up this morning the skies were clear and the sun was shining brightly. A good omen? Maybe. Midday dinner with Florrie seemed never-ending.

'Would you like some more pudding?' Florrie asked, raising the jug of custard.

'No, no thanks.'

'What's got into you today? I told you Lily Day's got herself a boyfriend and all you said was "Has she?". You ain't sickening for something, are you?'

Patsy knew she hadn't been listening. All week she had been deluding herself. She now knew with certainty that when six o'clock came she would be there, waiting.

As she got ready, Patsy offered up a silent prayer.

'Please, God, let him be there. Don't let him have been having me on.'

When she walked quietly down the stairs she sighed with relief at the sight of the closed kitchen door. Florrie was probably still snoozing in her armchair. If she was lucky, she would be able to creep out without Flo being any the wiser.

She walked in the opposite direction, taking the long way round. She was wearing a flowered dress and matching jacket. It wasn't very warm, but it looked nice, and the evening promised to be fine. Her hair had been brushed until the chestnut lights gleamed. She knew she looked good and the thought heartened her. There was a gnawing sensation in her stomach. It wasn't hunger, but apprehension as to whether she was doing the right thing.

At six o'clock prompt she was in the High Street and now, suddenly full of confidence, she walked towards Dunne's, the outfitters.

Half an hour later her feet were aching and she was beginning to feel cold. She wondered if she had missed him. Had he been and gone?

'Mad,' she muttered to herself. 'That's what I am, mad, standing here on a Sunday evening waiting for a ruddy gypsy. Face the truth, he's made a fool out of me. He never had no intentions of turning up.'

Still she lingered, reluctant to believe the truth. By now, she felt she knew every shape and every colour of every hat in Dunne's window, and of the ties, scarves and gloves. When the clock tower in the Broadway Centre showed a quarter to seven the anger really rose in her.

'Sod him,' she said aloud as she walked home.

For the next four days Patsy knew she was irritable. She imagined Peggy Woolston's face if she ever found out that she had gone to meet Johnny Jackson and he had stood her up. She told herself over and over again to forget it. How daft it had all been at the fair. That gypsy had been having a good old laugh at her expense, and she had been stupid enough to fall for it. She had cried on Sunday night. Not over him, but tears of anger because she'd let him make a fool of her.

*

'Mrs Holmes. Is Patsy in?' It was Thursday evening and Florrie felt pleased when Peggy Woolston popped her head round the door.

'Yes she is, love, upstairs. Gawd knows what's got into her these last few days. She don't want my company, or anyone else's come to that. She even snapped at Gran yesterday and that's not like her. I've never known her to be moody. A right bloody chip she's got on her shoulder about something. You go on up, love, and see what you can do to cheer her up.'

Patsy was ironing at the kitchen table, over which she had spread an old blanket topped by a scorch-marked sheet.

'Oh, it's you,' she said ungraciously as Peggy came into the room. 'If she's come to gloat,' she thought, 'I'll kick her down the stairs.' She didn't know if Peggy had found out about the date, and was still suspicious.

'What brings you here?' she asked, a touch of harshness in her voice.

'Well, I haven't seen you all week, so I thought I'd come round. Besides, I've got something to tell you.'

'Just let me put this lot away, then. Go and put the kettle on if you like.' Patsy folded the blouse, laying it on top of a pile of underwear. In a way she was pleased to see Peggy and she was fed up with ironing, anyway. She removed the flat iron, standing it on end in the hearth. As long as Peggy hadn't come to gloat. 'Does she know I waited nearly an hour in the High Street?' she asked herself. 'I'll die if she goes on about it.'

'Here you are. I've made the tea. You haven't got much milk, though.'

'It don't matter, as long as there's enough for us now. Flo will give me a drop for the morning.'

They munched a biscuit and sipped their tea, then Peggy licked her fingertips and pushed her frizzy hair back from her forehead. 'Well, get on with it. What was it you were going to tell me?'

Peggy waited a moment, then said, 'You're never going to believe it.'

Patsy was getting exasperated. 'For Christ's sake, spit it out. Can't be that important or you'd have blurted it out the minute you got here.'

'Well.' Peggy looked like the cat that had swallowed the cream as she pushed the ironing blanket to the centre of the table and set her cup and saucer down. She was enjoying keeping Patsy in suspense. She turned her eyes from the table and looked at Patsy.

'Mum sent me up to Harrison's to get fish and chips for our tea and who do you think was in the shop? Not buying fish to take away. No, they were eating it there, sitting down at the tables.'

Patsy reached down for the poker, scraping it along the fender as she lifted it. Eyes blazing, yet at the same time trying hard not to smile, she leaned towards Peggy. 'I'll kill you in a minute if you don't tell me what you're on about.'

'Johnny Jackson and his brother Tom.'

Patsy's heart sank and she felt her face go white. So she had come to rub it in.

'They want us to go out with them this Saturday. To a do at the Fountain.'

Triumphantly, Peggy waved a hand in the air. 'Well, say something! Blimey, it's not every day we get a date.'

A sense of weariness came over Patsy. She wasn't going to go through all that again.

Peggy's voice became persuasive. 'You know you want to go, so don't look like that. Besides, I bet we'll have a smashing time.'

Still Patsy said nothing. Staring at the rug beneath her feet she remembered the humiliation of waiting last Sunday.

'Oh, Patsy. You are down in the dumps, aren't you? What the hell is the matter with you?'

It was true she did want to go. Yes, she wanted to see Johnny again, but nothing in this world would make her go. She got up and took the cups out to the scullery and ran the cold tap on them.

'What did Johnny say when he asked you?' She stood with her back against the table and looked directly at Peggy. She felt she was her friend, but she wasn't quite sure.

'Nothing.'

'But you said . . .'

'Yes, I know I did. Tom told me this do was going to be a kind of social, not in the pub, in the hall next door and if it's fine they are going to have dancing in the gardens. He just asked if I'd like to go with them and bring a friend. Course, I told him I would and that I'd bring you.'

'And what did Johnny say to that?'

'I've told you. Nothing. He seemed chuffed but if you don't want to come, then don't. I can soon get someone else to go with me.'

Suddenly, Patsy was surprised by her own thoughts. Why shouldn't she go? She'd show him! Besides, the thought of Peggy taking another girl had made her jealous. Why she should feel jealous she didn't know, but she did.

'All right, I'll come if you want me to.'

'You're barmy, you know that, Patsy? I've been pleading with you to come for the last half hour, haven't I?'

As Patsy undressed that night she gave a little twirl in front of the long mirror which was set in the cupboard door. I'm going to a dance. I'll dress up to the nines and all! Johnny Jackson may be there, but he won't be the only pebble on the beach, so blow him.

There was plenty of fight in her and it would take more than the likes of him to put her down. Come Saturday, she was going to that dance and she was damn well going to have a good time.

Chapter Seven

OH, YES, SHE was pleased to see him. The mere sight of him had set her heart pounding. She wasn't going to admit it, certainly not to him, but she was glad that Peggy had persuaded her to come. They sat around a rustic wooden table in the garden of the Fountain public house, Tom and Peggy together on one side, Patsy and Johnny opposite them.

Only Patsy seemed to feel any embarrassment. The others talked and laughed with easy familiarity, Johnny and his brother cracking jokes non-stop. 'He's pretending he never left me standing waiting,' Patsy told herself, 'and I'm certainly not going to remind him. Not in front of the others.'

Tom Jackson looked a lot older than Johnny and was taller by about three inches. He was a raw-boned young man with a lean, weather-beaten face, dark hair and dark eyes that looked kindly at Patsy, perhaps sensing her discomfort. As if to show off, Peggy snuggled up to Tom, ran her fingers through his thick hair then, lowering her face, she stuck out her tongue and licked around his ear.

'Cut it out, Peg.' Tom's voice was harsh. Grabbing at her arm, he pulled her to her feet, pushing her in front of himself. Turning to face his brother he said, 'We'll be over in the hall. There's a bar set up in there. See yer later.'

Peggy shot a mischievous grin in Patsy's direction as Tom literally dragged her across the grass.

Left alone with Johnny, Patsy again felt embarrassed and she jumped when he took hold of her arm and pulled her round to face him. His manner was brash and swaggering again. 'Something wrong?' he asked, still brazenly smiling.

Sarcastic sod, she thought and had the urge to swipe her hand around his face. Instead, she blurted out, 'As if you didn't know.' Oh, blast! She had made up her mind to say nothing and now she'd come straight out with it and admitted she'd turned up last Sunday.

His head went back and he roared with laughter. Patsy's temper flared. The bloody nerve – she wasn't going to sit here and let him jeer at her. She gathered her skirt around her and picked up her handbag. His fingers closed tightly around her wrist, causing her to wince. She was forced to look at him again and she felt really angry. There it was again, that gloating smirk, showing his brilliant white teeth. As if that wasn't bad enough, he then gave her a cheeky wink.

Her anger got the better of her. She kicked out, seeking his shins, but the confined space between table and bench restricted the movement. She felt an overwhelming desire to reach up and tear those

black curls from his head and pull them out by the
roots, but he still had her wrist in a tight grip.

Slowly, not taking his eyes from her face, he
lifted her hand and held it against his cheek. Then,
lowering his head until his lips were level with her
ear, he whispered, 'Will you be my girl?'

Patsy flinched sharply and drew away from him.
Enraged, she was trembling in every limb. 'I'm
going home, Johnny,' she managed to mutter.

'No, you're not, and you're not going to make a
scene, neither. You're just going to sit there and be a
good girl while I go in the pub and get us both a
drink.'

She didn't answer but merely sat there, rubbing at
her sore wrist. She should go home, or at least go
and find Peggy. She couldn't help feeling it would
have been better if she hadn't come in the first place.
By now her heart was pounding. Johnny seemed to
be playing with her, joking one minute, serious the
next. If only he'd meant what he had whispered.

Gripping the edge of the table until her knuckles
showed white, she hung her head, her eyes tracing
the spaces between the planks that made up the table
top.

People seated nearby were laughing and their
chuckles made her look up. In spite of herself, she
had to smile. Johnny, carrying a tin tray on the
flat of his hand, his arm outstretched, was doing
an impersonation of a drunken waiter weaving and
stumbling, the glasses of beer slipping precariously

from one side of the tray to the other. He was so funny. The other people in the garden must have thought so, too, for they clapped at the impromptu performance. He set the tray down on the wooden table, and turned and acknowledged their applause with an all-embracing nod. Patsy gave in to the laughter that came welling up naturally from inside.

She slid further along the bench, making room for him to sit beside her. They didn't speak, but just sat holding hands. The coloured lights came on, lanterns strung between the trees casting soft, twinkling lights around the pub garden on this nice spring Saturday evening.

The strains of the band had ceased. Now from the hall came the discordant notes of an accordion. Time for a sing-song – all the old pub-turning-out songs such as 'Nellie Dean', 'Fall in and follow me', 'Show me the way to go home'. The social was going with a swing.

'Come on, let's go and join them.' Johnny smiled nicely at her now, adding as he got up, 'Or else Tom will be well and truly boozed.'

'It was lovely,' Patsy told him as they sat close together at a corner table in the saloon bar of the pub much later that night. 'I wonder where Peggy and your brother went off to.'

Johnny took a long drink of his beer and grinned. 'Ask no questions . . . There ain't no flies on Peggy, so don't start worrying about her.'

Taking a sip of her ginger beer, Patsy watched Johnny's face carefully over the rim of her glass. He had been real nice. He could dance well, too, doing the waltz like an expert. He hadn't minded a bit when at first she had stumbled. His hand firmly in the small of her back, he had guided her well until she had found it easy to match her steps to his. Two or three times she had found herself being thankful that she had worn the long taffeta dress Florrie had made for her at Christmas. It was dark green, a bit dull she had thought at the time, but tonight – with three petticoats underneath – the full skirt had stood out, flouncing nicely as Johnny had twirled her around. The Charleston had been a right laugh: too strenuous a dance for most, and neither Peggy nor she knew how to do it. That hadn't stopped the Jackson brothers. The two of them had gone on to the floor and together they had put on a show. The whole hall was in an uproar by the time the music had stopped. People in the crowd had encouraged them, hooting and yelling their approval.

Patsy knew she would remember tonight for a long time to come.

'Sorry, Patsy.' Johnny's serious-sounding voice broke into her recollections.

'What? What did you say?'

'I'm doing my best to say sorry for last Sunday.'

She was ready to forgive him anything. It didn't matter now. He had stayed with her all the evening and made her feel like a queen. He'd had eyes for no one but her. His hand stroked her long hair, from the top of her head way down past her shoulders, and when he bent and kissed the bare skin above the sweetheart neckline of her dress, she said aloud, 'It doesn't matter.'

Everything was all right now. She had a boy of her own. She belonged to someone.

When his lips brushed her ear and the quiet words came again, 'Will you be my girl?' she didn't hesitate.

'Yes,' she said, nodding her head. 'Yes, I will.'

So it all began.

All summer the weather had been good, even too hot at times. Johnny Jackson rolled the sleeves of his red shirt high above his elbows, leaving the tattoos on his dark arms clearly visible. His shirt was unbuttoned from his throat almost to his waist, the dark hairs on his chest lying damp and curly. Now August was almost gone and, with the coming of September, he had a problem.

He slammed the high, wooden doors closing in the ground where he lived with his family when they weren't touring. He ran towards his brother's Douglas twin-engined motorbike. He knew full well that Tom would be furious about his taking it. So what? What he didn't know wouldn't hurt him, Johnny told himself, still hoping against hope that Tom wouldn't find out. Sitting astride the bike he pushed it forward with his feet still on the ground, then slapped it into first gear. The motorbike shuddered, roared into life and accelerated as he operated the gear lever. Knees close together, hands gripping the rubber-tipped handlebars, he zoomed off down Mitcham Common Road.

He'd been seeing Patsy for five months now, on and off, and he knew he'd been unkind to her.

'I could have treated her a damn sight better,' he muttered to himself, leaning sideways as he took a bend.

'I'll have to tell her tonight. Can't just go off and disappear for a month and expect her to be waiting when we get back.' He turned a corner, the wheels dangerously near to the kerb. Patsy was a nice kid, but she was well . . . so innocent. Not a bit like that mate of hers, Peggy Woolston. He'd stake his life Patsy was a virgin. God, there'd been times when he'd wanted her, but he'd held back. Why? He didn't know himself. Even a proper kiss was improper to Patsy. Ought to give her the elbow really, he grimly told himself. More than once he'd let her down and, boy, she'd showed that temper of hers. A right little spitfire she could be at times, but she always came round in the end.

If he went off now, no, that wasn't right. *When* he went, for he had no choice. Ma said all the family went hop picking together, and every September that's exactly what they did. The whole Jackson tribe descended on Kent. But a whole month, maybe longer. He'd miss Patsy, yes he'd miss her like hell.

Patsy bit her lip anxiously. She was used to Johnny being late – often not turning up at all, but last night had been different. She knew he definitely had something on his mind. She had got so used to seeing him that when he went away for days on end she felt terribly lonely. When he failed to turn up he never offered any explanation, and that hurt. Then, days later, there he would be, waiting when she came out of the market and he would ask, 'You still my girl?' and always his eyes would be mocking and his lips smirking. Nearly always she exploded. She couldn't help herself. He was so smug, so sure she'd come round. When he wasn't there she told herself she'd tell him to get lost, but she never did.

These summer months, though, had been lovely. Walking on the common with Johnny, going up the park, he'd even taken her to Clapham fair. Sundays weren't just days spent with Flo any more. No, on Sundays she went out with Johnny. Florrie! Even saying her name made her feel guilty. Dear old Flo. She didn't want to upset her, but she was never going to understand about Johnny any more than Ollie was or, come to that, any member of the Day family. Each in turn had let her know their feelings. Their comments all ran along the same lines; in fact Patsy wondered if they hadn't all got together and made certain she knew exactly what they felt about

Johnny Jackson. Florrie's opinion made her smile. Not that she would dare let Florrie see her smiling.

'Lazy, bloody tyke,' was Flo's name for Johnny, if she referred to him at all – mostly, she just sniffed when Patsy was getting ready to go out.

Still, they all went on at her only because they cared. She knew most of what they said was true, but it made no difference.

The day had been a scorcher and this evening there still wasn't a breath of air about. Hanging around here at the Junction wasn't doing much for her temper and she'd just about decided to go when the bike ran in close to where she stood. Flashing her a wicked grin Johnny revved the engine hard before switching off the throttle.

'Shan't be a tick, love. Just going to park it round the back.'

'Show off!' she said to his back.

They walked away down the back streets and came out into the lane by the river.

Johnny broke the silence. 'Do you know anything about hop picking?'

'No, nothing at all, but I do know some people in Selkirk Street that go every year. Why?'

'Well, we go every year. All me family does, to the same farm down in Kent.'

Visions of furniture and cooking utensils being loaded on to flat carts came to Patsy. 'Scum bugs', Florrie called them. 'They live like tramps, camp out in fields, lowest of the low,' Florrie would say every September, watching them set off.

They had reached a lonely spot where the river ran under an old iron bridge. At least here there was a bit of a breeze. Patsy leaned over the parapet and pulled her long hair from her neck, letting it hang over one shoulder.

'Would you like to come with us?'

She stared at him in amazement.

'Well, will you come?' he asked with his usual grin.

'Oh, Christ! You know I can't. What about me job?' And what would Flo and Ollie say, she thought.

'Bugger your job. You work too hard, anyway.'

'Well, I can't live on fresh air, can I?'

Despite his joking manner, Patsy could tell he was serious. His face was tense.

'He really means it. He wants me to go!' The thought surprised her. 'What do you want me to go with you for? You go with all your family, you just said so.'

'You know why.'

'No, I don't.'

'Now, stop playing about. We won't get back to London till the end of October and you know very well I'd miss you.'

'Nice of you to say so.' She felt all at sixes and sevens, and this made her voice sound sharp.

'Don't be sarcastic, it don't suit you.'

Patsy stared at the ducks swimming lazily towards the bridge; their colours were really pretty.

'Tell me what you're thinking. Will you come or not? You can earn good money picking hops, you know.'

Patsy looked at him dubiously. 'I don't think Blower would let me have all that time off,' she said lamely, 'though he did say I ought to have a holiday soon.'

A dark glint came into his eyes and he caught hold of her wrists tightly. 'For Christ's sake, Patsy,' he cried, 'for once in your life make up your own mind about something. If it's not that old Florrie it's Ollie, and if it's not him it's the whole bloody Day family telling you what you can and what you can't do.'

His dragging Flo and Ollie into it really got her back up and out of sheer bravado she yelled back at him, 'You don't know nuffin' about me. My friends look after me, but I keep meself and I can look after meself.'

Ignoring her outburst, Johnny said, in an unusually quiet voice, 'I want you to come, Patsy.'

He moved nearer and held her in his arms. 'Think about it, will you love? I can't get out of going, me ma would blow her top, but we'll be gone a long time and I'd miss you. I would . . . honest.'

She put her head on his shoulder and sadly muttered, 'I don't know. I'll try. We'll have to see.'

Very subdued, and looking hot and bothered,

they walked back side by side, not talking. His face was strangely soft as he kissed her goodbye. 'You will try and come, won't you?'

'Yes, all right.'

He started the bike up and roared off without so much as a wave. Forlorn, Patsy walked home. She was between the devil and the deep blue sea. If she went hop picking God knew what Florrie would do. As for Ollie – well, she couldn't face that. If she didn't go, she'd probably lose Johnny.

Patsy had made up her mind and there was nothing she could do about it. Reluctantly, Florrie Holmes heaved herself out of bed. Gawd, what a night. What had got into that girl? She put her feet into her slippers and pulled her dressing-gown on. It had been bad enough these past weeks with her going out all the time with that Johnny Jackson, but to come right out and say she was going hop picking. Gawd above! She still couldn't believe it. Leaving her job, going off to Kent and with that bloody load of gypsies.

She tugged a comb through her tangled hair and tried to calm down. She hadn't slept but just tossed and turned all night and why? Because she'd worked herself up into such a state last night. She still didn't know if she was coming or going.

She'd helped take care of Patsy since the day she'd been born. She'd helped bring her into the world, and that was the truth. As a child, Patsy had been well behaved, kind and loving and always obedient, Ellen had seen to that. Admittedly, she had been cheeky at times, but this was only to be expected, growing up around here like she had and her poor mother out working every hour that God Almighty sent. Still, cheeky didn't mean rude, nor bloody obstinate. As a toddler, Gran used to call her a cockney sparrow. I know what I'd like to call her now – a daft little bitch! Ellen would turn in her grave if she knew.

Patsy was loved and fussed over by half the street. There wasn't one that wouldn't give her a helping hand. Wait till this got out!

It had been a nine day wonder when Ellen had turned up here pregnant and no husband in tow, but folks' contempt had soon melted. There wasn't anybody who hadn't ended up admiring Ellen. No mistaking, Ellen had come down in the world, the posh way she spoke gave the game away, but she asked nothing from nobody. She had worked hard, kept herself and Patsy clean and tidy and never got into debt. Yes, even up the market they'd got used to Ellen always being a bit refined.

'Where did I put those bleeding aspirins?' Florrie muttered under her breath, fumbling in the cupboard on the bedroom wall. 'I could drink a river dry.' She dragged herself through to the scullery. Her head was throbbing and her legs felt more swollen than usual. With the kettle filled and placed on the hob she stared out of the window, seeing nothing, and despite the warmth of the morning she shivered. Terrible things might happen to Patsy if she went off with those Jacksons, but what could she do? Suddenly, Patsy wouldn't listen to a word she said. That thought made Florrie sad.

As she poured the boiling water on to the tea leaves in the brown earthenware pot she remembered the last words Ellen had spoken to her: 'Do what you can for Patsy.'

Well, she'd done her bloody best, but there was little she could do now to stop her going with that Johnny Jackson, short of tying her up and locking her in. She had thought about that, too.

Alexander Berry walked quickly down the steps of the Town Hall. He had no qualms about taking an early lunch. His mind hadn't been on work all the morning. He took a chair at a window table in the small café and lit up his pipe.

'Only a cup of coffee for now, if you don't mind, Mrs Brown.'

Mrs Brown watched him sitting there. Mr Berry was one of her nice customers, always had a ready smile for her, but today he was down in the dumps.

If she did but know it, that was only the half of it!

Like his dear friend, Florrie, he was at his wits' end. He just couldn't get Patsy out of his mind. He didn't know what to do about her. There was such a strong similarity between Patsy's and Ellen's looks that sometimes his heart ached just looking at her.

He had also thought that Patsy had a similar character and personality to Ellen. Maybe the edges were rougher, her speech not so refined, but that was only to be expected. Never in a million years had he dreamed she would oppose him so violently.

He had been appalled when she'd taken up with that fairground lad. He thought at first he had been wise in giving her enough time to see for herself the boy was no good. Dear God, Patsy was the daughter he had never had. Her mother had been the one woman he had loved and he should have asked her to be his wife. Why, oh why hadn't he? If Ellen hadn't died so suddenly, maybe, just maybe, he would have plucked up enough courage to ask her. Taking his pipe from his mouth, he laid it down on the tin ash-tray and took the cup of coffee between his big hands. Ellen was the loveliest lady he had ever known. The trouble had been that she was well out of his class, and he had hesitated too long. He had loved her dearly and he missed her still.

Now, what could he do or say that would deter Patsy? She seemed to see Johnny Jackson as a nice young man who led an adventurous life, and who could blame her? Nothing in her life so far had been exciting – quite the reverse. Working from the day she left school, every week as humdrum as the last.

He understood only too well what the attraction was, and Patsy's feeling of having someone to belong to. What a pity she couldn't see the pitfalls. Why was it one couldn't put old heads on young shoulders? He sipped the dregs of his now-cold coffee and told himself that all he could do was sit back and wait. He would be there when Patsy needed him – and he knew only too well that that day would come.

Patsy couldn't put her own feelings into words. She hated seeing Flo and Ollie so upset. The easy, loving relationship between them had been there as long as she could remember. It was more a special kind of love. Since she had grown up she had come to realise that the same special bond had existed between her mother and those two dear people. Look how they had taken on the responsibility of caring for her when her mum had died. If it hadn't been for them, she would have been sent to an institution. What a pity they didn't like Johnny. How could she make them understand her feelings when she didn't understand them herself.

It was just . . . well . . . when she was with Johnny she had a sense of belonging.

Fred Jackson jerked on the reins of the two horses that were hitched to the cart and Johnny turned round and said, 'Here we go. You two all right back there?'

Fred was so like Johnny that it was easy to tell they were brothers. Patsy sat in the cart with her legs outstretched on a bed of straw. Beside her sat Daisy, Fred's wife, a slim young woman in her late twenties. Daisy was different from the typical fair-ground girl. For one thing, her hair was dyed red and she was quiet in her speech and was friendly. Patsy had taken to her straight away.

The day was warm, the sky cloudless and Patsy was beginning to relax.

'Your first time, going hopping I mean?' Daisy asked.

'Yes,' Patsy smiled her answer.

'You'll like it. It's nice out in the fields.'

With London behind them, and not one of them giving a thought as to how long the journey was taking, a lot of Patsy's fears were fading. She was discovering what it was like to feel free. Her head was not filled with thoughts of work. She was in a different world.

It was wonderful. The sun was shining, the fields were wide and open and the lanes green and leafy. Best of all, the air was sharp and clean.

'I sent me kids down with Ma. Christ, it's quiet without them, but it's nice to get rid of them once in a while.'

Patsy had been dozing when she heard Daisy's voice.

'Oh, how many children have you got?'

'Three, but it will seem more like twenty-three when we get there.'

'What? I don't understand.' Patsy pushed her bottom back, straightened her spine and leaned back against the side of the cart, watching Daisy's whole body shake with laughter.

'I don't suppose you do, love. You don't know what you've let yourself in for. About six vans left Mitcham before we did this morning. You should have seen them. They were crammed with Jacksons from all over and crikey, the kids, it will take me all my time to sort them out. God knows what you'll make of them.'

'Fred, Fred!' Suddenly Daisy raised herself and called out. 'When are we going to have a stop? My stomach thinks me throat's been cut and I'm dying for a pee.'

That lunchtime was the happiest part of Patsy's day. At the end of the narrow lane was a village, but Daisy and Patsy now lay on their stomachs, their chins resting in cupped hands, on the grass outside a pretty little pub.

'Hell of a time they're taking in there,' said Daisy, her voice sounding very loud in the quiet country-side.

'They haven't been that long,' Patsy began timidly.

'Aw, give over Patsy. You know as well as I do, or you should do by now, they're having a few pints and it's bugger us.'

Fred and Johnny certainly seemed a boisterous pair as they came out into the sunlight. 'Here you are then, me darlings,' they said in unison.

'Thank God for that. I was beginning to wonder

if you were going to stay put all day,' Daisy crossly told them.

They ate hunks of crusty bread and strong Cheddar cheese, washed down with gulps of cider straight from a quart bottle which was passed from hand to mouth.

Thirty minutes later and they were on their way again. Now they were in the Kent countryside, passing cows and sheep lazily wandering in the fields. Through Tankerton then Staplehurst – even the names of the places had a magic ring to them. At Paddock Wood Railway Station several horse-drawn carriages were waiting and Patsy turned her head in curiosity.

'They're waiting for the "'Oppers Specials",' Daisy told her with a laugh.

Patsy's raised eyebrows showed she didn't understand.

'From London Bridge they run special trains for the hop pickers. Get it? 'Oppers Specials!' This flat statement brought a smile to Patsy's lips. Occasionally Daisy told her more about the Jackson family and Patsy asked the odd question, but mostly they lay back and were quiet.

The sun was quite low in the sky when Fred guided the horses through a wide gate and into a field. That was when stark reality struck Patsy. The field was teeming with people. Old, shrunken men, healthy, bronzed lads, women, young and old, preparing meals over smoky, open fires and children were everywhere yelling, running, some even crawling.

'This is me dad, Patsy, and that's me mum over there.'

Those were the only introductions Johnny bothered to make. Mr Jackson was a heavy man. He was dark and Patsy thought he looked menacing. Both his arms were heavily tattooed, like Johnny's, and his collarless shirt, unbuttoned, hung loosely over his trousers, showing a chest covered with dark hairs.

He walked slowly all round Patsy. She could smell his sweat, but she didn't raise her eyes, just kept staring at his dirty boots.

'Bit scrawny ain't she, lad?' he said to his son, then turning his head he called, 'Lil, come over here and meet Johnny's girl.'

'I suppose I've seen worse.' Mrs Jackson spoke grudgingly as she looked Patsy up and down.

It was horrible to have to stand there like a naughty child listening to these people's sarcastic comments. Patsy stood up straight, tilting her chin defiantly and stared straight into Mrs Jackson's face. Who did this small, wizened woman think she was? A stranger might have put her age at between sixty and sixty-five, but Patsy knew from what Johnny had told her that Mrs Jackson was only in her mid-fifties. The outdoor life had played havoc with her skin and her hooded eyes were so deep-set that it was impossible to tell what colour they were.

'Well, we've all got plenty to do,' Mrs Jackson declared. 'You don't intend to stand there gawking all night, do yer?'

As she spoke again, Patsy caught the gleam of several gold teeth set among Mrs Jackson's front white ones.

Johnny, perhaps sensing how uncomfortable it was for Patsy, said, 'Come and say hello to me sisters.'

She slipped her hand inside his and pressed close to him as they walked across the field.

'Your mother doesn't like me. Perhaps I shouldn't have come.' Patsy was quite upset and Johnny looked gloomy.

'Oh, for Christ's sake, give yourself a chance, will yer? Now this is Sarah, Polly, Annie, Dolly and that 'alf pint over there is the youngest. She's called Maisie.'

'I'll never remember all your names,' Patsy told the group of women, trying bravely to smile at all these strange faces.

'You will,' Johnny told her, 'and never mind about the kids. Half of them don't know who they belong to, anyway.'

A strange feeling of melancholy came over Patsy. What was she doing here? She just wanted to run.

The dinner was a disaster and eaten out in the open field. Whatever did they do if it rained? Rabbit stew, the gravy pale and thick, and turnips – the only vegetable Patsy detested! She wondered where

the tables and chairs came from. Did they leave
them here or were they carted down from London
each year? The men ate standing up, mopping up
their gravy with doorsteps of bread.

'Thanks, Daisy,' Patsy said gratefully as Daisy
handed her a mug full of strong tea. Then, fearfully,
she asked, 'Where's the toilet and where can I have a
wash?'

You'd have thought she had asked the way to
Buckingham Palace. Everyone roared and hooted
with laughter. Mrs Jackson answered spitefully,
'You ain't come to the Ritz, you know.'

'Come on, Patsy, I'll show you.' Patsy felt Daisy
was the only friend she had there and her heart
warmed to her.

The long, barn-type wash house was primitive.
The closets were merely a wooden seat set across
deep holes in the ground, and the smell was awful.

'Make do for tonight, love.' Daisy's voice held a
note of pleading. 'Tomorrow morning you can
come with me, early. We'll wash down in the river
and use the bushes for big jobs.' Patsy's heart leapt
in terror. It had never occurred to her that conditions might be as bad as this.

'Oh, and don't forget to bring some bum paper
with you!' Daisy's manner was straightforward, but
seeing Patsy's face she added kindly, 'And don't
look so downhearted. Everything will look a lot
better in the morning.'

'I hope so,' said Patsy in a flat tone of voice.

Nothing had prepared Patsy for the sleeping arrangements. The small hut had one communal, makeshift bed which was planks of wood extended wall to wall, on top of which straw palliasses had been laid.

'Where are you sleeping, Daisy?' Patsy nervously asked.

'Me and Fred have our own hut further along the row. I'd best find me kids and get them settled. See you in the morning, love.'

In spite of sharing the bed with Mrs Jackson, two of her daughters and two small girls, and the fact that Johnny had disappeared without so much as a goodnight, Patsy was soon fast asleep.

It was a beautiful morning and the sun was streaming in through the open door of the hut when she woke up. It was not yet seven o'clock and the day promised to be hot. Untangling herself from the arms and legs of the still sleeping little girls, Patsy was glad to get outside into the fresh air. Inside the hut it was stuffy and smelly.

At a quarter to eight they moved off. What a weird lot we must look, Patsy thought to herself. There were toddlers in pushchairs, babies in perambulators, teenagers, mothers, fathers and grandparents. No one was allowed to stay behind. As they straggled through the lanes to the furthest field where picking was to begin, Patsy caught a glimpse between the hedgerows of the great Whitbread

Farms. There were rows of solidly-built brick dwellings and notice-boards pointing the way to toilets and washrooms. The conditions appeared luxurious compared with what she was enduring.

The hop field was lovely, green and cool. Labourers jerked the vines down, using long poles to disentangle the rough, twisting stems.

'You'd better sit here by me till you get the hang of it.' Patsy felt better. They were the first kind words Mrs Jackson had spoken to her. Whole families settled themselves each side of the long canvas troughs, and Patsy watched in fascination as fingers flew. They all had their own steady rhythm, stripping the dropping clusters of hops into the bins. Their skill and nimbleness astonished her.

No matter how she tried, which way she sat or which hand she used, Patsy couldn't get the hang of it.

'Yer silly cow! Hops, not leaves, go in the bin. You're no bloody good at it. I knew you wouldn't be. Farmer will dock us a bushel at weigh-in if the 'ops ain't clean. Pick all those bleeding leaves out, go on, get on with it.' Mrs Jackson's hand stopped just short of Patsy's face as she swung her arm towards her.

'You can tell the difference between 'ops and leaves, can't you?'

'Of course I can,' snapped Patsy. She was feeling homesick and longed for London. She missed her friends at the market and the easy camaraderie which existed there. Meekly now she said that she was sorry, but wondered why she had come to Kent at all.

'Bring them kids back here. Stop your gossiping and pick, that's what yer 'ere for, to pick. It ain't a bleeding 'oliday.' Mrs Jackson was just as strict with her own brood. She was so ruthless and overbearing that Patsy marvelled that her children put up with her, but they seemed to adore her, even if they did fear her at times.

By midday Patsy felt she had worked hard. Forbidden to pick, she had become everyone's dogsbody. Clearing away the stripped vines, crawling beneath the bins to retrieve fallen clusters of hops, climbing ladders to free snarled-up tendrils.

'*Break*.' The call echoed round the field.

The Jacksons believed in eating well. Masses of food was set out and all was consumed ravenously.

During the long morning Patsy had seen little of Johnny. He wasn't a picker. Using their own cart and horses, he and Fred had landed a plum job, carting the bagged-up bushels of hops to the oast houses, there to be laid out within the kiln to dry.

'See yer later, Patsy,' he now called, giving her a breezy wave and strolling off with his father and brothers in the direction of the Bull Inn.

Patsy's temper almost broke. *Her* throat was parched. Why couldn't he have taken her for a drink?

A huge cauldron of water, set over an open fire,

had come to the boil. The women filled their large teapots but all eyes were on Mrs Jackson as she stirred the steaming contents of a jug with a metal spoon.

Raising the spoon to her mouth, she slurped the hot liquid.

'Sop-me-bob, that's bloody good,' she cried and everyone laughed.

'Hurry up, Gran.'

'Let me have a drop, Gran.'

Even the children couldn't wait. The jug was passed from one woman to another, while Patsy wished that someone would pour the tea out. Satisfied grins appeared.

'Your turn, Patsy.' She put her head back and let the hot liquid pour down her parched throat. If the jug had not been taken from her hands she would surely have spilled the lot, for she was shattered by a fit of coughing. Her tongue was smarting and her throat burning.

'Crikey. What is it?' She wiped the tears away from her eyes and took a deep breath. Then another rasping cough caught at her. What the hell had they given her?

'It was only whisky.' Daisy's voice held a hint of apology.

'What?'

'Well, whisky, hot water and sugar. Hop-pop, Ma calls it. Here, drink this.'

Thankfully, Patsy grasped the mug of tea Daisy

had thrust into her hand. Looking up, her eyes still watering, Patsy caught Mrs Jackson sneering and as she looked at her the sun caught the dangling gold ear-rings she wore, causing them to glitter. Spitefully Patsy thought they matched her gold teeth. The thought also flashed into her mind that Johnny got his warped sense of humour from her.

Three days later and Patsy had learned to pick, but she hated it. She had such bad sunburn that the lids of her eyes were swollen and, even worse, there was a plague of flying insects in the fields. The backs of her hands were dotted with bites that itched like mad and her fingers were horribly stained from handling the green, scaly hops.

She also hated having to take her turn at helping to prepare the evening meal. Under such conditions she knew she didn't make a very good job of it. Cooking on open fires, sheltered only from the weather by a canvas awning, frightened her. Sparks from the fire flew upwards and it was a wonder to her that the canvas didn't burst into flames. Kettle, stewpot, frying pan – all were set among the heated embers. The heat burned her face and the smoke made her already sore eyes smart even more.

The last two evenings Patsy had gone with everyone else to the Bull. Tonight they were off again. The pub was packed to capacity with the men, the women and children lining the grass banks and verges outside.

'Stay outside with Patsy and the kids,' Fred ordered his wife.

'I don't see why I should,' Daisy said obstinately.

'Because you'll get me hand round your face if you don't,' he told her.

Daisy sighed. 'Come on then, Patsy, only for Christ's sake don't sit near Ma. I've had more than enough of the old bitch all day.'

Music blared out and the Londoners sang with gusto. Towards closing time the children were all tired and irritable and two Jackson brothers, each with more than a few pints inside him, wanted to fight each other.

Mr Jackson's brawny arms swiped at them both.

'I'll kill the bloody pair of you if you don't pack it in,' he yelled.

Patsy sat still on the grass and silently prayed that Johnny would stop drinking and walk back with her. He did neither.

It was the same routine the next day. The sun still beat down and everyone said how lucky they were with the weather.

'Patsy, go and find those two sons of mine, we need some more bushel baskets. The lazy pair of sods have probably got their heads down somewhere.' Mrs Jackson's fingers still flew in jerky movements as she spoke.

By now, Patsy had learned to take all the abuse in her stride and did her best to ignore it. As soon as she was out of sight she cheered up. This was a break from picking and an excuse to seek out Johnny. 'God knows, I haven't seen much of him since we got here,' she said to herself.

Ma was right. There they were, both of them, sitting on the ground, backs against the oast house, peacefully smoking cigarettes. She felt her temper rise. It *was* a bloody holiday for them.

'Johnny, your mother says she's waiting for baskets and I'd like to talk to you.'

Whether Fred was being tactful or just wary, Patsy didn't know. He rose to his feet and said, sheepishly, 'I'm going for a leak.'

Johnny's impish grin appeared on his face. 'I know just the place,' he said, pulling her by the hand.

She went with him willingly. She had no defence against him when he smiled at her. As soon as they reached the shelter of the trees, he drew her close to his chest.

'Oh, Patsy love. I've missed you.'

'That's good,' she said. 'You haven't made much effort to see me.'

With a finger he touched her cheek. 'Smile, come on, smile for me.' Then he put his hand on the back of her neck and drew her head forward. She felt a tingle ripple through her. She knew she wanted him to kiss her. As his lips closed over hers, she couldn't stop herself thinking he smelled of beer and sweat. Pulling herself away she told him, 'I don't want to go to the pub tonight. Can't we go for a walk – on our own?'

'Well, I suppose we can, first, then have a drink on the way back.'

'Blooming drink! That's all you think about.' Her impatience showed in her voice.

'Patsy, Patsy,' he said gently. 'I've told you we'll go for a walk and we will. What's the matter? Ain't you enjoying yourself?'

'Enjoying myself?' Now her voice was bitter and Johnny looked bewildered.

'I can't be with you all the time. I've told you I've missed you.'

'Have you?' she scoffed at him. 'Well, I haven't noticed it.'

'You're not in a very good mood, are you?' he murmured, making to put his arms around her again.

'Leave off, Johnny,' she cried as he tried to kiss her. 'I have to get back to work. Your mother will go mad at me. She only sent me for the measuring baskets.'

'All right, all right. Don't get out of your pram.'

'Well, it's not the same for you, is it? You and your brother seem to be having a lovely life of it.'

'Right, we'll go off on our own tonight. There, me darling, does that make you feel better?'

As he smiled at her, Patsy looked down at her appearance. She had a sacking apron around her waist, her hair was tousled and needed washing and her hands were filthy. She sighed. What a bloody mess!

'I'll have a good wash and tidy myself up directly after dinner,' she told herself, wishing earnestly that she could have a bath. Now, looking straight at him, she asked, 'Johnny. You promise? Just you and me? We can go off somewhere by ourselves?'

'I promise,' he said solemnly.

Yet, when she looked back and saw him standing there, grinning from ear to ear, she only half-believed him.

'Jesus, I'm lucky to have you for my girl.'

Patsy walked beside him feeling happy at last. They had spent the last half-hour walking around the lanes hand in hand. Johnny was so different when they were alone. He let go her hand, ran a few steps ahead and stopped, giving her an amused smile.

'I've no intentions of ever letting you get away from me, Miss Kent,' he told her, trying to assume a posh accent. Then he did a little jig.

Patsy laughed. 'You should be a comedian.'

He ran back and cuddled her close, his arms enfolding her tightly. Oh, he could be so nice when he wanted to.

'Are you glad we came for a walk on our own?' Patsy asked him.

'Yes. Yes, I am and we'll go back to the farm.' Gently he let his hand stroke her hair and quietly added, 'We won't go to the Bull for a drink.'

★

Patsy had never seen the farm so deserted and peaceful. In the dimness of the hut Johnny took her in his arms and kissed her just as he usually did, softly, gently and with great tenderness. Suddenly, he broke away and whispered hoarsely, 'We can't stand here, it's daft. Come on, we'll lie on the bed.'

Very calmly he caressed her as they lay together on the straw palliasse, his face so close to hers that their noses were almost touching. When his breathing became heavier and his grip firmer Patsy still made no protest, not even when his fingernails dug into her flesh. Then he moved his hands from her shoulders and slid them down inside her blouse. He could feel the agitated beating of her heart as she twisted her body and thrust him away.

'Johnny, please. Please don't.'

'Come on now, Patsy. What's wrong, darling?' He made a move to draw her to him, then stopped as he felt her whole body stiffen in his grasp. For a few moments he considered saying he was sorry, but he could not deny the irresistible urge that was burning him up. He lunged towards her, pulling her firmly against him, and brought his mouth down to cover hers, thrusting his tongue deep within her mouth. Patsy was terrified. This wasn't her laughing, carefree Johnny. This was a beast with burning breath and groping, scratching fingers. She beat on his back with clenched fists. Still he ground his body into hers, his breath now coming in short, hard gasps.

When he lifted her skirt and his hand forced her knees apart she shouted, 'No, stop it. Not like this. Please Johnny.'

Suddenly, he released her and sat up. 'Aw, Patsy, I thought you were supposed to be my girl,' he said, looking utterly dejected.

Her heart softened, just a little. 'I am, but Johnny—'

'No!' he cut her off. 'Either you are or you're not.'

Sensing her hesitation, he drew her back into his arms and as they fell back together on to the mattress he whispered, 'I wouldn't hurt you for the world.'

What followed was inevitable. Now nothing could have stopped Johnny. With his passion aroused his strength was too much for Patsy, and her struggles and the sound of panic in her voice only seemed to inflame him all the more.

When he lay flat on his back, his chest heaving, Patsy crawled to the end of the bed and stood in the small space in the hut and began to dress herself. Pushing himself upon his elbows Johnny watched her and as he gazed at her the urge came flooding back, sharp and urgent. Unable to restrain himself, he leapt from the bed and before she had time to protest he dragged her back to lie beneath him. His desire was no longer suppressed. There was no holding back – all thoughts of gentleness were abandoned. His passion was given full rein and Patsy's feelings were entirely forgotten.

Much later, Patsy groped her way to the door, making for the fresh air. She was surprised to see it was still light. It seemed hours since she had gone into the hut with Johnny. For a long time she sat on the grass, slumped against a tree trunk. With trembling hands she tried to tidy herself up but as she wiped her inner thighs with the hem of her petticoat and saw the bloodstains, ugly, hard sobs shook her body.

'I'm going down to the Bull. Do you fancy a drink?' Johnny was walking briskly towards her, smiling as if nothing had happened. 'Well, are you coming or not?'

'No I'm not.' Patsy's voice was choked with sobs.

'Aw, come on. Ma will wonder where you are.'

She began to cry in earnest now. The nerve of him. She wasn't going to face his family. Not tonight. She couldn't, she felt dirty, sore and bruised. She wouldn't be able to face anyone, least of all his mother.

She got up, ignoring him and stumbled towards the river. The sound of his laughter followed her. He had used her and now he was mocking her. She walked with head bent. Her hair, which she had washed with such care earlier that evening, hung down over her face. Her feet slithered over the uneven ground and she nearly fell into a ditch. She didn't care. She felt degraded and disgusted, as much with herself as with him.

'Oh, dear Jesus. . . . ' she started to say, but couldn't go on. What was she praying for? That the clock could be turned back? That the past hour could be wiped away? She realised it was too late to pray for the impossible.

Next morning, Patsy didn't want to go out into the open field. She was feeling a mixture of shame and fear. How she wished there was somewhere she could go and have a bath.

'Morning, darling, and how are you on this beautiful day?' Fred, teeth flashing, was grinning broadly. Mr Jackson was grinning, so were all of Johnny's sisters. Was she imagining it? Had Johnny been boasting? In her mind she could hear him telling them, 'I had 'er over.'

Were the men's bawdy comments directed at her? Were they being more vulgar than usual? Where could she go? Was there anywhere to hide?

The morning seemed endless. Mrs Jackson seemed more unpleasant to her than usual.

'You've had the right old 'ump all morning. For Christ's sake buck up,' Daisy told Patsy at break time.

'Yeah, come and have a drop of whisky,' Mrs Jackson told her, a sly sneer spreading over her lips. 'Then maybe you'll earn yer keep this afternoon, 'cos it's for sure you've done sod all this morning.'

'Now shut up, Ma,' Daisy cried in exasperation. 'Leave her alone, can't you. Maybe she's not feeling so good.'

'Not feeling so good!' Mrs Jackson snarled the words. 'You don't want to be worrying yerself over her. Stuck up, lazy bitch, that's what she is. Expects everyone else to work and wait on her. Well, it won't wash. Not with me it won't.' Rounding on Patsy now she screamed, 'Either you do your share or bugger off. We're not going to carry you – not any longer, we ain't.'

That settled it. She couldn't brave it out any longer.

Back in the hut, Patsy pushed her few belongings into two bass bags. Through the lanes and across fields she walked, asking directions once from a country gentleman. When she stopped to rest she turned, half-expecting to see Johnny. Would he come after her? Did she want him to?

Her head was throbbing, yet she couldn't keep her mind still as she sat in the train compartment. Why hadn't she listened to Florrie or paid attention to Ollie's advice? How could she face them? She had nowhere else to go. She felt nothing but despair.

The train drew into London Bridge and she knew she was nearly home. She was pleased to see crowds of people, all in a hurry, and street hawkers shouting their wares. The tram was crowded: standing room only. Familiar landmarks were gliding past as the tram rattled towards Tooting. Patsy felt beads of sweat roll down from her armpits. Soon she would have to face Florrie. Whatever was she going to tell her? Not the truth, that was for sure. 'Thank you,' she mumbled as the conductor helped her off when they reached the Broadway.

Florrie bustled up the passage as Patsy pushed open the front door.

'Blimey! I wasn't expecting you.' Her eyes roamed over Patsy in dismay. They took in her grubby skirt, her torn stockings and her untidy hair, but it was her face she couldn't believe. For a moment she was struck with terror. Patsy's eyes told her she had been to hell and back. There was so much she wanted to yell at her, to ask her, but every ounce of love and affection she felt for Patsy came to the surface. She moved closer to her and put her arms about her. Only her rough, red hands shook as she did what she always did when at a loss for words. She patted Patsy's back, with a steady rhythm, just as she had when she'd been a baby.

Patsy was stunned by Florrie's reception. She had expected accusations, even 'I told you so', and suddenly she realised how awful she must look.

'Come on, love, we'll have a cuppa. I've got the kettle on.'

Patsy tried to smile, but Flo's kindness and the love in her voice were too much. Johnny's terrifying attack and her own sense of guilt, plus the loneliness and despair she had felt on the journey home, all came together, choking her and the tears came spilling out from her eyes and down her cheeks.

Patsy looked around at the homely kitchen. The scrubbed table-top, the two well-worn armchairs, one each side of the fireplace, the china jugs hanging from hooks on the dresser, the best cups and saucers on the top shelf. Oh, it was nice to be home. She belonged here and she felt safe.

'Thanks,' Patsy said, taking the cup of tea from Florrie.

'Florrie,' Patsy whispered, her head low, her eyes downcast.

'Yes, love?' Florrie half-turned, offering rock cakes she'd set out on a plate.

'I'm sorry. What else can I say?'

'Nothing, love. Unless you're hurt. You're not, are you?'

'No, I'm all right,' then seeing Florrie's worried frown she added 'I am, really, Flo. I'd like another cup of tea though and then . . . could I have a bath?'

'I'll put the water on for your bath, Gawd knows you look as though you need one, but you can pour your own tea out. I'm not waiting on you just because you've decided to come home.'

Patsy giggled. She knew Florrie's gruffness was a cover-up for her pleasure at seeing her.

Clean and fresh, dressed in her nightclothes, Patsy sat in one chair, Florrie in the other, and they talked long into the night. Florrie told her all the happenings of the street, how she had beaten Ollie at cribbage. Patsy told Flo of the beautiful Kent countryside, but the Jacksons were never mentioned.

Florrie's legs were troublesome and the doctor had given her a letter to take to St James's Hospital, but she was more worried about Patsy. The girl was so pale and washed out and so obviously depressed that Florrie's pleasure at having her home had turned into concern. She had repeatedly asked Patsy if she was going back to work but got no reply. Instead, she just sat there looking small and defeated. Florrie felt she had to find some way of cheering her up. She couldn't hang around the house doing nothing. She needed to be with old friends and the market was just the place, but she seemed to have lost all her enthusiasm.

'I'm coming with you,' Patsy said in a matter-of-fact voice, appearing in the doorway with her coat on.

'No you're not,' Florrie said firmly.

'You can't stop me, so let's hurry up and get going.' Florrie was terrified of hospitals and was more than pleased to have Patsy go with her. Secretly, she thought that maybe an outing would do her some good, but she wasn't going to give in that easily. She widened her eyes at Patsy, trying to keep her voice quiet. 'It will only be a waste of time.

Nobody can't do nothing for my legs. You know it
and so do I.'

'We don't know any such thing.' Patsy came forward and took Florrie's hand. 'Look, it can't do any
harm to go and see what they have to say.' Then,
sensing Florrie's bravado was an act to cover up her
fears, more gently she added, 'We'll make a day out
of it, shall we? Perhaps have a bite to eat when we're
out, eh?'

Patsy could be tender-hearted when she wanted
and her gentleness made Florrie's heart tighten with
love.

The waiting-room was packed and the two of them
sat bunched up with four other women on a long
wooden bench.

Florrie had lost her fear, obstinacy having taken
over. It was all a waste of time her being there,
anyway. She wasn't going to let anybody operate
on her veins. Patsy was her biggest worry. She
looked at her, anxiously. Before she had gone to
Kent she had been bright, happy and bubbling; now
her face was pinched, her eyes dull and sunk in their
sockets. Was she ill? What had happened to make
her come home? Putting her hand on Patsy's arm
she asked quietly, 'Patsy, why don't you think
about going back to work? I'm sure you'd feel better
once you got back to normal.'

'I have thought about it and I'll start looking for a

job soon. I will, I promise.' Patsy's voice held a touch of bitterness.

Florrie couldn't believe what she'd heard.

'What would you want to look for a job for? You've got a job.'

'I couldn't ask Blower to take me back,' Patsy said dully.

'Oh, don't be so bloody daft. You haven't lost your job.'

The nurse at the reception desk drew a sharp breath of disapproval at Florrie's raised voice and bad language. Florrie pretended not to notice and leaned towards Patsy. Lowering her voice, she told her, 'You're talking out the back of your head, you know that, don't you? Blower knows you're home because he asked me yesterday when you were start-ing back. Fancy thinking he wouldn't have you. Can you see Gran's face if you told her you were looking for another job. She'd go mad!'

Patsy didn't answer, but her face brightened.

Neither of them heard the sister in charge the first time. Only when she called: '*Is* Mrs Holmes here?' in a very loud voice did Florrie rise to her feet. The sister bristled.

'Come along. Doctor has a full list this morning. We mustn't keep him waiting.'

Turning her head, Florrie made a grimace at Patsy before entering the white room and closing the door behind her.

Fifteen minutes later she shuffled out.

'Told you it was a waste of time, didn't I? Pills, that's all he's given me. Said I've got to take this paper down to the pharmacy department and get them now.'

Patsy was feeling a whole lot happier with the thought that she might still have her job on the market, and she smiled as she helped Florrie on with her coat.

'I won't take the bloody things.' Patsy let that pass. She'd see that Florrie did.

From St James's they walked through the back streets to Balham Station.

'Two hours we were in there,' Florrie moaned.

'Never mind,' Patsy said, doing her best to pacify Flo. 'There's a coffee stall in Balham Market. Shall we have a hot pie and a cup of tea?'

'Well, I could do with something. The smell of those hospitals gets right down me throat, but I'm not standing up at no stall. Eating out in the street indeed. I ain't come down to that yet.'

Behind the coffee stall was a café owned by the same family. 'It looks clean and respectable enough,' Florrie huffed as Patsy opened the door.

There were times when Patsy wanted to hug Flo. She was so down-to-earth and motherly, yes, and comforting. She'd always been there when needed, ready to fuss over her and feed her. Her gruff exterior was an act. She was afraid to show too much emotion, for fear of being thought soft. Nothing was really too much trouble. Florrie would go to any lengths when it came to looking after her. Suddenly, Patsy didn't feel quite so bad about what had happened in Kent. She would put it all behind her. Florrie wasn't her real mum, no one would ever replace her, but she was a darned good substitute.

The café was steamy and the air smelled of stale cigarette smoke, but the pies were good, succulent meat with thick, rich gravy and the tea hot and strong.

'Not bad at all,' Florrie said gratefully as she wiped her mouth with her handkerchief.

'Must have been good if you say so, Flo,' Patsy chuckled.

'That's a tout. You can tell just by looking at him.' Patsy looked ahead to where Florrie was pointing.

'What's a tout?' she asked.

'He spends most of the day standing in the shop doorway, trying to get folk inside to buy something. He's on to a good thing when the market's on.'

They were threading their way slowly between the stalls, heading for the tram stop. Patsy couldn't resist the temptation; she stopped to look into the windows of Chaplin's, a stylish shop on the street corner.

'Can I tempt you? We're giving a discount on everything today, special one-day-only offer.'

'No, thank you. Just looking,' Patsy quietly told

the man who wore a check jacket and a trilby hat set at a rakish angle.

'Go inside. It don't cost nothing to look,' he urged. Florrie had drifted further along the pavement.

'Patsy, what's the matter?' she called.

'Nothing, Flo. I'm just looking in the windows.'

The tout, sensing that he would have to win Florrie over, walked towards her.

'Why don't you come and sit down in the shop while your daughter has a good look round?' He smiled persuasively at her and took her by the arm. 'We have some really good bargains on offer today.'

Secretly pleased that he should take Patsy for her daughter, she allowed the tout to steer her back to where Patsy stood. Grinning now, she said, 'Suits me, love. If you want to go in I'm in no hurry.'

Patsy felt excited. It would be nice to see the inside of a proper shop. Most of her things were bought from market stalls, or were made by Florrie or herself. She couldn't help feeling amused, though, at Florrie giving in so easily to flattery.

Amusement soon changed to embarrassment.

'We ain't gonna buy anything! Patsy's just going to have a look round while I take the weight off me feet!' Flo brazenly told the smartly-dressed, black-haired assistant.

'Well, make yourself comfortable then,' the young lady told her as she pulled forward a gilt-backed chair. Florrie couldn't check a sulky sniff at the smallness of the seat, and as she noticed the long red fingernails she sniffed again, but she eased herself down on the chair, putting her shopping bag on the floor beside her.

Patsy felt guilty as she looked at her. In these elegant surroundings Flo looked dowdy. The hat she wore was new – well, new to her; it was a good quality brown felt, which she had paid fourpence for at the church jumble sale. Her coat had seen better days, though it was neatly pressed and the buttons had been renewed. A sudden thought came to Patsy. Never once had she heard Florrie complain that she was hard-up. 'She must have made a lot of sacrifices for me,' she thought. 'She is always so generous, and I've taken her a lot for granted.'

Patsy curbed the desire to look at the racks of coats and dresses. Instead, she lingered at the glass-topped counter below which hung blouses in every shade and colour.

'Oh, that is beautiful,' Patsy sighed, as the young lady held before her a green silk blouse. A professional at her job, the young lady gave Patsy a winning smile.

'Yes, it's one of our best. Goodness, it could have been made for you – the colour is almost the same as your eyes.'

Patsy knew she was being taken for a naive young girl. 'Try it on, it won't take a minute,' the assistant encouraged. Patsy fingered the material – it was beautiful. She allowed herself to be persuaded, but she felt awkward when the young lady remained in the fitting-room. The silk felt lovely against her skin. She got a bit flustered trying to do up the buttons, but the fingers with the long, red nails soon had them fastened.

'Go and show your mother, dear,' the precise voice told her. As Patsy stood in front of her, Florrie raised her hand and covered her mouth. It was like seeing a ghost. Only the eyes were different. Other than that, it was like looking at Ellen all over again. A lump came to Florrie's throat. The heavy lace collar set so well around Patsy's neck and the lace cuffs looked very prim and proper. Oh, she does look so nice, she thought.

'How much is it?' Florrie barked the question, though neither by nod or wink had she shown any opinion.

'Seven and six, madam.' Florrie gasped. 'It is one of our best lines, madam.'

'Go and take it off, Patsy,' Flo ordered, sticking out her chest. 'Blimey, they must think folk are made of money.'

Patsy looked crestfallen and turned away without a word. She took the blouse off and handed it out through the curtain. Donning her own clothes, she felt disappointed; but Florrie was right, it was too dear. Seven and sixpence for a blouse was an awful lot of money.

Florrie was already standing near the doorway when Patsy emerged from the dressing cubicle.

Besides her shopping bag, Florrie now held a white, oblong bag, its side emblazoned with the word 'Chaplin's' in large black capital letters. It was impossible to read anything from her expression as she thrust the bag at Patsy.

''Ere. You can carry this.' Without so much as a backward glance, Florrie led the way into the High Street, not even stopping when the tout asked, 'Are you glad you went in now, ladies?'

Not until they had turned the corner did she turn towards Patsy and let out a great belly laugh. It caused people to stop and stare, but Flo's laughter was so infectious that Patsy had to join in. Still laughing, Patsy managed to say, 'But, Flo, you said it was too dear.'

Wiping her eyes with the back of her hand, but still broadly grinning, Flo said, 'And so it bloody well was. You don't think I gave them seven and six, do you? Not on your life I didn't.'

'Well, how much did you pay for it?' She thought it was hilarious and had laughed so much that by now she had hiccups.

'Never you mind, it's my treat.'

'Florrie, no. Now come on, tell me. If you don't let me pay for it I won't wear it.'

'Well, it won't fit me, will it? Can you see me trying to squeeze my bosoms into that flimsy blouse?'

This thought set both of them off again, Florrie laughing fit to burst, Patsy grinning from ear to ear.

'Tell you what, you can pay 'alf.'

Seeing she wasn't going to win, Patsy said, 'Well, all right. Thanks, Flo – but you still haven't told me, how much?'

'Four bob.'

Patsy shrieked, partly in disbelief, partly in sheer pleasure. 'How did you manage it?' she wanted to know.

'When you've lived as long as I have you learn to beat these so-called clever ones at their own game. I offered her three and six at first. I knew I wouldn't get it for that, but she came down a lot, didn't she?'

'Florrie, you are amazing!'

'Yes, I know.' She smiled shrewdly now. 'But there's one thing I want you to promise me.'

Without thinking, Patsy blurted out, 'Anything.'

'I want you to stop moping about the house. Get yourself back to work in the morning. You will, won't you?'

Patsy sighed. She wanted to, very much, but she didn't fancy facing Queenie or Blower, come to that. Quietly she answered, 'All right, Flo. I will, I promise.'

Florrie had to hold her tongue as they rode home on the tram. What she was dying to add was, 'And stay away from that bleeding gypsy,' but since Patsy had not mentioned him since she'd come home from Kent, she thought it wiser to keep her mouth shut.

Chapter Eight

THE FOLLOWING WEEKS were depressing for Patsy. The weather was cold and windy and although she told herself repeatedly to forget Johnny, her life felt empty without him.

She was glad to be back on the market. Even though the work was hard, she liked her job and loved the people. They were the nearest she had ever had to a real family – they didn't belittle her. Here she was treated as one of them. Each night when she returned home Florrie fussed over her, and Ollie would pop in most evenings, but Patsy showed little enthusiasm for anything other than her work.

It was the second Saturday in October and it had been the usual busy day. Shortly after half-past six, Blower insisted that Patsy get away home. She was grateful as she felt exhausted. As she made her way between the stalls, her shopping bag full of bits and pieces and the top piled up with fresh vegetables, she saw him. From a safe distance she stopped, took a deep breath and let it out slowly. Johnny looked more foreign than ever. His curly black hair had a blue sheen. Tanned and brawny, he lolled against the wall with an air of indifference. There was nothing she could do but go towards him.

'How's my girl, then?'

Oh no, not again. I'm not letting him start that all over again. She shook her head and made a great show of setting her bag down between her feet. She found it impossible to say anything.

Johnny, leaning towards her, laughed. 'Aren't we clever. Got home all on our own, didn't we?' he said in his teasing manner.

Taken aback, Patsy stared at him for several seconds. 'I shouldn't have gone with you in the first place.'

'Well, it don't matter now, does it?' At this point he bent to pick up her shopping, while with his free hand he took Patsy's arm and propelled her towards the café. The tea he bought her was hot and sweet and she gratefully began to drink it. She tried to keep her eyes away from his face, but he leaned across the table, put a finger beneath her chin and raised her face to the level of his own.

'Will you come out with me tomorrow?' he asked cheekily.

She made no answer, just continued to stare into his dark eyes. It would be even worse if she said yes this time and again everything went wrong. But she had thought of him constantly and missed him so much, even if she'd tried not to admit it. Her hands were dirty from her day's work, one nail was broken, and she was ashamed of them as he took them in his own and began moving his thumbs backwards and forwards across her palms. With a flourish, he raised one of her hands to his lips and with a mocking smile, he kissed it. She snatched it away.

'What the hell do you want of me?' she demanded.

He grinned. 'I just want you to be my girl – that's all.'

'Why, you two-faced beast,' Patsy exploded, but suddenly the humour of the situation made her smile.

'You're smiling, you're really smiling. Go on, admit it, you missed me.'

Patsy hesitated, then gave a nervous giggle.

'Come on, love, let's start afresh. Say you'll be my girl,' he wheedled.

'Oh, Johnny,' was all that Patsy could find to say.

They walked down Strathmore Street in silence, Johnny still holding her hand tightly. He opened the gate and set her shopping bag down inside the front garden.

'Six o'clock at the Broadway?' Johnny asked quietly.

'All right,' she said, giving in gracefully.

So Patsy began to smile again and Johnny constantly told her she was his girl.

Six more weeks and it would be Christmas again.

For the past four mornings, Florrie had stood at the bottom of the stairs listening to Patsy vomiting.

'Oh, Gawd blimey, she's pregnant.' As the thought struck Florrie she had to grab the banisters to stop herself from falling. How could you have been so blind, she told herself. She'd been thinking Patsy had eaten something which had turned her stomach, but four mornings in a row! How could she have been so bloody daft!

Slowly she straightened up and looked into the mirror hanging on the passage wall. She looked as if she was going to be sick herself and for the first time in a long time tears pricked behind her eyes. Oh, the poor kid. Was history repeating itself? Her thoughts went back to lovely Ellen and how hard her life had been. Maybe if she had lived Patsy might have listened to her, and things would have been different. Men, she sniffed to herself, are all tarred with the same brush; not one of them is worth bothering about. Sadness gave way to anger. Patsy had knocked about the streets long enough, seen other girls falling for babies year in year out, and should have had more sense than to get herself into the same mess. She put her hand to her eyes, angrily brushing away the tears.

'It's got to be that bloody Johnny Jackson.' Sighing deeply she muttered to herself, 'I'll end up swinging for him.'

In the kitchen she laid out two cups and saucers. Impatiently she thumped the top of the kettle, willing it to boil quicker, but she merely succeeded in causing a draught which put the flames out beneath it and had to strike another match to relight the jet. As she made the tea, Florrie gazed out into the back yard. It didn't seem very long ago that Patsy had lain in her pram out there and she had looked after her while Ellen had worked herself to death in the market.

Patsy had been a smashing baby, good as gold. When she'd put her pram out front there wasn't a passer-by who hadn't stopped to tickle her under the chin. Now here she was, only a kid herself, and pregnant. Then Flo's mood became very aggressive. How dared that sod touch her? Come to that, why the bloody hell had she let him?

She found Patsy not yet dressed, with her arms resting on the edge of the sink, her shoulders shaking as she retched and heaved. When Florrie placed a hand on her arm, Patsy almost jumped out of her skin.

'Oh, it's you, Flo,' she gulped, wiping her mouth.

'It's all right, my love, come and sit down. No, don't cry, don't upset yourself. Besides, crying won't solve a bloody thing, now will it?' Patsy sat down and hid her face in her hands, rocking herself back and forth.

'Florrie, what am I going to do?'

The sadness in her voice almost broke Flo's heart. She stood helplessly by Patsy's side. She had the desire to put her arms around her and hold her tight, but refrained from doing so. Instead, for the second time, she vowed silently to herself, 'I'll kill that bleeder, even if I have to swing for it. I'll kill him.'

She stroked Patsy's cheek softly. 'We'll get it sorted out, love. Come on now, wipe your face. Let's have our tea, though I expect it's gone cold by now. Come on, it will be all right, you'll see.'

But in her heart she knew it wouldn't be all right.

Gran Day clutched the sides of her armchair and didn't say a word for a full minute after Florrie told her.

'Poor bloody mite. She's still only a child herself and she's not like some of the sluts around here.' Drawing in her breath and letting it out in a great gasp she bawled, 'That bleeding sod will wish he'd never been born. Did she tell you what happened? He didn't rape her, did he?'

'No, no, I'm sure it wasn't like that.' Florrie was a bit frightened. Gran's face was bright red and her chest was heaving. 'From what I can gather, it happened while she was away hop picking. She ain't really told me much at all, just keeps saying he only loved her.' Flo's main thought at the moment was to pacify Gran.

Gran heaved herself to her feet, waving her arms and bellowing like an angry bull. 'If he did attack her, my God he wants to watch out. There's many a man around here, besides my lot, that will be out to get him. Patsy herself may be a bastard, but you and I know, Flo, there's no one about there who would dare say so out loud. Is there? Come to that, no matter what suspicions they might have had, not one person would have chanced referring to Ellen as anything other than Mrs Kent. If it does turn out that he raped her, there'll be a queue form to see he gets his bloody desserts, you mark my words.'

On and on Gran ranted until suddenly she said, 'You stay here, Flo, I'm going over the road to see her.'

'Well, all right. But, Gran, go easy on her. You know what I think? Patsy felt she'd found someone to need her, someone of her own, when she met that Johnny.'

'Aw, shut up, Flo. You're just making excuses for her. She's got all of us, ain't she? Ain't we always treated her as one of our own?'

'Yes, yes, of course we have. But she's always known that she's had no *real* family of her own. Just go easy on her, will you?'

Using the crutch that Jack had made for her, Gran laboured her way up the passage, out of her own front door and across the street. Heaving Florrie's door open by swinging her hip against it, she stood just inside and called up the stairs, 'Patsy, love, it's me, Gran. Come down, I want to talk to you.'

Patsy, who had been dreading this moment, came to the head of the stairs. 'All right, Gran, I'll be down in a minute,' she said quietly.

When Patsy came into Florrie's untidy kitchen,
Gran had to choke back a cry. Not only were
Patsy's eyes swollen and red from crying, but she
looked ill. She wasn't chirpy and lively any longer
and yet she looked so young. After a moment of
hesitation, during which Gran told herself to leave
sentiment aside for the time being, she came straight
to the point.

'Right! Now, Patsy, you'd better tell me what
happened. Because if you don't, Gawd knows what
my boys are going to do. They'll be bound to think
the worst.'

Patsy hung her head and gulped back the tears.

'It's no good you being obstinate.' Gran's voice
was softer now. 'Did he attack you, Patsy? That's
what you've got to tell me.'

Patsy looked afraid. 'No, not really. He said he
loved me.' The words were dragged from her. 'He
was nice to me at first. We had been for a walk.'

Gran's face flushed. How could she be angry with
her? 'Gawd almighty, been for a walk!'

Patsy raised her eyes and looked into the face of
the woman she'd known all her life as 'Gran'.
Bloated and old she might be, but Patsy loved her
dearly. Now all she could find to say was, 'I'm
sorry, Gran. I'm so sorry.'

The pathetic tone of Patsy's voice affected Gran
deeply. Gruffly she spoke. 'What's done is done, my
love. Do you want to get rid of it? It can be
arranged, you know.'

Patsy lowered her head and shook it. 'Johnny will marry me, I know he will. I'll be all right.' Gran's hand flew to her throat. Christ, no, she thought, but she had the sense to keep her thoughts to herself.

Nothing, she felt, could be worse than seeing this lovely, gentle girl married to that shiftless youth. Tied into his tribe of a family, they'd eat her alive. That tattooed, dark-skinned fellow – horrible! She clenched her fists tight against her sides. I'd like to do for him myself, she thought. Aloud she asked: 'Do you really want to wed him, Patsy? He's not a steady bloke, and you told me yourself you don't like his family.'

'I know, Gran, but Johnny's different. He's a nice boy.' That was too much for Gran. She couldn't help herself.

'Boy! He ain't no boy! He's a man, and he bloody well knew right enough what he was letting you in for.'

Patsy dropped her head down on to her chest, but not before she had given Gran a defiant look.

Gran spat words at her now. 'Patsy, now just you listen to me. It won't help to adopt that attitude. You haven't lived here with us all your life for us not to know you inside out. You'd never get along with him, you wouldn't be happy. That Johnny is no better than the rest of his tribe. He's a selfish sod.'

'Johnny is not like the rest of them,' Patsy interrupted. 'He's kind.'

'Well, we'll see, won't we? In my book he's scum.'

Seeing the look in Patsy's eyes, Gran's rage evaporated. She opened her arms wide and Patsy flew into them. Gran gently stroked her long dark hair, seeing how the weak rays of the morning sunshine shining through the window brought out its chestnut glints. The trouble with this child, she told herself, was that she saw that Johnny through rose-coloured glasses. What would she do if he refused to marry her? And Christ help her if he does, she added to herself.

'Gran, I know Johnny could be different if we did get married. Do you think Florrie will let him come and live here?'

Lord above save us! The way this kid was accepting the situation. Bring that bloody sod to live here, above Flo and opposite me! She hadn't formed an answer before Patsy again whispered, 'Gran.'

'Yes, love?'

'Don't make me have the baby taken away, will you?'

What could she do, what was there left to say? She took hold of Patsy's two hands, stroking them with her own calloused ones. 'No one is going to make you do anything you don't want to. We'll all stand by you, Patsy, you don't need telling that.'

Patsy's green eyes were filled with fear and her voice was pleading. 'Gran, I want to be married.'

'Yes, I know, love, but you might not feel the same way later on and then it would be too late.'

'I don't care, Gran. I want my baby to have a father.' Gran was about to give a sniff, which would have told plainly what she thought of Johnny Jackson as a father, but she checked it swiftly as Patsy, in a voice so low that Gran only just heard her, said, 'I want my baby to have a name, a real name, not like me.'

The lump that came up in Gran's throat almost choked her. She leaned forward in her chair, crossed her arms about her large chest and gave way to her distress. Those last few quiet words of Patsy's had said volumes. Now the sobs that were racking her old body and the tears that were streaming down her face were all for this bewildered girl who sat beside her. For her Patsy, whom she had helped bring into this world, whom she had loved and done her best to help, as she had Ellen before her.

Florrie was right. In spite of everyone, Patsy felt she didn't really belong. Her heart ached with the thought of how lonely Patsy must have been since the death of her mother.

'Gran, what will Grandad say, and Blower and Danny?' Suddenly, Patsy cut her words off short. Her huge green eyes looked terrified.

'What on earth's the matter, love? Have you got a pain?'

'No, Gran. Nothing like that.'

'Well, what is it, then?'

Patsy's face had lost every vestige of colour and Gran felt fear clutch at her own heart.

'For Christ's sake, tell me what's wrong.'

'Ollie.' Just the one word was enough. Gawd above, yes. Who the hell was going to volunteer for the job of telling him? A great big bloke he might be, but he was as soft as butter where Patsy was concerned.

Gran hedged. 'You can leave Grandad and the boys to me. Lord knows, it won't be easy, but we'll see. Come on now, wash your face and bring me a flannel to wipe mine, then you can help me back over home.'

As she waited, Gran thought about the future. How would Florrie react to his living upstairs? Yet, if they did get married, they'd have to have somewhere to live. What was worse was the thought of that blasted Johnny Jackson coming into contact with her family every day. That would be asking for trouble.

Gran followed Patsy out into the street. Never in a million years had she dreamed that Patsy would get herself into trouble like this. She was the one girl around here she'd have laid money on would keep herself to herself. God knew how they were going to get it sorted out. Choked with apprehension, she thought: 'One thing's for sure, she'll have to grow up fast now.'

★

They were married at ten o'clock on a Wednesday morning in the first week in December, in an office at Wandsworth Town Hall. Ollie and Florrie were the only witnesses.

'Be happy,' Ollie had told her.

Florrie had hugged her, but said nothing.

Johnny, being twenty-three, had needed no one's consent. Patsy, still not quite seventeen, had had to apply to the County Court, as she still came under their jurisdiction. She had suffered agony while waiting for the officials' decision and the look of scorn on their faces was something she would never forget.

In less than a fortnight Patsy was asking herself if this husband of hers was really the Johnny with whom she had walked, laughed and been happy. Already she had doubts about really loving him. She had come to realise Johnny was lazy, cunning, didn't wash himself as often as he should and, worst of all, he was a liar.

Every morning she pleaded, 'Please Johnny, get up before I go to work.'

'Leave me be,' he would order her, pulling the bedclothes up over his head. He had no intention of getting a job.

Monday morning again, and at a quarter to six she came into the bedroom with a steaming mug of tea. Playfully, she nudged him a few times. 'Sit up, Johnny, and take your tea.'

Suddenly, he threw back the covers, patted the mattress and grinned at her. 'Get in, come on Patsy, come back to bed.'

She gave a deep sigh. 'I can't. You know very well I can't. I have to get to work and there isn't time, I'll be late.'

'Bugger your work. You mean you don't want to!' He spat the words out bitterly.

'That's not fair, and you know it. If I laid in bed all morning I'd lose my job. Then what would we do for money? That's another thing, Johnny, what about when I get bigger and have to pack up work? Please get up. You could find a job, I'm sure you could, if you'd only go out and look for one.'

Pulling himself up, he clenched one fist and the anger in his eyes frightened Patsy. 'You're a bloody cold fish,' he yelled at her. 'Why don't you tell the truth. You've gone off me, that's if you ever did feel anything for me in the first place.'

'Now you're being daft,' Patsy commented drily.

'Oh yes?' He picked up the mug of tea and flung it at the wall. Patsy looked with despair at the stain already spreading over the wallpaper.

'I'm beginning to hate the sight of you. All you wanted was someone to give a name to your bloody baby. That's another thing. How do I know it's my bleeding kid? Even my brothers have asked me that.'

Slowly, Patsy walked away from him and stood at the foot of the bed. This wasn't the first time he had worked himself up into a rage, but it was the first time he had made such an accusation. When she spoke her voice was quiet. 'I try to love you Johnny, but this is the wrong time. I have to go to work.'

He spluttered a mouthful of curses. 'You've hit the nail on the head there all right. "Try to love me." You shouldn't bloody well have to try. To anyone else it would come natural, but not to you, oh no. You're so damned cold-blooded it's a wonder you don't suffer from frost bite!'

Patsy felt the anger rising within her and she retaliated. 'You could have made love to me last night, but you weren't here. It was turned three this morning when you came home, and you had had so much to drink I had to help you into bed.'

His mouth tightened in anger and his eyes blazed. 'What the hell's it got to do with you what time I came home? That's another thing. Home you call it – these poxy two rooms and a scullery. What with you and that old hag downstairs, it's a wonder I ever come back.' He pulled his features into a sulky grimace and spoke in a voice that was supposed to mimic Florrie.

' "Patsy, love, you shouldn't be carrying that heavy bucket. Patsy, dear, you should rest more, put your feet up." All that old bitch cares about is her precious Patsy. She don't give a tinker's cuss about me. All she did was help trick me into marrying you.' He threw himself backwards, banging his head on the brass bed-rail and let out a thunderous curse. 'Right, clear off if you're going, only don't expect me to be here tonight. I ain't going to be made a laughing-stock of any longer.'

Patsy bit her lip as she walked from the room, asking herself why she bothered to argue with him. It was a certainty he'd still be in bed if she came home at midday, and expecting her to get his dinner.

That evening he was there, propped up by the wall at the entrance to the market. He held out his hand to Patsy and gazed at her like a lovesick dog. Wearily she looked at him, staring into those deep, dark eyes. This man could change in a second from being a humorous, charming lover to a raging bully. Firmly Johnny took her arm and together they went home.

The weeks turned into months and Patsy did her best to stay cheerful. Married life was not at all as she had imagined. She put up with Johnny's whims and bad temper and the fact that he stayed away, often for days on end. Sometimes, lying awake at night, she'd ask herself why she had been such a fool. Johnny was never going to leave his tribe, get a steady job and settle down. Other nights, she would not even try to sleep, but would sit at the window for hours on end trying to understand him. Why had he agreed to marry her if he had no intention of living with her? She had made all possible allowances for him and had hoped and prayed that the tension between them would lessen.

It wasn't an easy pregnancy and there were many days when she dragged herself to the market wishing she could have stayed in bed. The mornings were bitterly cold and often a frost gleamed on the pavements. Life was much harder in the winter. There was coal to buy, and making ends meet was an endless worry. All Johnny seemed to do was spend dinnertime in the pub and the rest of the day kicking about with his brothers. Did they make enough money at summer fairs to live on during the winter? If they did, she had never seen any of it. How did he think she coped? A while back she had managed to save a few shillings to buy baby clothes, but when she'd gone to the tin, tucked away at the back of the cupboard, it was empty. She had told Johnny that was a mean thing to do but he had only laughed. Sometimes she wallowed in self-pity, then she pulled herself together. She had to go on for the sake of the baby. Did she do right to decide to keep it? At least it would have a name.

The start of another week. Johnny had been home all over the weekend, the first time Patsy had seen him for two weeks, and it hadn't been a happy time. He seemed intent on bickering, unable to discuss anything in a quiet, rational way and at loggerheads with Florrie the whole time. She felt weary tonight as she pushed open the front door. Immediately, she knew Johnny had gone, for Florrie's kitchen door was wide open and she kept it shut tight when Johnny was about.

'Come and have a cup of tea with me, Patsy,' Florrie called.

As she sat down, Patsy thought Florrie's kitchen had never looked more cosy than it did that evening. It was dusk outside and the flame from the gas mantle cast a warm glow. She kicked off her boots and stuck her feet out towards the roaring fire. It felt so good to be able to relax and there was such a sense of peace. She had lived her whole life in this house and it held so many memories of her childhood, her youth and, most of all, her mother.

'Count your blessings,' she told herself. 'You have Florrie, dear old Flo, yes, and Ollie, especially Ollie. With two people like them to care for me, what have I got to complain about?'

Florrie handed her a cup of tea and as she did so she looked at Patsy's pale face, noticing the lines of tiredness. 'Gawd help me,' she thought. 'I'd give anything not to have to tell her, but what else can I do?'

Aloud she blurted out, 'The rent man came this morning.' Patsy raised her eyes and instinctively knew something was wrong.

'What about it? He comes every other Monday. I left my book and the money out on my kitchen table.'

The look on Florrie's face was enough; no explanation was needed. They both sat in silence for what seemed a long time. The centre of the fire dropped, sending sparks up the chimney and still neither of them moved.

Quietly, Florrie broke the silence. 'We can't leave it there. It's not the first time.'

The bottom fell out of Patsy's world.

'Did you pay mine for me, Flo?'

'No, love, I couldn't. I didn't have enough.'

Patsy caught the choked sob in Florrie's voice. Straining forward she put her hand out to rest on Flo's knee.

'Tell me, Flo, how many times? Please, don't beat about the bush, just tell me.'

Florrie's face was full of concern for her. She should never have got mixed up with the likes of him. 'Bleeding thief,' she muttered for the umpteenth time that day. 'You see, love, the first time I thought you'd just forgotten to leave it out. Then a fortnight ago, I thought you were a bit short and didn't like to say so.'

'So this is the third time. That's six weeks I owe now.'

Outwardly Patsy tried to stay calm and controlled. Inwardly she was seething. So that was why he had come home.

Florrie, too, was trying to suppress her anger. Soothingly she said, 'No, you don't. You're only the last two weeks in arrears. I told him you'd pay four weeks next time.'

Patsy felt sick. Where would she find four weeks' rent? The rent man wouldn't wait.

'So, for the last month you've paid my share of the rent as well as your own? Why didn't you say something, Flo?'

'Forget it,' Florrie ordered. 'I managed. I'm only sorry it had to come out now.'

They lapsed into brooding silence again.

'Listen,' Flo said, rising from her chair. 'Why don't we forget about it for the time being? I'll make us another cup of tea and then I'll cook us a nice bit of fish and we'll 'ave our tea together. How does that sound?'

Patsy's eyes shone with unshed tears as Florrie squeezed her arm reassuringly. In the scullery, Flo placed the large black frying pan on to the gas stove. Patsy had gone upstairs to freshen up. While the fish was cooking, Flo decided she'd get her best tablecloth out and set it nice to cheer Patsy up if she could. As for that bloody Johnny Jackson, she wished he'd sling his hook for good. Lying, thieving, conniving sod. Full of hot air and promises. He'd never set foot in this house again, not if she had her way he wouldn't. Blast him. He don't give a damn about Patsy, takes her on, that's all he does. Thieving bleeder.

After a restless night, Patsy had come to a decision. There was nothing she could do about repaying Florrie at the moment, but she could go to Mitcham and have it out with Johnny. As she sat in the tram, anger bubbled inside her. The way he had treated her was bad enough, but to steal her rent! He knew full well it would be Florrie who had to face the rent collector. Been laughing up his sleeve for a month now, probably thinking what a soft cow Florrie was not to have let on. Only came home this weekend to pinch the money. Soon cleared off again, hadn't he? Bloody coward.

Rage was still giving her Dutch courage when she arrived outside the hoardings surrounding the ground on which the Jacksons lived. She had no idea what she was actually going to say to him. She was not prepared for the sight which met her eyes as she stepped through the door set in the wooden screens on which advertisements were posted. It was unbelievable. On this large area of waste ground stood several Romany-type caravans. None appeared to be in a state of good repair. Originally, most likely, they would have been gaily painted, but now the paintwork was cracked and chipped and the front steps broken and dangerous. She stepped back in fear as two pigs came scuffling and grunting towards her.

Further ahead a wooden hut had been erected on stilts. Beneath it, chickens and even ducks were picking over what appeared to be rotting fruit and vegetables. The ground was littered with animal droppings. At the far end seemed to be a tip.

Heaven only knew what paraphernalia lay beneath the piles of rusting old iron and tin.

Patsy felt terrified. A horse and cart was being recklessly driven towards her. She stepped back against the fence and it drew to a halt within inches of her, penning her in. Within seconds, half the Jackson tribe were grouped around her, the women laughing shrilly at her panic. Mrs Jackson grinned at her, the gold teeth still very conspicuous.

'To what do we owe this pleasure?' she sarcastically asked.

Displaying far more courage than she felt, Patsy said, 'I've come to see Johnny.'

''Ave you now? Supposing he don't want to see you?'

'Please, Mrs Jackson, I need to talk to him.' Patsy was ashamed of herself for pleading, yet she felt it was safer to placate his mother. She didn't want to be turned off the place without getting to see Johnny.

'He's over there.' A bony finger pointed the direction. Picking her way warily, she walked towards the van. Johnny stood in the doorway looking down on her, contempt showing in his face. He spoke first.

'Well, what the 'ell are you doing here?'

'I've come for my rent money,' she told him, doing her utmost to sound bold.

'Don't know what you're on about,' he answered, but he looked sheepish.

'Johnny, don't let's play about. I have to get to work. You know very well I always leave my rent money out on the table every other Monday morning.'

'So what?'

'So, including yesterday, it's been missing three times. That's six weeks' rent. I want it back, Johnny. I need it.'

'Are you calling my son a thief?' The suddenness with which Mrs Jackson sprang forward frightened Patsy. That woman was enough to scare anyone. Tugging her black shawl around her narrow shoulders, her wrinkled face blazing, she screeched, 'No son of mine stole your bloody rent, you cheeky bleeding bitch.' She advanced towards Patsy, her face contorted with hate, her eyes narrowed into evil slits.

Patsy's heart was beating wildly, choking her with its pounding, but she stood her ground. 'No one else could have taken that money.' She turned to where Johnny was still standing on the caravan steps. 'Why won't you admit it? You know I can't afford to lose it.'

Johnny leaned sideways and spat on to the ground. 'Piss off,' he said, causing even the children to laugh.

Patsy felt her throat tighten with the tears her temper wouldn't let her shed. Why had she come? What was the point in pleading? Surely by now she should know he had no principles; but she wasn't going to go away with her tail between her legs. She clenched her fists so tightly that her fingernails dug into her hands. How she wanted to claw those nails down Johnny's face, so that he would never leer at her again. She put one foot on the step towards him, but old Mrs Jackson was quicker. She pushed Patsy aside so fast that she made her miss her footing. She flung one arm out to save herself as she struggled to regain her balance, but her feet slid from under her.

It seemed as if every female member of the Jackson tribe was leering down at her.

'You snared our Johnny into marrying you,' one shrill voice came at her.

'Who else was knocking you off?' another voice spat at her.

Patsy rose to her hands and knees and then managed to stand up. Torments and jeers were coming at her from all sides. She had to dodge quickly when she saw Mrs Jackson rushing at her with a knife in her hand, screeching like a scalded cat. Never in her life had Patsy heard such vile obscenities from a man or woman, and the venom with which they were uttered made her reel.

Mrs Jackson spat at her now. 'You listen to me, my girl. My Johnny's place is here with his family. We don't consider 'im married, nor never would he have been if we'd got wind of it. You're no better than your bloody mother was. A brothel-bred git, that's what you are, and if you're not off my land in two minutes I'll set the bleeding dogs on yer.'

Mrs Jackson's temper had risen to such a pitch that Patsy felt she was capable of using the knife any moment. Street kid as she was, all her instincts told her she was no match for this foul-mouthed harridan, but she wasn't going to let Johnny get off so lightly. He stood close now, a snigger curling his lips. Like a thing possessed, she flung herself at him, lashing out at his tormenting face. Fred Jackson came from behind and caught her wrists, yanking her away. In the struggle, all three of them went down, falling over each other and hitting the ground with a thud.

By now, she was shaking from head to foot. As she rose, Johnny's hand whipped out, striking her across the side of the face. It almost knocked her senseless. Two men frog-marched her to the gate, her feet dragging along the ground.

The wooden door slammed and she was alone in the street. She leaned against the wall, trying to get her breath. She could still hear obscenities ringing in her ears. A pain shot through her stomach and then she was vomiting against the hoardings.

Ignoring the curious glances of passersby, she wiped her eyes and mouth and strode off, oblivious of everything and everyone. She was desperate to be home and, without waiting for a tram, she marched off down the pavement.

God, she'd had some insults slung at her today. Incensed at the injustice of it all, her footsteps kept pace with her thoughts. She had been so humiliated.

That old witch would pay for it one day, and so would Johnny. Brothel-bred was she? No one could call her that and get away with it. 'If it takes me years and years, I'll get them for that. As for him, he'll get his come-uppance. I don't know how, but I swear to God I'll get him. I will, I will, I will,' she vowed.

Florrie was paying the milkman when Patsy pushed down the latch of the garden gate. One glance and her lower jaw dropped in horror. The milkman took the jug from her shaking hands to prevent her spilling it all.

'Whatever's happened?' she gasped, staring at the raw wound on Patsy's face.

'Best get her inside,' the milkman advised. He could smell the stale vomit down the front of her coat and see the filth that clung to her.

While Patsy sat in the bath, Florrie hurried to the pub for a quarter bottle of brandy. An hour later Patsy was clean and warm, seated in front of the fire, the eiderdown from Florrie's bed wrapped snugly about her, the inevitable mug of tea clasped between her hands. However, this time it tasted different – the result of Florrie lacing it liberally with brandy.

'You're not telling me you went on your own and faced that lot, are you?' Florrie sounded so incredulous that Patsy half-smiled.

'I just wanted to have it out with Johnny, though

I think I knew that I hadn't a chance in hell of getting the money back from him.'

Flo's old eyes stared at her. 'I told you. Never mind about the blasted money. We'll scrape it together somehow. My Gawd, gal, you took a chance. That lot could have maimed you for life.'

Wisely, Patsy answered, 'I know that now. The old girl nearly did.'

'Yet you had a go! You stood up to them.'

'As much as I could, for what good it did me.'

'Was Johnny there?'

'Of course he was.'

'What did he have to say for himself?'

Patsy lowered her head, twisted the eiderdown with her fingers and stayed silent.

'Denied it, did he? Bloody sod. I wish to Christ you'd asked Ollie and Blower to go with you.'

'No, no.' Patsy interrupted the flow of Florrie's anger. The blood rushed to her face as she remembered what the Jacksons had said about her mother. Her mother had been a wonderful person, worth a hundred of any of that lot. They'd even doubted Johnny was the father of her baby. She didn't want anyone to know about that.

The silence seemed endless. Florrie wanted to know a great deal more but she couldn't bring herself to ask. There was a sort of steely calmness about Patsy now and it worried her. She had seen the bruises on Patsy's body and thighs. The Jacksons must have really torn into her. God knew what would happen when Ollie and the Days got to hear of it. All hell would be let loose.

'Come on Patsy.' Flo spoke as calmly as her anger would allow. 'Let's get you upstairs and into bed.'

Despite everything, Patsy slept the day away. It was evening before she got up to make herself a drink. As she sat sipping her tea there was a slight tap at the door and Ollie came in.

'How are you, my love?' he began, sitting down opposite her in what had been her mother's chair. For once Patsy was unable to relax in his presence. Leaning towards her, he gruffly asked, 'Why didn't you come to me, Patsy? Whatever made you go over to Mitcham on your own?'

Patsy shrank back. Now she was for it. Florrie must have told him everything. Rising, Ollie bent over her, tilting her head towards the light. He gasped in horror. The whole of one side of her face was cut and bruised, showing signs of turning black and blue. Near to her ear were more lacerations. He touched her cheek with his finger. Patsy turned away, refusing to look at him. He took two steps backwards, struggling to control his anger.

'He did this? Johnny did this to you?' he spluttered.

Patsy seemed to shrink, her head lowered, her hair falling forward hiding her face.

Ollie thrust his hands deep into his pockets. His blood was boiling. 'I'd strangle him with my bare hands if he were here this minute,' he growled to himself. Nobody, least of all that filthy Johnny Jackson, could attack Patsy like this and be allowed to get away with it. It was no good, his anger was uncontrollable. Almost unaware of what he was doing, he went into the scullery; his hamlike fist slammed against the wall and deep guttural sounds came from his mouth. 'By Christ, I'll see he pays for this. If it takes to the end of my days, I'll make him sorry he ever laid a finger on Patsy.'

Florrie, kicking open the door, made Patsy jump. Her nerves were so on edge that her body gave a convulsive jerk.

'Pie and mash for all of us,' she declared, depositing a large basin on the table. The tension eased as they ate. No more words were necessary. Yet the pain tore Ollie apart as he looked at Patsy's bruised face and he let his thoughts dwell on what a horrific experience that morning must have been for her.

By half-past nine, Florrie had cleared the table, washed up and put a stone hot-water bottle into Patsy's bed before saying 'Good-night.' Ollie lingered. Patsy found herself thinking, not for the first time, how nice it would have been if Ollie had been her father. She had never known the happiness of having two parents. Ollie kissed her gently on the forehead.

'Good-night, sweetheart. God bless you,' he murmured. With a surge of affection for this big man whom she had known all her life, Patsy threw her arms around him and laid her head on his chest.

In the doorway, Ollie hesitated before he said, 'Patsy, I've settled up with Florrie about the rent, so stop worrying. Sleep well,' he told her as he quietly closed the door.

She couldn't bring herself to go to bed but sat letting the tears run unchecked down her face. Her eyes were drawn to the only photograph she had of her mother and Ollie taken together. She gasped in astonishment. It was as if it had come alive! There was no colour in the picture, only brown and white. Previously she had thought it portrayed her mum as stiff and lifeless, but now she looked different. She was beautiful and elegant and her hair, skilfully wound into earphone plaits, was actually shining. Her pale blue eyes smiled at her reassuringly. Ollie's cheeks were red, his eyes twinkling and he was smiling. She put out a hand to touch the frame. It was strange, as if these two people were joining together, telling her they loved her. She blinked and the moment was lost, yet somehow she felt strangely comforted.

It was three o'clock in the morning when she woke. Her legs felt as heavy as lead and her shins burned as if hot rods were running through them. She stretched her feet and gave a shriek. Oh no, not cramp again! Easing herself to the edge of the bed, she pressed her feet on to the cold linoleum and sat there taking slow, deep breaths.

The pain eased and she made to get back into bed, but the sheets felt wet. Feeling for the box of matches she struck one and lit the candle in a saucer on the chair beside the bed. The wick spluttered for a second before the flame took hold. Lifting the saucer high, she saw the bloodstains.

It was dark and cold in the scullery as she fumbled to light the gas mantle. She boiled the kettle and poured the water into the enamel bowl, gave the flannel a good rub of bar soap and washed her legs and between her thighs, rinsed the flannel out twice and wiped her face, wincing as she drew the cloth over the sore, bruised places.

As she raised her arms to pull a clean nightdress over her head, the pain came. The intensity of it had her gasping. She stood still and taut, not daring to move, feeling very frightened. 'Stay calm, don't panic,' she told herself. 'Go down and wake Florrie up, she'll know what to do.'

Hand over hand, holding on to the furniture for support, she groped her way towards the door. Reaching the head of the stairs she rested. Then, suddenly, without any effort, she was going forward and downward.

Florrie and Ollie sat each side of the hospital bed watching Patsy drifting in and out of consciousness. They had been there for hours, wishing to be near in case she woke up and asked for them, but the only word she had whispered was 'Mum'.

Patsy had been home from hospital for two weeks,

and Florrie was at her wits' end. She had tried everything she knew to lift Patsy out of her depression,
but to no avail. The Day family had been marvellous. Queenie, Blower and Danny had all been to
visit her, bringing with them gifts of eggs and fruit
in the hope that she would start to eat. Even the
flowers they brought didn't cheer her up. Queenie
begged her to go with her to visit Gran, who dearly
wanted to see her, but even that wouldn't get her
outside the front door.

Then one Sunday afternoon she put on her coat,
tied a scarf over her head and told Florrie she was
going for a walk. Just as she used to, she walked up
to the common. By the time she reached the avenue
of trees it was four o'clock. It had been a day typical
for the end of March – fine and dry with a strong
wind. Now, as the evening began to draw in, the
wind had turned harsh and cold. For the past half-
hour she hadn't met a soul – it was as if she was
alone in the world.

As she walked, she thought back over the past
months and wondered how she had endured them.
Why was it, she asked herself, that one never came
to know one's own mind until it was too late. Her
mum used to say that experience was the most
expensive commodity in life. She had said that
everyone made mistakes and mistakes had to be paid
for.

Well, she was paying all right. Seventeen years
old and she'd been married, lost her baby and been

abandoned. She had put her faith in the wrong people. She had convinced herself that Johnny had loved her. He probably did, at least as much as he was capable of loving anyone, but he was weak and easily influenced by his family. She realised now that he could never settle down and get a regular job. She had thought that her love could change him. How blind she had been!

She had thought that being married to Johnny would give her an identity, establish her name as Jackson. Growing up with the name of Kent hadn't bothered her until her mother died, when the whole, stark truth had come to light.

She was a bastard. In all probability, Kent was a fictitious name, invented by Mum in order to hide her real identity. What about her mother's parents – her grandparents? Where were they? As far as she knew, they had never acknowledged her existence.

She had tried to sort it out in her mind for ages, but felt she'd never know the truth. The reality was, no one wanted her – not legally. The way she saw it, she was unclaimed – belonging to no one.

They could say what they liked, this much she knew. There had been some good in Johnny. He had been kind to her at times. He hadn't been forced to marry her, that was one thing in his favour. Then, again, he probably never would have done so if they hadn't gone to the registry office without telling his family.

What a wedding it had been. Not so much as a

buttonhole, let alone a bouquet! No family to kiss
and hug her or to whisper congratulations. Not
even a new dress! What happened to those school-
girl dreams of a white wedding, proudly walking
down the aisle on your father's arm in a long dress
with a train? Well, that would have been out,
because she'd never had a father. As for a reception,
there hadn't been one. Even the poorest of families
put on a bit of a do when there was a wedding, but
no one had felt inclined to mark her special day.

She paused to select a dry patch of grass beneath a
tree and flopped to the ground. As always, Ollie,
Florrie and all the Day family had been marvellous
to her, but she didn't want their sympathy. She
choked back a sob. Tears were welling up again and
she had an overwhelming urge to give way – to cry
and cry and cry.

'No!' she rebuked herself. 'Stop wallowing in
self-pity. You've shed enough tears these past few
weeks to fill a bucket.'

She wiped her eyes and stood up. She was envel-
oped in silence. Even the birds seemed to have gone
to bed.

Most families would be cosily gathered around
their warm fires, having Sunday tea. Here she was,
all alone. Was she glad Johnny had married her? She
considered for a moment, but wasn't sure of the
answer. One thing was certain though, he didn't
want her now. Well, good riddance to bad rubbish!
It must have been the biggest mistake of her life

when she had given in to Peggy Woolston's coaxing and taken a ride on that roundabout at Hampton Court Fair.

Chapter Nine

WINTER HAD PASSED and given way to a long, hot summer. There was a maturity about Patsy now. Her life was back to normal: working on the market during the week, spending Sundays doing her washing and ironing and taking long walks in the evening. August Bank Holiday was approaching and the market would be busy over the weekend.

As it was a very warm day, Patsy was taking her afternoon break outside in the yard. Seated on an upturned wooden box, her body leaning back against the wall, she thankfully sipped her tea. Hearing the sound of horses' hooves on the cobbles, she raised her head. It would be Danny coming in from his rounds. It was Danny's cart, but a stranger was up on the box. Blower was across the yard in a few quick strides.

'Hello, there. Where's Danny?' he wanted to know as he cast a shrewd eye over the man who was attempting to get down from the cart.

His movements were awkward. He twisted his body so that one foot touched the ground before the other. When he was standing beside Blower, Patsy was surprised to see that he had a club foot. An ugly iron structure, about three inches in height, had been mounted on to his right boot.

'Are you Blower, Danny's brother? I'm Eddie Owen.' In no time at all he explained what had happened. Danny had been taken ill. The ambulance men seemed to think it was appendicitis.

'How did you become involved?' asked Blower.

'My dad owns a small general store at Colliers Wood. He buys almost daily from Danny. My mother died a year ago and Dad can't leave the shop to go to market himself.'

'Oh, yes. I remember Danny telling me about your mum and dad. The name didn't click. Sorry, Eddie.'

'That's all right.'

'Don't you work in the shop?'

'No, not much. My mother would never let me and since her death I have tried but I haven't really taken to it.'

Turning now to Patsy, Blower asked, 'Can you find a mug of tea for Eddie? I expect he can more than do with one.'

Patsy poured tea into one of the pint mugs the men preferred, and as Eddie accepted it she took the opportunity to study him. Ollie was tall, but this man was taller by at least an inch. As he bent his head and looked at her, she thought she had never seen such beautiful eyes. They were huge and brown and the lashes were so long. Many a girl would like to have lashes like those. He smiled at her and those eyes glinted merrily. She felt he was a happy man and kindly with it.

'I'm sorry, I don't know your name.' Even his speech was different from what she was used to hearing. Feeling flustered at meeting this unusual man with a cultured voice, she answered too quickly: 'Patsy Kent.' Her hand flew to cover her mouth. Why had she said Kent and not Jackson? She felt her cheeks burn as she blushed.

As Blower rejoined them he took his wallet from his back pocket and, opening it, he spoke to Eddie. 'You must let me pay you. You've gone to a lot of trouble for us today. In fact, you've saved our bacon, getting those orders delivered.'

Shaking his head, Eddie put a restraining hand on Blower's arm. 'There's no need, really. Thanks all the same, but Danny's done me many a favour in the past and I'm happy to do a hand's turn for you.'

Blower hesitated for a moment then thrust his wallet back into his pocket. His thoughts were racing ahead. This would have to happen now, one of the busiest weeks of the year. He couldn't spare men off the stalls, yet those orders had to be got out and delivered. Miss one customer, especially this coming weekend, and he could kiss that business goodbye.

As if he sensed Blower's thoughts, Eddie asked: 'Would you like me to do Danny's round? He is obviously going to be off sick for a while.'

Blower pondered for a few moments. Eddie was

presentable, well dressed, spoke nicely and would go down a treat at the big houses. yes, even at the convent. But would he get through the round in time? Climbing up and down from the cart, first finding out what the cook or housekeeper needed, back to fill out the order, back again to the house loaded down with boxes . . . Eddie couldn't do it, not with his gammy leg, but who else could he get? There weren't many he could trust with two horses.

Inspiration came to him in a flash.

'Patsy, how would you like to go on the rounds with Eddie all this week? You know the places Danny calls on, and I know you've helped him with his books many a time. You could nip up to the houses, get the orders and run them back to Eddie.'

Eddie wasn't a bit put out by the implication that his club foot would slow him down, but Patsy was. She'd have loved to be out in the sunshine for the next five days but she felt embarrassed. Blower was insinuating that Eddie couldn't manage on his own.

'It would be a good solution, that's if you wouldn't mind.' Eddie spoke as if he genuinely did want her to go with him.

'Yes, all right, Blower. Shall I come in at the same time in the morning or shall I make it earlier?'

'Thanks, love. The same time will do. I'll have the boys load up the cart all ready for you both.'

It was a beautiful morning. Everything was working out well, just as Blower had said it would. At each tradesmen's entrance Patsy was met with the same queries: 'What about Danny?' 'How is he?' 'When will he be back?' 'Send him our regards.'

She assured all the females that Danny was receiving the best of attention! She and Eddie worked well together, gradually getting into their own routine and Patsy found him to be utterly fair when weighing up the goods.

At one o'clock they pulled off the road. Eddie put the nose-bags on the horses and left them to feed, while he and Patsy sat on the grass and ate their own packed lunch.

When she left the market at the end of the day, Patsy was pleased to think that tomorrow she would again be spending the day with Eddie Owen.

Happy, she almost ran to work next morning. As Eddie came towards her in the yard he was even taller than she had remembered him. His shoulders were so broad and his muscles moved as he walked, but those eyes! The darkest brown and so large, they dominated his whole face. He was smiling at her – such a warm, friendly smile. Oh, yes, it was going to be another lovely day!

Each lunchtime Patsy sat close beside him, her knees often pulled up to her chin, learning all about him, her green eyes sparkling, engrossed in what he had to say. One day she told him about herself, about Johnny and how Kent was no longer her legal name. She talked of Florrie and Ollie so much that Eddie felt he not only knew them, but liked them.

Patsy was at ease with Eddie and talked to him more than she'd spoke to anyone for months. What few questions Eddie put to her were asked in such a way that she knew he wasn't being nosy, but that he really cared.

'Goodnight, Eddie.' It was Saturday evening, the week was over and she had no idea what arrangements Blower had made for next week.

'Patsy, wait a minute.' She turned back with a smile as she heard Eddie call. 'Patsy, I've been thinking. Monday being Bank Holiday, would you like to come out with me?'

She hesitated and he added, 'You could come back for tea and meet my dad.'

Still she didn't answer and he turned away. 'It doesn't matter if you don't want to.'

'No, no, it isn't that I don't want to, honest it isn't. It's . . . it's . . .'

'Tell me, I won't be offended.'

'I always go somewhere with Ollie and Florrie when it's holiday time and I don't like to disappoint them. We only take a tram ride in the afternoon, something like that. Flo, especially, will be looking forward to it.'

Eddie's face brightened. 'Listen, listen to me. Why don't you bring them home for a late tea when you get back? My dad would be pleased to have the company.'

Her eyes lit up and she grinned broadly. 'Could I?

Better warn you, though, Florrie's a bit of a character.'

'I already know that from what you've told me. To tell you the truth, Patsy, I can't wait to meet her.'

'Well, if you're sure. It would be a nice change for all of us, but who's going to get the tea?'

'Me and Dad, of course. You wait and see, we'll surprise you.' He put his hand gently under her chin and tilted her face upwards. 'You will come, won't you?'

She stared up at him for a moment. He wants me to go as much as I do, she thought.

She smiled again. 'All right, we'll be there. Thank you.'

'Between five and six, then, on Monday.'

'Are you ready, Patsy?' Florrie called from the bottom of the stairs.

'I won't be long.'

Florrie looked at Ollie standing in the doorway. Like her, he was all dressed up and ready to go.

'I've never known that girl take so long over dressing herself.'

'Don't fret yourself,' Ollie calmly told her.

'Oh, dear Lord, I hope she won't be disappointed. She's set such store about going to tea with these Owens.'

Ollie shrugged. 'It was nice of them to ask. Patsy

really seems to like this Eddie. Anyway, we can judge him for ourselves when we get there.'

As it happened, they hadn't been for an outing. It had turned out to be a typical Bank Holiday – pouring with rain!

Later, sitting beside Ollie in the tram, Florrie sighed. As if reading her thoughts, Ollie glanced across to where Patsy sat. She had certainly taken pains with her appearance today. He smiled a little sadly. It was such a long time since Patsy had been anywhere or looked so pretty and lively as she did today. He hoped all would go well.

All three of them gazed appreciatively at 'Owen Stores', its plate glass windows facing down Marlborough Road. The flat above had to be approached from the back. Even the yard was clean and well kept, and high flowering shrubs grew against the rear wall. Eddie stood at the top of the steps, the front door wide open, waiting to welcome them. This pleased Patsy; he must have been watching out for them.

As Eddie ushered them into the living-room his father rose from an armchair. At once, Patsy could see from whom Eddie got his looks and his height. Mr Owen was a big-framed man, though not so straight in stature now as he probably had been when younger. He wore cavalry twill trousers and a three-quarter length cardigan, which looked as if it had been hand-knitted, over a blue cotton shirt, the top two buttons of which were left undone. On his feet he wore carpet slippers. How comfortable he looked; there would be no standing on ceremony with him.

Mr Owen faced Ollie first, gripping him firmly by the hand and saying, 'Welcome to our home, Mr Berry.'

'Thanks for inviting me and my friends. Please call me Ollie.'

The open face spread into a smile. 'Pleased to know you, Ollie, and I'm Frank.'

Turning now to Florrie, Frank Owen gave a deep, rumbling laugh. 'So you're Florrie. I'm right pleased to meet you.' No one could have taken offence either at the laugh or the words.

Florrie answered in the same vein. 'Sounds like my reputation 'as preceded me, Mr Owen.'

He laughed again. 'Let's have your hat and coat, and please call me Frank. I shall call you Florrie.'

As Patsy was unfastening her coat Eddie made to help her. His father nudged him aside. 'Oh, yes, I see what my son means. You are pretty and your hair is lovely. I'm so glad you've come to see me.' Cheeks flaming, Patsy was only able to mutter, 'Thank you.'

The three men stood by the window, already deep in conversation. Patsy had been apprehensive, but not any more. Flo tugged at her arm. 'Cor, it's real nice here and I like Mr Owen . . . and your Eddie.'

'Oh, leave off, Flo. He's not my Eddie.' But

Patsy had to agree it certainly was nice here. They were in a big, airy room with lace curtains at the windows and carpet all over the floor, right up to the skirting boards.

'Now then, come and sit up. You, Ollie, sit there, better let the youngsters sit next to each other and you, Florrie, sit here, next to me.' Frank Owen set everyone at ease.

It was a marvellous tea. The table was laid with a linen tablecloth edged with lace. There was a bowl of salad topped with slices of hard-boiled egg, tinned red salmon, crusty bread and real butter. To follow they had jelly, blancmange and tinned peaches. Then came small fancy cakes. They ate so much no one felt inclined to move away from the table.

Florrie was in her element. Her offer to make a fresh pot of tea had been readily accepted. Gathering the rose-patterned cups and saucers in front of her, she filled and handed them around as if she was the hostess.

'Would you like to see the rest of the flat?' Eddie asked. Patsy needed no second bidding. Eddie's bedroom was decorated mainly in white and one wall, lined with shelves, held numerous books. His father's room had a slightly feminine touch, no doubt from his wife's influence, and Patsy felt sad for Mr Owen. The third bedroom was a mixture of guest-room and office. The kitchen was a delight. Painted yellow, it had a recess at one end where a wooden table and two chairs were placed. Patsy guessed Eddie and his father had most of their meals there. The place was so big and they had it all to themselves – no one living above or below.

There was one more surprise and it brought forth a cry of pleasure from Patsy. A bathroom! A large copper geyser was on the wall above the long white bath. She had never seen anything like it before. 'A bit different from Flo and me having to fill our old tin bath,' she thought to herself. This one had taps and a plug to get the water out. No scooping out the dirty water with a dipper until the bath was emptied enough to be dragged to the yard.

A white china toilet with a wooden seat and long chained handle stood grandly in one corner. She thought of the times in the middle of the night when she had had to put her coat on over her nightdress and go down into the yard to use their draughty, outside lavatory!

'What luxury,' she exclaimed to Eddie.

'Dad had it installed for Mum,' he told her.

Seated in the comfortable front room, watching them together, there was no doubt in Florrie's mind that Patsy was happy being with Eddie. Who would have thought it possible that they would all get on so well? Ollie was sitting back in his chair, relaxed, very much at home. Frank Owen and his son were good 'uns, was Florrie's verdict.

There was a strange sense of loneliness and uncertainty about Eddie as they said goodbye. He thought Patsy looked so small and young. Acting on impulse, he kissed her, very gently, on her cheek. His action even surprised himself.

'Thank you for coming,' he murmured. She turned and walked slowly, almost reluctantly, down the stairs.

'You will come again,' Frank Owen said to Florrie.

'Try and stop me,' she grinned then, pausing at the door, she said, 'Thanks for today.'

At the end of the day Florrie was full of gratitude.

'I think our Patsy has done all right for herself. She'll be fine this time, that Eddie is a good lad,' she remarked to Ollie when they were alone.

Wisely, Ollie shook his head. 'Don't rush your fences, Flo. It's early days. I agree Eddie is a nice young chap and his father is a good, likeable man, but take it steady, let things take their course.' He didn't dare voice his thoughts. Lurking in the background was Johnny Jackson. He wished Patsy all the luck in the world, he was happy that she had found a decent friend, but could never forget that she wasn't free.

That Bank Holiday was to set the pattern for many similar gatherings. Sometimes they all met at Ollie's house, with Florrie taking charge of preparing the food, a task she enjoyed and was proud to do.

The following months saw the friendship be-

tween Patsy and Eddie deepen. Life was good now
and Patsy was happy. They went for walks, they
picnicked by the river, occasionally they went to
Brighton, where Patsy watched, fascinated, as the
sea rolled in. Often Eddie had wanted to take her in
his arms and kiss her. Always he told himself not
yet, Patsy wasn't ready for more than friendship.
They often talked for hours on end. She told him all
about her childhood but only gave sketchy details of
what life had been like with Johnny. How she
wished that she could erase that episode from her
life.

Eddie told her all about his background. He had
been born in the main bedroom above the shop
twenty-three years ago. Because of his withered leg,
his mother would not allow him to attend the local
school, preferring to send him to a private establish-
ment where he had received a good education. Even
so, he had had to endure taunts from the other boys,
who would call him 'gammy leg' or 'club foot'.
Never able to take part in school sports, he had
been somewhat withdrawn, living his life under his
mother's protective wing.

It was from his father that Patsy learned more
intimate details.

'My wife was to be pitied more than blamed,'
Frank Owen had told her. True, she had cosseted
and coddled Eddie, but he stressed it had been a
traumatic experience for her when, at his birth, the
doctor had informed her that their son had a

withered, shortened leg. Mrs Owen's mind had immediately registered 'cripple', despite the fact that he was otherwise a fine, healthy baby. From that moment, she had set out to shield Eddie from the world. Coming to believe her crippled child was a cross she had to bear, she rejected all suggestions that he should be trained for any specialised employment, although academically he was very bright.

Since the death of his mother, Frank Owen told Patsy, Eddie had stretched himself more. He had enrolled at college for several courses and become a frequent visitor to the library.

'My wife was never one for books,' Frank had sadly remarked. 'Being a bookworm never got anyone anywhere,' she had often rebuked Eddie.

One day Eddie confided to Patsy that his greatest ambition had been to become a fine athlete. An impossible dream. However, he was a member of a sports club and Patsy later learned that he trained regularly, with a dedication that was incomprehensible to the other members. Knowing this, Patsy felt she had never met anyone who tried so hard.

By now, Eddie was a regular visitor to number twenty-two. Florrie was content, for the two of them seemed so close and she took pleasure in hearing Patsy constantly laughing. There was no doubt in Ollie's mind, when he saw them together, that they were happy, but he couldn't help having misgivings. What seemed so simple might be impossible. The fact remained that Patsy was already married.

Christmas was drawing near, and on the eighteenth of December Patsy would be eighteen.

'I'll take you to London as a birthday present,' Eddie declared.

The morning was bright and crisp. There had been a sharp frost overnight which had left the pavements with a slippery, silver gleam and their footsteps made a crunching sound as they walked. Patsy was excited. To see places with a special person was to see them with double enjoyment.

First they visited Trafalgar Square. They gazed up one hundred and forty-five feet at Nelson on his column, sat on the edge of the fountains and fed the pigeons, then Patsy looked in awe at the four bronze lions. Through Oxford Circus down to Bond Street they walked. Patsy pressed her face to the shop windows.

'Crikey! Do people really pay these prices?' she wanted to know.

By lunchtime they had arrived at Marble Arch. Watching Patsy's face as she stared in wonderment, Eddie said, 'This archway was originally an entrance to Buckingham Palace.'

'What? I don't understand.'

'It was, truly. It was first erected there in 1828 and twenty-three years later it was removed and brought here to the north entrance of Hyde Park.'

Patsy stared at him in disbelief. 'You're making it up.' It delighted Eddie to watch the different expressions on her face.

'I'm not, it's absolutely true.'

'All right, clever clogs. I'll believe you, though thousands wouldn't,' she said cheekily.

'Have you had your fill of sight-seeing? Because I'm starving!'

'And where are we going to find a café around here?' she asked.

With a mocking bow, Eddie offered her his arm. 'You, miss, are having your birthday lunch at Lyons Corner House.'

Two or three times during their meal Patsy had to draw in her breath to stop herself from saying 'Cor', as waitresses served them course after course. 'I wouldn't like to have to do all this washing up,' was what she did say.

'Well, you haven't got to, so shut up and eat your dinner,' Eddie laughingly answered.

When finally they left the Corner House, Patsy pulled a red woollen hat from her bag. The hat, together with the scarf she wore, had been Queenie's birthday present to her. Pulling the woollen hat down over her ears, she tied the scarf and pulled on her gloves. Looking down at her, Eddie was amused. He thought she looked like an elf and the very sight of her tugged at his heart strings. She was so vulnerable, exposed to life on her own, and he wanted to take care of her. No, it was more than that. At that moment he knew just how much he loved her. He wanted her for his own, to be his wife, never to have to spend a day without being able to see her.

Both of them were exhausted when they eventually entered Flo's kitchen, though neither would have admitted it. Patsy's great green eyes sparkled as she related the events of the day to Florrie, who needed no reassurance that Patsy had had a great time.

'And how about you, lad? You enjoyed yourself, did you?' Eddie didn't answer Florrie. He just smiled a knowing smile and nodded his head towards Patsy who was sitting by the fire, boots off, toasting her toes on the fender. His look said it all. Florrie knew what he was telling her and if he made Patsy happy then that was good enough for her.

They spent Christmas with the Owens. The weather was terrible, with biting, freezing winds blowing on Christmas Day, which was dark and murky. Inside was a cosy scene; the dancing flames from the fire were mirrored in the old furniture while lighted lamps and coloured candles showed up the richness of the drawn brocade curtains. Frank played cards with Ollie, and Florrie was full of admiration for the effort father and son had made to make the room look lovely. A small tree stood on a side-table, shimmering as the light caught it. Every tiny ornament was silver, sparkling against the green of the branches. So simple yet enchanting. The day was filled with gaiety and Patsy felt they were together just like a real family.

The evenings were lighter now and Eddie and Patsy walked arm in arm as usual. They passed courting couples and married people out with their children and Eddie wished with all his heart that he and Patsy might be man and wife, though he had never said so out loud.

It was as if Patsy was reborn. Since she had had Eddie as a constant companion, laughter rippled from her mouth and merriment shone constantly from her huge, green eyes. Life to her now was wonderful. To some, they must have seemed an ill-matched pair – she so short and he so tall and walking awkwardly. It didn't worry Patsy. She didn't care about his leg. If it bothered her at all, it was because of the inconvenience the heavy boot caused him.

One Sunday afternoon in April, Patsy walked to Colliers Wood. She was going to have tea with Eddie and his father. Signs of spring were everywhere. A great many people were about, taking advantage of the sunshine. Even the grass looked greener along the banks of the railway line and the slight wind was refreshing against her face.

Arriving at the shop, two things puzzled her. The shop door was showing a 'Closed' sign and the blinds were drawn down over the plate glass windows. Shops such as Owen's relied heavily on Sunday trade.

The front door at the top of the back staircase stood ajar, which made her even more uneasy. Entering the front room, Patsy took the situation in at a glance. Frank Owen was sunk back in his armchair. He looked ghastly.

'I've sent for the doctor,' Eddie quietly told her.

Patsy pulled up a chair and sat beside Mr Owen. He tried to straighten himself up but fell back, giving Patsy an apologetic look, but at the same time letting her know he was glad to see her. She returned his look with equal tenderness and love, for this man had become very dear to her. He had welcomed her to his home, encouraged her friendship with his son and never once had questioned her past, though she knew he was well aware of the facts. There were so many reasons why Patsy held this man dear to her heart, the main one being that he had given her Eddie.

On arrival at the Infirmary, Frank Owen was barely conscious. Shortly afterwards, he slipped into a coma, from which he never roused, and at six o'clock he died peacefully.

It surprised Patsy how well the funeral was attended but, as Ollie pointed out, Frank Owen had been in business in the district for a great many years.

In reality, the truth didn't hit Eddie until after the

funeral. In Tooting they had seen nothing of him. Patsy couldn't understand why he was staying away. Didn't he want to see her? Didn't he need her any longer? She wanted to go to him, but instead she let a full week pass, and again felt as if her world had fallen apart.

Sunday arrived, and on a sudden impulse Ollie declared they were all going to Colliers Wood.

Eddie was jerked into action when the three of them arrived and Patsy gave him a slow, understanding smile as he did his best to make them welcome.

After having a cup of tea, Florrie gave a curt nod of her head, indicating that Patsy should follow her into the kitchen. As Florrie and Patsy left the front room, Eddie stood up and, resting his hands on the mantelshelf, he stared into the empty grate.

'Hadn't you better start thinking about opening up the shop?' Ollie started the conversation apprehensively. For the first time in their acquaintance, Ollie saw resentment on Eddie's face. 'Tell me to mind my own business if you like, lad, but something has to be decided. The place has been shut up now for a fortnight and it can't be doing the stock much good.' Eddie kept his eyes cast down and made no reply.

Ollie tried again. 'The perishable goods will have to be thrown out. Besides, have you given any thought to the customers? You could end up losing them all.'

'So what?' Eddie's voice was sharp. 'Mostly they only use our shop for odds and ends, anyway.'

Eddie's tone saddened Ollie. The shock of losing his father so suddenly, plus the responsibility of being left a business to run, was weighing heavily on him. Suddenly, he heaved a great sigh and his features seemed to relax. 'Ollie,' he said hesitantly, as if unwilling to burden someone else with his problems.

Ollie leaned forward, placing his hand on Eddie's arm. He felt he had to encourage him to talk. 'Try telling me what your plans are. I don't want to influence you, but if I can help in any way . . .' He didn't finish the sentence, but just sat back and waited.

Eddie heaved another great sigh. 'It's Patsy, really. There are so many obstacles in the way. I love her so much and I want to marry her.' He paused, forcing a smile. 'I know it sounds daft, but I think I've loved Patsy from the moment I set eyes on her in that market yard. She was so different from any other girl I'd ever met. My views haven't changed since I've got to know her better. She is different. She has a kind nature, she's fun to be with, it never seems to bother her that I have a deformity and she never pities me. I can't stand pity.'

Slowly, Eddie lowered himself into a chair. 'If Patsy were to go out of my life now I wouldn't know what to do. I know we can't be married, yet I can't stand the thought of living without her.'

Ollie sat quietly, studying Eddie. He was lost for words. What could he say? The only sound in the room was the ticking of the clock.

Eddie broke the tension. 'When my mother was alive, she had me convinced that I would never marry, that no girl would look at me twice. Then I met Patsy. Meeting her was like a miracle to me. I don't want the shop. I'd rather have a proper job, earn a weekly wage and have Patsy for my wife.'

Thoughtfully, Ollie asked, 'Have you told Patsy all this?'

'No, but I have contacted the Jacksons,' Eddie said bitterly.

Incredulity showed on Ollie's face. 'You've done what?'

'Well, I wrote two letters but never got any reply. Then I hung about the place until I met Johnny Jackson.'

Ollie still couldn't believe what he was hearing.

'I told him how things stood and asked him if he would divorce Patsy.' The embarrassing memory of that meeting came back to Eddie. He couldn't voice the details – not even to Ollie.

'What was his reaction?' Ollie forced himself to ask. Eddie gave a wry smile.

'Violent, to say the least. The whole Jackson clan ganged up on me. Told me I was welcome to Patsy – but no divorce. Then they threw me off their land.'

Ollie nodded. In his mind he could picture exactly

what treatment Eddie had received. 'No need to describe the Jacksons to me, lad. They've been a thorn in my side ever since Patsy took up with them. Incidentally, it's not their land, it belongs to the Coal and Coke Company. Originally, the family settled there as squatters and over the years it's become more trouble than it's worth for the Company to invoke the law and evict them.'

Ollie hesitated. 'You know, Eddie, Patsy was so young and susceptible when she met Johnny, who could blame her? At the time his way of life must have seemed glamorous.'

They were both absorbed in their own thoughts. Ollie took his tobacco pouch and filled the bowl of his pipe, packing down the tobacco tightly before striking a match. Drawing, he had the pipe smoking nicely now. He wondered what the outcome would be. Just how could he help? He wasn't sure.

'Eddie, haven't you got to go to London this week to see your father's solicitor?'

Eddie lifted his head and nodded. 'Yes, why?'

'Well, why not use the opportunity to seek professional advice?'

'What! You mean disclose all the facts about Patsy having been married? Lay all her private life open to a stranger?'

'Well, if you two do want to get married, the truth will have to come out eventually. Talk to Patsy, only she can decide. You know, sometimes the end can justify the means.'

'I'll think about it,' Eddie said huskily. 'Thanks, Ollie, thanks a lot. You really do care for Patsy, don't you?'

'As if she were my own,' Ollie assured him.

Brooding on Ollie's advice improved Eddie's confidence. Best of all, he was with Patsy again. She lay stretched out on the stubbly grass, his coat spread beneath her. The park was crowded most Sundays and today was no exception.

'Come on, let's walk.' Eddie bent over Patsy, pulling her to her feet. Taking her arm, he flung his coat over one shoulder and they began to walk away from the crowds.

Eddie had never seen Patsy look brighter, more relaxed or happier, as if she hadn't a care in the world. She looked lovely in her spring outfit, with her hair tied back with ribbon. Beneath a great leafy tree he drew her to him, bent his head and kissed her. It was a tender, gentle kiss.

'There has never been any other girl in my life. Only you, Patsy, I love you.'

'I love you, too, Eddie.'

He looked pleased, but surprised she had actually said the words out loud.

'I know we can't get married, but we can't go on living apart. I want you for my wife, for us to have a family.'

Patsy moved away from him. 'Eddie, you know we can't.'

He stared at her calm face. 'You don't mean that, Patsy. There has to be a way. We will get married.'

It was as if she had not heard him. 'I am already married,' she whispered.

He reached out roughly, jerking her round to face him.

'You've just said you love me,' she protested.

'I do. I want to be with you, all the time, every day.'

She sighed deeply. 'Just to spite me, Johnny will never divorce me.'

She had known for a long time that Eddie loved her. It was in his every action. How could she tell him how she felt? Without him now, no day would have any meaning.

Eddie pulled her to him. His lips covered hers, demanding now, forcing hers apart and there was an answering yearning from Patsy. Time stood still. Their arms were entwined, their longing for each other obvious in every movement.

Reluctantly, Patsy pulled away.

'Now say you will marry me.' Eddie's voice was pleading and deadly serious.

'We will have to wait a while.'

'Oh, no, we won't,' he told her convincingly. 'I don't intend to wait any longer for you, my love. You are coming to the solicitor's with me and we'll see what he has to say.'

Patsy floated on air. Her problems no longer seemed insoluble. Her Eddie, with his charming smile and winning ways, had come right out with it. He loved her. He wanted her to be his wife.

That night, when Patsy went in to say goodnight, Florrie needed no telling that things had come to a head. Patsy smiled at her in a sweet, slow way and her eyes glowed with an inner light.

Alone, Florrie felt her lower lip tremble and angry tears sting her eyes. When she got into bed, she lay for a long time thinking of Patsy, unable to sleep. She deserved happiness so much. Please God, let things work out well for her this time.

Through the window, Patsy could see the Houses of Parliament. Big Ben had already chimed three strokes, making her aware that Eddie had been closeted in the solicitor's office for half an hour. The waiting-room in which she sat was sparsely furnished with just a few straight-backed chairs and a table which held back numbers of magazines. Her intention to remain calm was fast receding.

At last, the connecting door opened. 'Come in please, Mrs Jackson.' The voice was deep, but kindly. 'I'm Mr Topple,' he said holding out his hand. 'I'm sure we shall get along fine. That's right, you take the chair next to Edward.'

Mr Topple was scarcely older than Eddie, but in appearance he was every inch Patsy's idea of a professional man: dressed in a sober dark suit, his brown hair closely cropped and on the bridge of his nose sat pince-nez spectacles.

'Now, Mrs Jackson, this is purely an informal discussion. I hope you will trust me to give you good advice and not to lead you astray.' He was teasing her, and Patsy relaxed, cheered up and smiled at him. 'No doubt you are aware that I recently acted for Edward's parents, and my father took care of their affairs over a long period of time.' He paused and cleared his throat. 'I have known Edward since we were boys. I shall do everything I can to sort out his problems.'

Patsy felt her face flush and her heart lurched; she was probably Eddie's biggest problem.

Mr Topple studied Patsy's face and then took the bull by the horns. 'Divorce for you, Mrs Jackson, would be the obvious answer. Unfortunately, as the law stands, that could prove to be very difficult. Unless of course, you are very rich. Very few working-class women have been known to bring a petition.'

Seeing the puzzled expression of woe on Patsy's face, Mr Topple leaned across his desk and again smiled kindly at her.

'Oh, yes, you may not want to believe it but the law can work entirely differently for the rich. Unfair, but true, I assure you. There was a time when the church courts dealt with all matrimonial matters, and those who wanted a divorce had to obtain a special Act of Parliament. The law has been changed slightly to allow a husband to obtain a divorce through the law courts but only on the grounds of his wife's adultery. A few society ladies have been known to engage a barrister to plead their case to the church courts, but even then the law allows only the one ground on which she may do so – and, again, that is adultery.'

Mr Topple removed his glasses and Patsy's eyes fixed on the sore mark across his nose made by the spring clip. Then she sighed, leaned back in her chair and closed her eyes. 'It's useless, isn't it?' She sounded exhausted. Dreading the answer, it took a lot of courage for her to ask her next question. 'I'll never get a divorce will I? Not this year, next year, not ever.' She opened her eyes and now her voice was bitter.

'My husband left me, Mr Topple. He never wanted me, he never provided for me and he was cruel, yet unless he wishes it I have to stay tied to him for the rest of my life. That's what you are telling me isn't it?'

Now it was Mr Topple's turn to sigh. 'I wish I could say it wasn't. But truthfully I can't.'

A long silence followed, until Eddie said: 'How about the money left to me by my father?'

Mr Topple shook his head. 'It wouldn't be enough. Barristers' fees alone would swallow it up.' Turning to Patsy, he spoke quietly. 'In your husband's case, could you prove adultery?'

Just as softly, Patsy answered, 'No.'

Mr Topple pulled himself to his feet, drew in a deep breath, and looked at them both. 'Here's what

I want you to do. Give me a few days to ponder on this matter and to take further advice. Meanwhile, try not to worry. The question of Mrs Jackson's divorce has not been dismissed out of hand. For the moment, let's just say it has been left in abeyance.'

Patsy considered this. Her face was serious. She was confused, but wished with all her heart that she could believe this kind man might still be able to perform what to her would be a miracle. She reached across to where Eddie sat and he took her hand between both of his and held it tight.

'However, there is something more pressing that has to be dealt with.' Mr Topple's voice was business-like now. 'This only concerns you, Edward.'

Patsy made to rise. Thrusting out his arm, Eddie checked her. 'Stay, Patsy, please.' His eyes sought those of his old friend who was now his adviser. 'All my future plans include Patsy. What is my business is also hers. I would like her to stay.'

'In that case, you should consider reopening your late father's shop with her help.'

They each showed different reactions to this bombshell. Eddie's face glowed with enthusiasm while Patsy's eyes showed doubt.

Mr Topple glanced from one to the other. 'If, at a later date, you decide to sell the property, which is entirely freehold, the market value would be greatly increased were the business to be functioning. On the other hand, should you be so unwise as to leave the premises lying idle, the property would deteriorate, thereby diminishing in value. In other words, there would be no goodwill to sell. If you both decided to reopen the business, it could add considerably to your resources.'

They walked along the embankment, each lost in thought. Warning bells were ringing in Patsy's head. Yes, she wanted to cry out . . . She couldn't bring herself to put the rest of her thoughts into words.

'Patsy,' the serious tone of Eddie's voice made her look up. 'Besides the business, my dad left me more than two thousand pounds. I'd give every penny of it to make you free so that we could be married.' He moaned and murmured, 'Oh, Patsy . . . Would you . . . Will you consider . . .' He couldn't seem to say the words outright.

'Edward Owen, you don't know what you are letting yourself in for.' With an exaggerated attempt at flippancy, she added, 'I haven't got red glints in my hair for nothing. From now on you are saddled with me!'

Eddie's eyes widened and his mouth opened, though no sound came from his lips. For a moment he stared at her in disbelief.

'Are you saying what I think you are?'

Patsy laughed merrily. 'Well, one of us had to come out with it. You've been beating about the bush long enough.'

'Honestly? You mean it? You will come and live with me?'

Shyly now, Patsy hung her head and very quietly said, 'Yes, I will if you want me to.'

Suddenly, his arms were around her, holding her close. She heard Eddie make a sound like a sob, which he tried to stifle. They just stood there, clinging to each other.

When at last Patsy drew back her eyes were glistening brightly. Eddie lowered his head and his words came firmly. 'One day you *will* be my wife. I'll take an oath on that. Until then, we'll face the consequences together.'

Chapter Ten

EVERYTHING WAS SETTLED, though not to everyone's satisfaction.

'Gawd help you,' was Gran's only comment.

'Hope you're not taking on more than you can chew,' Blower said thoughtfully.

Patsy's emotions had been mixed until the final day arrived. Now she watched Eddie carry her cases up the steps, dragging his foot clumsily. Inside, almost shyly, she closed the door and stood with her back against it. No more doubts. This was her home now. She and Eddie would live here as man and wife. The past was over and done with and she wasn't going to let it ruin her future.

Like newly-weds they got ready for bed. Eddie watched Patsy undress and he could hardly believe she was actually here beside him in the bedroom. He resolved to make her so happy she would never have any regrets.

What a wonderful way to wake up. The sunshine was streaming in through a chink in the curtains and Patsy was smiling as she made a sudden effort to sit up, but Eddie threw his arms out of the bedclothes and drew her back down into the double bed.

Patsy's small shape melted into his big arms as she lay cuddled up against him. His arms tightened about her body and she smiled again, only this time it was a long, slow, womanly smile. Eddie chuckled and ran his fingers up and down her spine and then slowly drew her naked body close to his. There was no shyness between them now. She had never imagined that sex could be so wonderful, never thought it could arouse such emotion within her.

Much later, she in her red dressing-gown, Eddie in pyjamas, they had breakfast.

'God, it's great to see you so happy,' Eddie told her. Happy! She was in her seventh heaven.

The following morning, promptly at nine o'clock, Florrie arrived. She removed her hat and coat, donned her floral overall and took charge. Around Patsy's waist, Florrie pinned a coarse sack. Eddie was ordered to wear a khaki-coloured dust coat.

Between the three of them, wonders were performed. Shelves were scrubbed and cupboards cleaned out, all in accordance with Flo's commands.

'Put some elbow grease into it, go on, I want to be able to see my face in that counter. Throw those packets out, they're damp. Clean the inside of those windows.' Talk about a forewoman! Florrie never let them rest, urging them, laughing with them, as they all worked side by side. The end result was well worth while. The windows sparkled, the counter gleamed and Florrie announced, 'Good. Anyone could eat their dinner off of that floor.'

Upstairs, Patsy went through to the kitchen to prepare a meal, while Florrie sank down gratefully into an armchair. She wouldn't admit it, not to save her life, but her knees were aching like mad.

Eddie put his hand on her shoulder. 'Thanks, Florrie.' It was said with intense feeling. Then he again said, 'Thanks, Flo . . . for everything.' He emphasised the words by pressing his fingers into her flesh.

'Get away! Don't try your charm on me, but I could murder a cuppa. Surely to Christ you know how to brew a pot of tea, don't you?'

Each knew what the other was thinking. Eddie wasn't just saying thanks for her working today. He was telling her he was grateful that she hadn't made a fuss over Patsy coming to live with him.

The atmosphere was nice and easy as they ate their meal. Florrie, aware of their intimate glances, banged the table. 'Do you only get one cup of tea around here?'

'For God's sake, fill her cup up, Patsy, or we shall never hear the last of it,' Eddie said, grinning broadly.

Later, Florrie put her feet up on a stool. Eddie sat in the big armchair and Patsy was on the floor, her back resting between Eddie's knees. Florrie began to snore gently. Tilting her head up, Patsy smiled impishly at Eddie and the look on her face said it all. It had been a good day, a good beginning and tomorrow they would open up the shop for business.

'I'll manage very well, stop worrying and get yourself off,' Patsy firmly told Eddie as he made out the list of goods they needed from the warehouse. Waving him off from the top of the steps, Patsy told herself how lucky she was to have found such a man. To walk straight into a home like this, furnished with such good pieces chosen by Mr and Mrs Owen over the years. She didn't even want to rearrange much, everything was perfect. She washed the breakfast dishes, made the bed and dusted the living-room, humming all the while.

Sharp at nine o'clock she turned the swinging card to show 'Open'. She didn't know how she got through the morning, so many customers came into the shop. Some gave her a cheery 'Hello', others quizzed her, showing undisguised curiosity. When Eddie stepped through the door at lunchtime she was bubbling over; she couldn't wait to tell him how many customers she had served.

When they closed the shop, Patsy cooked their first proper dinner. It was a merry meal and they toasted each other: 'To the first of many.' Afterwards, Patsy lay on the floor, her young body stretched out. Eddie reached down and laid his hands on her long hair, which now hung loose over her shoulders. His heart was bursting with love and pride.

This blissful state lasted a week before the neighbourhood was buzzing with the news that Eddie Owen had brought a girl to live with him over the shop.

It wasn't unheard of for a man to live with a woman without marriage, but it was rare. The most popular opinion was that this hussy had seized her chance and cottoned on to the cripple because he'd got money.

Patsy's first reaction to the gossip was to ignore it. It was only what she had half-expected. Many times she was on the verge of losing her temper. When one customer boldly asked ' . . . and when are you and Mr Owen thinking of getting married? Set the date yet, have you?' Patsy had to bite back her retort, which would have been, 'Mind your own business.'

The gossips had a field day and rumours ran riot.

'She has an 'usband already.'

'She's left her old man in the lurch, took up with Owen for what she can get.'

Even though these women made a pretence of whispering, Patsy heard every word – as they intended she should.

Then came the first confrontation.

'I'll not be served by 'er!' a middle-aged woman snorted. The colour flooded up into Patsy's cheeks.

Moving aside, she bent low, making a pretence of stacking tins beneath the counter.

Eddie looked at the woman and he was filled with helpless, blind rage.

'Maybe you'd like to take your custom else-where.' There was a silence. Eddie was tempted to throw her out of the shop.

'Why should I?' the woman snapped. 'I've been coming here for years. Both your dad and mum, when they were alive, were glad enough to serve me.'

With great difficulty, Eddie held his temper in check. Several customers were waiting to be served and all seemed to be holding their breath. How would young Owen handle this? Forcing himself to remain calm, Eddie said, 'I will also be very glad to serve you, providing you show respect to my wife.'

'Yeah, give her a chance. She ain't done you no harm,' one sympathetic voice called.

'You can give her all the chances you like, but she ain't gonna get an inch from me, 'cos the point is she is not his wife. Already got one 'usband, she has. Bloody gold-digger.'

'That's enough.' Eddie's voice rapped out like a shot from a gun. 'If you're not out of here in two minutes, I'll throw you out.' Turning impatiently to the other customers, he told them rudely: 'And that goes for any of you that feel the same way.'

'All right, I'm going, but I'll tell you this. I wouldn't buy my cat food in here from now on.'

With that, she slammed the door shut, narrowly missing Eddie's fingers.

'Take no notice of her. She's a spiteful bitch.'

'Jealous, that's her trouble.'

The other customers smiled at Patsy and pretended sympathy, but all the while they were waiting for the next turn of events. The incident upset Eddie badly. This wasn't what he had brought Patsy here for. His aim had been to surround her with love, care and respect. These women, with their acid tongues and biting sarcasm, professed to have such strict moral codes but, suspected Eddie, in their private lives they were no better than anyone else.

Most days were good and the nights were fantastic. Sex was an expression of their love and even just lying in Eddie's arms was magic. Patsy sometimes felt it was a dream, too good to be true. What did it matter if she wasn't legally married? In everything but name she and Eddie *were* man and wife; at least that was what she kept telling herself.

Danny called in daily. 'How's my chirpy sparrow?' he would call, going through to the yard to talk to Eddie. Queenie came, bringing her boys, and Eddie gave them sweets and lemonade from the shop. Some Sundays, Ollie and Florrie came for the day and Patsy would show off, making special dinners and light, fluffy sweets. On other Sundays, after they had shut the shop, they went 'home' to Florrie, where they ate traditional roast dinners, followed by treacle pudding served with a great jug of custard. Patsy now felt it was like having a real family of her own.

Some customers still persisted in making snide remarks, though only after making sure that Eddie was out of earshot. One morning, alone in the shop, Patsy sighed as she saw Mrs Colbourn and Mrs Whitehead coming in together. These were two customers she dreaded having to serve. They were a smarmy pair and crafty with it.

'Half a pound of tea, half a pound of butter and a nice big piece of cheese, please, me ducks,' Mrs Colbourn said, a smile on her face which spread from ear to ear.

Something alerted Patsy. She cut and weighed the cheese, wrote the price on a slip of paper then added the cost of the tea and butter, before placing them on the counter.

'That will be one and ninepence please, Mrs Colbourn.'

'All right, love, just put it on the slate,' Mrs Colbourn said, reaching for the cheese. 'I'll settle up with your husband later on.'

The reference to Eddie being her husband had been deliberate, and had brought a guffaw of amusement from Mrs Whitehead. Their game was so obvious. Patsy's hand shot out, covering the cheese.

'I'm sorry, Mrs Colbourn, we don't keep a slate.' She couldn't resist adding, 'Of course, you could come back when my husband is here. Maybe he will allow you credit.'

'Why, you bleeding bitch!' Mrs Colbourn stepped back, her mouth agape. She hadn't expected this slip of a girl to see through their ploy, and be sarcastic into the bargain!

Thick and throaty, both women yelled abuse at her. Patsy had stood enough. This time she decided to give as good as she got. White-faced and trembling with temper she let go.

'You two must think I was born yesterday. You thought you would try it on with me, didn't you? Well, it hasn't worked. Go on, get out and next time try the Co-op. See if they'll put it on the slate for you.'

Patsy couldn't fathom the expression on Eddie's face after she had given him an account of the happenings. First, he covered his mouth with his hand and took a couple of deep breaths before saying anything. Even so, his words came out mixed with a kind of stuttering laugh.

'Oh, Patsy, I underestimated you . . . and they certainly don't know you round here! Tried to come the old soldier, did they?' He collapsed against the counter, no longer able to hold back his laughter. He wished he could have seen his Patsy having a go. Patsy watched in amazement as he doubled up. His laughter was infectious and she had to join in. They were both mad, clinging to each other, laughing fit to burst.

*

There was one occurrence Patsy kept entirely to herself.

In the butcher's one morning she had been shocked when a mere lad of ten or eleven had boldly told her, 'My Dad says you're a whore 'cos you ain't married to Mr Owen.' She had bought chops for their dinner, not caring much whether they were fat or not, just glad to get out of the shop. Walking back, the same boy and two younger lads were swinging from ropes tied to the lamppost. As she passed they began to chant in unison, 'To bed, to bed, but not to wed. Eddie Owen's not right in the head.'

What chance did she stand against this lot?

She pulled herself up straight and held her head high. She wouldn't let them beat her. She was happier now than she could ever remember, and bigots weren't going to drive her away.

'Christ almighty!' This profane exclamation from Eddie made Patsy jump. Still seated at the breakfast table, Eddie held out the letter he had just read. The outside of the envelope had been franked 'Topple, Topple and Bradshaw', so Patsy knew it was from the solicitors.

'Read it. Go on, read it.' For the first time since Patsy had known him, Eddie was shouting at her, his face showing anger. Hesitantly, Patsy reached for the sheet of notepaper. Eddie drew it back. 'I'll read you the gist of it.' His eyes scanned quickly over the typed words. 'Here it is.' Pausing, he raised his head and looked at Patsy. 'Sorry I blew my top, Patsy, but listen to this. "We have approached Mr Jackson with the view to his wife obtaining a divorce. He is unwilling to co-operate . . . blah blah . . . there is no feasible way Mrs Jackson may bring her own petition . . . we have pursued this matter through all the legal channels . . . furthermore, as matters stand, we envisage it may be years before the law is amended." ' He tossed the letter down on to the table. 'For God's sake, when?' he shouted.

'Eddie, why get yourself so worked up?' Patsy asked, trying to appear unruffled. 'You didn't expect Johnny to agree, did you? I'd have been surprised if he had.'

'I know, I know all that, but . . .' he stammered.

'But what?' Suddenly she was afraid.

'You might want to call it a day. The customers' snide remarks, the frustration. I wouldn't blame you.'

'Now you listen to me, Eddie Owen.' Patsy banged the table so hard the cups rattled in their saucers. 'I'm here because I want to be with you. I love you. How many more times do I have to tell you?' Facetiously, she added, 'Besides, I like being able to have hot baths.'

'Patsy, oh, Patsy. Was there ever anyone like you? Come here.' Drawing her within his arms, he held her gently, his lips against the top of her head.

Minutes passed before he told her, 'Mr Topple wants to see us a week today. Ten a.m., in his office.'

'What for?'

'Well, we won't know that until we get there, will we?'

This time Patsy had to sit for only fifteen minutes in the bare waiting-room before an extremely smart young lady came to tell her, 'Mr Topple would like you to go in now, please, Mrs Jackson.' Beneath a smart tailored jacket the young lady wore the new-length hobble skirt. She looked very sophisticated and Patsy couldn't help wondering whether it was education or breeding that enabled one to obtain employment in a lawyer's office. Probably a bit of both, she decided.

Mr Topple leaned across his desk and held out a firm hand in greeting. 'May I call you Patsy, as Edward does? "Mrs Jackson" doesn't seem appropriate in the circumstances, does it?' The colour mounted in Patsy's cheeks. *He knows we're living together. Oh, well, he had to know some time.*

'Why, yes, of course,' she answered.

'Sit yourself down then, Patsy. I think I may have come up with a solution that at least goes half-way to solving your problem.' He stopped briefly. 'Someone else has had an idea.' He gestured towards Eddie, who swallowed and looked away self-consciously. 'One, I might add, of which I heartily approve.'

Patsy felt she had been right. Mr Topple was a kind, understanding man, but the thought of Eddie having an idea which he hadn't divulged to her niggled a bit.

'How would you feel about changing your surname?' Mr Topple's raised hand stopped Patsy from protesting. 'I know. I understand this is a delicate matter. But whereas divorce seems out of the question, there is no earthly reason why you should not take Owen as your surname.'

Patsy sat back in her chair, leaning against the side arm in order to look directly at Eddie. He nodded his head and smiled at her. She was getting irritated. Oh, it was easy enough to sit here and talk about a change of name, but that wouldn't make the slightest bit of difference. She might just as well call herself the Queen of Sheba. The neighbours would still know her as Patsy Jackson, married to one man and living in sin with another.

Mr Topple tapped his desk with his fingers. 'By deed poll,' he said.

'Sorry?' Patsy hadn't been listening.

Slowly and deliberately, Mr Topple explained. 'A deed poll is the most formal method of legalising the change of one surname and in practice is the method most commonly used. If you wish, I will prepare a formal deed which you will be required to sign, once in the name of Jackson and then in what will be the name you intend to use henceforth. However, the signing will have to take place before a solicitor from another firm. You may safely leave the matter in my hands.'

Obviously, he expected some comment from Patsy, but when none was forthcoming he rose from his seat. 'Well, that's about as far as we can take matters this morning.'

Patsy assumed they were free to go. She shot a look at Eddie, who was putting a hand nervously through his thick, dark hair. At the door, Mr Topple took Patsy's hand between his own and said, 'Don't look so worried, my dear. When Edward has outlined his plans to you, you may view the future more optimistically.'

They passed several men, wearing long black gowns, with grey pigtailed wigs on their heads. She assumed they were barristers returning to their rooms after having appeared in court. She longed to ask Eddie why his father had dealt with a London solicitor rather than one nearer home, but she wasn't going to be the first to speak. Eddie owed her an explanation, she told herself peevishly.

The sun was shining on the broad, slow-moving Thames and gilding the great dome of St Paul's Cathedral in the distance. Patsy stopped to remove her jacket, folding it carefully before placing it over her arm. This lovely August day was turning out to be a scorcher.

'Are you hungry?' Eddie had broken the silence.

'A bit,' she sullenly answered.

'Don't say it like that. We only had toast before we left. You must at least want a cup of coffee.'

Patsy couldn't hold out any longer and she half-smiled. 'My throat's parched, but you know coffee always makes me more thirsty. I'd rather have tea any time.'

'Well, come on, then.' He held out his hand and they grinned at each other.

'Eddie. What did Mr Topple mean?' She couldn't hide her curiosity any longer.

'Not now. Later,' he told her and his face warned her to leave the subject alone for the time being. Eddie hailed a passing taxi.

'Where to, mate?' the driver asked.

'Covent Garden Market, please,' Eddie told the driver before getting into the back with Patsy.

She allowed herself a wry smile. This was the life, riding around London in a cab. All too soon the taxi drew to a halt, and the driver was asking for his fare.

While Eddie was paying him, Patsy stood gazing. What a sight! Used as she was to working on Tooting Market, what she saw still astonished her. There were porters with boxes balanced high on their heads, barrows each so heavily loaded they didn't seem safe, more crates of fruit and vegetables than she had ever seen in her life and men bawling orders from all directions.

'Why have we come here?' Patsy asked as Eddie came to her side.

'Best breakfast in all London,' he said with an odd note in his voice.

Patsy gasped as she entered the café. The brilliant sunshine that poured in through the open doorway combined with the steam from the urns and the heat from the kitchen beyond to make the place stifling. Almost immediately a woman came from behind the counter, gave a delighted shriek and wrapped her arms around Eddie. Patsy couldn't hide her surprise as she watched Eddie bend his head and plant a kiss on her cheek. As they drew apart, the woman half-turned and, taking in all the occupants seated at the tables, she waved an arm calling loudly: 'Look who's here, lads.'

Great bursts of laughter accompanied warm greetings.

'How are you, mate?'

'Eddie! Long time, no see.'

One man, whose stomach rested on the edge of the table, struggled to his feet and held out his hand. 'By God, Eddie, I'm glad to see you. Why have you been such a bloody stranger?'

Eddie put his arm across the fat man's shoulders and very emotionally said, 'It's great to see you, Joe.'

Patsy felt strangely alone, sitting at a table while Eddie did the rounds, shaking hands, slapping backs.

'I'm Mary.' The woman who had embraced Eddie wiped the surface of the table and placed a condiment set in the centre. 'No need to look so down in the mouth, love. I've known Eddie since he was a nipper. His mum and dad were nice people and I'll tell you something else, you've got yourself a good bloke there.' The woman looked common, her cheeks well rouged and her hair dyed a bright shade of ginger, yet Patsy smiled at her. She couldn't help herself, for Mary's nature was so warm and friendly.

'How is it everyone here seems to know you?' Patsy asked as Eddie sat down next to her.

Eddie looked uncomfortable. 'I used to work here.' Patsy gravely considered his admission. It wasn't a crime, was it, to work on a market? Yet Eddie had dragged it out as if it were a skeleton in the cupboard.

'What, on the stalls?' she asked.

'No, over there in the wholesale warehouses. I used to be in the accounts office.'

'Didn't you like the job?'

'Oh, yes, I did, very much so.'

'Well then, did you leave, or what?'

'I left.'

'Why, for heaven's sake, if you liked it so much?' He lowered his head and Patsy only just caught the two words he mumbled: 'My mother.'

Patsy kept silent and wondered what was coming next. Rather self-consciously, Eddie added, 'She meant well, she just thought the travelling was too much for me.' Patsy was dismayed as she saw the hurt in his eyes, but was saved from making any answer as Mary, setting plates down in front of them, said, 'Here you are, my dears, get that inside you.'

Thick slices of bacon, fried bread topped with tomatoes, two eggs and two sausages. 'Blimey!' The word jumped from Patsy's mouth and Eddie gave her a subdued grin.

There was an awkward silence between them as they ate. There was so much Eddie wanted to say, but he couldn't. To Patsy, it seemed as if Eddie was miles away, shutting her out for the first time since they'd known each other.

'I'm pregnant!' If she had wanted to drop a bombshell, well, she had succeeded. Eddie's head came up with a jerk. His large, dark eyes, protected by those long, thick lashes, seemed to glisten with tears, but she couldn't be sure, because he had turned his head away.

Before she could say more he asked, 'Have you ever been to Kew Gardens?'

His question surprised her so much that she turned away so that he shouldn't see the disappointment in her face. She couldn't reply. He had said nothing about the baby. Was he pleased or annoyed? She couldn't even make a guess.

This time, Patsy was included in Mary's hugs and kisses as they made to leave the café. Ribald remarks and flowery language were jokingly called after them as the porters saw them off.

In the Strand, Eddie hailed another cab. 'Botanic Gardens, Kew, please.' The taxi weaved in and out of the traffic to the Surrey side of the Thames, making for Richmond.

Patsy was always to remember her first sight of Kew Gardens.

'Oh, isn't it beautiful?' she exclaimed. The scent of flowers was everywhere as they walked past splendid displays. They lingered in the aviaries and gazed in wonder at a Chinese pavilion set in the middle of an ornamental pond.

'This has got to be my favourite,' Patsy declared, sniffing the perfume the blooms gave off here in the rose garden where they now stood.

Much later, they came to what Eddie told her was a gazebo. To Patsy it was a place where she could sit down and admire the view.

After what seemed an age, Eddie took her hand. 'I told Mr Topple I was considering emigration – to Australia, probably.'

Patsy felt herself go numb with shock. It was as if the ground had been knocked from under her feet. The thought of him going off to another country, leaving her. No. They were going to spend the rest of their lives together, that's what he had told her, over and over again.

'Darling, let me finish. You've jumped to all the wrong conclusions.' The concern was there in his voice. To Eddie, the look on Patsy's face had made it obvious what she was thinking. 'I didn't mean *me* go to Australia. I meant *us*.'

Relief flooded through her, yet doubts crowded her mind. He took hold of her with such force that she fell against him. He put his arms about her and brought her head against his chest.

'Patsy, oh, Patsy,' he said with sorrow. 'I can't for the life of me seem able to get you to trust me. What can I say? Whether you believe me or not, from the day you came to live with me you became my wife. Not just until it suited either of us, but for life. All right, we can't have a marriage certificate, but to me that doesn't make the slightest difference. As God is my judge, I regard us as married. Everything we have is ours. Everything we do, we do together. To me, you are my wife and as soon as we can change your name you will be known as Mrs Owen.'

It was the longest speech she had ever heard him make and she was so moved she wanted to bawl her eyes out. With a smile now he said, 'I must say, I never thought of a deed poll. We have Mr Topple to thank for that.'

Patsy had not yet been able to grasp all the implications and Eddie's only anxiety now was that she might start to worry.

'I'm sorry, Patsy, to have sprung it on you like this. I didn't want to say anything before because I didn't know if it would be possible. I still don't. There's the question of passports, whether the

Foreign Office will grant them, but at least I've made tentative enquiries. Now we shall have to wait and see what answers Mr Topple comes up with.'

Patsy sighed. 'Well, you've obviously been giving it a lot of thought. But why? Is it because of me and all the gossip?' Eddie was aware of Patsy's intense look.

'Yes, in a way that has something to do with it, but mainly it's for us. In a new country you'd be Mrs Owen, no one would be any wiser as to whether we were legally married or not.'

He paused and a deep chuckle came from his throat. 'Australia might be a good place for my son to be born and brought up in.'

Patsy flung herself at him, her fists pounding his chest. 'You beast,' she cried, but the overwhelming joy on his face was very apparent. 'You are pleased, aren't you?' Her voice still sounded uncertain.

'Pleased,' he said. 'I'm over the moon.'

Now they both started laughing. Eddie stood up, put his arms around her waist and raised her up until her face was level with his.

'Put me down,' she yelled. 'It's not fair, you're so much taller than me.' Still grinning, he lowered her to the ground and ruffled her hair.

'Yeah, but you're prettier than I am. In fact, Mrs Owen, you are beautiful.'

Things were bound to work out for the best. Eddie had a way of making her feel beautiful and all nice inside.

Chapter Eleven

IT WAS JUST six-thirty when they walked past the Red Lion in Colliers Wood. The evening was warm and men were grouped together on the pavement, enjoying an early pint. Eddie and Patsy were almost past when a voice hailed them.

'Eddie, where have you been? There's been a right old schemozzle down at your place.' Men nodded their heads in agreement. 'Someone called the police.'

Patsy's hold on Eddie's arm tightened, the colour draining from her face. Quickening their steps, they hurried across the green and turned the corner. The largest of the shop windows had been smashed and fragments of glass were all over the pavement as well as covering the inside. The shop door was ajar, but before entering they had to step over an enamel bucket which lay on its side on the step. Inside, the floor was swimming with water. A short, wiry man poked his head in at them.

'Round the back, the copper's round the back,' he told them.

A few women were loitering in the lane. With a triumphant grin one called out, 'They've got your mum down at the station.'

Patsy's face showed her bewilderment. Another pushed her face close to Patsy. Her lips curled up, she growled, 'It's all your fault. If it wasn't for you there wouldn't have been none of this bother.'

'What? I don't know what you're on about. I wasn't even here,' Patsy angrily shouted back.

'Get away with you, now come on, let my . . . wife pass.' Anger was throttling the words in Eddie's throat, but the women had sensed his hesitation.

'That's just it,' the ringleader cried. 'She ain't your wife. Her 'usband came looking for her, and what did he get? Dirty water thrown all over him, that's what.'

Eddie practically pushed the women aside, guiding Patsy in front of him up the steps.

'Evening sir,' a policeman greeted them as they entered the living-room. Patsy made for a chair and sank down into it, gripping her hands tightly together.

'Do you want to go and lie down while I try and sort this out?' Eddie's voice was heavy with anger, but the pressure of his fingers on her shoulder let her know it was not directed at her.

'No, no, of course not. I'm all right, but what did that woman mean about my mum being taken to the station?'

'That'd be Mrs Holmes, I expect, ma'am,' the officer chipped in.

Eddie made an impatient gesture. 'Go on, go on. What about Mrs Holmes?'

'Well, sir, she was taken into custody more for her own good, like. She wanted to take on the whole street it seems. Wasn't satisfied at having a go at the Jacksons.'

'Oh, my God.' Patsy sat up straight in the chair, but Eddie, in spite of everything, had to suppress a smile. He could well imagine Florrie doing battle!

'I was told to remain here because the shop is wide open,' the policeman said, looking very ill at ease, and Eddie guessed he had no right to be up here in their living-room.

'What exactly happened?' Eddie asked.

'Well,' the policeman cleared his throat, 'it was mostly over when we arrived. The Jacksons had scarpered by then. Seems Mrs Holmes was doing a bit of cleaning when one of the Jacksons demanded to see his . . . erm . . . wife.' He covered his mouth with his hand for a moment, as if to cover his embarrassment.

'Then what?' Eddie's patience was growing thin.

'Seems the lady wasn't believed when she told him neither of you was in. One word led to another. She threw a bucket of water over them and they threw a brick through your window.'

'Have you charged Mrs Holmes with any offence?' Eddie asked.

'I wouldn't know, sir. You can find out more at the station.'

'We'll be along as soon as I've seen to the shop.'

'Right, sir. I'll be on my way, then.'

Crouching, Eddie took hold of Patsy's hand. 'I'll be as quick as I can, love. Why don't you put the kettle on? We could both do with a cup of tea.'

Tom Rider stood in his doorway. 'Saw you coming, Eddie. Everything all right, mate?'

'Mate' was a good term between these two, for that's exactly what they were. Moving aside, Tom asked, 'Aren't you coming in?'

'I won't, Tom, if you don't mind. We have to get to the police station to find out what's happening to Mrs Holmes.'

'That's the stout lady that was at your place, is it?'

'Yes, she helped to bring Patsy up.'

'Well, I'll tell you this much. She's got guts, that woman has. Me and my missus was going to butt in when them buggers were having a go at her, but she didn't need no help. I'll tell you another thing, if we ever have another war, you'd better be glad she's on our side!'

They both laughed. Eddie again pictured the skirmish. 'Would you make the shop window secure for me, Tom?'

'No problem. I was going to come along anyway, as soon as I'd finished me tea.'

'Thanks, Tom. I'll away and sweep up the glass.'

'Leave the glass, Ed. There's a few that will help me to clear up. You want to remember, mate, not everyone around here is against you. There will be gossiping old bitches wherever you go. Sod 'em, I say. Get on with your life and don't let them worry you.'

Eddie handed over the keys and then shook Tom's hand.

'Go on, mate,' Tom said, pushing Eddie towards the gate. 'I'll lock up and the keys will be here when you get back.'

It was cool inside the police station and Patsy shivered as if someone had walked over her grave.

'May we see Mrs Holmes, please?' Eddie asked the desk sergeant, who gave a deep chuckle before saying, 'You most certainly may.'

Both Eddie and Patsy had half-expected to find Florrie locked up in a cell. Instead, when a young constable opened a door and said, 'Here we are,' they were both dumbfounded. It was the station canteen with policemen everywhere, eating and drinking, playing darts, while Florrie, seated at a table, was fooling around with a pack of cards.

She greeted them loudly, telling the room at large, 'Here they are! I told you they'd come for me, didn't I?'

Patsy ran across the room and flung herself at Florrie, hugging and kissing her. Patsy could hardly believe it, but there wasn't a mark on Florrie, thank God.

'Are you all right?' There was a note of relief in Eddie's voice as he asked.

'Course I am, son,' she assured him, but Eddie thought he detected a tell-tale sob in Florrie's voice. He drew nearer and gently kissed her cheek.

With an exasperated movement of her arm, she all but knocked him sideways. 'Oh, get on with yer,' she cried, blushing madly. 'Go and see someone about getting me out of here. Been here long enough, I have.'

The police sent them home in a Black Maria.

'By God, news travels fast,' said Flo. All the Day family had gathered into Gran's house, concern showing on their faces. Danny came over to where Florrie was sitting.

'Here, drink this,' he ordered. She took several slow sips of the whisky and it cetainly seemed to have a quick effect on her.

'Shut up. Now listen, all of you,' she said, 'and I'll tell you all about it.'

Everyone in the room was angry when Florrie had finished her stormy version of what had happened.

'We'll go over to Mitcham mob-handed,' was Danny's hasty decision.

'Yeah, we'll have our day now,' Blower declared.

'No you bloody well won't,' argued Ollie. This surprised them all and they looked at him questioningly.

'It won't do any good to start a full-scale war. There are other ways of dealing with the Jacksons. It's easy to see what they're after. Patsy is happy, doing well for herself – and that is what's annoying them. Well, believe you me, their day will come. I personally will see to it.'

'What you gonna do, Ollie? Shoot the bleeding lot of them?' Grandad's words broke the tension. Everyone burst out laughing and even Ollie gave a wide grin.

'Well, you ain't going back to Colliers Wood tonight,' declared Gran. It was settled. Eddie would spend the night at Ollie's house and Patsy would stay at Queenie's.

Eddie sipped the hot coffee Ollie had made and, quite suddenly, he gave a great shudder. 'Is there ever going to be any peace for us?' he asked.

A feeling of frustration swept over Ollie, for he didn't know the answer.

Eddie leaned towards Ollie. 'One thing's for sure, we're never opening up that shop again. I don't care what happens, I'll have it boarded up tomorrow.' He pushed his hand up over his forehead and through his thick hair. 'Patsy doesn't deserve all this hassle.'

Ollie got to his feet and sighed in despair.

'Jealousy, that's what it boils down to, Eddie. Did you really believe it would be any different? The business means money, and some folk begrudge you that. Probably, that's how Johnny feels. He didn't want Patsy, but since he's found out that she's doing so well, he's not going to let you forget the fact that he is still legally her husband.'

After moments of silence, Eddie implored: 'Tell me what to do, Ollie.'

'Well, lad, I think you have to make your own decisions.' He grasped Eddie's shoulder, putting pressure, trying to reassure him. 'Things have a way of working themselves out, but . . .' Ollie was too overcome to continue.

For what seemed like hours, long after Queenie was asleep and breathing steadily, Patsy lay pondering on the eventful day's happenings and asking herself about the future. She had tried hard to settle to her life at Colliers Wood, but some people wouldn't live and let live. There were days when she felt nostalgia for Tooting, the Day family and her job at the market. Yet life without Eddie now didn't bear thinking about.

Soon she would be able to use the surname of Owen. Would that make any difference? She doubted it.

That breakfast at Covent Garden had been an eye-opener. Eddie had once told Blower that he had never had a job, well, she couldn't blame him for concealing that fact. She had embarrassed Eddie by asking why he had left. What a shame his mother had been so over-protective. She must have loved

Eddie dearly, wanting only to shield him, but it had had the reverse effect, simply making him more conscious of his deformity.

The visit to Kew Gardens had been wonderful, but fancy choosing such a place to tell her his amazing news. Go and live on the other side of the world! She would be burning her boats. No familiar faces, no big family of Days and she'd miss Florrie and Ollie. Oh, God, how she'd miss them. There would be no one to run to in times of trouble – no family at all.

Yet, the thought struck her, she would have her own baby. Yes, she supposed she was lucky, she had a good man, one who truly loved her. Eddie was willing to give up everything for her, to start a new life together.

She placed her hands on her stomach. Who knows, we might end up with a big family of our own.

Settling down further in the bed she snuggled up to Queenie and, with a deep sigh, murmured to herself, 'Count your blessings and be thankful.'

Chapter Twelve

SOON, THE SHOP was completely boarded up and a black and white sign informed everyone that the Royal Arsenal Co-operative Society had acquired the premises. All decisions had been made. Eddie had made several trips to see Mr Topple and Patsy was still quite unable to believe the outcome. It was as if it were all happening to someone else.

'We have enough capital to qualify for Australia,' Eddie had said in a strong voice. 'With the cash my father left me and the proceeds from the business and premises we shall be quite well off.'

Eddie was happy that his plans were progressing so well. Laughingly, he had patted her cheek. 'No language problems either, since we've decided on Australia, so smile and stop worrying.' Easier said than done.

Eddie and Patsy stood in front of a tall building which housed several solicitors' and accountants' offices. At nine-thirty in the morning Wimbledon Broadway was buzzing with activity as they scanned the brass plates attached to the wall. It took only a minute to find the one they were seeking.

'May I help you?' a spinsterish type of woman asked when they reached the first floor.

'We have an appointment with Mr Grey,' Eddie told her.

'Name?' For an answer, Eddie extended a letter for her inspection.

'Take a seat.' This receptionist certainly didn't waste words. A good ten minutes passed before they were shown into an office, and by then Patsy was like a cat on hot bricks. A short, dapper man with a thin moustache greeted them with a curt 'Good-morning.' He waved them to seats and immediately turned his attention to the papers which lay on his desk. When finally he raised his head he nodded towards Eddie.

'Your name is?'

'Edward James Owen,' he firmly answered.

'Ah, yes, Owen. Actually, today's business does not concern you, but I can well understand your presence.'

Mr Grey's eyes lowered to the papers again. 'Owen, yes.' Patsy felt her cheeks flame up and beneath her breath muttered, 'Pompous pig.'

'Mrs Jackson.' The force with which Mr Grey pronounced her name brought Patsy's head up with a jerk. His hand stretched across the desk holding out a document, on the bottom of which appeared to be a blob of red sealing wax.

'Read it through,' he ordered. 'If you comprehend the facts, sign it.' Patsy hadn't missed the note of sarcasm in his voice.

' . . . Do solemnly and sincerely declare that I

absolutely and entirely renounce relinquish and abandon the use of my said former surname of Jackson.' Well, that was no hardship. ' . . . Assume, adopt and determine to take and use from this date hence the surname of Owen in substitution of my former surname of Jackson.'

She only glanced over the remaining paragraphs. In all records, transactions and signing of documents she would use the name of Owen. She authorised and required all persons to describe and address her by the adopted name of Owen.

Wonderful! On paper it sounded fine. She suppressed what would have been a scornful snigger. How did she go about 'requiring' people to call her Mrs Owen?

Patsy rose, hesitantly. 'Yes, yes, come to the desk.' Mr Grey's voice was intolerant. 'Sign there, and there,' he indicated spaces. 'No, not your first initial, write your full names: Patricia Eleanor Jackson, followed by Patricia Eleanor Owen.' The scratching of the pen on the thick paper sounded loud while Patsy did as she was bid.

'Thank you. All formalities are completed.' His speech was sharp and clipped now. 'No doubt you will be hearing from Mr Topple. Good day to you both.'

Eddie was already half-way out of the door. Carefully, Patsy retrieved her handbag and gloves from where they lay on the floor. She had a great desire to face Mr Grey and say ' . . . and good luck to you,' but instead she gave a tug to her hat and made what she hoped was a dignified exit.

The rain was coming down in sheets. What a morning this was turning out to be.

'In here, let's get in under here,' Eddie's words were barely audible above the wind as he tugged at her sleeve and drew her under a glass covered entrance. In just a few minutes they were both soaked, he more than she for he wasn't wearing a hat. The rain was trickling down from his hair, even a few drops hung from the end of his nose.

They shook themselves like a couple of shaggy dogs. Patsy took her handkerchief and reached up to wipe his face. He caught hold of her hand, gently smiling. 'Hello, Mrs Owen,' he said quietly, then bent and kissed her, long and hard, on the lips. When he released her his eyes stayed fixed on her face.

'Some day, we'll be married properly, that's a promise,' he declared. Then suddenly, he burst out laughing, which upset Patsy. 'Look,' he cried, his finger pointing. 'Look at the walls.' Posters proclaimed: 'Jesus is the Saviour of all Mankind. Knock, and the door shall be opened unto you.' They were sheltering in the entrance to the Salvation Army Hall.

'This isn't how I planned it at all, but it seems very appropriate.' Eddie's voice was filled with emotion and his hands shook as he withdrew a flat jeweller's box from his coat pocket. Its covering, once royal blue velvet, was now faded and one corner had a greyish stain, as if water had been spilled on it. He held it flat on the palm of his hand before opening it. On the silk lining lay two gold rings.

'I've had them made smaller. I hope they fit. They were my mother's.' He laid the box on the window-ledge and, taking her left hand, he slipped the thick, plain gold band on to her third finger, then the second ring, which had a half-circular setting of diamonds. For the second time since they had come into the shelter he bent and kissed her and, when their lips parted, he still held on to her, holding her close.

When Patsy did look up into his beautiful dark eyes her own green eyes were bright and shiny, moist with tears. Almost timidly he said, 'Now you are Mrs Owen.'

If only that were really true.

It was still pouring as they half-ran to the tram terminal.

'To hell with going home,' Eddie cried, signalling a cab. 'I'm taking you to lunch at the Dog and Fox up on Wimbledon Common.'

Never had there been a happier meal. His eyes laughed down at her and she gave him mischievous glances. She wasn't dressed for these posh surroundings, but it didn't matter. No one else existed. The two Owens had eyes for no one but each other.

Their wet coats were steaming by the time they got home.

'What are you laughing at?' Eddie asked as he rubbed her hair with a towel. She stared at him helplessly, she couldn't speak for laughing. 'Tell me what's so funny,' he demanded, tickling her, which only made her worse.

'You . . . married . . . me . . . in the Salvation Army Hall,' she got out at last.

Eddie put his arms about her. 'Where better, my darling?' No two people had ever been happier on their wedding day.

Now there were only two more days to get through. This evening would be spent in Strathmore Street. Where else? The Days' house bulged at the seams. The whole street seemed to be popping in and out to say their farewells to Patsy and Eddie. Patsy had planned a long, quiet chat with Flo and Ollie, but at the moment that seemed impossible.

'Blimey, we've got a house full tonight,' Queenie said as she handed round the food.

Grandad Jack gazed down at Patsy affectionately and gently touched her cheek. 'Who would have thought that our little Patsy would be going to Australia to live?' Blower, already half-drunk, just stared at her in a melancholy way. The booze flowed freely and everyone carried on with the party except Eddie, Ollie, Patsy and Florrie who, at midnight, made ready to leave.

All goodbyes were said noisily, all embraces were

clinging, until it was Gran's turn. With her characteristic cockney humour she said, 'You look after her, lad, or you'll have me to answer to,' but she couldn't prevent her voice from shaking as she held Patsy in her arms and murmured, 'God bless you, Patsy.'

The sound of the Days still singing their heads off over the road only served to make number twenty-two seem more desolate. Florrie had been strangely quiet all evening and, in a way, that had made it worse for Patsy. 'Should I be putting thousands of miles between us?' she tormented herself.

Ollie took himself off into the front room and sat there in the dark, reminiscing. He had had what he considered a privileged childhood. He had loved both his parents and adored his older brother, Jack. He remembered vividly how upset his mother had been when Jack had left home. Ten years older than himself, Jack had got mixed up with bad company. Whatever the dirty business was he had been involved in, no one ever knew. He hadn't stayed around to face the music. Postcards had arrived from time to time, sent from different parts of the world. Then his mother had died and within six months his father had followed her. On both occasions Ollie had tried to trace Jack, but without success.

Ollie's bachelor life had seemed fine until Ellen had come into his life. What about Ellen? The memory of her face and voice flooded to his mind.

She had been different from any other woman. With Ellen had come Patsy. From the day she had been born, she had become part of his life. He felt a physical longing. If only.

Now, even Patsy was going. She and Eddie would be living thousands of miles away, among strangers. He put his head down, no longer able to control his sadness. Losing Patsy was tearing him apart.

When the door opened and Patsy came into the room, Ollie could not hide the sudden tears which came to his eyes. He reached out and Patsy threw herself into his arms.

Early the following morning Florrie kissed Eddie, but she only hugged Patsy tight for a moment before pushing her out into the passage and closing the door, all without saying a word.

Now there was no one to see the tears stream down her cheeks unchecked as she thumped her chest with clenched fists.

Ollie came out into the street to see them off, clutching each in turn in a great bear-hug. At the corner, Patsy stopped and looked back. The lump in her throat nearly choked her. She closed her eyes, screwing the lids up tight. All night long she had lain awake, counting her blessings over and over again. It hadn't made the slightest bit of difference. Australia was still on the other side of the world, and the only family she had ever known was here in Tooting.

She stood rooted to the spot, seeing Ollie standing there, alone, on the doorstep. Where was Florrie? The thought that she had abandoned Florrie made Patsy shudder. Fat old Flo, with her huge bosoms and bad legs, wedging herself into her tatty armchair. With a sudden jerk Patsy seemed to see the inside of number twenty-two: small rooms, narrow stairs with worn linoleum, back yard and outside lavatory. In a flash she knew that trappings didn't mean a thing. What mattered was knowing that people loved her, had fought to keep her, would go on loving her even if she deserted them and went to live thousands of miles away.

There was a terrible sadness on Patsy's face as she raised her eyes to stare at Eddie. He had no need to ask what was wrong.

He took a handkerchief from his pocket and gently wiped her eyes. In a voice choked with emotion he said, 'Oh Patsy.' It was a full minute before he could continue.

'I love you so much, Patsy, it's like a knife being thrust into me when I see you so upset. No one is forcing us to go to Australia. It's not too late to change our minds. I could still cancel everything. Do you think I haven't thought about what a wrench it would be for you to leave Florrie and Ollie?'

Patsy moved closer. Her arms went around his

waist, she buried her face in his jacket and let it all out. Great dry sobs racked her body. A man turned the corner and stopped to light his cigarette, cupping his hands around the match against the wind. Ragged boys ran past, bowling their iron hoops, which clanged loudly as they forced them down the centre of the road, and litter whirled along in the gutters.

Eddie and Patsy were oblivious to it all as they stood on the corner clinging to each other.

An exclamation came suddenly from Eddie's lips: 'Oh, God.' How young she was, how small and thin and what a rough hand life had dealt her so far. 'How could I have been so thoughtless?' he angrily asked himself. To take her away from all the love she had ever known just because a few spiteful women scorned them. Silly, stupid women who knew no better. As to the Jacksons, they could go to hell! He'd find some way to deal with them.

He bent low, cupping Patsy's face with his hands, holding her still for his soft lingering kiss. Releasing his hold, he turned her about and quietly told her: 'We aren't leaving England, no matter what.' Then, giving her a gentle push, he added, 'Go on. Go and tell Ollie.'

The sadness left her face, she brushed her hand across her eyes and to Eddie she looked incredibly beautiful.

'Thank you. Thank you,' was all she could think of to say before she started to walk back down the street towards Ollie, and then she was running, her long chestnut hair bobbing on her shoulders, and Ollie was holding his arms wide, as every man does to a child he loves.

Chapter Thirteen

IT WAS AS if all hell had broken loose. Half the popu-
lation of Strathmore Street seemed to be crammed
into Florrie's back kitchen. Eddie's hand had been
shaken and his back slapped so many times that he
began to feel dizzy. 'Good on yer, lad. No one ever
won a battle by running away,' seemed to be the
general opinion of all the men.

Grandad had the last word. 'Just settle where it
suits you, boy. Take good care of our Patsy and
you'll be all right. Don't let the Jacksons worry you,
either. Any more trouble from them and we'll sort
it out once and for all. Bloody murdering sods, the
lot of them.' Every male member of the Day family
nodded his head in agreement and Eddie had had to
suppress a smile as he pictured the Jackson tribe in
full flight with the Day family in hot pursuit.

Florrie and Gran were wailing like two scalded
cats. Aprons thrown over their heads, they were
really giving vent to their feelings.

'Aw, give over, please!' Patsy had an arm around
each of them as she pleaded. But neither of them
was listening.

Ollie pushed his way through the throng and
stood looking down at the three of them; on his face

was a grin which spread from ear to ear. 'Leave 'em be, my love. It's sheer relief, that's all it is – though why they have to make such a racket is beyond me.'

Gently he pushed Patsy until her back was against the wall then, taking hold of both her hands, he spoke softly and the intensity of his feelings was apparent in his voice. 'The past few weeks have been an agony of waiting for us all. Now it's all over. You're the only family I have, the only family I have ever wanted from the day I met your mother. All that matters now is that we get you and Eddie set up in a decent home of your own.' He paused and gave a little chuckle. 'Somewhere not too far away, so that we can visit you.'

Patsy began to feel that she and Eddie had been very selfish; they had been so wrapped up in their own troubles that they hadn't given a thought to others. Family ties – and God knew these rough and ready folk, packed into this small room, were her family in every sense of the word – loyalty to them had to count for something. With the din that was going on it was difficult for Patsy to make herself heard, so she stood up on her toes and put her lips against Ollie's cheek. As she did so, she saw Eddie watching her from across the other side of the room. The look on his face was soft with longing, and as he smiled at her her young face lit up and she smiled back. Silently they mouthed to each other: 'I love you.'

★

Eddie had been quite content to leave everything to Mr Topple. The young solicitor had been very understanding – indeed, he had laughed; and Eddie had the feeling he wasn't all that surprised at their decision to stay in England. Patsy had worried that Eddie would lose financially. He had coaxed her doubts away.

After hours of discussion, and endless viewing of properties, they were moving to number six Navy Street, Clapham Common – not a million miles from Tooting.

The rapid honking of a horn came from below. The removal van was here. It was almost time to leave. Patsy was wearing her new coat, which had a fur collar. 'It feels good around my neck, and it's so warm!' She smiled happily as she snuggled her head against the fur.

'Any regrets?' Eddie asked quietly.

'No.' Her eyes met his without wavering.

Eddie was silent now, thinking back over past events. He was sure no man had ever loved a woman more than he loved Patsy and he had only one regret. If only he and Patsy could be legally married. To make her his wife was his dearest wish. Patsy never broached the subject now but he didn't need telling that the thought that she was not his wife in the eyes of the law was always uppermost in her mind. One day, he solemnly vowed, one day!

Patsy broke into his thoughts. 'What about you,

Eddie? You were born in this house, and your mum and dad worked hard in the shop downstairs.'

'Shush. Shush,' he said, placing his fingers over her lips. 'We've been over all that, and everything else. Besides, from today we are both going to look forward and put the past behind us.'

Navy Street was not the sort of place where Patsy had ever thought she would be fortunate enough to live. It was a short side road with tall well-built houses with spacious rooms spread out on three floors, an inside lavatory and a bathroom. Florrie had arrived before them and had gone through the house opening windows and lighting fires in the downstairs rooms.

Eddie had paid two women to clean the rooms on the ground and first floors thoroughly. The top floor of the house was let to a single lady. The rent she paid would be useful and because the premises weren't being sold with full vacant possession the asking price had been that much lower. By the time the removal men had all the furniture in place, collected their tip and departed, Ollie had arrived and Florrie had the kitchen table laid with a grand meal: boiled ham, tomatoes, pickles and a huge dish of mashed potatoes. She had made and brought with her a deep apple pie. Setting a tin of evaporated milk down on to the table, she had to have something to moan about. 'You can't have any custard, ain't found the milk saucepan yet, no jugs neither, so it's milk straight out of the tin over your pie, or go without.' It turned out to be a very jolly meal, which Eddie ended by raising his mug of tea high in the air and proposing: 'Here's to the first of many happy gatherings in Navy Street.'

'Hear, hear,' the others chorused.

'Cooee, cooee,' a voice interrupted from the hall-way. Patsy rose and went to open the door. Too late; it opened as she reached for the handle.

'Hallo there!' A woman crossed the space between them, greeting everyone as if they were old friends as she placed a flowering pot plant down on the table. 'Just my way of saying, "Good luck in your new home",' she said to Patsy.

She was a tall big-boned woman with a jolly smil-ing face and fair hair pulled back tightly from her face. She was wearing a brightly-coloured flowered dress and a white cardigan which was so baggy that it almost reached her knees.

Florrie's eyes were focused on the woman, but they gleamed with amusement.

'Well, I'll be blowed!' the tall visitor gasped. 'Florrie Holmes! I never expected to see you again, not in this life I didn't.'

'Kitty Palmer!' Florrie gasped in return, and cast her eyes heavenward as if asking for divine help. 'I've known Kitty since we were kids at school together,' she mumbled. 'She used to live alongside me in Strathmore Street.'

Her face flushed up as she made this statement,

and she hurried on, saying to Kitty Palmer, 'I've always felt a bit guilty about the way you were seen off. Wasn't nothing I could 'ave done about it at the time, but I still felt guilty.'

Kitty put her arm out and patted Florrie's shoulder. Very quietly she said, 'Not to worry. It is all a long time ago now,' and she smiled as she sat down in the chair that Eddie had pulled up for her

Ollie came to the rescue, made all the introductions, and Eddie confirmed that Mrs Palmer was their tenant from the top floor. She didn't overstay her welcome, but drank the cup of tea which Patsy handed her, said her goodbyes and went.

Florrie hastily got to her feet and followed her up the hallway. 'I am right pleased to see you again, you know, Kitty. Life's funny, ain't it? Come full circle we 'ave, eh?'

'Yes, you're right there, Flo, and I'm more than pleased to see you again. Will you be coming over often?'

'As often as I can. You can bet on that. Like me own, Patsy is. I'll tell you more another time. You could do me a favour though, if you would. Keep your eye on Patsy, will you, Kitty? She's among strangers up here. I'll be glad when the baby arrives.'

'I'm more than pleased that a nice couple like them have bought the house. I worried a bit about who I'd get downstairs. I'll do me best Flo, I'll give an eye to her.'

'Thanks, Kitty. You'll find out – two of the best, they are.'

Florrie had hardly put foot back inside the kitchen than Patsy was pleading, 'Come on, Florrie, tell us all about it.'

'All about what?' Florrie asked, playing for time.

Patsy knew her too well. 'Oh, come on, you're bursting to tell us. What did you mean when you said Kitty was seen off?'

'Well—' Florrie paused dramatically, crossed her arms and heaved her bosoms up while all three of them cast looks at each other and tried hard not to laugh. It was Ollie who broke the silence.

'I remember Kitty living at number sixteen, but it was a long time ago. I can't recall why she moved.'

'She didn't move. She was chucked out!' The words exploded from Florrie. Now she had everyone's attention.

'The trouble with men is that they don't think. Number sixteen is where Mr and Mrs Masters used to live. Only youngsters they were when they first came to our street. She had four kids in five years. Two boys, one after the other, then twin boys. Twins were about five when their mother died, can't remember what she died of. At the time Kitty was a slip of a girl, in service she was, big 'ouse up on the common, used to come to see her mum, she lived other end of Strathmore Street. Masters cottoned on to Kitty straight away. Well, 'ad to 'ave someone to see to his kids, and don't think his own creature comforts weren't one of his main reasons either. Oh no, 'ousekeeper he told everyone when he moved Kitty in. But I'll tell you this – there wasn't many as believed him.'

Florrie had to pause in the telling and Patsy moved closer to Eddie, who immediately covered her hand with his own. Unconsciously Patsy shivered: this story was hitting too near home.

Florrie saw Patsy's reaction and, having now got her second wind, she leaned forward and wagged a finger at Patsy. 'Every man is not as good as Eddie, as well you know to your cost.'

Now it was Eddie's turn to feel uncomfortable. He wished Florrie had never started telling them this account of Mrs Palmer's background.

Florrie broke the tension by grinning at them.

Ollie knew that nothing would prevent her from finishing her tale, so he calmly said, 'Get on with it, then. I suppose there is an end to this story?'

'Too right there is.' She was off again. 'Twenty years Kitty lived with Masters. A damn good mother to them boys and a wife to him. He was killed in some accident in the factory where he worked. Wasn't cold in his coffin and them sodding boys of his had Kitty out of 'ouse and 'ome. Wasn't as if they needed the 'ouse. Three of them were married, other one was in the Army. Trouble was, Kitty hadn't a leg to stand on, Masters 'ad never married her. Them buggers 'ad no feelings. Out she went with nothing.'

'How about a fresh cup of tea?' asked Eddie, tactfully, as he got up and went out to the scullery and filled the kettle.

Patsy busied herself collecting up the cups and clearing the table, and as she did so she made up her mind that she would always be kind to Kitty Palmer.

It took some time for Eddie to decorate their home: three rooms on the ground floor and two bedrooms and a bathroom on the first floor. He gave a lot of thought as to what he would eventually do. Their money wouldn't last for ever. Should he buy a business or should he try for a job? Each day he shelved the problem.

Patsy had never completely lost that morning feeling of nausea and Eddie insisted that she register herself with a local doctor.

Doctor Healy was friendly and the most unlikely-looking doctor you could imagine. He was a big young man, red-faced and rugged, dressed in a white coat that showed his shirt beneath was open at the neck.

'Morning, Mrs Owen,' he said, and nodded amicably to Eddie who had insisted on going to the surgery with Patsy.

Doctor Healy asked a lot of questions, examined

Patsy behind a screen and pronounced her fit and well. He did suggest that she rested during the afternoons. 'Come and see me again, two weeks from today. By then I will have made a reservation for your delivery.'

As they made to leave his office he put a hand up on to Eddie's shoulder and held him back. 'Have you always worn an iron on your shoe?' The question was asked in such a way that it gave no offence.

'Always,' Eddie answered without embarrassment.

'How long since anyone took a look at your leg?' This question caught Eddie off guard. It was a long time since anyone had made a direct reference to his deformity. Sensing Eddie's uneasiness, Doctor Healy thrust out his arm and the two of them shook hands. 'Another time, eh?' The doctor spoke quietly. 'You know things have improved somewhat. You could at least have a medical shoe made.'

Eddie promised to think about it and all the way home the thought whirled round and round in his head. To be rid of this iron on the bottom of his boot! It must make walking that much easier and surely his legs wouldn't ache as much as they often did now. The kind of boot he had worn all his life was clumsy, to say the least. Let things settle down a bit, see Patsy all right and the baby born, and he promised himself he would go and see Doctor Healy again.

★

Their life took on a pattern. Each morning they had breakfast together in what Patsy called their 'sit-down kitchen', because it was so large and had a scullery leading off from it where the washing-up could be done at the long earthenware sink. The garden at the back of the house was delightful, long and wide with plenty of flower-beds shielded from the wind by tall trees and heavy shrubbery. The weather was still bad: frosty mornings and bitterly cold winds that stripped the trees of their remaining leaves and sent them whirling over the grass. Patsy longed for the summer and imagined their baby sleeping peacefully in its pram beneath one of the trees.

Mainly because Eddie insisted, Patsy did put her feet up of an afternoon. They compromised. She refused to go upstairs to their large bedroom, where she said she felt out of things on her own. Instead she lay on the settee in the front room. Patsy loved this room. Wide as well as long, the wall facing the door held a huge marble fireplace, and at the far end of the room four tall windows formed a bay. Some of the pieces of furniture that had belonged to Eddie's parents were genuine antiques and there were also Dresden porcelain figurines that his mother had collected over the years. Set out now, together with one or two other items which Eddie had bought, they gave the room an intimate comfortable look.

One afternoon Eddie came in and caught her

doing a little jig in front of the fire. 'Everything is wonderful,' she cried as he set the tea-tray down on to a side table. Her mood was infectious and he laughed out loud. Despite her bulk he lifted her off her feet and whirled her round and round. 'And you're the most wonderful thing of all,' he told her. As she clung tightly to him, with her arms around his neck and the bulge of the baby between them, she wondered what she would do without him. Her lips trembled at the very thought.

Patsy now attended a clinic for expectant mothers at the South London Hospital For Women, which was where Doctor Healy had booked a bed for her confinement. It was at this clinic that Patsy made her first friend in the neighbourhood, Amy Andrews. Amy lived with her husband in Clapham Manor Street which adjoined Navy Street. They already had two adorable children: Laura, who was four years old, and George who was just two. Amy was expecting her third baby around the same time as Patsy was expecting her first. At least to the world at large it was Patsy's first. Wild horses wouldn't have dragged from her lips the fact that she had been married to Johnny Jackson and had miscarried one baby already. She shut her mind hard and fast to that episode of her life. She *was* Mrs Owen, and no one would ever force her to admit otherwise.

Ted Andrews and Eddie Owen met outside the hospital, and hit it off from the start. The Andrews weren't that much older than the Owens and the two families became great friends. Outings became a regular thing. With Clapham Common so near there was plenty to see and to do as they walked across the grass and fed the ducks on the pond. Ted and Eddie pushed the youngsters on the swings, which brought shrieks of delight from Laura and loud squeals from baby George.

One Sunday, when Florrie wasn't coming for the day because her legs were bad and Ollie had decided to stay at home with her, Amy invited Patsy and Eddie to tea. She put on a lovely spread with home-made cake and sherry trifle to follow their salad. The two men volunteered to do the washing-up and the two young women stretched themselves out in armchairs.

'Do you want a boy or a girl?' Amy asked, breaking the silence.

Patsy grinned. 'I don't mind which – but I think Eddie would like a boy.' She placed her hand on her stomach, feeling the baby, then as she felt it kick, she started to laugh. 'I think it's a boy.'

'Why? Because it feels like a footballer?' They laughed together. 'If it is what will you name him?'

'Either Frank Alexander or Alexander Frank.'

Amy swallowed. 'What a mouthful,' she said. 'Why those names?'

Patsy explained that Frank had been Eddie's father, and that Ollie, whom both Amy and Ted had met on several occasions, had been like a father to her. 'Ollie's real name is Alexander,' she added.

'What if you're wrong, and you have a girl?' Amy asked as she got to her feet and walked across to the table and filled two glasses with orange squash.

'Ellen,' Patsy replied without hesitation, 'after my mother.'

Handing one glass to Patsy, Amy asked, 'How old were you when your mum died?'

'Not quite fourteen. That's when Ollie became my guardian, and he and Florrie have looked after me ever since.'

'No wonder you think so much of them,' Amy murmured.

Patsy went to bed that night thinking that the Andrews were nice unaffected people, and counting herself lucky to have found such friends. The fact that Patsy was so happy and contented was reason enough for Eddie to think that his decision to cancel all plans to emigrate to Australia had been the right one.

It was five o'clock in the morning when Patsy shook Eddie awake.

He practically fell out of bed in his scramble to help her. 'Shall I make you a cup of tea?' It was the only thing he could think of to do.

'Better forget the tea and go and telephone for the ambulance,' she told him as the pain in her back took hold and she clenched her teeth.

'I'll help you downstairs first,' he said and as she settled herself on the edge of the bed he knelt and eased her feet into her slippers. She put her arms into her dressing-gown and drew it round her as far as it would go.

'Right, time to go,' she told him, doing her best to smile as she waddled across the room and out of the door.

Five hours later Eddie, trying hard to stop the trembling in his limbs, followed a nurse down the long corridor. The faint antiseptic smell made him feel sick.

'Told you it would be a boy,' he whispered as he bent over the bed, thinking how small she looked lying there.

'Old knowall,' she smiled up at him, then her arms came out from under the sheet, stretched up to his neck and pulled his head down to her face. As they kissed each other their tears mingled.

This time they were tears of joy.

When a nurse came into the room holding the baby, tightly wrapped in a shawl, and placed him in the crook of Patsy's arm, they both gazed at him in wonderment. A band around his tiny wrist declared him to be Alexander Frank Owen, born on the second of April, 1924.

Eddie stammered his thanks to the nurse, grinned at Patsy, sank down into the chair at the side of the bed, closed his eyes, thanked God – and gave himself up to the gratifying feeling of being a father.

Chapter Fourteen

SUMMER HAD ARRIVED. The streets were dry and the sun shone down from a cloudless blue sky. On really hot days the overflowing dustbins in the back alleys smelt awful, despite the efforts of an army of dustmen that came round collecting the garbage every Monday morning.

The fine weather brought the street traders out in force. 'Any rags, bottles or bones? Any old rags today?' Harry, the old rag and bone man, dressed in his long greasy overcoat with a length of thick string tied around his middle, would call in his sing-song voice as he pushed his handcart along.

'Penny a pound pea'o.' 'Cherries, ripe che---rry, tuppence a pound now ladies,' the barrow boys would shout as loud as their lungs would allow. This brought the women out in their droves. Pea-pods, weighed on shiny brass scales and shot straight from the scoop into aprons held out wide, were then shucked by the ladies of the street as they sat on their doorsteps and nattered an hour away. Children were thrilled when their mothers sported out for some cherries, dangling pairs on to their ears pretending they were ear-rings, their lips and fingers soon stained purple as they gobbled the plump fruit.

Not all the street vendors pushed handcarts. There were still a lot of horse-drawn vehicles about, and where there are horses there are always piles of dung. This was not an opportunity to be missed. Galvanised buckets and shovels in hand, women soon had the mess cleared up. 'Great for the old man's allotment,' they would declare as they carried their prize indoors.

Patsy had settled down well, neighbours had accepted her and Eddie for what they said they were, husband and wife. Kitty upstairs proved to be a good tenant and a kind friend. Indeed, there were times when Patsy felt afraid. Everything was going so well. What had she done to deserve such happiness? Alexander thrived and Patsy rejoiced in the fact that she could stay at home all day and care for him. Eddie still hadn't got a job, though he did have one in the offing, with Hunt and Nichol, the same firm that he had once worked for in Covent Garden. So much had happened so quickly.

When the question of the baby's christening had arisen it had been decided that they would go back to Tooting, so much easier for both Florrie and Gran Day to attend. 'We'll never hear the last of it if we don't let them provide the tea afterwards,' Eddie had said.

'Hmm,' Patsy had mused; not only the tea, but the booze-up as well.

St Nicholas's church on the corner of Church Lane at Amen Corner had been packed. Ollie's pleasure at having the baby named after him showed clearly on his face, while Gran and Florrie were in their element as they clucked and cooed over the new addition to the family.

It was during the evening, when – as Patsy had foretold – the drink was flowing freely, that Doctor Healy had dropped in at Eddie's invitation to wet the baby's head. Edging Eddie into a corner he had quietly said, 'I've made an appointment for you to see an orthopaedic specialist at St Thomas's Hospital on the Embankment.'

Eddie's eyebrows had shot up. 'Bit quick! I haven't really had time to think about it.'

'Then it's about time you did. Can't do any harm,' was what Doctor Healy said out loud. What he thought to himself was that the matter had been neglected for far too long already. No one should have to clump about with a three-inch iron extension fitted to the bottom of a boot. It looked hideous, and he still hadn't fathomed out why an otherwise good-looking intelligent young man had had to go through his life dragging this freakish-looking contraption when surely something could have been done at least to improve, if not to cure, the problem.

Later, when Eddie told her about the appointment, Patsy was all for it. She was excited at the very thought that Eddie might walk normally.

'That will never happen,' he told her. 'At the most all they'll do is make me a different shoe.'

'Oh you, you're an old pessimist,' she said, chivvying him.

At the first appointment the specialist did not mince his words. He came straight to the point. He could offer no cure. Quietly and calmly he told them both, as they sat close together facing him in his tiny office.

'The malformation of your leg and foot, Mr Owen, has deteriorated over the years rather than improved. In my opinion, the neglect has been scandalous. What I do suggest now is that you have an operation. Metal rods could be inserted in the leg to give added support. No promises,' he quickly added. Then he went on to endorse Doctor Healy's feelings about a surgical shoe. 'No problem there,' he stated. 'Built up from the inside, it will look a whole lot better and be a damn sight less awkward.'

After Eddie had spent two weeks in hospital the result, they both agreed, was well worth while. The surgeon had done a good job. There hadn't been much that he could do with the leg, other than what the specialist had suggested. The foot he had been able to straighten. Two pairs of shoes had been made by experts. The shoes for the right foot no longer had an unsightly iron lift to give the height, their only outward difference from an ordinary shoe was in a slightly thickened sole. The support lift had been skilfully fixed to the interior of the shoes by craftsmen.

Eddie's bearing was completely different. He now held himself up straight and, although he still dragged his leg slightly, he strode along with much more confidence. He got a job: full-time employment in the accounts department of Hunt and Nichol. He was back earning a living, among men he liked and trusted, and as Patsy was quick to tell Florrie, you didn't need to be clairvoyant to tell that he was really happy to be back at Covent Garden again.

Life was so good! Now and again the thought that Johnny Jackson was a dog in the manger niggled Patsy. He hadn't wanted her. Never had, once he had found out that she expected him to go out and earn a living for the pair of them. So why wouldn't he agree to a divorce and let Eddie marry her? The fact that she wasn't Eddie's wife in the eyes of the law still hurt. One day, she promised herself, all the Jacksons – the whole damn tribe of them – would get their come-uppance. The obscene, offensive comments they had flung at her about her mother's past had hurt more than the physical blows she had suffered at their hands.

'I've got a long memory,' she vowed. Meanwhile she did her best to put such thoughts to the back of her mind and get on with living her life. God Almighty knew she had plenty to be grateful for.

Saturday was her favourite day. Eddie didn't have to go to work, and more often than not Ollie brought Florrie up to Clapham for the day. They made the most of the glorious weather. Florrie and Patsy usually ate cold pork pies and suchlike out in the garden at lunchtime, while Eddie and Ollie took themselves up to the Manor Arms for a drink, and baby Alex lay on a blanket and slept in the shade.

Alexander! Patsy only had to look at him or to see Florrie fussing over him and a wide grin would spread over her face. He was the best baby in the world. He was always smiling, holding his little hands up to his face as if he were counting his own fingers. The lady doctor at the clinic was pleased with him: he had gained five ounces last week, his first tooth was nearly through. All this Patsy knew Florrie would relate in detail to Gran when she got back to Tooting.

Come the evening and Ollie wouldn't hear of Patsy cooking a hot dinner. Instead he would press half a crown into her hand and tell her to be quick. She needed no second bidding. She would stand in the queue in the steamy atmosphere of the fish and chip shop and, like all the rest of the hungry folk, she'd spend a blissful ten minutes of anticipation, while the fish sizzled in the great pans of boiling fat. Back home with her large newspaper-wrapped parcel she'd find the table laid, the plates warming in the oven and a plate full of thick slices of bread and butter ready placed on the table. ''Twas a feast fit for a king,' Eddie would declare as he licked his fingers and collected up the dirty plates.

When autumn set in the cold was bad enough, but the rain made things ten times worse. It came pelting down day after day and the wind never seemed to stop howling. It was difficult for Patsy to get the baby's napkins dry and aired. Eddie would come home soaked to the skin, yet he never complained. As Christmas drew nearer the pair of them were like a couple of kids themselves as they bought and wrapped presents and toys. It was without a doubt the happiest time of Patsy's whole life.

This wonderful state of euphoria stayed with Patsy throughout the whole of the next year and finally, as Christmas approached once more, she knew she was pregnant again. Eddie acted like a dog with two tails when she gave him her news.

The New Year was hardly started when it became apparent that all was not well in this England that young men had died for in order that it might become a land fit for heroes. The economic recovery of 1920 hadn't lasted. Money became tight, prices of all foodstuff rose alarmingly, so what little wages men were getting went nowhere when it came to feeding their families.

The month of May should be the nicest time of

the year as the buds on the trees are bursting with blossom and spring takes a firm hold promising that summer is on the way.

'*Star*, *News* or *Standard*. Get yer paper 'ere. Miners out on strike. *Star*, *News* or *Standard*, a penny.' The loud cries of the paperboys rang out down the back streets as they lugged their heavy canvas bags and made the most of the crisis in order to sell more papers. It was the first of May, 1926.

The whole of the working classes seemed to be on the side of the miners. On street corners and in the pubs, among men and women alike, the strike was the main topic of conversation. Eddie came back from the Manor Arms in a very serious frame of mind.

'It's the bosses and the owners who have brought this about,' he told Patsy as he unlaced his shoes and stretched his legs out beneath the table. 'Two thirds of the coal-miners have been locked out of their pits because they won't agree to these lower wages proposed by this Samuel Commission. Hard to say if the miners will win their case – should do by rights – but the working man has never come out on top yet. Not when fighting the bosses, he hasn't.'

Patsy set his supper of bread and cheese down in front of him and set about making the cocoa. She hadn't any idea what the Samuel Commission was, but Kitty upstairs had a brother who was a miner in Yorkshire. Only that morning she had been telling Patsy of the appalling conditions in which the men had to work, bent double and more often than not knee-deep in water, and all for wages so low that men with families couldn't live on them.

It's an ill wind that blows no one any good. For the next couple of days the newspapers had a field day. Talks between mine-owners and the unions were reported, and even the fact that the government was interfering was detailed on the front pages. Suddenly the whole country was plunged into a general strike. There were no trams, buses or trains. All the newspapers disappeared from the streets. Industries shut down and the docks lay idle. Everywhere there was uproar. 'Stay indoors,' Eddie urged Patsy, as he left to walk to work.

That was all very well but she had to go shopping, for bread if for nothing else. As she came up the side of the common and turned into Clapham High Street she immediately wished she had heeded Eddie's advice.

It seemed as if all hell had been let loose. Professional men from the upper classes had decided to teach the workers a lesson; they had rallied to the government's cause and were driving lorries and buses.

The ordinary man in the street wasn't going to stand by and watch that!

In the centre of the main road a tram had been overturned, which showed just how far some men were prepared to go to bring all forms of transport to a halt. Fights had broken out, grown men grappled with each other, and Patsy had to pull the pram quickly to one side as two men, doing their best to knock the stuffing out of each other, rolled along the pavement. The noise was deafening and it was many a long day since Patsy had heard such foul language. She decided she would be much better off at home.

Two days later, when things were getting desperate for everyone, a strange thing happened in Navy Street. A horse-drawn cart, driven by Eddie Owen, pulled to a stop in the centre of the road. On the cart were several milk churns. A great cheer went up as the women ran to fetch jugs of all shapes and sizes and Eddie carefully ladled out the precious milk to each family. 'How did all this come about?' was Patsy's first question when she was finally able to talk to him on their own.

'I heard there was this milk pool being set up in Hyde Park, so I made my way there. I was dead lucky really, cadged a lift most of the way.'

Patsy grinned. It was typical of her Eddie to make light of his efforts. 'They didn't just give you the milk, did they?'

'Not exactly. No deliveries had been getting through, gallons were going to waste, so some bright spark thought of Hyde Park as a central location. Shopkeepers, all sorts, were there to pick up the milk. A delivery yard had loaned a few horse and carts and they were asking for volunteers to deliver milk to the hospitals. I took some churns to

St James's and to the Women's Hospital, and the loader put on an extra four for me to distribute as I thought fit.'

'I love you,' Patsy told him as she flung her arms around his neck and planted a smacker of a kiss on his cheek.

The strike lasted only nine days. The unions called it off without imposing any conditions. The miners didn't go back to work. Indeed, it was to be several months before the pits were working again and then it was only on the employers' terms.

The summer months seemed to drag as Patsy's legs and ankles swelled and she wasn't able to walk as far as she would have liked. She was, however, very happy indeed when on the twentieth of August, 1926, she gave birth to another healthy son. This time she and Eddie argued over the choice of his name. 'Let's choose a name that can't be shortened,' she pleaded.

In the end they had him christened David Edward.

People said that Alex was like Patsy, but there was no mistaking who the new baby took after. His eyes were big and brown, his hair thick and dark, exactly like his father. From the start Alex was very proud of his brother, and neither Eddie or Patsy could quite believe how good life was turning out for them.

Chapter Fifteen

As Eddie boarded the tram for home, the post office clock struck midnight. This was late for him to be out, even on a Saturday night. Tonight he had been to a boxing match with Dave Mitchell. He felt elated. He had felt for some weeks now that there was something in the wind and tonight his suspicions had been confirmed.

Dave Mitchell was overseer for the whole of Covent Garden and had previously worked for the same firm as Eddie now did, Hunt and Nichol. Overseer was considered a most important post. Dave had the capacity for the job, and was popular among the men. Being six foot two inches tall and brawny with it, no one treated him with disdain; any trouble, and Dave quelled it before it got out of hand.

Although Eddie worked in an office most of the time, there wasn't much that went on in the market that he didn't get to hear about. In the four years that he had worked for Hunt and Nichol he had come to know that Jack Dwyer and his gang were the ones to watch.

It was common knowledge that warehousemen and porters kept their families supplied with a few oranges, apples and whatever delicacies were in season. It was accepted as part of their dues. What Jack Dwyer was up to was another matter all together. Jack himself was a bully. The previous afternoon there had been a right old rumpus.

Dwyer had been drinking; he'd burst into the wage clerk's office and demanded that he and his gang be paid their day's wages there and then. 'Why?' the clerk had asked. The market was nowhere near clear, there were still vans waiting to be loaded. Dwyer had become violent.

White with rage, Dave Mitchell had appeared. 'I said I'd give you a warning,' he had yelled. 'Well, you've had your last one. You're off our lists, even for casual labouring.'

Later, on the grapevine, Eddie had learned that Dwyer and his gang had been taking whole loads of fruit and vegetables and selling them to hotels. In a roundabout way it was Eddie who had rooted them out. He had alerted Dave Mitchell weeks earlier to the fact that the invoices for goods brought in did not always tally with quantities sold to buyers. He had had to say something about it, for dealing with irate growers who knew when they were being sold short wasn't a task that he relished.

'I should have known that it was Dwyer,' Dave had said to Eddie when they had met for a drink that evening before the boxing match. 'We shan't be seeing him again. Dwyer is a big talker – likes to brag. I couldn't act before, though, not until I had proof. Well, yesterday, he took one risk too many. I'd given him several chances but being warned off meant more than financial loss to him. It meant loss of prestige. It meant the scorn of the other porters. To redeem himself, Dwyer had only one answer, violence, I wasn't having that and he had to go.'

Dave had called for two more beers then grinned, and slapped Eddie on the back, before informing him, 'You're getting promotion, mate. You deserve it.'

The tram clattered on towards Clapham Common. He couldn't wait to tell Patsy his news. The fact that he had succeeded in what was virtually his first attempt at full-time employment did a lot for his own self-esteem. He suspected that fear of poverty remained strong in his Patsy. As a child she had seen it help to kill her mother. Patsy took nothing for granted. He was well aware that daily she thanked God for all the privileges that the two of them enjoyed, and for the fact that they had two bright healthy boys. Now she would be as pleased as he was that his job was even more secure.

Patsy opened the street door as Eddie strode up the garden path. 'You're late,' she called.

'Yeah, sorry, love.' He kissed her cheek and held her to him. She was thrilled when he told her that he was going to be promoted, as much for him as for herself – he deserved it.

It was almost one o'clock by the time he had finished telling her, and Eddie noticed that Patsy's head was dropping. Only by a great effort was she preventing her eyes from closing. He put his hand out towards her and he felt all his love for her surge up within him. Of all the good things that had ever happened to him, having Patsy as his wife was by far and away the best.

'Come on, my darling,' he said gently, raising her up out of the chair. 'Let's go to bed.'

There was real pleasure in Eddie's voice when, over dinner the following Wednesday night, he said, 'I saw Blower and Charlie up at the market this morning. They've come up with a cracking idea for August Bank Holiday.'

Patsy was all ears: she loved anything to do with the Days. 'Hurry up then, tell me,' she urged Eddie as he tantalised her by calmly going on with his meal.

'All right, all right,' he replied, knowing that he would get no peace until he did tell her. 'All the family have agreed that it's murder trying to take everyone out for the day on public transport.'

Patsy put down her knife and fork and grinned widely at him.

'It's nigh on impossible!' As she made that statement, they both burst out laughing. The same picture had come to the mind of each of them. Fancy trying to get Gran, Florrie and more than a dozen kids on to a tram or even a train, never mind the rest of the clan.

'Blower's talking about hiring a chara, from Orange Coaches at Tooting Bec. Brighton is where he suggests we go for the day, on the Monday.'

Patsy's face was beaming. 'I'll take the boys and go down and see Gran tomorrow.'

'I thought you might. Can't wait to put your two pennyworth in, can you? Afraid you'll be left out of something?'

She rapped the back of his hand with her spoon. 'I'm only teasing,' he cried. 'Stay down there all day, I'll come down and bring you home when I finish work.'

The friendship between Amy and Ted Andrews and Patsy and Eddie had become very firm. The Andrewses had been invited over to Ollie's house, Gran had liked them, which was as good as a seal of approval, and Ted now often went with Eddie down to the Selkirk to have a drink with the men of the Day family.

Amy and Patsy had a lot in common. Amy had given birth to another little boy just three days after Patsy had had Alex. The Andrewses had named their boy Thomas. He and Alex were already, at four, firm friends.

Patsy was round at Amy's bright and early the next morning. 'I'm not going to stop,' she called down the passage to Amy, as she lifted Alex from the foot of the pushchair and unstrapped David from the seat.

'Why not?' Amy asked as she filled the kettle and lit the gas jet beneath it.

'Cos I'm going to get the tram and go down to Florrie's for the day. I want to see Gran an'all.'

'You've still time for a cuppa, surely?' Amy asked her as she kissed Alex and picked up David. 'Come on, the pair of you come and see Tom. He's playing with his bricks in the front room.' Having settled the three children with plenty of toys to keep them occupied, Amy came back down the hallway and into the kitchen. 'Right,' she said. 'Let's have it.'

Patsy watched as Amy emptied cold tea-leaves down the sink, warmed the pot and made a fresh brew. 'Well, come on, then, tell me!' Amy cried, impatience getting the better of her.

'How do you know that I've got anything to tell you?' but there was a smile on Patsy's lips as she asked.

'How do I know? It's written all over your face. You're bursting with news of some kind.'

'Oh, all right,' Patsy gave in, sat down at the table and accepted the cup of tea that Amy poured out for her. Half an hour later Amy was shaking with laughter as she got up and went and brought the children out to the kitchen to give them a glass of milk. 'Did Charlie Day really get a bathchair from the nuns?' Amy asked as she giggled.

'Yeah, course he did. And Grandad pushed Gran up and down Strathmore Street in it. Everything I've told you is true. If you have a day's outing with the Day family, you can bet your bottom dollar that there's never a dull moment.' All three children were fascinated as they watched their mothers fall about laughing, and Alex demanded to know when they were going to get on the tram and go and see Gran.

'Don't forget, will you, Patsy? Ask if there's room on the coach, if Ted and me and our three can come to Brighton!'

'I will,' Patsy promised as she bumped the push-chair down the front steps. 'I expect there will be room. Eddie said they weren't taking outsiders, only family and friends. See you,' she called back over her shoulder as she set off up Clapham Manor Street.

Nine times out of ten, Bank Holiday Mondays turned out to be wet and cold, and the best-laid plans always went wrong. This year they were lucky. The coach had arrived on time, everybody had been seen on safely with Gran and Florrie having the whole of the back seat to themselves. The sky was cloudless, the sun shone down, and the only complaint was that it was too hot.

On arrival the men helped to settle the women and the children on the beach, near to the edge of the sea, and then by mutual consent had taken them-selves off to have a drink. 'The pubs shut at half-past two, so we'll see you all about three o'clock.' Blower made this statement loud and clear.

His sister Queenie wasn't going to let the men clear off just like that. 'Wait a minute,' she yelled after them, as they began to troop off up the beach. 'We've all only got bits and bobs with us to eat, the kids will be starving by three o'clock.'

'Keep yer 'air on,' Chalkie, her husband, yelled back. 'Blower's got it all sorted out with the driver. He's gonna take us all up to Black Rock. He knows a good place up there, where we'll get a high tea.'

'That suit yer, Sis?' Blower called to Queenie.

'Yeah. Just as long as it is three o'clock, and no later!' She, as usual, had the last word.

They ate their sandwiches and drank lemonade from the bottles, took the children's shoes and socks off, tucked all the little girls' frocks into their knickers, which made the boys laugh, and went *en masse* down to the sea, leaving Gran and Florrie to doze in their deckchairs in peace.

There was a breeze down by the water's edge and Patsy thought it utter bliss as she wandered up and down, letting the sea lap over her bare feet, and she took deep breaths of the salt air. The children were playing in the water with happy unconcern, the bigger ones jumping the waves while the toddlers endlessly filled their gaily painted buckets and ran tirelessly to and fro to fill the holes they had dug in the sand.

Patsy was full of joy as she watched Alex and George venture out further until the water was up to their knees and her laugh was like that of a young girl as they turned and ran back through the foam.

The tide was on the turn, coming in quite fast now, as the women gathered up the children and herded them all safely further up the beach.

'I could murder a cup of tea,' Gran called as Queenie came into sight.

'Me too,' Florrie nodded towards Patsy.

'We'll go up to a kiosk and get a tray. Probably be able to get some ice creams for the kids,' Queenie volunteered.

'We'll go with you,' Amy and Patsy said in unison.

Alex was happily building a sand-castle with the help of George and Laura, and Patsy knew that Florrie wouldn't take her eyes off them. The three women set off with four youngsters in tow: Amy had Tom by the hand, Queenie had hold of Annie, one of her nieces, and Patsy held David's hand on one side while Billy, Annie's twin, clutched Patsy's other hand tightly.

They came up the steep slope instead of climbing the steps that would have taken them on to the lower promenade. They found themselves in the midst of a miniature fair, mainly small roundabouts and various slides. Squeals of delight burst forth from all four children, and their plea to be allowed to have a ride couldn't be ignored. Queenie went and paid the man while Amy and Patsy lifted the children into the car of their choice. All three of them waved cheerfully as the music played loudly and the roundabout came around. Every one was laughing and talking at once as the ride came to a stop and they ran to lift the children down.

Patsy watched in horror as the old woman came out of the pay desk and walked towards her. She had seen this happen in a nightmare, but had never really believed that it would come about in broad daylight. She raised her head high and their eyes met.

For a second they looked at each other, and Patsy shuddered as she saw the hatred in Mrs Jackson's glance. She hadn't altered: she was still a wizened-up old woman with wispy grey hair and a mouthful of gold teeth. 'Who fathered them this time?' She spat the words at Patsy and her attitude was savage.

When Patsy pulled David and Billy closer to her side, and did her best to ignore Mrs Jackson, the old woman took a step forward and with venom in her voice she hissed, 'You can't pass them bastards off on my Johnny!'

'Gawd almighty, I'll kill yer! You old witch!' It was Queenie, until then rooted to the spot, who screamed these words and sprang into action. Never a small woman, she towered over Mrs Jackson – she raised her great arm and would have knocked her head off her shoulders if the older woman hadn't ducked beneath the blow.

'Leave her, Queenie,' Patsy pleaded, tugging at Queenie's dress. 'Can't you see that's exactly what her scheme is? I know her too well of old. Get us all riled up, and before you know it she'll have the whole mob of her family down here. And if we don't come off worse, she'll call the police.'

Mrs Jackson threw her head back and let out a horrible cackle of a laugh.

'Please, Queenie, leave it,' Patsy pleaded again. 'Look, the kids are frightened. Let's go.'

Very reluctantly Queenie stepped back and turned away. Patsy took her handkerchief from her pocket and wiped it around her face, as if she could wipe away all the loathing she felt for this woman who was still screaming obscenities at her, as she turned and walked to where Amy was standing with the children huddled round her.

'Thanks, Amy,' Patsy managed to mutter as she lifted David up in her arms and hugged him close to her chest.

Queenie's breath was coming in short sharp gasps and her face was bright red with anger.

'Let's cross the road and go in the café and have a cup of something ourselves before we take a tray back down on to the beach,' Amy suggested. Seated at a round table, with large cups of steaming tea in front of them and the children happily sucking orangeade through a straw, Queenie asked Patsy what she wanted to do about Mrs Jackson.

'Nothing. Nothing at all,' Patsy quietly answered. 'What would be the use? Tell the men, and God knows what the outcome would be. Don't let's spoil the day any more than it has been. Please, Queenie, don't say a word, especially not to Eddie or Ollie – they would be so upset.' The sob in Patsy's voice nearly had them all in tears.

'All right. If that's the way you want it. I won't say a word.'

Patsy knew what a good friend she had in Amy as she leaned across and squeezed her hand. Not one question had she asked, yet Patsy knew that she could rely on her to hold her tongue.

Amy watched as Patsy sipped at her tea, and saw the tears spill over and run down her cheeks. Although Patsy quickly brushed them away and smiled bravely at the children, Amy felt sad for her. So Patsy had a past that she would rather forget. Well, it was none of her business. It wouldn't alter the fact that they were good friends. Poor Patsy! Poor Patsy!

Queenie brought them back to normal. 'If we don't hurry up and take some tea down to Gran, she'll skin us alive and eat us up.' The kids all laughed, especially when Billy said, 'We gotta get our ice creams before we go back.'

Everyone was smiling as Queenie said, 'Of course we 'ave.'

It was a very thoughtful Patsy who helped shepherd the children down the steps to the beach while Amy and Queenie trod carefully as they each carried a tray of tea.

'One day,' Patsy muttered to herself. 'One day.'

Chapter Sixteen

'I KNOW, I know,' Eddie said as Patsy hurried him off to work. 'You can't wait to open your letter,' he teased. 'I hope Ollie is all right up there in Liverpool.'

'So do I,' answered Patsy, giving him a great big hug. She stood watching him go down the garden path and didn't close the front door until he was out of sight. Her mood was very thoughtful as she went back into the kitchen. She poured herself out another cup of tea, and settled down to read what Ollie had to tell her this time.

It was two months since Ollie had received the first of a batch of letters from a law firm based in Liverpool. He had brought that letter to Clapham for her and Eddie to read and they had spent the whole of that weekend discussing the fact that it informed Mr Alexander Berry that his brother Mr Jack Ronald Berry had died in New Zealand.

Both she and Eddie had fired questions to Ollie, nineteen to the dozen, but he hadn't known the answers himself.

'Jack was very much older than me,' Ollie had told them. 'He left home, went to sea when I was still a lad.'

'Did you never hear from him?' Patsy was eager to hear the ins and outs of this missing brother who had never turned up since she had known Ollie, and was now dead.

'Yes, we did for a while. Coloured postcards from all around the world. I remember taking them to school to show my teacher. I'm sure I showed them to you, Patsy, when you were a little girl.'

'Well, what happened?' Eddie quietly asked that question.

Ollie shrugged his shoulders. 'We seemed to lose touch. When my parents died I did try to trace him, but my attempts came to nothing.'

That first letter had opened up a whole can of worms. Apparently, although Jack Berry had died in New Zealand, he had had business interests in many countries. Ollie had been advised to contact the firm of solicitors in person. Apparently there were a lot of legal formalities to be gone through and, as Jack Berry's only surviving relative, Ollie's signature was needed on several documents.

Ollie had been away nearly two months. Apart from the fact that she missed him badly, Patsy was worried sick. Why was Ollie staying in Liverpool so long? Surely he hadn't still got papers to sign. Was he ill? Patsy's imagination ran riot. Ollie wouldn't stay up there in a strange city unless there was a very good reason for him to do so, but then why on earth didn't he say so. All his previous letters had been vague; he told her all about the city, the hotel he was staying in, and about the great ships that were in the docks, yet he never said what he was actually *doing* or why he was away from his own work for so long. If he wasn't careful he'd get the sack. Today's letter wasn't much better.

It was a horrible dismal day. It had been raining when she got up, and it hadn't stopped. All the morning Patsy hadn't been able to get Ollie out of her mind. Even when she was reading to the boys her thoughts were miles away, and Alex complained that she was reading too quickly and that she wasn't stopping to let them look at the pictures. She was glad when it was time to get their lunch.

They heard the letter-box rattle and Patsy was about to get up when David slipped down from his chair. With his mouth full of potato he said, 'I'll get it.' He came back and climbed up to sit at the table, then pushed a long brown envelope towards his mother. 'Postman's been again,' he told her, and she had to smile to herself at how quickly he was growing up.

Patsy slit open the envelope and after reading only a few lines she felt this letter wouldn't make her feel any happier than the one from Ollie had. It was from the County Council. The local school had reserved a place for Alexander Owen from 27th March – the beginning of the summer term and only three weeks away. Alex wouldn't be five years old until the second of April. The writer of the letter also suggested that David Owen might like to attend the half-day infants' school. Lose both her boys at once! By the time Eddie came home from work she had worked herself into a right old state.

They had finished their dinner and the boys were in bed before Eddie asked, 'What did Ollie have to say?'

Patsy reached behind her for the envelope. 'You'd better read it,' she said tossing it across to him.

Eddie unfolded it and began to read. Patsy got up, refilled the kettle and put it on to boil. Then she sat down again, and picked up the pages of the letter as Eddie laid them down, and read them through again herself.

Eddie sighed heavily as he folded the pages of the letter and replaced them in the envelope. 'Doesn't seem as if he's coming home yet, does it?'

Patsy leaned her head back against the chair and closed her eyes. What was happening? 'What do you make of it all?' she softly implored of Eddie, and without waiting for him to reply she very quietly asked, 'Do you think that he's come into a lot of money, from his brother, and he won't come home at all?'

Patsy's voice had been little more than a whisper, and Eddie knew that she was near to tears.

'Oh, Patsy, how could you even think such a thing? I know you're worried about him, but Ollie will tell us everything he has to tell us in his own good time.'

Eddie's heart ached for Patsy. He could imagine how she had been letting her thoughts run wild. Ollie meant everything a father would to Patsy, and she must have been torturing herself for days now because he had been away so long. He got up, went round the table to where she sat, pulled her to her feet and took her into his arms.

'You don't believe what you just said, do you? You don't need me to tell you that you are the most important thing in Ollie's life, bar none.' He felt her tremble and for a few moments he stood, just stroking her hair. 'What about this tea?' he suddenly asked. 'The kettle will have boiled dry if you leave it much longer.'

Patsy broke free from his arms, rubbed the heel of her hand across her eyes and flew to the gas stove. As she stood pouring the boiling water on to the tea-leaves in the pot she called to him over her shoulder.

'I had another letter by the second post today. You'd better read that one as well.'

Having scanned the pages, a teasing glint came into Eddie's eyes. 'Well, you must admit it would be good for the boys to have other children to mix with,' he said, knowing how loath she would be to let them go.

Patsy's big green eyes became shrewd with what Eddie privately called her disgruntled mood. Then suddenly she grinned, mischievously.

'Changed your mind, have you?' he asked.

'Decided you'd be pleased to have them off and away from under your feet?'

'No, I haven't.' Still she grinned like a cat that had got at the cream.

Eddie's eyes narrowed. He couldn't make out what she was up to. Patsy lifted her hand to push a strand of hair back from her forehead and as she did so she laughed. 'Just what are you scheming?' Eddie asked as he advanced towards her. 'And don't tell me "nothing", I know you too well by now.'

Patsy turned her gaze upwards to Eddie's handsome face and looked directly into his huge, dark brown eyes. A shiver of excitement went through her as she told him, 'I shan't mind the boys being at school too much. Another seven months and I'll have a new baby to look after.'

'My God! How long have you known? Are you all right? Hadn't you better sit down?'

The next second they had hold of each other tightly and were both laughing. They stood there clinging, she with her arms around his waist, he with his head laid on her hair. Several minutes passed before Patsy said, 'I'll go and see that the boys are all right.'

She walked quickly through into the hall and went upstairs to the bedroom. No further words were necessary. Eddie was pleased that she was pregnant again, and the ecstasy of the past few minutes was enough.

★

Patsy had to live through another three weeks of uncertainty before she finally got the letter which told her that Ollie was coming home. She was there on the platform waiting when the train bringing him from Liverpool drew into Euston Station. She couldn't see him, had he missed the train? Oh, don't be so daft, she chided herself, but her restlessness was growing by the minute. Backwards and forwards she paced, moving her handbag from one hand to the other, fiddling with the buttons of her coat, then she saw him. His head covered with thick bushy hair towered above most people. For a moment she hesitated; there was something different about him. He was wearing a new overcoat, and the thought struck her that Ollie was still a very attractive man. Suddenly, as she pushed her way through the crowds, his eyes locked on to hers – those lovely, kindly eyes that she had been familiar with for as long as she could remember, eyes that she had always known she could trust. Dear, dear Ollie. Patsy ran the last few yards and his arms came around her, gathering her to him, and she felt safe again.

'Here! Here! What's all this? Anyone would think I'd been away for years, the way you are carrying on.' There was tenderness in Ollie's voice, but the lump that had gathered in Patsy's throat was threatening to choke her. Slowly they began to walk up the platform.

Patsy couldn't utter a word. Her eyes were filled

with unshed tears, and her heart was full of love and gratitude for this man. Without Ollie her life would have been so vastly different. The very thought made her shudder.

Dinner was a happy meal, a real family gathering. Naturally Florrie was there. She not only wanted to know what had kept Ollie in Liverpool for so many weeks, she wanted to know all the ins and outs of everything when it came to discussions of Jack Berry's affairs.

Ollie was strangely uncommunicative about giving details. 'There's not much to tell,' he insisted. 'Heck of a lot of sorting out for the legal fellows to do. Seems Jack really did see the world. Had his finger in all sorts of pies in all sorts of places.'

Further than that Ollie would not be drawn. He changed the subject. 'So, we're going to have another addition to the family, Eddie tells me.'

'Yes, that's right, early October.' Patsy smiled at them all, and again thought how lucky she was to have all these people to love her and to care for her.

'Daddy said he wants Mummy to give us a baby sister, but David and me don't want a girl.' Alexander was quite proud of the statement he had just made, and of the laughter it brought from the grown-ups. 'We don't mind another brother, do we, David?' he added, amid more bursts of laughter.

★

Easter, then Whitsun, came and went. The affairs of Jack Berry were hardly ever mentioned, though Ollie did ask Eddie to go to the City with him and introduce him to Mr Topple.

'I'd like a firm of solicitors much nearer home to handle the sorting out for me,' had been Ollie's explanation, but he had added an extra reason for using Mr Topple's firm. 'They used to be your father's solicitors, Eddie, and he certainly handled affairs well for you when your father died. Mr Topple was also very good and extremely kind to both you and Patsy, as I remember.'

Eddie agreed that everything that Ollie had said was true, and added that he would gladly vouch for Mr Topple and make the introduction.

The boys being at school opened up a whole new world for Patsy. She helped out at fêtes, organised coffee mornings and attended open days for parents. With the coming of summer again, they went on several outings with the Andrews family, mainly to parks and gardens and very often just up to the common. One very hot Sunday afternoon at the end of July, Amy and Patsy were seated in deckchairs under the shade of a great oak tree on the far side of the common. Ted and Eddie had taken the children, armed with a bag of bread, to feed the ducks.

Suddenly Amy said, 'My mum and dad have been married forty years this coming weekend. We're going home, down to Southend – my aunt and uncle are putting on a surprise party for them.'

Patsy opened her mouth to reply, but Amy was quicker. 'Come with us,' she said, blunt and genuine as always.

Patsy blinked at the suddenness of the invitation.

'I mean it,' Amy assured her. 'My family would give you a terrific welcome.'

'I'm sure they would, but we've promised to go to Florrie's. We haven't seen Gran for nearly three weeks, and if we don't go there'll be hell to pay. She'll begin to think we've murdered the boys.'

Patsy hoped that Amy hadn't noticed anything strange about her voice. The pat excuse she had trotted out made her feel guilty. It wouldn't be a total lie – they would go to Tooting next weekend – but Patsy would very much have liked to go down to Southend and join in the celebrations for Amy's parents.

'So why didn't you accept the invitation?' Eddie wanted to know when Patsy told him about it later that evening.

'You know very well why I didn't,' was Patsy's rather sharp reply.

Eddie heaved a great sigh. 'Oh, Patsy, you're not going to use the same old excuse. You're too thin-skinned, that's your trouble. You imagine half of what you worry about.'

'Do I? Well, there was a time when it would have

worried you that we aren't legally married. It doesn't seem to bother you so much these days.'

'Of course it bothers me, but we have gone over this so many times and what's the outcome been? There is nothing whatsoever I can do about it.'

Patsy knew that she should leave the matter there. Eddie was getting annoyed; every now and again she couldn't help it, she had to let her feelings show. Time and again she had felt awkward for whenever the subject of an anniversary was raised, someone in the company would ask how long she and Eddie had been married. She hedged, but try as she might she was never able to stop her cheeks from flaming up. She certainly wasn't going to lay herself open to such questions at Amy's parents' ruby wedding party. It was the sort of question that would be bound to come up. It was bad enough that Amy had witnessed that show-down with Johnny's mother at Brighton though she had never mentioned it.

Eddie's attitude softened. He wished with all his heart that he could give Patsy the one thing that she yearned for so much: marriage.

God knew he hadn't wanted it to be like this. From the very start he had wanted to make Patsy his wife. She had never treated him as a cripple. Before he had met her his life had been drab and meaningless. Her love had given him a new level of self-esteem; they had two fine healthy sons, another baby on the way; who could ask for more? His feelings for Patsy had never altered. He would swear that no man had ever loved a woman more than he loved his Patsy.

Taking her hand between both of his, he said, 'Oh, Patsy, my love, you still don't know what you mean to me.' His voice was gentle now, as he stood gazing down at her, seeing the copper tints in her hair and her lovely green eyes glistening with unshed tears.

'You're beautiful. Life without you doesn't bear thinking about. Remember the Salvation Army hall? Well, that was our wedding day and don't you ever forget it. I've never thought of you as anything other than my wife.'

His words, spoken so softly and with such feeling, made her tears brim over. She couldn't believe the wonder of them.

'Ssh!' He pulled her gently against him, patting her back as Florrie had done when she was a child.

The first few days of October were a bonus. 'An Indian summer,' Patsy said to herself as she got off the tram at Clapham South, 'this will help shorten the winter.' It was more than two hours later when she came through the main entrance of the Women's Hospital, and she was very relieved to see Eddie standing at the bottom of the steps waiting for her. She tired so easily these days and her legs were swollen and painful from the moment she got out of bed. She would be glad when this pregnancy was over and the baby was safely born.

She stood still and let go of Eddie's arm. It hadn't really sunk in until that moment. 'Twins!' She said the word out loud, and Eddie stared at her in amazement.

'You're not serious?' He lowered his head, looked into her face, saw that she was, and all he could utter was one word: 'Incredible'. Then he flung his head back and laughed out loud.

People passing by looked at him as if he'd gone mad. He didn't care. He stepped back, drew himself up to his full height, and said in a voice deep with emotion, 'Mrs Owen, you are wonderful!' Suddenly serious, he said, 'It's hard to take in, isn't it.'

Patsy smiled. 'Yes, I haven't got used to the idea myself yet. I couldn't for the life of me believe the doctor when she told me. You don't mind, do you?'

'Mind! We'll have a grand family, won't we!'

Patsy heaved a sigh of relief. 'Now can we go home?'

It was then that he realised how tired she was. As they walked slowly towards the tram stop Eddie was silently praying, 'Please God, keep her safe.'

Hardly had they got home than the rain came – just a light shower at first, and then, without warning, it suddenly turned into a deluge. Huge drops fell with rapid splashing sounds, lightning lit up the sky and the thunder roared. 'Thank God, Kitty has met the boys from school,' Eddie said as he went round making sure all the windows were shut. 'I'll just pop up and see that they're all right.'

The wind seemed to have risen, the rain was lashing down and in no time at all the gutters and the eaves were overflowing.

It had become very dark and the noise was terrifying; even the glass in the window frames was rattling. Patsy was glad when Eddie came back downstairs. 'They're doing a jigsaw puzzle and Kitty has promised to cook them pancakes for their tea. I said I'd go up for them at seven o'clock. You know, Kitty is thrilled to have them – she must get very lonely at times.'

'Yes, well I think we're lucky to have Kitty to fall back on, and the boys do love her.' Patsy had to yell her reply to make herself heard above the storm.

There was a great clap of thunder. Patsy jumped, and Eddie saw how pale she was. 'Only a summer storm, it will pass in a minute,' he said, trying to sound reassuring.

'Summer! It's October!' she declared, but the wind did seem to be dying down, and the noise was not so loud.

With the curtains pulled, and a fire burning brightly in the grate, they ate their tea from trays on their laps. At a quarter to seven Patsy said, 'Isn't it quiet without the boys? I'll come up with you to get them. It will give me a chance to say thank you to Kitty.'

As they reached the top of the second flight of

stairs, Kitty opened her door calling out, 'You shouldn't have climbed the stairs, Patsy. Are you all right?'

'Yes, I'm fine,' Patsy managed to answer – but her breathing was bad and it was obvious that she wasn't all right. Eddie guided her into Kitty's brightly-lit living-room and turned to assure the boys that their mother just needed to rest for a few minutes. Groping behind her for the comforting feel of an armchair, Patsy lowered herself slowly down into it.

'I'll be all right,' she whispered through lips that were trembling as Eddie knelt down beside her and loosened the neck of her dress. She did her best to sit up, but fell back, beads of sweat standing out on her forehead. 'You're going to the hospital,' Eddie stated firmly, making for the door. He turned round to see Patsy pushing herself up by the chair arms, her face grey with determination.

'I'm coming down,' she said. 'I've got to get my case. It's all packed, and I know where it is. Will you see the boys into bed for me, Kitty?'

'Oh, love, you don't have to ask – you know that. Just get yourself off to the hospital. I'll stay downstairs with the boys till Eddie gets back.'

Patsy smiled her thanks and then drew the boys towards her, kissing each in turn. Both were a little afraid of what was happening, and David began to cry.

'Come on, now,' Kitty soothed. 'Let your mum

go, and we'll finish our jigsaw and then if you get yourselves ready for bed I'll tell you a story.' Patsy, relieved that the boys were in such good hands, went from the room and leaning heavily on Eddie made her way down the stairs.

At the hospital Eddie felt very much alone as he sat in the visitors' waiting-room, wringing his hands together, praying that Patsy would be all right. Twice he got to his feet as a nurse came into the room, only to be told, 'Go home, Mr Owen, it will be some time before there is anything to report.' He stood irresolute; he'd much rather stay and be near Patsy.

Daylight came, and the Day Sister would stand no nonsense. 'You're not doing yourself or your wife any good by staying here,' she sharply told him. 'Get yourself home. Get some rest. Have a meal.'

'Expectant fathers!' she muttered, as she went back into the ward.

Outside in the High Street Eddie stood still, leaning against the wall, oblivious to the noise of the traffic and the great carthorses' steady clip-clop as they passed pulling loaded flat carts and open wagons. Even the cries of 'Wall Street Crash' from the newspaper vendors failed to penetrate his despondency. What if Patsy should die? *No, No*, he almost screamed aloud. He couldn't bear this waiting. He had to do something, he'd go home, take the boys to school.

As he held out the coppers to the conductor for his fare on the tram his eyes held an expression that would have been hard to identify. They were the eyes of a man desperate for consolation.

Thirty-six hours passed before Eddie was allowed to see Patsy – the longest, loneliest hours he had ever experienced. 'She's had a bad time,' a doctor told him as he stumbled after him down the long white corridor. 'I'm afraid she won't be able to have more children after this.'

Eddie could scarcely refrain from saying, 'I don't care.' All that mattered to him was that Patsy was and would be all right. It seemed an eternity since he had brought her in to this hospital, and since then he had died a thousand deaths. If it had been that bad for him, what about Patsy? She must have suffered terribly! Did she think he had deserted her?

At last. The doctor pushed open a door of a side ward, held it back and motioned for Eddie to pre-cede him into the room. With three great strides Eddie was at the end of the bed, and there he stopped dead. His eyes widened with surprise. Patsy was sitting bolt upright against a mound of pillows.

Exhaustion showed in her red-rimmed eyes and the two spots of bright colour on her cheeks, and yet her green eyes twinkled roguishly at him. He flopped down into a chair at the side of the bed. Relief flooded through him, leaving him feeling as if he had fought a war single-handed. He wanted to put his arms around her, to kiss her, to tell her how agonising the past hours had been, but most of all he wanted to tell her how much he loved her, needed her, adored her. Oh, he'd never be able to make her understand. He couldn't find the words to express just how he felt. He sat there, silent, his head bent forward as if in prayer, until Patsy's fingers closed around his hand. He raised his head and as their eyes met the love they felt for each other was there for all to see. No words could have declared it more clearly.

Numerous visitors came over the next few days. Most were turned away. Even Queenie was cowed in face of Sister's stern warning: 'Husband and parents only, if you please. Mrs Owen needs her rest.'

This statement didn't deter Florrie or Gran in the slightest. 'I ain't come all the way from Tooting to see me great-granddaughters and be turned away by the likes of 'er,' sniffed Gran as Queenie pleaded with her mother to keep her voice down.

Florrie wasn't going to be outdone. 'That's me daughter in there,' she stated in a voice loud enough to be heard out on the common. 'I'm not moving from here till I see that she's all right. Might 'ave milk fever for all I know. And what about the babies? Is there some reason why you ain't letting us see 'em?'

Sister gave up. How did that nice Mrs Owen come to have relatives like these? 'Ten minutes! I mean it. And do try and be quiet and don't upset Mrs Owen.' She flounced off with a twirl of her white apron, but she wasn't quick enough not to hear Gran say, 'Bloody cheek! As if we'd upset our Patsy.'

'Twin girls!' Florrie said in hushed tones as she gazed into the cot.

'Oh, they're bloody lovely!' was Gran's only comment.

'You'll have to wait till I get out of here before the pair of you start unwrapping them to see if they've got all their fingers and toes.' Patsy was smiling gently as she spoke. The very fact that these two dear old women cared enough about her to travel from Tooting and satisfy themselves that the hospital was looking after her and the babies, was not a matter for laughter to her. That's love, she told herself. Real family love.

Staff from other wards kept finding excuses to come in and look at the twins. 'They really are the most beautiful babies,' they all declared. Long ago Eddie and Patsy had agreed that if the baby was a girl they would name her Ellen and now because they thought that Emma linked so well with Ellen that was the name they gave to their other daughter.

Chapter Seventeen

PATSY SANG SOFTLY to herself as she rolled out pastry on the table in the middle of the kitchen. She wouldn't have believed it was possible for anyone to feel as happy as she did now. It was Christmas Eve and she was really looking forward to tomorrow. In front of the dresser the twins lay one each end of a large wooden cot. The kitchen was quiet and warm and Ellen and Emma slept peacefully. They were one year old. Time had passed so quickly – they had been crawling for weeks now and were already doing their best to stand.

For her and Eddie, 1930 had been a good year. Others hadn't been so fortunate, and this knowledge upset her greatly. Hundreds of men were out of work, and it had become a common sight to see women patiently standing in long queues where voluntary organisations were handing out free food. Things were worse in the North. Half the time she was afraid for Eddie. He would attend every meeting, get himself on to any committee that promised to help find jobs for the men. In May there had been a hunger march.

Three hundred and fifty marchers, including a few women, had met up in Hyde Park. These poor desperate souls had walked from Scotland, Wales and all corners of the country to bring their plight to the attention of the government. For three days she hadn't seen anything of either Eddie or Ollie who had both been in Hyde Park, manning the soup kitchens, helping out wherever they could. Well, they would, wouldn't they? These two men of hers, they were the salt of the earth.

The thought of Ollie caused her to stop singing. Why had he given up his job at the Town Hall? He spent a lot of time up in the City, still dealing with his brother's affairs she supposed. This was another thing which puzzled her. He never mentioned Jack, though Patsy had expected to be told whether he left a great deal of money or at least what kind of businesses he had been involved in. Eddie told her that Ollie spent a lot of time with Mr Topple. She couldn't see what for. Jack hadn't set foot in England for years before he died so how on earth could Mr Topple sort everything out? Well, she wasn't going to tax her brains thinking about it; she was going to enjoy this Christmas and thank God for all his blessings.

She still had a lot to do. There was going to be a crowd for Christmas dinner. Ollie had been staying with them for the last three days; he had his own bed in the boys' room, for he regularly slept over at the weekends. A put-you-up was ready for Florrie in the front room, Kitty was coming down from upstairs for the whole day and Ted and Amy

Andrews and their brood would help to swell the gathering. What with that lot, and all the children and their presents – boy, thought Patsy, they were in for a great time!

'Morning, my love!' Ollie had come into the kitchen without her realising it, breaking in on her thoughts.

'I thought you were going to have a lie-in? As soon as I'd finished this pie I was going to bring you up a cup of tea.'

'I'm up now. You carry on, I'll brew a pot. Have you had breakfast yet? I heard Eddie go out before four this morning.'

Patsy took the empty mixing bowl and rolling-pin to the sink, glancing into the cot as she passed. 'I got up with Eddie, fed them,' she said, nodding her head to indicate Ellen and Emma, 'and no I haven't eaten. Let's have a cuppa first then I'll do us a fry-up. It will save a meal; call it brunch, cos you won't get anything else till dinner tonight.'

'Did Eddie say they were busy on the market?' asked Ollie as they ate the plateful of breakfast Patsy had cooked.

'They have been this past week. Seems Christmas is Christmas no matter what.' Then, becoming very serious, Patsy asked as she poured each of them a second cup of tea, 'What's the weather going to do over the holiday?'

Ollie gave a satisfied sigh, patted his stomach, grinned at Patsy and said, 'Mmm, that was good!

As to the weather, only God knows.' He got up from his chair, went to the kitchen window and drew back the short lace curtain. 'The sky looks full of snow, but it's far too cold for snow showers. It's more likely that everything will freeze.'

'Good God, I hope not. Things are bad enough for those that can't afford a bag of coal without a great freeze-up. What's the matter with the government, Ollie? Surely there is something they could do. 'Tisn't as if they don't know that people are starving, that kids haven't got a pair of boots to their feet. After all, the men aren't asking for hand-outs – all they want is a job. Why all of a sudden is there no work about? What happened to all the jobs? Don't tell me again it's a world-wide problem! I'm only interested in the state of affairs close to home, and God almighty knows they're bad enough.'

Though Ollie knew how upset Patsy got whenever this subject was discussed, and knew she did her utmost to help any family she heard of as having a particularly bad time, he had to grin to himself. Between Patsy and Eddie they ought to be able to put the world to rights.

'Quite a few organisations will be out on the streets today, delivering food parcels and coal, so stop your worrying. No one around here will be cold or hungry over this holiday, and I can promise you that.' He didn't tell her that he would be one of the main contributors. 'Patsy, I need to talk to you.'

She was bending over the cot, loosening the

covers, checking that the babies hadn't got their noses pressed into the pillow.

'Look, will you stop fussing and sit down?' Ollie spoke to her as he had when she was a child. 'I need to talk to you seriously.'

She straightened up, turned to look at him, her eyes full of questions.

'Now there's no need to look at me like that. Just come and sit at the table, and listen to what I have to say.' He sat down opposite her and placed a manila envelope on the table between them. His voice was quite firm as he said, 'We have to talk about the Jacksons.'

A piece of coal fell to the hearth and one of the babies sighed in her sleep, but otherwise you could have heard a pin drop! The colour drained from Patsy's face.

'No!' She sounded as if she were frightened. 'No,' she repeated and this time she sounded resentful. 'I knew things were too good to be true. Going too well. Why in heaven's name do you have to bring *them* up, today of all days?'

'Now just you be quiet a minute, Patsy,' he ordered as he drew an official-looking document from the envelope. Without giving her a chance to say so much as a word, he went on talking. 'This document is a land deed. You remember the waste ground at Mitcham where the Jacksons lived?' Ollie paused, and Patsy nodded her head sullenly. She didn't want to be reminded of Johnny and his family, not today. Not ever.

Ollie kept his eyes on her face as he continued. 'Well, you always knew it belonged to the Coal and Coke Company. The Jacksons may have lived on it for years, but they were squatters.'

'So?' Patsy's curiosity was aroused now.

'The Company decided they had had enough. They put the land up for sale, and I bought it.'

'What?' Patsy hissed the word out from between clenched teeth. 'Whatever for? What can you possibly want with a piece of rotten old waste ground?' A sudden thought struck her. 'If you've got thoughts about throwing the Jacksons off that land, how are you going to go about it? You said yourself that the Coal and Coke Company have been trying for years to evict them. If a great company like that couldn't get them off, how are you going to manage it?'

The sad look on his face made her fall silent. 'You ungrateful bitch,' she thought to herself. 'There's Ollie doing his best for you, just as he always has done – though God knows where he got the money from – and all you can do is yell at him.'

'I've asked myself those questions several times, but that's beside the point now. I did buy it.'

'Oh, Ollie,' Patsy was up and out of her chair, flinging her arms around his neck, 'what am I going to do with you?'

'There's more to tell,' he confessed. She threw

back her head and laughed so loud the babies woke up. 'Now, see what we've done between the pair of us! Come on, my lovely,' she whispered as she lifted Ellen out first. 'Your grandad can hold you for a moment.' Ollie held out his arms and took the baby, a wide smile on his face as he gazed at her. Patsy went back over to the cot and picked up Emma, cradling her in the crook of her arm as she sat down again. 'Well, come on then,' she grinned at Ollie. 'Let's have the rest of this story.'

He didn't hesitate, just plunged on in. 'I had a contracting firm close off the part where the Jacksons had their caravans and on the other part of the ground, the bit that lies well back from the road, I've had three houses built.'

Patsy stared at him in total disbelief. Like someone in a trance she got up, put the baby on to her hip and with her free hand filled the kettle and put it on the gas to boil. 'I'd better make the twins something to drink,' she mumbled.

'I never revealed my identity. The Jacksons have no idea who the purchaser was. Mr Topple conducted all the legal transactions for me. He also took the Jacksons to court and asked for an eviction order against them.'

Patsy made no reply. It was as if she hadn't heard a word. Yet inside she was laughing merrily. What a man Ollie was! He'd sworn years ago that he would pay back all the hurt she had suffered at the hands of the Jacksons. It was as if Ollie could read her thoughts and he now savoured the rest of the telling. 'The courts didn't refuse the application because I offered the Jacksons, through an estate agent, alternative accommodation.'

Patsy's mind raced ahead of him. He was mad! He had to be. He'd evicted the Jacksons from what was now his land and put them into brand-new houses. She couldn't see the point. They'd never pay the rent. It took all her will-power to sit still and listen.

'Does Eddie know what you've done?' She shot the question at him, making both the babies jump. Rather sheepishly, Ollie told her that he did.

'Mind you, when I told him that I was going to tell you today, he did say rather you than me. In fact, he told me to be ready to duck!'

Slowly and carefully Ollie changed Ellen over so that she lay on his left arm and with his right hand now free he unfolded the document and laid it flat between them. He lifted his eyes to meet those of Patsy and, with love evident in the sound of his voice, he said, 'Rightly or wrongly, Patsy, this is my Christmas present to you. The whole thing, land and houses, notarised in your name. Those people are now living in houses that belong to you.'

The silence seemed to go on for ever. She couldn't think of a single thing to say. Ollie finally spoke.

'Take your time, my love. All my instincts told me I was doing right. To be honest, looking at you now, I'm not so sure. It's up to you. Whatever you decide, Patsy, is all right with me. Sit tight for a while is about the best advice that I can give you.' They both stood up at the same time and with the two babies clasped between them they gave each other a kiss – just a peck on the cheek, but that small action said it all. Then they stood back and smiled at each other.

'I must go out,' Ollie said, putting his arm into the sleeve of his overcoat and shrugging it on to his shoulders. 'After all, it's nearly Christmas and you're not the only one with things to do.'

At the door he stopped, turned and faced her. 'Just remember one thing, Patsy: you owe the Jacksons nothing. Quite the reverse is the truth.'

Neither Patsy nor Eddie could remember a Christmas like it. It began at a quarter to six in the morning when the two boys burst into their room shouting, 'Mum, Dad, Father Christmas has been.'

'Well I never! What did he bring you?' Patsy's tone was full of laughter as she nudged Eddie to move over and make room in the bed for Alex and David to climb in with them. 'Come on, give me a cuddle for Christmas,' she said, pulling the boys close, one on each side of her. They tried to clamber over to Eddie's side and Patsy tickled both boys which only made them giggle and shout all the more.

'You're worse than they are!' Eddie exclaimed. 'You'll wake the whole house up.' Laughing and giggling, Patsy got up and went downstairs to make tea for everyone. Christmas had begun.

During the whole of the holiday Patsy kept her mouth shut and her thoughts to herself regarding the present that Ollie had given her. She had done her best to close her mind completely to the whole matter.

Now, it was the day after Boxing Day. Patsy sat before the fire in what she still thought of as her beautiful front room. Florrie sat opposite her, warm and contented; she'd enjoyed every minute of the holiday. Patsy was far away, lost in deep thought. Was something troubling her, Florrie wondered, or was it her imagination? Either way she'd get to the bottom of it. Patsy got up and took two logs from the box in the hearth and threw them on the fire, pressing them firmly down with the long brass poker. Slowly she sat down by the fire and stared again into the flames.

Florrie couldn't keep quiet any longer. Patsy's deep frown was worrying her. 'What's up, love? Want to tell me about it?'

'Nothing, really,' Patsy mumbled.

'Now, don't give me that. Any fool can see you've something on your mind and, as you well know, I ain't no fool.'

'You wouldn't believe me if I told you,' Patsy said.

'Well, we won't know that till you stop mucking about and get on with it.'

Patsy turned her head, and again she said, 'You won't believe it. But knowing you, you'll find out sooner or later, so I suppose I'd better tell you.' She stood up and, with her elbow resting on the mantelpiece, told Florrie everything.

During the telling Florrie didn't interrupt once, but her face grew redder by the minute. Patsy ended the story and then, in a voice that struck Florrie as infuriatingly quiet, added, 'Ollie said all the Jacksons are now living in houses that belong to me.'

'Gawd blimey, you're right! I don't bloody well believe it!'

'Calm down, calm down!' Patsy thought that if Florrie didn't take a hold of herself she'd blow a gasket.

'Think of it! Spending good money to house that bleedin' lot. He's got to be off his 'ead. You know what it is, don't you? He's come into money from that brother of his, and it's turned his brain.'

Florrie paused to draw breath, and Patsy laughed to herself; she would not dare let Florrie see her laughing – the mood she was in, she'd just as likely swipe her one – but to say that Ollie was off his head! Nothing could be further from the truth. She'd looked at it from all angles and Ollie came out of it as a very wise man. She'd made up her mind to take his advice. She was going to do nothing about the Jackson family at the moment but let them think that they had beat the system, that their ship had come in. She would burst their bubble in her own good time.

'You've not been listening to a word I've said,' Florrie complained.

'Sorry. I was thinking,' Patsy replied. 'What were you saying?'

Florrie did what she always did when she was put out; she made a face and heaved up her bosoms. 'I was telling you. You be careful about what you decide to do, I shouldn't 'ave to tell you this but perhaps you've forgotten what a rotten lot of bleeders those Jacksons are. I warned you before, so did Gran, and a fat lot of bloody notice you took then.'

Patsy stepped nearer and took hold of Florrie's hand and as she slipped her arm around her shoulders she put her lips to Florrie's cheek and kissed her. 'How about a Guinness?' she asked. 'After all, Christmas isn't over yet.'

'Get on with you. Charm the sparrows out of the trees, you could! But don't run away with the idea that that's the end of it, cos it ain't. Not by a long chalk, it ain't. I'll 'ave a few words of me own to say to Mister Alexander Berry, you see if I don't.'

Patsy poured the Guinness from the bottle into a tall glass, making sure she put a good head on it. She passed the glass to Florrie without saying anything. It was always wise to allow Florrie to think that she had had the last word.

Chapter Eighteen

ALL THE HOPES of better things ahead and feelings of goodwill to all men seemed to vanish as the new year got under way. January, with dreary mornings and long dark evenings, didn't do much to boost the morale of men who had no jobs to go to. Over the Christmas period many men had voiced the opinion that 1931 would see the turning of the tide, and things would begin to look up. With February only a week away such was not yet the case. Eddie had been partly laid off, and was working for only three days a week. Still, as he repeatedly told Patsy, three days in work was a lot to be grateful for when you looked around and saw the state some families were in.

Patsy felt she had to lower her head as she passed Clapham Labour Exchange. The ever-lengthening queues never failed to make her feel sad. The men stood shivering in clothes so thin and patched that the bitter cold winds blew right through them. Hands in pockets, flat caps on their heads, eyes that showed utter despair, they presented a picture of a woebegone wretched lot who had been robbed of their manhood and left with no hope for the future. The twins in the pushchair, as she hurried by, did bring a faint smile to the face of one or two men, but even that made Patsy feel guilty. Her children were warmly clothed and well fed. Eddie still had a little money left, from the sale of his father's shop, safely tucked away. They could manage, just, on a day-to-day basis. Many of life's treats were thanks to Ollie, including winter coats for each of them.

'My Christmas present,' he had laughingly told Patsy when she had objected to the cost.

Eddie had also told her to stop worrying when she had protested to him that Ollie had no job now and yet he spent an awful lot of money on them. 'Ollie's got plenty to do. Why do you think he spends so much time in the City?'

'I don't know! That's the whole point. No one tells me anything,' Patsy had yelled in exasperation.

Eddie soothed her. 'Ollie told me that some money was beginning to trickle through to London from Jack's various business deals. I'm sure he'll tell us all about it when things are finally settled.'

Patsy had to be content. At least what Eddie had told her went some way to putting her mind at rest. There had been times when her imagination had run riot as she thought of Ollie spending all his money, buying land, having houses built. If prosperity had come to Ollie she was glad – no one deserved it more, and the timing was fortunate. Having Ollie for their grandfather was beneficial to her children in more ways than one. He didn't spoil them, any more than he had spoilt her when she'd been a child, but he did make sure that they didn't go short of anything that was essential and, more than that, he gave them love, and his time – two very special commodities.

In return, Alex and David loved and respected him, and the twins would giggle with delight the minute Ollie came into the room.

Like all mothers Patsy was finding that each of her children had a very distinct personality. Alex: if she were honest, she loved him best of all her children and there were times when she felt a sense of guilt because of this. He was her first-born, named after her beloved Ollie; perhaps she was entitled to love him most.

David. He was so very much like his father that she felt it was a bonus to have been given him for a son. More contented than Alex, he asked nothing more of life than that which came easily.

Ellen and Emma: she rolled their names around her tongue, slowly, lovingly. She had certainly been blessed to have been granted two such beautiful, healthy little girls. Did her memory play tricks? She didn't think so. She could see her mother in both of them, and she often prayed that they would grow up to be as kind and as gentle as their grandmother had been. Her mother had given up her own family and a life of ease in order to bring her up. It was only since her death that Patsy had realised exactly what that had meant. She had been too young to appreciate the sacrifices that her own mother had made.

Never to have been married! The thought struck Patsy with such force that she couldn't get it out of her head.

She went about her daily tasks as always, washing the smalls in the sink while the sheets from the beds boiled in the copper, filling the scullery with hot steam. When things got better and Eddie was back on full time she intended to ask him if they could get one of the new gas coppers. Each week it was more difficult to find enough fuel, mainly old wood, to burn under their copper to boil the water.

Outside the back door, she was running the washing through the mangle ready to peg it on the line when Kitty put her head out of the top-floor window and called down to her. 'Patsy, when you've finished that lot, I'll make us a cuppa. Bring my milk up with you when you come, it'll save my legs up and down them stairs.'

'I hope it's not going to rain,' was Patsy's thought as she looked up at the sky, which was rapidly becoming darker. 'If it does the washing can stay out. I'm certainly not going to clean and hearthstone the front steps today.' She put her own two bottles of milk just inside the passage and picking up the third one she made her way up to Kitty. She tapped on the door and, as she did so, she heard Kitty's voice telling her to come in. Kitty was sitting in an armchair by the window, embroidering a small linen cloth. The tea cups were set out on the table and a large slab of gingerbread lay on a flowered dish. 'Make the tea will you, Patsy? The kettle is boiling,' Kitty called as she raised her eyes from her sewing.

Patsy didn't go straight through to the scullery, but went and stood watching Kitty put delicate stitches into the cloth. The colours of the pattern that Kitty was working were so pretty that Patsy exclaimed, 'That's really beautiful. Who are you making that one for?'

Kitty loved Patsy to come up to her rooms for the occasional chat and she was hoping she would stay a while. She put her work down, eased her bulk up out of the chair and went to the table. 'Go get the tea, an' I'll tell you.'

Patsy brought the pot to the table and, taking a teaspoon from one of the saucers, she gave the tea a good stir before she sat down facing Kitty. 'So, what's to tell? You're always doing embroidery of one kind or another. Who's this cloth for?'

'It's to be a wedding present. Lil, up the corner shop, 'er daughter's getting married. Should think 'erself bloody lucky an' all that the fellow is going to wed 'er.'

'Why?' Patsy demanded, as she poured out the tea and watched Kitty cut two slices from the slab of gingerbread.

'Cos it takes two to make a bargain. The girl's as much to blame as the fellow, but every time a girl finds 'erself in the family way it's the bloke that gets called all the rotten bastards. Well, Lil's girl can count 'erself lucky, fellow's gonna do the right thing, stand by 'er. Mind you, he ain't much of a catch: no job and not much prospects of finding one, the way things are going.'

Patsy made no reply as she thoughtfully sipped at her tea. The very same question that had been on her mind for days would have to come up now. And from Kitty of all people. Kitty herself would have been a darn sight better off if she'd got Mr Masters to marry her. Patsy didn't want to hear this. She wished she'd never come up the stairs that morning.

Kitty suddenly added fuel to the fire. 'Out of work or not, I suppose any father is better than none. Once a child is born and labelled a bastard it must stick for the poor kid's whole life.'

'Stop it!' Patsy wanted to scream. This was too near home. Her goodbye to Kitty was curt, and her thanks for the piece of home-made gingerbread that Kitty had carefully wrapped in greaseproof paper for the children was not at all gracious. She couldn't help it; her temper was slowly getting the better of her.

The wind had got up, keeping the rain off, and most of the washing was dry by the time that Patsy went into the garden. The flat irons were heating up on the kitchen range and she spread the thick ironing blanket across the table. She took the padded iron-holder from the hook where it hung underneath the mantelshelf, lifted a red-hot iron, spat on it and held it close to her cheek to check that it wasn't too hot. Anger was making her careless, and she almost burned the side of her face.

She got through the ironing in record time, her actions fast and furious, her thoughts whirling round and round in her head as she argued the point with herself. What would be the feelings of her children, when they grew up and became aware that she and their father had never been legally married? They would inevitably find out. Did it really matter? Yes, it does to me. She was outraged by her own question. Eddie said that the whole matter had become an obsession with her. Obsession or not, it rankled and she was never going to feel any different. Time and time again she had added up things on the plus side. Eddie was marvellous. She couldn't ask for better. Four wonderful, healthy children, a nice home which was warm and dry and enough food for all of them to eat, good clothes on their backs and boots on their feet. Could she ask for more? Yes, she could. And she would.

She folded up the freshly ironed sheets and hung them over the line in the scullery to air. It was time to wake the twins from their nap and take them with her to meet Alex and David from school. She raked a comb through her long hair and wound it up into a bun which she fixed securely at the nape of her neck. By the time she had finished she had decided it was time that she did something about

Johnny Jackson. He had had things his way for far too long. Now it was her turn.

First, she was going to go and see Mr Topple. Everybody else seemed to go to him for advice so why shouldn't she? She remembered when she had lived over the shop with Eddie, and how some of the customers had treated her with contempt. The unpleasantness she'd had to endure then! But Mr Topple had been kindness itself to her. He'd made all the arrangements for her and Eddie to emigrate, yet even when she'd changed her mind and they had decided to stay in England he hadn't seemed at all put out. Quite the opposite: he'd said then that if ever she needed his help or advice she was to go and see him. Well, now she was going to do just that.

By the time her two boys came racing out of the school gates, arms open wide, faces raised for a kiss, Patsy was feeling much better-tempered. She wouldn't change her mind. The very next time that Florrie came over to Clapham she'd get her to see to the twins and she'd be off. On her own to see Mr Topple the solicitor.

With the coming of spring, the hopes of men and women alike rose. Those with wireless sets listened to the daily news broadcasts with a sense of renewed optimism. Most ignored the fact that the queues outside the labour exchanges didn't grow any shorter, that there were riots in India because under the leadership of Mahatma Gandhi the people wanted independence from British rule, and that a man named Adolf Hitler was stirring up trouble in Germany. The brighter weather brought hope, living was cheaper, coal was not such a necessity, and the men could walk longer distances in search of a day's work.

During the warm, dry days of early May, when Eddie wasn't working, Patsy would cut sandwiches and they would spend as much time as they could out with the children in the fresh air. Despite all the poverty, girls walked on the common in pretty brightly-coloured dresses, their boyfriends sporting open-necked short-sleeved shirts. Some older men wore Panama hats, while others tied knots in the four corners of their handkerchiefs and spread them on top of their heads. Motherly women would stop and talk to Patsy about the children, always admiring the twins, whose long hair, which she always had tied back with silky ribbons, now showed the same copper-coloured glints as her own. Alex and David ran about wearing only a pair of shorts, and their little bodies were already nicely tanned.

Watching Eddie kick a ball to the boys, or on his knees, happy as a lark, tickling and teasing the two girls, she would tell herself he was just a big kid himself. Sometimes she felt such love for her family that she would get a tight feeling in her chest, as if a hand were scrunching it up. Sometimes she was afraid – her life was too good to be true.

In the back of her mind was the ever-nagging problem of Johnny Jackson. Twice she had visited Mr Topple in his chambers, and as she had expected he had been most helpful. He had advised caution. She had checked with the house agents and discovered it was now twenty-one weeks since any of the Jacksons had paid rent. She would play the waiting game a little longer. At least she was now fully aware of just where she stood with regard to the law. The circumstances were such that Mr Topple had urged her to try and get Johnny voluntarily to admit to his own adultery. Unable to resist a slight grin, he had lowered his voice and said, 'Whatever means you resort to, in order to get this admission, I don't think I want to know about.' At that moment Patsy's reaction had been to hug him. He was proving to be not only a great ally, but a very good friend.

As the days wore on, Patsy became more and more determined to act against the Jacksons. She wanted badly to get the matter settled, yet she dreaded the confrontation that had to come. The Whitsun Bank Holiday had brought the typical Bank Holiday weather. Saturday and Sunday had been bad enough with the rain coming down non-stop. Monday had been worse, a filthy day, dark skies, cold winds and the rain still lashing down.

'Talk about spring,' Florrie muttered. 'Good job the 'oliday is all over. What d'you think? Shall I take 'em all to the pictures this afternoon? Get 'em out from under your feet.'

It was the Tuesday morning, and they were standing side by side at the sink, peeling potatoes for the midday meal, when Florrie made her suggestion. For a minute Patsy was flummoxed – Florrie must have been reading her thoughts. She had finally come to a decision, and had thought she would have to wait until the boys were back at school before she could put it into action. Now Florrie was giving her a golden opportunity.

Patsy stood at the front gate and watched as her four children happily trooped off down the road. Already they were pestering Florrie to say that they might have an ice-cream in the interval.

'Well,' Patsy said out loud as she got herself ready, 'I hope it all works out.'

Then, still speaking aloud, she added, 'I've just got to make sure that it does.'

The tram was a long time in coming and Patsy felt a strong urge to turn round and go home. Once on board she relaxed a little and rummaged in her handbag for pennies to pay her fare. By the time she reached Tooting Broadway and had to change trams she was smiling faintly to herself. The tram shuddered to a halt at Mitcham fair green, the end of the journey; she had no option other than to get off. She had walked as far as the Three Kings Pond when she had to stop. She was having difficulty in breathing, so many memories were rushing through her mind, horrible memories that she had fought to put behind her.

She forced herself to walk on, and then she was standing on the very spot where the Jacksons had lived for so long, and where they had tormented her so badly. No tall hoardings enclosed the site now. The ground was covered in stubbly grass, and stinging nettles grew everywhere, bounded only by a wire mesh fence. Patsy had to turn away. Her heart was thumping like mad – she mustn't panic now. She trod warily along the narrow lane until the ground sloped downwards; here she stopped again, and gazed down on three two-storey houses. Even from this distance she could see they weren't in any way pretentious. They were just solidly-built ordinary dwellings.

She heard the sound of the dogs rushing towards her before she saw them. They came bolting out of the bushes, charging at her – three of them, all Alsatians, and they skidded to a halt forming a semi-circle around her. The noise of their barking was deafening and their great fangs terrified her.

The weather had been miserable when she had set out and now it started to rain again. The lane was muddy and Patsy felt that if she stood still much longer, she would become bogged down; yet she couldn't move for fear that one of these huge dogs might sink its teeth into the flesh of her leg.

For what seemed an eternity she cowered there,

feeling terribly frightened and with all her limbs trembling.

'Down! Down, I say, and stop that blasted racket.' With the voice came the sound of running footsteps. Thank God for that! Someone was coming. Patsy sighed with relief.

As the man came into sight, he called out in a rasping voice, 'What the bloody hell are yer doing round 'ere?', and as he drew nearer he yelled again, 'Down! Down I tell yer.' The three dogs dropped down on to their bellies, their front paws spread flat each side of their heads, their ferocious eyes still focused on Patsy. She still didn't dare move.

Glaring at her, the man continued to yell at the top of his voice. 'It's yer own damn fault, whoever you are. You've no sodding business being on this land, you're trespassing! Me dogs are only doing their job.'

The man was very close to her now and every instinct told Patsy that he was a Jackson. Could it be Tom? Or Fred, perhaps? He was scruffy-looking, his collarless shirt open almost to his waist showed a heavily tattooed chest, black braces hung loosely down over baggy corduroy trousers. To say that Patsy wasn't frightened any more would be untrue, but she stood her ground and spoke in as firm a voice as she could manage. 'I'm well aware that this is private land. I'm here to see Johnny Jackson.'

The man looked perplexed as he stared at her. She was well dressed, her tone of voice was one of authority, and by the look of her she wasn't hard up.

Pulling the collar of her camel coat up high, and tightening the belt around her waist, Patsy quietly asked, 'Well, are you going to move these dogs away from my feet and inform Mr Jackson that I'm here?'

The man's face exploded into instant anger and he thrust his chin out towards her. 'Who the bloody hell are you? Inform my bruvver that you're 'ere! You've got nerve, I'll give yer that. Now take my advice, and sling yer bleeding' hook, we don't 'old with the likes of you around 'ere.'

He had raised his voice and shouted the last few words which had set the dogs off snarling again, but they lay where they were, making no attempt to move.

Keeping her voice as steady as she could Patsy said: 'That's what your family told me nine years ago, that they didn't hold with the likes of me.'

'What!' He scowled at her. 'Don't know what yer on about. Go on, clear off, before I really set the dogs on you.'

Patsy had come too far now to feel nervous. Her temper was rising, but she forced a smile, albeit a cynical one. 'Your mother used that same threat when I was here last. Now, are you going to fetch your brother or shall I walk down to the house and find him?'

'Who the hell are you?' the man asked again, but a lot of the boldness had gone from his tone.

If it hadn't been for the three dogs that still lay so alarmingly close to her, Patsy would have took a step nearer to him. Instead, she stood up straight and, sounding a lot braver than she felt, she told him, 'I'm Patsy Kent, that was. A brothel-bred git, according to your mother.'

He rushed at her, letting out a deep growl, and grabbed her. Patsy thought her time had come. He would kill her, and if he didn't the dogs would. She could smell his hot stale breath and feel his fingers digging into her neck. The dogs were out of control now, leaping up in the air, snarling and panting. She knew she was fighting for her life as she kicked and struggled to break free.

'Cut it out! Do you 'ear me? Cut it out.' The shouts were coming from down the lane as another man came tearing towards them. He stopped suddenly, as if unsure what to do. 'Let go of her,' he ordered, grabbing the other man, who was still holding on to Patsy, and pulling him away. 'Now lock those dogs up. Go on, lock them away, before they really hurt someone!'

Patsy staggered as the first man released his hold. She had to fight to get herself under control and she still had to gasp to get her breath. Her assailant gave a low whistle, turned and went back the way he had come, the dogs racing ahead of him. She felt her whole body sag with relief. Those dogs were vicious. She found herself suddenly free and as she looked at her rescuer, she knew without a doubt that she was facing Johnny Jackson.

Time had not dealt kindly with him. His thick black hair still grew long at the sides and back of his head, but the crown was shiny and bald. He looked even more swarthy; he must have broken his nose, and it had failed to heal properly. He was watching her, puzzled. Then a look of total disbelief came to his face. 'You? Patsy?' he stammered.

'Yes, Johnny, it's me,' Patsy snapped.

Everything around suddenly seemed abnormally quiet as they stood facing each other. The rain was heavier now and Patsy was getting soaked.

A gloating smirk spread about Johnny's mouth as he eyed her up and down from top to toe. 'Ain't done bad fer yerself, 'ave yer Patsy? What yer come back for, d'yer still wanna be my girl?' His voice was filled with sarcasm, and when he threw back his head and roared out laughing, Patsy's hand itched to swipe him around the face, but she was too busy trying to wipe away the blood that was trickling down her leg.

'You should 'ave known better,' Johnny said, still grinning. 'Remember? We always guard our land with dogs.'

By now Patsy's nerves were so taut she wanted to scream. It took all her will-power to speak firmly. 'It is not your land!'

'Oh yeah,' he sneered, 'an' what would you know about it?'

'A lot more than you think,' she told him, and had the satisfaction of seeing the grin disappear from his face and a baffled look come into his eyes. Keeping her voice as steady as she could, Patsy pressed her point home. 'I own this land!'

Johnny Jackson might have been only a fair-ground worker, but he was no fool. Instinctively he knew she was telling the truth.

Patsy gave him no time to react to her statement. Boldly she added, 'I also own all three houses which you and your family are living in.'

His face exploded in anger. 'You bitch, you bloody bitch.' The words came out as a snarl, and his arm came forward and upwards with his fist clenched.

Patsy was quick, her manner as ferocious as his now. 'You do,' she screamed, 'you lay one finger on me and I'll have the police here so fast you won't know what's hit you. I'll also see that every damn one of you Jacksons are evicted from my properties.'

'Jesus Christ Almighty!' He brought his clenched fist up again, but it was his own forehead he thumped. 'You vindictive cow!' He roared at her.

'Vindictive! Well, if that's not a case of the kettle calling the pot black, I don't know what is. For years you've never wanted me but you made damn sure no one else could have me. I don't give a monkey's what you or your family call me, but I'll tell you this, Johnny, either you do what I want or I'll see that not you nor any member of your family go on living in my houses.'

They were both shaking with anger, but it was his eyes that fell away first.

'Right,' Patsy said, with a confidence she was far from feeling, 'now that we understand each other, shall we go down to one of my houses and have a talk?'

As she walked down the lane behind Johnny, Patsy shuddered. She was soaking wet and very cold and the thought of what still lay ahead did nothing to lift her spirits. She dug her hands deep into her pockets and renewed her determination.

Patsy looked around the messy room in disgust. 'You'd better take that wet coat off.' There was laughter again in Johnny's eyes, and she knew he was mocking her. He had already removed his own coat and she knew it made sense for her to do likewise. They sat opposite each other and the sight of him sickened her.

His calico shirt had no collar, but a brass stud hung limply from the top buttonhole. His sleeves were rolled up beyond his elbows, and the well-remembered tattoos were visible on his forearms. His eyes, especially when he laughed, still held some of that boyish charm that had captivated her so long ago, but his body had run to fat.

He gave her a roguish grin, but Patsy had the feeling that it was sheer bravado when he said, 'Me missus 'as got her eye on you.'

Patsy felt herself tremble and the thought struck her that perhaps his mother was in the house. Twisting her body round, she saw a woman lolling against the door-jamb of what appeared to be the kitchen. She was lighting one cigarette from the stub of another, yet she never took her eyes off Patsy for a second and Patsy felt that she had watched her every move since she had entered the house.

The woman was quite tall and at first Patsy thought she must be turned fifty. But when she looked more closely she could see she was probably no older than herself, though she had the tough, hardened look normally associated with older people. She was no beauty, and certainly not well groomed. Her body was thin to the point of scrawniness. Her red, rough hands were dry and knobbly. Long ginger-coloured hair was parted at the centre and scraped back into a plait. Her complexion was ruddy, telling that she spent a lot of time out of doors, yet her face somehow had a pinched look. It was obvious she mistrusted Patsy on sight.

Considering the state of the house the woman's physical cleanliness was remarkable. Her cotton dress was a faded navy blue, perfectly plain, but as clean as her body and face. Compared to Johnny she appeared respectable and tidy.

Suddenly she grinned, but only with her lips. Patsy stared into her blazing eyes and was frightened at the violence she saw mirrored there.

She found herself leaning backwards as the woman spoke. 'I was about to ask who the 'ell are you but I guess I don't 'ave to. It will be all over the tribe by now. You're the biddy who tried to foster her bastard off on Johnny. What d'yer want this time? From the look of yer, there ain't much that you're in need of.'

The woman deliberately blew a cloud of smoke in Patsy's direction and Johnny threw back his head, laughing uproariously. In what sounded like a proud declaration he said, 'That's Mary, me wife.'

It was Mary who shouted now, 'Yeah an' we've got five young uns, all legal Jacksons, make no mistake about that. So whatever bloody trouble you think you've come 'ere to stir up today, you can damn well ferget it, yer saucy bitch.'

Patsy considered this statement and inwardly she smiled. It was more than she could have hoped for. Mary and Johnny did not know it, but they were playing right into her hands. She gave an exaggerated groan as she looked at Mary. 'So, the family accepted you. You must be a trusting soul if you believe that Johnny was never legally married to me.'

Mary stubbed her cigarette out in a tin ashtray,

and her voice was solemn as she answered. 'I ain't
no bloody whore, so don't go running away with
any bleedin' ideas of that sort. I've bin with Johnny
a long time now, he chose me and I chose 'im and
we've stuck together through all sorts of trouble.
Don't let my skinniness fool you. I'm tough enough
to 'andle a couple of big bruisers any day, and you
don't scare me one bit. I could kill you as quick as
look at you, an' I will too if you don't soon state
what you've come about – and then sling yer sodding hook out of my 'ouse and git yerself back to
yer bloody fancy man. Anyone's only got to look at
yer to see some poor bugger is keeping yer.'

Patsy was furious, but she held her temper in
check. 'Tell her, Johnny!' The words were rapped
out sharply and Mary came forward, felt for a chair
and sat down.

Johnny looked from one to the other, his features
twisted with anger. 'You tell 'er.'

Neither anger nor fright showed on Patsy's face.
She remained outwardly calm as she said huskily, 'I
own the whole of this ground, and all three houses
in which the Jackson families are living are owned
outright by me.'

Johnny remained silent. Mary stood up, reached
for her packet of cigarettes and box of matches.
Embarrassed, Mary threw one word at Johnny:
'True?'

Johnny only mumbled gruffly, 'Would seem so.'

The silence hung heavily until Patsy spoke.

'Seeing as how none of you have bothered to pay me any rent for almost six months, I would be quite within my rights to have the lot of you evicted from my properties.'

Patsy flinched as Mary roared at her. 'I'm on to you an' your game. Don't think I'm not. Where the sodding 'ell did you get the money from for this airy-fairy scheme you seem to 'ave dreamed up? Come to that, why the 'ell 'ave yer got it in for the Jackson family? What 'arm did they ever do to you?'

Patsy could hardly believe what she was hearing. Her laugh was cynical as she faced them. 'Where the money came from is no concern of yours, and my scheme – as you call it – is for real. That much you'd better believe. If the whole tribe of you wish to go on living in these houses, then Johnny has to agree to allow me to divorce him.'

'What d'yer wanna divorce for, after all these years?' demanded Johnny. 'We was never wed properly anyway.'

Patsy ignored the interruption and turned again to Mary. 'It will be best for all of you if you make him see sense. Persuade him to let me divorce him, please. It will be quick and simple, and it won't cost either of you a penny.'

'Come into a bloody fortune, 'ave yer?' Johnny sneered, then without waiting for an answer he shook his head. 'Can't be bothered. Sorry an' all that, but I ain't getting mixed up with lawyers and bloody law courts. Nah. You ain't gonna drag me through all of that, not on yer life yer not.'

'That's telling her,' Mary encouraged him.

Patsy sighed deeply. 'All right. But you can't have it both ways.'

'And what's that supposed to mean?' Johnny's voice was heavy with sarcasm.

Patsy made no reply. Getting to her feet, she slowly put her coat on.

Mary gave a cackle of a laugh. 'Going, are yer? Are yer sure yer wouldn't like to stay an' take a jar of tea with us, or maybe even something stronger, seeing as how you've had a wasted journey.'

Johnny still slouched in his chair, a grin spreading over his face from ear to ear. Standing directly in front of him, Patsy took from her bag a small card.

Looking straight into his eyes, she spoke in a firm voice that left him in no doubt that she would no longer be intimidated by him or members of his family. Bending low, she held out the card until it almost touched the tip of his nose. 'That is the name and address of my solicitor. You have a choice. Either you pay him a visit, before the end of this week, do exactly as he asks, sign any document he puts in front of you – or come next Monday I'll have the bailiffs here and every last one of you cleared off my land.'

Johnny came to his feet like an uncurled spring. Anger flamed his cheeks, his clenched fists beat the air and his voice was sheer blood and thunder as he roared at her. 'You cow! You mean it. You really mean it, don't yer? You'd put us, our kids and all the family, out on the streets. Gawd above, you've turned out to be a spiteful bloody bitch an' no mistake.'

Obscenities were being screamed at her by Mary as Patsy made her way down the short hall and let herself out of the front door.

Men, women, teenagers and toddlers stood huddled in both doorways of the other two houses. She could hear their mutterings but there were no threats of violence. Hatred was apparent in the eyes of the adults, but the time when they could browbeat her was long gone. All she wished for was to be shot of the lot of them. To wipe clean away the period of her life that had been entwined with theirs. Ollie had had the forethought to give her the wherewithall for this scheme. Would it work? All she had ever wanted, from the moment she'd set eyes on Eddie, was to be his wife.

She straightened her shoulders, held her head high and walked back up the lane, praying silently that God would see that Johnny did as she had asked.

Early the following Monday morning, Patsy went to London. When all the preliminary greetings were over and Patsy was seated, Mr Topple went behind his desk and sat down facing her. He leaned back in his chair and with almost a boyish grin said, 'You did well, Patsy. Very well indeed. Mr Jackson has paid me a visit. Mr Berry has insisted that we engage the services of a very good barrister to represent you, and you'll be delighted to know that proceedings to obtain your divorce are already under way. So, my dear friend, you may now safely leave matters in my hands.'

There was no more discussion. She was around the desk, being held in arms that made her feel safe.

'Patsy, you aren't happy unless you have something to worry about, are you?' Eddie spoke casually as he slowly buttered his toast.

Patsy, beside him, was very still. She stared at the official letter that lay in front of her. 'It's all happening so quickly now.' She added, a little wistfully, 'Do you think it will go through all right?'

Eddie, in his usual practical fashion, put down his knife and gave Patsy his full attention. 'How many more times do I have to tell you, my darling, money speaks all languages. This barrister is costing a small fortune and that is why you can be sure that there will be no last-minute hitches.'

Patsy pushed back her chair with a scrape. 'I hope you're right,' she muttered as she went to see what the twins were up to.

Both Ollie and Eddie did their best to reassure her that there would be no further complications. Nevertheless, Patsy spent sleepless nights worrying over what ordeals she might have to face in court.

When, finally, the day arrived Ollie was there by her side as usual, holding on tightly to her hand, and she soon found that she need not have got so upset.

There were few people in court, all strangers, and the public gallery was empty. Earlier in the entrance lobby, her barrister, in what had seemed to Patsy almost a conspiratorial whisper, had informed her that he had asked the court's discretion as to her own adultery. Her cheeks had flamed up as he had patted her arm and said, 'Far better to admit to cohabitation than to have some busybody coming forward, claiming to show cause as to why the decree nisi should not be made absolute.'

Johnny admitted that he had cohabited with an Irish woman named Mary Best for seven years, and that they had five children.

It was all over quite quickly. The judge granted Patsy a decree nisi. Now all she had to do was wait.

Chapter Nineteen

NOVEMBER THE FIFTH, Guy Fawkes night. At about six o'clock that evening the Owens were to have a bonfire party in the garden, and all their children's friends and their parents had been invited. Now it was just ten o'clock in the morning, and fireworks were the last thing that the Owens had on their minds.

Patsy sat at one side of the kitchen table, and Eddie sat opposite her. Her divorce papers lay spread out between them. The dream that had tantalised her for so long, could now come true.

She couldn't describe how she felt: one moment she wanted to giggle, the next she was very near to tears. All the frustration and bitterness would become a thing of the past. She was free of the Jacksons. It hadn't only been Johnny that she had had to fight, but his mother and father, his brothers and sisters – every one of them had been against her from the very beginning.

Now she could look back on the time she had spent with Johnny with at least a little compassion. They had both been so young; far too young to have entered into a marriage that was doomed from the start. Johnny came from a race of near-gypsies, a tribe of people who led a life entirely different from that which she herself was used to. An outsider, an intruder, was how his family had seen her and she really couldn't blame them. What she had resented were the spiteful lies, the thieving and the venomous taunts.

'Hey, hey, remember me? I'm still here!' Eddie broke into her thoughts and brought her back to the present. He got up and moved his chair so that he could sit beside her. 'Patsy, listen to me.'

She raised her head, and through her tears her eyes were shining as she looked into his.

'I know, I know, it's been a long time. But it's over now.' Suddenly she found herself smothered in Eddie's strong arms, while he hugged her tightly.

Minutes passed before he spoke again and when he did his voice too was choked with emotion. 'I've told you time and time again, a marriage certificate won't make an atom of difference to me. As far as I'm concerned, you've been my wife since the day you came to live with me above my father's shop.' His mood changed from being serious, and he grinned at her. 'Still, if you really want me to make an honest woman of you, you've only to say the word.'

'Oh, you!' She pushed him, and he caught hold of her around the waist and said very quietly, 'Come on, we've plans to make and things to do.'

By midday they were seated in the lounge of the vicarage, talking to the Reverend Mr Whitehead, the vicar of St Nicholas's church which stood on the corner of Church Lane and Mitcham Road in Tooting. It was the church where Patsy herself had been christened, and both their two boys and the twins had also been christened there.

'I'm pleased that you have come and told me. I'm also astounded, and that's putting it mildly,' Mr Whitehead exclaimed as he beamed at them. A small man, turned sixty, with a round face that seemed to wear a permanent smile, he was popular with most of his congregation, especially the younger members. 'Of course you realise that you will have to have a civil ceremony?'

Eddie gave all the necessary assurances, and the vicar's smile grew even broader. 'In that case, all will be well.' He opened up his leather-bound diary, turned some pages, nodded his head a few times, then raising his eyes and peering at them over the rim of his spectacles, he said, 'New Year's Eve. Seems a fitting day to me. Will that suit both of you?'

'Oh yes!' It was like a cry of joy as Patsy spoke those two words and Eddie looked at Mr Whitehead and they laughed together.

Word got around. It was impossible to keep a thing like that quiet. Some nasty-minded people still laughed at them. Most laughed *with* them. Ted and Amy Andrews were flabbergasted.

Ted slapped Eddie on the back, and his body

shook with laughter as he said, 'If you've got any skeletons in the cupboard – and who the hell hasn't? – I've always believed in leaving them there! But, boy, this is a good one! What an excuse for a booze-up.'

'Hey, just you hang on a minute, Ted,' Patsy cried out in protest, 'we're not having any do, never mind a booze-up.'

'That's what you think, Patsy me darling,' Ted declared as he lifted her off her feet and swung her around in his arms.

'Yeah, an' I'm making the wedding cake,' Amy pronounced firmly.

'Are you ever going to sit down and stop fiddling about? You're like a cat on a hot tin roof!' Florrie was smiling to herself as she moaned at Patsy. Gawd above knew tomorrow would be the answer to all her prayers.

Her Patsy, her little girl from the minute she'd opened her eyes upstairs in this very 'ouse. She'd be sleeping in that same room tonight, that's if she ever let any of them get any ruddy sleep! Thank the Good Lord he'd let her live long enough to see this come about. Eddie Owen, one of the best men God ever put on this earth, and him and her Patsy were going to be married tomorrow. Properly married, in God's 'ouse.

'Damn!' Florrie had been so busy talking to herself that she'd dug the needle into her finger. She was supposed to be sewing ribbons on to the dresses that the twins were going to wear. Poking her finger into her mouth she sucked at it and continued to thank the Almighty for the way things had finally turned out.

Christ knew it had taken long enough to get shot of those bloody Jacksons. Ollie had been cunning! He'd given Patsy the means to get her divorce. What about the day Patsy had come back from Mitcham, black and blue she'd been, used 'er as a bleeding punch bag those Jacksons 'ad, and that rotter Johnny had stolen her rent, not once, but week after week. Ollie had sworn that day that he'd live to see them put down. He'd be like a cock with new feathers when he took Patsy down that aisle tomorrow.

Two days ago there'd been a civil ceremony up at Lambeth Town Hall, Eddie and Patsy were legally man and wife now. That hadn't stopped Patsy from telling Eddie that he was to stay in Clapham on his own, she didn't want to set eyes on him until they met in church. Cheeky cow really! Florrie again laughed to herself. Many a man wouldn't 'ave stood for it. Patsy wasn't very big, but when she said something she meant it. Kids and all, she packed 'em all up and came 'ome, as she put it.

Not that I'm not tickled pink over it, and she knows damn well I am. Married from the 'ouse in which she was born and bred. You got to admit it seems only right. The kids weren't in the 'ouse, oh no, only you and me tonight, Florrie, Patsy had stated firmly. Off to Queenie's she'd taken the two boys. Emma and Ellen were tucked up over in Gran's 'ouse – well, there'd 'ave been all 'ell to pay if old Gran hadn't been allowed in on some of the arrangements.

Patsy came through from the scullery carrying a tray with cups and saucers and a teapot set out on it. She set the tray down on the kitchen table, then turned and let herself out into the back yard. Bending, she lifted the stone flowerpot off the milk bottle and picked up the quart of milk. It was a bitterly cold night but she hesitated before going back into the warmth of the kitchen, and glanced up at the sky. Clear and bright – no fog, no wind, just hundreds of stars shining. Everything was going to be lovely for tomorrow.

She and Florrie drank their tea in silence, each totally aware of how much love they felt for each other. An ill-assorted pair some might say: a rough and ready, fat woman, and a small slim young woman whose mode of speech didn't even compare, yet no mother and daughter ever had a closer or more loving relationship.

'Come on, Florrie, let's get you into bed.' Patsy saw her safely tucked up in her downstairs bedroom, then she rinsed their teacups under the tap and left them on the wooden draining-board ready for the morning.

Finally she walked quietly upstairs to bed. She undressed, put her dress on a coathanger and hung it behind the door. Then she got into bed. She closed her eyes, but sleep wasn't going to come that easily.

She could still feel, and almost see, her mother here. How many times had her mother leaned over her in this room, and kissed her goodnight? Had her own life run along the same lines as her mother's? Not really. Her mother had conceived her in love, the fact that her father had been killed before they could be married was an act of God, and life hadn't worked out so well for her mother after that.

She, Patsy, was being given a second chance. All the bad things were in the past. In the morning she was going to church to have her future life with Eddie blessed by God. She knew her mother smiled, she approved; and Patsy was smiling to herself as she finally fell asleep.

The whole house was in an uproar. The comings and goings of half the street were making Patsy nervous. In the end she had had to shoo her own children from the house because she was very near to tears. They looked so lovely, and Alex seemed so grown-up dressed in his first proper suit. Florrie had been transformed. She wore a loose-fitting navy blue dress and long coat; her hair had been washed and set and now peeped from beneath her flowered hat. 'Don't you dare cry!' Patsy had called after her as she went out to join Gran in one of the wedding cars.

Alone, now, Patsy took a deep breath. This was no good. If she didn't stop it she would be crying herself in a minute, and that would never do. She heard the sound of more motor cars out in the street and knew it was nearly time.

She stood back to look at herself, once more, in Florrie's full-length mirror. Her oyster cream dress with its lace bolero was simple but graceful. It was mid-calf in length, low-necked and long-sleeved, and she wore silk stockings and soft kid shoes.

The door opened and Ollie stood there looking very smart in his best suit. He didn't say a word, but came slowly towards her. There was such a light in his eyes and such a soft, sweet smile on his face that Patsy felt a lump in her throat. Once again the tears stung behind her eyelids, and she had to blink rapidly to stop them from spilling out. His arms went gently around her and his lips brushed her cheek. 'I'm so proud of you, Patsy, and so happy for you.'

'Thank you for everything, Ollie,' she whispered as she picked up her small spray of yellow freesias and maidenhair fern.

Solemnly Ollie offered her his arm and she, smiling up into his face, took it and went from the room and down the narrow passage and out into Strathmore Street. A crowd of neighbours shouted, 'Good luck, Patsy. Gawd bless yer!' and Patsy turned to wave to them before getting into the white-ribboned chauffeur-driven car.

Patsy was surprised at the number of people in the church and she hesitated for a moment, until she felt Ollie put slight pressure on her arm, and then she was walking up the aisle on the arm of the man who had always treated her as if she were his daughter.

Even the weather was doing its best: winter sunshine filtered in through the stained glass windows, reflecting on the pale stone walls and conveying a sense of warmth and welcome.

All heads were turned in her direction but Patsy could now see only one man. He was waiting for her at the altar. Then she was standing by his side, and from his great height he looked down at her. There was no need for him to speak. The look that went from his eyes into hers said it all.

The words of the Reverend Whitehead were awe-inspiring, yet even he was smiling. 'We beseech Thee O Lord to bless this union . . .'

Patsy's heart, as she listened to the beautiful words, felt as if it would burst with happiness. In front of a congregation, a minister of the church was declaring that she could live for the rest of her life as Eddie's wife. In the silence that followed Eddie leaned towards her and slowly lowered his head and his lips touched hers. When she eased back from his kiss, he gazed down at her. 'All right now, Mrs

Owen?' he asked in a whisper. 'Yes! Oh, yes!' she whispered back.

He bent and kissed her lips once more, and she closed her eyes and said a silent prayer.

Outside the church, on the grass and pathways, their friends were milling about them. 'I've never been kissed so much in my life,' Patsy declared to Eddie as they both kept smiling while more and more photographs were taken.

'This one will be for posterity,' exclaimed Blower Day as he focused his Brownie box camera, having taken some time to group Alex, David, Ellen and Emma around their parents.

Everyone roared wth laughter. 'Yeah,' Blower's brother Danny called, 'try explaining that one to your grandchildren.'

It was all good-natured fun. No offence was meant or taken, for Patsy didn't give two hoots now – they could laugh all they wanted to, and she was able to laugh with them. There were no more dark hidden secrets, life was an open book from here on, and she was determined to enjoy it to the full.

There was a surprise in store for her when, nearly an hour later, they all poured out of the cars in front of the Selkirk public house.

Thinking only that the men had decided that they should all go for a drink, she gasped with delight as she entered the saloon. Four long tables were set out parallel to each other, with a fifth table running along the top, and all were laid up in style for a wedding reception.

Queenie whispered into Patsy's ear, and she looked up at Eddie, who nodded, acknowledging that he knew who was responsible. She left his side and made her way to where Gran and Grandad Day stood.

She wanted to say so much to these two dear people who, like Florrie and Ollie, had taken her – and her mother before her – to their hearts and made them part of their family. This wonderful, thoughtful gift to be shared with all their friends was too much and Patsy burst into tears.

The laughter that greeted Patsy's tears was loud and long, particularly when Grandad Jack took Patsy in his arms, rocking her back and forth, and Gran said, 'Well, I'll be buggered! Supposed to be the 'appiest day of her bloody life and what does she do? She stands there bawling.'

The meal was over. The cake had been cut, the champagne corks had all been popped and speeches made by several of the men. The one that gave Patsy the greatest happiness came from Ollie, who ended by saying in a voice filled with emotion, 'It has been a great privilege to have been allowed to be a surrogate father to Patsy.'

Hours later, Gran and Florrie were seated in armchairs at an open upstairs window, looking down in amazement on the scene below.

'We've seen some street parties in our time, eh gal? But never nothing like this. The world and 'is bloody wife seem to 'ave made their way to our street tonight.'

Gran leaned further out over the sill and agreed with Florrie. 'Tell you what, Flo, 'alf the stall 'olders from Tooting Market are down there. Can't wonder at it though, most of those costers still remember Ellen, God rest her soul, an' everyone of 'em 'ave known Patsy since she were a nipper.'

The whole street was packed with chairs on the pavement outside every house, and the centre of the road was a mass of moving figures. Gran's piano had been pushed out into her front garden and Grandad Jack was belting out all the old songs on its yellowed keys, stopping only to fortify himself with another pint of beer. Blower, Danny and all other male members of the Day family were manning a bar, which they had set up on the wall in front of Queenie's house. Bonfires had been lit at each end of the street, and coloured lanterns were strung across the roadway.

Eddie and Patsy were doing their best to speak to everyone and thank them for coming. They were forced to separate to make way for a group of running children, and when they came together again, he asked, 'Happy?' She looked up at him, nodded and smiled, and he smiled back and they continued their walkabout. Patsy hadn't realised just how much she missed the camaraderie and the hustle and bustle which came with these down-to-earth market traders. They hugged her tight, kissed her and repeatedly asked, ''Ow are yer, darling? 'Ow is it we never see yer these days? Ain't gone all posh, 'ave yer, since yer moved up to Clapham?'

The air was filled with laughter and noisy singing, the smell of burning wood and an appetising aroma from three braziers on which jacket potatoes and chestnuts were roasting. It was very cold, but no one was bothered. The world was in a deep depression, there was wholesale unemployment bringing with it the evils of poverty and poor health among the working classes, but tonight the crowd gathered together in Strathmore Street didn't care.

As the last day of 1931 drew to a close, the mood of the crowd seemed bent on enjoyment. The bonfires were still piled high, burning well and children, up late on this New Year's Eve, shrieked every now and then as great showers of sparks shot up through the air into the far-reaching beyond.

A wireless set was brought out into the street and a silence settled over the crowd as a circle was formed and arms were linked.

Boom, boom. Big Ben rang out the old year and brought in 1932.

'Auld Lang Syne' was sung with gusto. Eddie and

Patsy broke away, and Florrie and Ollie were well contented as they watched the pair of them kiss and wish each other, 'Happy New Year.'